A Deadly Rejection

LM Milford

ISBN ISBN 978-1-913778-02-6

Text © 2017 LM Milford

Cover art by Jessica Bell
Formatting by Polgarus Studio

For Mam and Dad, for all your support over the many, many years

Acknowledgments

This one could take a while. Writing this book may have been my own work, but I've had a lot of support in the editing and production. First, a big thank you to Keshini Naidoo for the first structural edit and some great feedback. To Donna Hillyer for her help with editing and polishing and to the lovely Helen Baggott for her proofreading skills.
Credit also goes to Jessica Bell for the gorgeous cover, which I'm delighted with.

A huge thank you to my Twitter crew, specifically Mel Sherratt (#keeponkeepingon), Jane Isaac, Rebecca Bradley and Susi (SJI) Holliday for their unstinting support. I couldn't have kept going without you. There are others, but there's not enough space to list you all!

And finally to my fantastic family and friends for never saying 'You can't write a book', and particularly to my Dad, whose question in April 2017 'When is this book going to be published, then?' really got me going.
You've all been my cheerleaders from start to finish and I can't thank you enough. Drinks on me at the next family party!

And to Paul, who has the honour of living with a crazy, scatty writer. Thanks for everything x

Chapter 1

It was the smell that drew the spaniel to the clearing. She loved anything dirty and smelly; the smellier the better, in fact. She didn't even mind being hosed down by her owner when they got home, as long as it wasn't too cold. It was worth it.

The long grass and brambles crunched under her paws as she leapt through the undergrowth. Coppin Woods was her favourite place for a walk. She paused a moment, sensitive nose twitching as she sniffed the air. Yes, it was definitely getting stronger. She wasn't entirely sure what it was but that wasn't important.

She could hear her owner calling her name, but she carried on running.

When she found the clearing, she stopped stock-still and began to bark; a warning bark rather than the joy of spotting a rabbit. By the time her owner caught up to her, she'd circled the car with the engine running and the hosepipe running from the exhaust into the car through an open and duct-taped window. She'd scampered back to the edge of the clearing whimpering. This wasn't what she'd been expecting.

The smell of car fumes was drifting all around the clearing. She watched as her owner rushed forward and tugged at the door handle of the car. She barked a warning and ran to his side, but he pushed her away. The door wouldn't open and, finding a rock on the ground, her owner smashed the car window. Coughing, he leaned inside and switched off the engine. Flicking open the door lock, he dragged the driver from the car and laid him on the ground.

'Can't tell if he's breathing,' he muttered, pulling out his mobile phone. The skin on the driver's face was burned and blackened, as were his hands.

Soon an ambulance, fire engine and police car were pulling up at the end of the track that led to the clearing. The paramedics ran to the clearing, carrying their heavy equipment, but after a short examination, they were shaking their heads.

'Gone, never stood a chance,' said one.

'I'll never understand why they do it,' replied the other.

'Peaceful, I suppose,' remarked the police sergeant who had just joined them.

The spaniel was twitching and pulling at her lead while her owner spoke to the police officer. She no longer thought that smell was interesting. She wanted to go home.

Chapter 2

Had it really come to this? Daniel Sullivan stared around the church hall at rows upon rows of fuchsias stretching away from him on long trestle tables. He loosened his tie, trying to get some relief from the mugginess of the room. He could see the gardeners trying to open windows to let in cooler air, but they were fighting a losing battle now the sun was getting onto the windows. Not that he cared. This was definitely the worst job he'd been sent on as a news reporter.

'Would you like another cup of tea?' Moira Turner, secretary of the Allensbury Fuchsia Society and organiser of the annual show, appeared behind him, clutching a cup on a saucer.

'No, thanks.' Dan tried to smile but the previous three cups of tea had done nothing to remove the brick of carrot cake that had settled in his stomach. The woman who made it would never have won anything at the Allensbury Flower and Produce Show's cake baking competition. That was another crap job he'd been sent on. Moira Turner was smiling at him expectantly.

'What do you think of the flowers?'

'Oh, erm, they're lovely. Very pretty. My mum would love them.' But I don't, he added silently.

It was clearly the right thing to say because the woman beamed.

'We've got a fantastic crop this year.' She looked around at the

3

plants affectionately as their owners made frantic last-minute adjustments to their arrangements. 'Judging them is going to be terribly difficult. Have you got everything you need?' She gestured towards Dan's notebook, peering at the lines and squiggles of his shorthand.

'Yes, I think so. All I need now is the result.'

'You're going to ring John for that later, aren't you? At about seven?'

'Yes. Unfortunately I've got a lot of other jobs to go on, so I'd better dash now.' Dan smiled apologetically, trying to make himself sound incredibly busy. The only thing he really wanted to do was get the hell out of this room.

'Oh, of course. I was just so pleased you were able to come down and your photographer has been to take some pictures too. So exciting to be in the local paper again.'

Dan smiled but inside he was cringing. The fuchsia show was in the paper every single year and yet this woman was so pathetically excited by it.

He said goodbye to her and walked out to the dirty, dented Peugeot he had been assigned for the day.

With a sigh he threw his bag into the passenger's footwell and swung into the driver's seat. He rubbed his face with both hands. He needed to get back in the game, away from these crap jobs, and back to the real stories.

When he returned to the office, he found his flatmate Ed Walker tapping desperately at his keyboard, eyes glued to the computer screen.

Dan opened his mouth to speak, but Ed held up a hand.

'Sorry, mate, I'm just on a deadline for this court copy. I'll be done in about four minutes.'

Dan sniffed and headed off to the gents. Everyone else got better jobs than him, he thought. Ed got to cover court, Emma Fletcher got to cover crime, and he was stuck with flower shows.

As he walked back to his desk, he saw Emma push through the double doors at the end of the office, a takeaway coffee in one hand and a dog-eared notebook full of scribbled shorthand in the other.

She smirked at Dan and then stopped by the desk of news editor Daisy King to give her the rundown on what she'd learned from her daily visit to see the police.

He hated to admit it, but Emma was very good at winkling out stories, getting people to say things they shouldn't. That didn't stop him being furious that he'd been passed over for the crime job. He'd thought he was the obvious choice. Instead the editor had chosen Emma, the more qualified, experienced reporter. Unfortunately Emma knew how Dan felt and took pleasure in making him feel bad about it.

Ed stood up suddenly, making Dan jump. 'Daisy,' he called, 'that copy's in the basket.' He stretched his arms above his head.

'Thanks,' Daisy replied. 'Now where's the rest of it?'

Ed pulled a face when she'd turned back to her computer.

'It's never enough, is it?' he said to Dan. 'No rest for the wicked. How was your flower show?'

Dan rolled his eyes, but before he could say anything Emma arrived at her desk beside him.

'Another flower show? You must be getting good at those now. Did you manage to uncover any murder among the montbretia? Carnage among the chrysanthemums?'

Dan glared at her. 'Shut up.'

She smiled. 'Very mature.'

Dan was about to retaliate when Ed cut across him.

'Anything good today, Emma?'

'The usual murder and mayhem. Well, apart from the murder bit.'

Ed laughed. 'I'm sure something will come along sooner or later. Maybe Dan will murder Daisy if she sends him to another flower show.'

They both laughed as Dan stomped away muttering something about getting a cup of tea.

Once he'd finished his tea and the bulk of the fuchsia show copy – all 150 words of it – Dan found himself at something of a loose end. Clicking into his email account, he refreshed his inbox, praying something interesting had arrived.

A new message popped up and his eyes widened. It was from one of the council officers, James Wilton, and the subject read 'Private and confidential'.

He sat up straight. Officers weren't allowed to talk directly to the press, and last time Dan broke that rule, by speaking to Wilton as it happened, it had resulted in a twenty-minute bollocking from Daisy demanding to know why he couldn't follow the rules and whether he was trying to stop the council speaking to the paper at all. His ears had burned for the rest of day after that one.

He checked over his shoulder that no one could see his screen and opened the message.

'By sending this to you, I'm putting myself at great risk,' Wilton had written. 'I don't know how long I've got before we get found out and I need someone to know why I did it. I can't trust anyone at the council. I can't cope with the guilt any more – I have to tell someone. Dan, I know I got you in trouble before when you were asking questions about that previous application but you're the only one who will have the balls to see this through. Please, please help me. You're the only one who can. Come to the council offices tomorrow (or perhaps tonight by the time you read this) before the planning committee and I'll explain the content below. This time I won't tell anyone I've spoken to you.'

The email was timed at seven-fifty the previous evening and was marked as having been delayed by the spam filter.

Dan hit print and then quickly crossed to the printer to collect the pages.

Wilton had forwarded an email trail, which consisted of a list of numbers being passed back and forth. Dan stared at it. The format of the letters and numbers was familiar. What on earth had James Wilton got himself into?

'Another cup of tea, mate?' Ed appeared, waggling a mug under Dan's nose and making him jump. 'You'll burn a hole in that piece of paper if you stare at it any harder.'

Dan quickly put the pages face down on his desk and then turned to hand his mug to Ed.

'You OK?' Ed asked. 'You look a bit … funny.'

'I'm fine. Just gagging for a cup of your lovely tea.'

Ed laughed. 'Now I know something's definitely up. You never compliment my tea.' He walked away chuckling and collected mugs from a few other people.

Dan turned back to his email. The rest of James Wilton's note contained instructions of where to meet him and how to get into the offices without being seen. Dan hit the reply button.

'I'll see you then,' he typed. There wasn't much else to say.

He took a deep breath. This was it, he was sure of it. This was bound to be something huge, otherwise Wilton wouldn't risk another verbal warning for speaking to the press without prior approval. At last, this could be the story he'd been waiting for.

Chapter 3

The rest of Dan's afternoon passed in a blur of writing up press releases about a charity whist drive, a toddlers' group doing a sponsored walk and a local artist nobody having a show in the town's tiny art gallery. Ordinarily it would have made him furious, but his mind was now on bigger things: the email folded up in his bag ready for tonight.

There was a slight cough behind him and Daisy appeared clutching a thick wedge of paper.

'Everything alright?' she asked.

'Fine,' said Dan.

Raising an eyebrow, Daisy thumped the papers onto his abnormally tidy desk and pointed to the front cover.

'Planning committee tonight,' she said. 'I notice you didn't pick up the agenda and committee papers when you came in this morning. Perhaps you'd like to actually prepare for the meeting, so you know what to expect.'

'Sorry, I've had so much stuff on today, I forgot.'

Daisy leaned down onto his desk, her head close to his, and spoke in a low voice.

'I know exactly what you've been doing today; I set the workload, remember. It's not been anything taxing and I expect you to set an example to the younger reporters. They look up to the seniors and at the moment you're not the kind of role model I'd like them to pay attention to. Get it right, Dan, prove me wrong.'

Dan took the inch-thick agenda from her. 'Then give me something good to work on.'

Daisy tapped the agenda. 'Start there. You've become so slapdash, Dan, and it's not like you. You need to do something about that.'

'I will.'

'You'd better.'

Daisy walked back to her desk and Dan began to thumb through the papers. Then something caught his eye.

'Elliot's Walk?'

'What?' Ed's head popped up over the top of his computer monitor.

'Why does the name Elliot's Walk ring a bell?'

'God knows. It's too nice for court papers, presumably?'

Dan frowned. Flipping open the agenda he read through the Elliot's Walk application. It was a proposal for yet another housing estate, this time on an area of scrubland in southern Allensbury. If he remembered rightly, local residents were dead set against the plan because they wanted to use the land for allotments. When he saw the number of houses that were proposed, Dan gave a low whistle. He could see why they were objecting. It would be overdevelopment.

Developer FGB Contracting, a Kent-based construction company, had bought up the land and was claiming their plan for houses was the best option for the town. At the last committee meeting, he remembered, the councillors had passed a similar application in the west of the town.

'Wasn't there an application for houses on that bit of land next to Elliot's Walk last year?' he asked Ed.

Ed shrugged. 'I don't know, mate. I never cover planning, unless the world has a meltdown and you're all off covering that.'

'I'm sure there was an application last year that got turned down, but I can't remember what it was.'

Ed walked behind Dan and peered over his shoulder. 'I don't know why they would turn it down; they keep saying we need thousands more houses.'

'That's why I was surprised at the time. But I can't remember the details.' Dan stared at the plans and snorted.

'What's up?' Ed asked.

'It's been recommended for approval by the officers. The residents are going to have a tough time getting it turned down.'

He continued to read the papers and then frowned. 'No objections from the residents?' That in itself was odd. Those residents weren't the type to have nothing to say about the application.

He felt a flicker in his stomach, that feeling he used to get on his previous newspaper. On his current diet of county fairs and flower shows, that flicker had been squashed but there had been a time when a story would fill his mind completely and make him forget anything else existed.

That was the one thing his ex-girlfriend Lucy had hated about the job. Or maybe it was just the way he'd tackled the job that she had hated.

'You don't really care about me at all, do you?' she'd shouted at him, tears flowing freely down her cheeks. Mascara had smeared across her face but she hadn't cared.

'Of course I do,' Dan had tried to insist but she'd cut across him.

'You shut me out. It's almost as if you're worried I'll steal your damn story.'

'I didn't think you would be interested.'

'Of course I'm interested. I'm your bloody girlfriend. Or at least I'm supposed to be. You spend so much time at bloody work, we don't have anything else to talk about. So I want to hear about what you've been working on.'

'Sometimes I can't tell you. You know that. I don't interrogate you about your day.'

'That's because you just don't care, do you? You don't care what kind of day I've had. The only time you care is when you could get a story out of it.'

'That's not true,' Dan had half protested, knowing she was probably right.

'It is true. You don't care about anyone but yourself and until you learn to put people before your bloody stories, you'll never have a proper life. Count me out. I've had enough.'

She'd stormed away with a flick of her long, blonde hair, slamming the door behind her. Dan had thought she would get over it and they would carry on as normal. But she had meant it. He'd tried to phone her but she wouldn't answer and then her best friend brought over a box of his stuff and asked for the clothes, CDs and toiletries Lucy had left there.

That had been two years ago. It wasn't his fault that he cared about his job, that he loved what he did. Maybe the job just wasn't compatible with relationships.

At five twenty-five, Dan began to put his things into his bag. He checked that his notebook, three pens and the planning agenda were inside, and slung the bag across his shoulder. His stomach was still flickering. Could James Wilton really have something big to tell him?

Ed looked up in surprise and checked his watch. 'You're going to planning already?'

'No, I've got something to do first.'

Ed raised an eyebrow. 'Listen, mate, you OK? I know we were teasing you a bit before—'

Dan shrugged. 'Does it bother me that I get all the shit jobs? Yeah, I don't want to be stuck here for the rest of my life.' He gestured towards the news desk. 'But how am I supposed to prove myself if all I get is fuchsia shows and county fairs?'

'You did make a monumental fuck up though.' Ed frowned.

'I know, but ...'

'Do you know how long it took me to rebuild the relationships I have at court? That you broke?'

'I've apologised for that. How many more times do you need to say it?'

Ed's face softened. 'Keep the faith, mate, you'll get there.'

'I've been in this place for four years and I've stagnated. I need a big story, something to get me out of here, get me to the next step.'

Ed gave him a sympathetic look. 'To be honest, the court beat isn't all that exciting, a lot of sitting around and then getting threats from the scumbags you report on. At least you get to talk to nice people.'

Dan smiled. 'Thanks for trying to make me feel better.'

'Did it work?'

'A bit.'

'Excellent. Look, I'll put the leftovers in the fridge for when you get back.'

'Cheers. What are you making?'

Ed smirked. 'That would spoil the surprise, wouldn't it?'

As Dan made to leave the office, Daisy stopped him.

'Remember, I need you to file all your copy from tonight's meeting before you go to bed. We're light on filler copy so I'm probably going to need all of it.'

Dan nodded.

He left the office and strode up the hill to the town hall. He checked his watch. He was going to be late for James Wilton.

He arrived at the town hall, a grand Georgian style building on the High Street, and pounded up the stairs to the second floor.

Normally he took the stairs slowly and looked at the portraits and creepy blank-eyed statues but today there was no time. He paused at the top of the stairs and looked up and down the corridor. James Wilton had said to turn right at the top of the stairs and it was the door right at the end of the corridor.

He reached the door and pressed his ear to it. He couldn't hear anything. He turned the handle and pushed open the door. The room was empty. All the computer screens were dark. Dan stepped inside and shut the door quietly.

He perched on the corner of a desk to wait for Wilton and looked around. It was an open-plan office, not very big but with desks set for six people in a hexagon shape. All the surfaces were completely clear. Dan didn't know how people managed in a paperless office.

The *Post*, by comparison, was a paper-full office. There was tons of the stuff and the newspaper files of back copies were what gave the newsroom that lovely dusty-old-book smell. As he turned to look around, he knocked a letter opener to the ground. He picked it up and put it back on the desk and continued to wait.

He glanced at his watch. He'd now been waiting for ten minutes. Where was Wilton? Surely he hadn't forgotten.

By five fifty-five, Dan's foot was tapping. He was going to have to go to the planning meeting or Daisy would kill him.

He slipped out of the office, closing the door quietly behind him. He walked quickly to the stairs and headed down to the first floor where the main council chamber was. As he turned a corner, he collided with three councillors who were whispering intently. He recognised David Edmonds, Paul Sanderson and Johanna Buttle.

Edmonds glared at him. 'Do you mind?'

'Sorry,' Dan said, glancing at Buttle's feet. Yes, as per usual her pointy shoes were in place. You could always rely on Johanna Buttle to brighten the place up. She wasn't a tall woman, but what she lacked in height she made up for in large breasts. She always wore very fashionable clothes and very pointy shoes, as if she were trying to prove that councillors could be on-trend. Usually she smiled at him and made an effort to talk, but today she seemed distracted and looked rather pale.

Paul Sanderson on the other hand was very tall, taller than Dan, and suited up like all the older councillors. He was late-thirties at the most but his usually kind, cheery face looked grim and his skin was flushed. He seemed to take advantage of Dan's arrival, saying, 'Excuse me,' and ducking inside the council chamber. Dan stepped back and allowed Buttle and Edmonds to go ahead of him.

On the floor of the chamber, dark wooden benches with leather cushions were arranged in semicircles facing a raised dais where the mayor would take his seat as chairman. A ledge ran along the back of each bench to give the councillors somewhere to rest their papers. A microphone sat in front of each person to allow any comments to be heard around the room. There was always a series of red flashes just before the meetings as the councillors tested their microphones were working.

Without another glance, Buttle made her way to the benches kept for the committee members, while Edmonds went to the other side of the room, sitting in the other side of the horseshoe of cushioned benches. Dan made his way to the table kept for the press, which was positioned behind the seats where Buttle and Sanderson had their heads together, whispering urgently. Looking over at the seats where the planning officers sat, Dan was surprised not to see James Wilton. Maybe he'd been running late and had gone to find Dan. He was about to stand up, intending to return to the office, when the wooden double doors flew open and Richard Drimble, mayor and chair of the planning committee, strode into the room.

Dan sat down and pulled out his notebook and pen. He frowned.

A set of meeting papers lay on the desk in front of him, but it had a different reference code to the one in his bag. People were still milling about on the floor of the chamber and, looking up, he noticed the public gallery was filling up. Wooden railed, it ran across one wall of the room and looked down on the councillors seated below.

Some councillors had already chosen their seats for the evening, but others were still sharing gossip or speaking to members of the public.

They all looked surprised by Drimble's sudden entrance and scuttled into their seats, while he took his on the raised dais at the front of the horseshoe of wooden benches.

Dan saw his eyes flick towards the public gallery and a frown of surprise flashed across his face.

It was odd to have this many people at a planning meeting. He thought he recognised a few faces from the Elliot's Walk Residents' Association.

Drimble struck impatiently at the desk in front of him with a gavel. When the chatter didn't immediately cease, he struck the desk two more times and people became silent. The meeting began in the usual way with the councillors introducing themselves and Drimble explaining what to do in the event of a fire and where the toilets could be found.

Drimble rubbed at his eyes as he introduced the first application, a very dull one about a conservatory being built in someone's garden. Why you needed planning permission for that, Dan could never understand. As the officer began a long complicated speech about the ins and outs of the application, Dan felt his attention already beginning to wander.

The ceiling of the council chamber was undoubtedly the most interesting bit of it. It wasn't quite the Sistine Chapel but it was elaborately decorated. Cherubs danced across a pale-blue background, waving pink ribbons. Each one was balanced on a beige-coloured panel bearing the months of the year in Latin.

Chin on hand, Dan stared upwards as the woman's voice droned on. That crack in the ceiling was definitely bigger than a month ago, he thought.

Someone cleared their throat just behind him, making him jump. A slight titter ran along the row of wooden chairs behind him and Dan peeked over his shoulder in surprise. There weren't normally people sitting there. He also recognised them as being from the Elliot's Walk Residents' Association. If there were no objections, why were so many of them here?

As the meeting slowly progressed, people were becoming restless, fidgeting in their seats and beginning to whisper. One woman earned a glare from Drimble when she got a rustling bag of toffees out of her handbag and started to hand them round. Dan had never seen a planning meeting so busy. What could they all be here for? His answer came when the Elliot's Walk application was announced and a whisper ran around the public gallery. The woman even put away her toffees.

'Application CB two-six-seven-eight, Elliot's Walk development for two hundred dwellings,' said Richard Drimble, looking around at the committee and glancing towards the gallery.

Then he looked at the pages in front of him and frowned down at the planning officer sitting in the bench closest to the dais.

'Harriet, are these the right papers?'

'Yes, sir.'

'Are you sure?'

'Yes. Those are the ones I was given.'

Drimble raised an eyebrow but let the issue go. Dan looked down at his papers. It did say two hundred, but he could have sworn he'd read one hundred and forty six earlier. And now the format of letters and numbers in James Wilton's email made sense. They were planning applications. Before he could pull out his old agenda, Drimble motioned for the planning officer to begin.

'Here we go,' Dan heard a man say in the row behind him.

The planning officer gave her introduction and then Drimble called on the applicant's representative.

'Mr Anderson to speak on behalf of FGB Contracting,' continued Drimble.

A swarthy man stood up and moved to the microphone. A hiss of disapproval ran around the gallery.

Anderson glanced at David Edmonds, who was peering at his planning papers and seemed to be trying to catch Johanna Buttle's eye.

'You have three minutes, a bell will sound at two,' Anderson was told.

He smiled. 'Members of the committee,' he began, 'the Elliot's Walk development is one of two projects which FGB Contracting has put before you. This area of Allensbury needs some attention and homes are the only option. This development is for one hundred and forty-six homes. They will attract families and will drastically improve a terribly rundown area.'

Another hiss went round the gallery and people began to mutter again. Drimble raised his eyes to the gallery and shook his head. The hissing stopped.

Dan couldn't believe his ears. He looked down at the planning agenda in front of him again. The area marked for development wasn't wasteland but a grassy area in a part of town that was already very well developed. It was the only green space for miles around. But surely he's misheard; had Anderson actually said one hundred and forty six homes? He stared at the papers in front of him. It said two hundred. But Anderson was still speaking and Dan tuned back in, wondering how so many 'family homes' could fit onto such a small area. One hundred and forty six would have been pushing it; two hundred was unimaginable.

He knew the council had looked at buying the land but the developer had asked for silly amounts of money and so the plan had been shelved. Had it been the idea all along to buy the land and then force the council to give permission for housing?

Anderson continued to drone on with the air of a man who was repeating what others already knew.

'Parts of this area are already very developed, it's true,' he said. 'But we've had a lot of feasibility studies done, at great cost, I might add, and there is no alternative use.' He spread his hands wide and looked appealingly at the committee.

Dan looked at Drimble, his pen automatically taking notes in shorthand. The mayor was staring at Edmonds, who was frowning.

'Leave it as a proper green space that all the residents can enjoy,' shouted a woman from the public gallery. All eyes swivelled to her and Anderson gave the committee a wounded look.

Edmonds rolled his eyes and tutted, while Drimble calmly looked up at the gallery and said, 'Quiet, please. Your representative will get a chance to have his say in a moment. Carry on, Mr Anderson.' He fixed the man with a stare and the latter started to fumble with his paperwork.

'In short, we don't see any other way to use this wasteland,' he repeated.

'It won't be wasted if they let us use it properly,' Dan heard the man behind him mutter. A bell dinged to mark two minutes of Anderson's speech and made him even more flustered.

'This area of land is too valuable to leave it unused; wasteland, or a green space, would attract fly-tipping and other antisocial behaviour. We just want to make Allensbury a nicer place for people to live and with this land looking the way it does that simply is not happening.'

The bell dinged again marking the end of his three minutes and Anderson gathered up his papers, thanking everyone for listening.

A quiet whispering began in the gallery as Anderson returned to his seat at the back of the room. When Drimble cleared his throat, everyone stopped talking.

'Right,' said the mayor. 'This is slightly unorthodox but we've had a last-minute request for objections to be raised and I've decided to allow it.' A ripple of whispers flowed through the councillors in the hall. Drimble looked surprised as Councillor David Edmonds got to his feet and requested to speak, but he nodded.

'Yes, Councillor, what is it?'

'I have to protest here, Mr Mayor. We have rules for a reason in these situations, and if they are not adhered to, then we're making a mockery of our own procedure. Why have a procedure if we ignore it?'

But Drimble was shaking his head. 'Sorry, Councillor Edmonds, but this is an extenuating circumstance and I'm prepared to allow it.' He turned towards a man seated behind Dan, leaving Edmonds to sit back down, red-faced.

'Kevin Turtle to speak against the application,' Drimble said.

There was a spontaneous round of applause as the man sitting behind Dan made his way to the front. Again, Drimble banged his gavel for silence.

The man was neat and precise-looking, dressed in a dapper three-piece suit and neat red-spotted tie. He even had a matching handkerchief tucked in his top pocket. He looked like a retired banker. Dan recognised him as the chairman of the residents' association. Taking his seat at the microphone, he waited to be given his indication to start.

'When you're ready, Mr Turtle, you have three minutes,' said Drimble.

'Ladies and gentlemen, the problems of this site have been rumbling on for eighteen months,' began Turtle. 'But the most disgraceful fact is that the local residents were not informed about these latest plans before you tonight. We've had very little time to mobilise ourselves to attend this meeting and object.'

A hiss ran around the room and Richard Drimble frowned and scribbled a note. He looked at the planning committee councillors and several of them looked equally baffled. Johanna Buttle was staring fixedly at the desk in front of her.

'The residents have consistently opposed any schemes for housing, not least because it does not allow enough space for the number of dwellings suggested,' Turtle continued. 'It is not only unfair for us, the current residents, but also for any future residents who might live there. The proposed dwellings are billed as "family homes" but they are mostly one- and two-bedroom flats. What kind of family will fit into them? And, more importantly, on such a built-up area, there will be nowhere for their children to play, except in the road, because there is no allocation for green spaces.

'But perhaps most importantly this land has never been earmarked for residential development so I cannot see why this company has even been allowed to consider these plans.'

Dan glanced at Drimble. He was leaning forward in his seat with his eyes fixed on Turtle.

'We, the residents, would love to have allotments there and this area could also include space for a children's play area. If the company would be prepared to do so, the residents' association would like to arrange terms to buy the land, paid for in instalments with interest as is proper, until its value has been paid off. That way everyone would get what they want. Whatever decision you take, please, please don't allow them to build these godawful flats,' he finished, just as the three-minute bell dinged. 'Thank you, ladies and gentlemen.' Turtle stood up and returned to his seat, giving the public gallery a cheeky thumbs-up as he went.

Drimble looked around the room. There was a pregnant pause as everyone waited for him to speak. He cleared his throat. Dan saw everyone in the public gallery lean forwards.

'Well,' said Drimble. 'We've heard from both sides of the application. Does anyone have any comments or questions?' The councillors all sat quietly, not looking at him. Dan saw Johanna Buttle cast a glance at Paul Sanderson who sat beside her. He met her gaze and both looked uncomfortable. Dan could understand why. He had some questions of his own already. There was something very wrong with this application. Was this what James Wilton wanted to tell him? Meanwhile, Drimble was looking around him in amazement.

'No one? Well, I have a question even if you don't. I want to know why on earth this application is recommended for approval.'

There was complete silence in the chamber and Drimble continued. 'Can anyone explain why a developer has been allowed to propose building houses – and so many – on land not earmarked for residential development?' he asked, turning to glare at Harriet, the planning officer who sat alone on her bench. 'And why it has been marked for approval? There also seems to be some discrepancy between the numbers quoted by Mr Anderson and those that appear on the papers.'

Dan felt himself almost nodding in agreement. He desperately wanted to look at the papers in his bag but he didn't dare take his attention away from what was happening. The planning officer rifled through the pages in front of her and then looked up at Drimble.

'I don't know, sir. I wasn't working on this application.'

'Then who was?'

'James Wilton.'

The flicker was back in Dan's stomach.

'And where is Mr Wilton?' Drimble asked.

'I … I don't know. He wasn't in work today.'

Dan noticed Buttle and Sanderson glance at each other and then look at David Edmonds. He was staring at Richard Drimble.

'But this application must have gone through several pairs of hands and numerous discussions before it came to us today. How was it not picked up at an earlier stage?'

Harriet looked over her shoulder at the head of planning who stood behind her at the back of the room, leaning against the wall. He recognised the appeal for help and moved to sit beside her.

He switched off the microphone in front of them and they whispered together for a moment.

A frown creased his face as he looked down at the papers. He whispered something in her ear and Dan saw her shrug her shoulders and shake her head.

The man cleared his throat and reached a hand towards the microphone.

'Mr Mayor, there seems to be some kind of mix-up with the papers – this isn't the version of the application we signed off. I'll have to request that we defer the decision while we work out what has happened.'

But Drimble was already shaking his head. 'It bothers me that this application was marked for approval when it breaks our rules about land use and number of dwellings.'

Johanna Buttle raised her hand.

'Yes, Councillor Buttle?' said Drimble.

'I hate to say this about a plan for regeneration, Mr Mayor, but I agree with you,' she said in a quiet voice.

There was an angry snort. Dan looked up, realising it had come from David Edmonds. He had stiffened in his seat and was red in the face.

'Elliot's Walk isn't in my ward,' she continued, 'and I like the idea of the area being used, but I can't see that housing would be the best option.' Paul Sanderson was gazing at her in amazement. Then he too raised his hand.

'Yes, Councillor Sanderson,' said Drimble.

Sanderson took a deep breath. 'I agree with Councillor Buttle,' he said. 'It seems very wrong that non-residential land should be built on without anyone raising an eyebrow.'

Dan saw Drimble cast a quick glance at Edmonds. The latter was glaring at the two younger councillors. Drimble thought for a moment and a whisper rippled around the public gallery.

'I don't think we can support this one even if it goes back to the planning office for a rethink,' said Drimble. 'I propose we refuse the application for this development. All those in favour?'

Gradually all the planning committee members raised their hands.

'Any objections or abstentions?' There were none.

'Application refused,' said Drimble.

There was a moment of stunned silence and then cheers broke out in the public gallery. Kevin Turtle jumped to his feet, punching the air and hugging his wife.

Drimble banged on the desk with his gavel, trying to make himself heard over the din. Once everyone returned to their seats, Drimble glanced at his agenda.

'That seems to be everything for tonight. Thank you to the members of the public who attended, thank you, members; meeting concluded,' he said.

Dan watched Drimble for a moment as he collected his papers together, a frown creasing his face, and then turned to Kevin Turtle. 'Any chance of a comment, Mr Turtle?' he asked.

'Delighted to help. Hmmm, what shall I say to be magnanimous in victory?'

Dan smiled.

'How about "We are very pleased to see this latest plan fall by the wayside and will continue to fight any proposals that we consider to be against our interests. We live in hope that there may come a day when children from the nearby housing developments can play safely and allotments can be formed as a relaxing place for those that want them. We thank the committee for its good sense in in taking this decision" – does that sound all right?'

'Great, thanks.' Dan started to turn away and then turned back to face Turtle. 'You said earlier that the residents knew nothing about this application?'

Turtle nodded. 'Yes. There should have been advertising and letters to all the residents but there was nothing.'

'How did you find out?'

'An anonymous letter was pushed through my letter box yesterday advising me to check online for the agenda for this meeting. Once I'd seen what was happening I mobilised the troops.' He gestured towards the people packing up their belongings in the gallery.

'Did you mention it to your local councillor?'

'I did and he said he would be here, but there's no sign.' Turtle rolled his eyes.

'Do you still have the letter? Could I see it?'

Kevin Turtle nodded. 'I'll be coming into town tomorrow, I can bring it to you.'

Dan thanked him and turned to his bag, but he didn't have time to look at the original papers before a council officer was trying to shepherd him from the room. Clearly she was keen to get home. He looked up just in time to see Edmonds fighting his way across the chamber towards Buttle and Sanderson. They'd clearly seen him coming because they exchanged a look and quickly ducked out of the door.

Dan followed them just in time to hear Sanderson say, 'We're for it now.'

'I don't care,' Buttle replied, squaring her small shoulders. 'My conscience is clear. This isn't why I joined the council. I couldn't live with myself if—' She spotted Dan listening and broke off.

The pair hurried away along the corridor and down the main stairs. Dan felt someone brush past him and saw the mayor striding away, disappearing into his parlour.

Stowing his notebook and pen into his bag, Dan checked his watch. It wasn't as late as usual but he still had a lot of work to do. A glance over his shoulder showed Edmonds having what looked like a whispered argument with Anderson from FGB Contracting. They saw him watching and Edmonds drew the other man away into a corner.

Dan hurried down the stairs as quickly as he could. He ducked into a doorway on the ground floor and dragged the old meeting papers from his bag. The Elliot's Walk application did say one hundred and forty-six. What was going on?

Chapter 4

'I want a word with you about your story,' said Daisy as Dan and Ed arrived at the office the next morning for the early shift. Getting them both up and into the office for six forty-five was always a challenge, especially as Ed was normally exempt from them as court reporter.

'Ok. What's the problem?'

'Are you sure you got the result right?'

Dan raised an eyebrow. 'Yes, I'm sure. I was there, remember?'

'They refused it? But I checked the agenda online and it said it was recommended for approval.'

Dan walked over to stand by her. 'They reversed the decision. Something weird was going on.'

'What do you mean?'

'The papers were different.'

'You're not making any sense.'

'The papers in the meeting were different to the ones you gave me yesterday.'

'What?'

'That's what I thought. That must be what James Wilton wanted to—'

As soon as he said the words, he regretted it.

'You are talking to an officer? After I told you not to?'

'But it could be something big.'

'A refused planning application? Really?'

'If I could just—'

'No, Dan. It was made clear that we leave the officers alone.' Dan began to protest but she held up a hand. 'Pursue the story if you think there is one, but stay away from James Wilton.'

When the other reporters started trickling in from about eight o'clock chatting about what they'd done the previous evening and the day ahead, they found Dan urgently tapping away. The juniors stopped and stared. They had not seen Dan working so determinedly for a long time. In fact, he was researching, trying to get it clear in his head what was happening. He had pulled several sheets of A4 paper from the printer and they were now covered in his illegible scribbling. He'd already emailed James Wilton the previous evening asking what had happened to him and could they meet again.

'I know something is going on, James,' he had written. 'Something was up at last night's meeting. We need to talk.'

But before he could answer any, or all, of the questions buzzing around in his brain, Daisy loomed up at his side clutching the news desk diary.

'We're getting a picture of the opening of the new book department in Fenleys,' she said, naming the town's big department store, and handing him the photographer's booking form.

'OK.' Dan jumped up, grabbing his notebook and pen.

Daisy stared. 'You're not usually this enthusiastic. What did you have breakfast?'

Dan shrugged. 'The usual.'

'Well, it seems to have had a very unusual effect.'

Daisy seemed inclined to find out the details of his breakfast menu, but Dan was desperate to get out of the office. If he hurried, he could try and speak to James Wilton before getting to Fenleys. He tried to take the form from Daisy's hand, but she held onto it.

'I like seeing your enthusiasm back, Dan. This is the type of thing I want the juniors to learn from you, but don't go overboard.' She let go of the form and as he moved past she said, 'And don't go near the town hall.' Dan looked at her. 'I mean it,' she said.

As he headed down the office, he smiled. Daisy knew him all too well.

But just as he reached the pavement, a voice called his name. Brendan, one of the paper's photographers, was climbing the hill towards him, puffing and panting under the weight of heavy camera kit.

'You off to Fenleys?' he asked, and when Dan nodded, he fell into step beside him. Brendan was a good talker and didn't often need a response so Dan became lost in his own thoughts, nodding occasionally. The walk to Fenleys took them past the town hall. Dan looked up at it, and debated internally what to do next. He had to speak to James Wilton, but he knew Brendan would let it slip if he bailed on the Fenleys job. He realised Brendan was standing two steps ahead, looking back at him. Without realising it, he'd come to a complete halt while he was considering his options.

'What's up?' Brendan asked.

'I need to pop in to see someone.' Dan gestured towards the town hall. Brendan looked at his watch.

'You've not got time. We'll be late for this job. I've got somewhere else to be when I finish.'

'OK.' Dan caught him up and Brendan began to chatter. Dan looked back over a shoulder, chewing on a fingernail. James Wilton would just have to wait.

Chapter 5

'What the hell happened in that meeting? You know how you were supposed to vote!' Councillor David Edmonds was red in the face and spittle flew onto the skin of his victim. Johanna Buttle shrank back against the wall as he leaned in. 'Well?' he yelled in her face.

'I couldn't do it. It would have looked so obvious. I think it was a step too far.'

'You're not in this to think. You're in this to vote how I tell you. And remember why?'

'I know, I know.' The woman was shaking. 'But Drimble would have worked it out. I think he's already on to us.'

'Rubbish. He knows nothing.'

'He's not as stupid as you think,' she said, her voice shaking. Edmonds snorted.

'You don't need to worry about him. You just have to worry about me. I'm the one who knows your secret.'

'I wish I'd never told you,' she whispered.

'I bet you do,' he said spitefully. 'But suffice to say I know and you will continue to do as I tell you until I say otherwise.' She shrank back against the wall. 'You won't ever defy me again,' he said. 'Or the newspapers will find out your secret.'

'You wouldn't?' she cried desperately.

'Oh I would, believe me.'

'But what would I do?'

'I don't care. It's in your interest to make sure you vote the right way in future.'

'Your way,' she whispered miserably.

'Good girl,' he said quietly. 'You follow my way or I'll make you very, very sorry.' He slammed his hand into the wall beside her head and he strode away leaving her cowering.

Chapter 6

It was only the thought of what James Wilton could, or would, tell him that got Dan through interviewing Timothy O. Cooke. He was a minor author of Allensbury history but contrived to make the invasions and wartime exploits of the town sound entirely boring. But, as Fenleys was a local, family-run department store, it prided itself on promoting local talent and Cooke was to be the focus of the opening of the new book section. It was all Dan could do to keep his mind on Cooke's latest boring anecdote while his brain tried to puzzle through the mysteries of last night's planning committee.

When they finished at Fenleys, Brendan hurried away to his next job, leaving Dan to wander back to the office. There was no hesitation this time and he headed up the steps into the town hall. He asked for James Wilton at the reception desk but, after the receptionist called the planning office, she put down the phone receiver shaking your head.

'Sorry, James isn't here today. Can anyone else help?'

'No. I'll call him tomorrow,' Dan replied, heading towards the door.

When he walked into the reception area at the *Post*, the receptionist stopped him, waving an envelope.

'Mr Turtle dropped this in for you. He said it's only a copy so you don't need to worry about returning it.'

'Thanks,' Dan said, taking it from her.

When he arrived back at the office, Daisy looked at her watch.

'What kept you?' she asked. Dan waved his takeaway coffee cup, his cover story for his late return. He went back to his desk.

'You were trying to chat up that poor girl in the coffee shop again, weren't you?' asked Emma disdainfully.

'No,' Dan replied shortly.

'Good, because last time I saw you it was painful. That poor girl was mortified.'

'Oh, shut up. You're just jealous.'

'Of you?' Emma scoffed. 'I don't think so. I feel sorry for her.' Dan opened his mouth to argue just as Emma's phone rang. 'Saved by the bell,' she said, picking up the receiver.

Dan sat down, keen to file his Fenleys copy so he could get back to the planning inquiry.

Emma stood up, suddenly making him jump. 'Thanks, I owe you one.' She banged the phone down and began to hurl her mobile phone, notebook and pen into her handbag. She kicked off her high heels and slipped on a pair of trainers, then dashed over to Daisy's desk, eyes shining.

'A body's been found at Coppin Woods,' he heard Emma say. 'By a dog walker.'

'What happened?' Daisy asked.

'They're not sure. Apparently it was in a car and someone might have set fire to it. My contact was a bit vague about that, but said the police are all over the woods and they've cordoned off one of the clearings not far from the car park.'

'Get down there. Take a photographer with you and let me know as soon as you know anything.'

Emma ran down the office and disappeared through the double doors.

Chapter 7

When she got to the woods, Emma was out of luck. She and Brendan were kept back at the police cordon, so far away from the scene that they couldn't really see anything. Brendan had already almost fallen into a ditch hidden in the undergrowth at the side of the muddy track they stood on, while he was trying to get a clear shot of the car. They had been allowed to pass the first cordon, which had been in the car park, and to walk up the track to the second cordon.

'Look,' said Detective Inspector Jude Burton, shooing them back from the police tape, 'if you let us get on with our job, I'll be able to give you the details much more quickly.'

'We were told it was a fire.'

Burton rolled her eyes. 'Chinese whispers, eh?'

'Why are you here? It must be something serious.'

Burton gave her a patient look. 'Emma, you know the score. There's been a death and we have to treat it as suspicious until we're told otherwise.'

Emma's ears pricked up. 'It's suspicious?'

'Don't get over-excited. You know they all are until we establish otherwise. That's not for reporting at this point,' Burton said, placing a hand on Emma's notebook page to stop her writing anything.

Emma scowled and then noticed Burton's feet. For once she was not wearing her trademark heels. Instead a pair of running shoes, covered in crime-scene booties, stuck out of the end of her well-tailored suit trousers.

'Don't even think about smirking, or you get nothing at all,' she said, seeing where Emma's eyes were fixed.

'No stilettoes today?'

'Can you imagine trying to walk in them on this ground?' Burton held up her left foot. She looked down at Emma's feet. 'I see you had the same idea.'

'And you can't tell me anything else?'

'Nothing at the moment.' Burton raised a manicured hand to stem Emma's immediate complaint. 'You know perfectly well that I'll tell you what I can as soon as I can. And don't try the pleading eyes,' she said with a grin. Emma stopped immediately and pouted. 'My girls may only be three and five years old but they're well-practised in that look. If I'm immune to them, then I'm immune to you.'

She moved to stand in front of Brendan who was still trying to take photographs of the scene.

'Oh, come on, at least let us get some pictures,' said Emma, nudging Brendan and pointing as a crime scene investigator rustled out from behind the car and began speaking animatedly to a uniformed officer.

As Brendan raised the camera, the officer turned in their direction and shouted, 'Sir.' Burton looked over her shoulder.

'Excuse me.' Her eye caught something over Emma's shoulder and she smirked. 'Looks like you've got competition.' Burton turned away, blonde hair glinting in the sun, and walked quickly across to the other officer who spoke quietly in her ear. Emma's last view was as they both turned and disappeared towards the still-smoking car.

'What are you doing down here?' Brendan called to someone who was making their way across the soft grass towards them.

'Oh, for God's sake,' Emma muttered. It was Chris Fryer, a so-called freelance journalist who was trying to make his name by scooping her. He'd not succeeded yet and she wasn't going to let it happen now.

'Hi, Emma, fancy seeing you here,' he said, swinging a camera off his shoulder.

'Having to take your own pictures as well these days?' she asked.

'You get the whole package when I'm around.' He leered at her. Emma's lip curled with contempt. He moved to stand next to Brendan and began to snap the same pictures. 'What have we got?' he asked Emma over his shoulder.

'Like I'd tell you. What's the matter, can't you get the police to talk to you?'

He laughed irritatingly. 'I can always get Burton to talk to me.'

Emma snorted. 'I thought she hated you.'

'That's just her way of flirting. She can't be seen to favour me.'

Rolling her eyes, Emma moved away and dialled a number on her phone. She was aware of Fryer trying to listen to her conversation and moved further.

'Hi, Daisy. Yeah, Jude Burton is here and she's being really cagey. She said, off the record, that there's been a death and there's a forensic team all over the car, which makes me think there's something pretty serious. She's not giving anything away at the moment. No, we're stuck at the cordon, which is a good distance away from the car. We've got some pics but they don't really show much and there's not a whole lot to write at the moment. Yeah, I will, and I'll keep you posted.'

She clicked the phone off and returned to glaring at the police officers working on the crime scene.

'I don't think that'll make them work any faster,' said Brendan, making her smile.

'It's something to do that doesn't involve talking to him, isn't it?' she replied, nodding towards Fryer, who was desperately trying to wave at Burton. The DI clearly saw him but turned away without acknowledgment.

Emma laughed. 'That's your idea of flirting, is it?'

'I'm wearing her down. It's a long game.'

Suddenly the activity around the car increased. 'Get a picture of that,' Emma said to Brendan.

Chapter 8

The following morning DI Burton and DS Mark Shepherd watched Dr Eleanor Brody across the skinny white body on her mortuary table.

Burton respected Brody a lot. She wasn't a large woman but she commanded whatever room she was in. Once she finished a post-mortem she always covered the body modestly and spoke of them by name. Her curly brown hair was tied back in a no-nonsense ponytail and the overhead lights flashed on her wire-rimmed spectacles as she turned away from the sink.

She calmly dried her hands on a paper towel and made a note on her clipboard before turning to face them. Even the scratching of her biro sounded loud in the silent morgue.

Burton pulled a face at Shepherd. It was not her favourite place and she didn't want to spend any longer there than she absolutely had to. Shepherd grinned and rested his broad shoulders against the wall. He seemed to take up a lot of floor space.

'What do you have?' Burton asked.

Brody frowned. 'A very confusing puzzle.'

'What do you mean?'

'You would think that the carbon monoxide would have got him, right? That's what usually happens with this kind of suicide.'

'Right, and …?'

'His lungs are clear and there's no cherry pink colouring to his skin that I can see.'

Burton and Shepherd both stepped forward.

'What?' asked Shepherd, frowning.

Brody directed his gaze to the slimy red lungs in the nearby dish. The twisted expression on Shepherd's face showed his disgust.

'There's no carbon monoxide damage whatsoever.'

'So he wasn't gassed, then?' Shepherd asked.

Brody nodded.

'More so, someone has gone to some trouble to cover up his identity, burning the face and the hands. You couldn't do that to yourself, could you?'

'You can't identify him?' Burton asked, looking down at the charred face.

'Not by fingerprints or by looking at his driver's licence, and his wallet is empty,' Brody said. 'It will slow us down in identifying him, but there's other ways to do it.'

'There's no way the burns could have come from the car?' Shepherd asked.

'You saw it,' Brody said. 'There's some flame damage, but that's from someone deliberately burning his face and hands. Maybe they were hoping the whole car would go up, but when it didn't – there wasn't enough accelerant to set the whole car alight – they resorted to setting it up to look like suicide.'

'So, you mean—' Burton began but Brody held up a hand. Clearly she didn't want to spoil her moment.

'Well, yes, I thought you'd like to see this. Can you help me, please?' She gestured to a nearby lab tech. He helped her to turn the body gently onto its side.

'What am I looking at?' Burton asked, peering at the skinny white back of the corpse.

'Here.' Brody's finger pointed to a small stab wound to the right-hand side of the man's spine.

Burton stared down at the body, her eyes widening. 'Is that what I think it is?'

Brody nodded. 'A puncture wound, quite a deep one, at least four inches. Mr Wilton here was stabbed, and he was definitely dead before he went into the car.'

When Burton walked into the CID office clutching two takeaway coffees, she found Shepherd perched on the edge of his desk gazing at a pretty, young uniformed woman. It seemed the woman was gazing back, which made Burton smile. All the uniformed officers loved Shepherd, even the men. He had a knack of listening with his full attention, no matter how crazy their idea or request was.

The woman was holding out a sheet of paper, which Shepherd was just in the act of taking. The paper waved in the draught caused by Burton pushing open the door and Shepherd stood up quickly. Too quickly. He sent a stack of precariously balanced folders whooshing to the floor.

'There was something inevitable about that,' he said to the uniformed officer, who grinned. Shepherd placed the piece of paper on top of his computer keyboard and stooped to pick up the deluge from the floor.

'Here, let me help you.' The woman stooped too and began to gather up the papers. 'Which folders do they go in?'

'They're all marked up.' Shepherd was nothing if not meticulous. In his work at least. His private life was somewhat less in control. 'Don't worry, I'll sort them out later.' Both stood at the same time, hands full of papers and laughed as they were unsure where to put them down.

'Are you trashing the place?' Burton asked, approaching the desk.

'Something like that.'

'What's that?' Burton asked, nodding at the piece of paper resting on Shepherd's computer keyboard.

'Take it. Alice brought it up.' Shepherd indicated the paper with an elbow.

Burton stepped forward, putting the coffees down on the neighbouring desk and picking up the paper. She scanned through it as Shepherd and Alice tried to find space on the desk for all the disordered pages. They finally managed it and turned to Burton who was sipping her coffee while looking at the page.

'A missing person?' Burton said, peering at the report.

'Yes, ma'am. You see…'

'Call me sir; I'm not the queen.' Burton paused in her reading and looked up. 'When did this come in?'

'Wednesday mid-morning. The woman was reporting her husband missing.'

'Have you spoken to her?'

'Yes. She said they had a row while they were out at dinner; she stormed off home and expected him to follow.'

'But he didn't?'

'No, she assumed he'd gone to stay with his brother in a sulk, but when she called the brother he hadn't seen him since last week.'

'What did she do then?'

'She waited till office hours and called his work but he wasn't there.'

'And she reported him missing.'

'Yes, but because he's an adult we didn't take action at the time.'

Burton looked at Shepherd, holding out the piece of paper to him. 'The description sounds like it could be the body in the car.'

'That's what I thought,' said Alice.

'Good work. Thanks for bringing it up here.'

Burton turned and began to walk slowly into her office, sipping at her coffee.

Shepherd gave Alice a thumbs-up as she left the room. He followed Burton into her office, missing the longing look Alice gave to him as she exited the main office door. He stood in Burton's office doorway, hands in trouser pockets, looking at her.

'What do you think?'

Burton's brow was furrowed. 'It shows initiative. That can't be said for a lot of our uniforms.' She looked up and saw the scowl on Shepherd's face. 'OK, I'm probably being a bit unfair.'

'I meant about the missing person.'

Burton was silent for a moment. 'I don't see why we don't call Brody and make the suggestion. It might help speed things along. But not a word to anyone else. We don't want it getting back to the family if it's not him.'

As she put a hand out towards the phone, the device rang. Burton and Shepherd looked at each other. Burton lifted the receiver.

'Hello? Oh, hi, Eleanor, I was just about to call you myself. I'll put you on speakerphone. Shepherd's here too.'

Brody's voice sounded tinny through the small speakers. 'Hi, Mark,' she said.

'Hi. We've got something for you.'

'I've got something for you too.'

'We think we might have an ID for the body,' said Burton.

'That's funny. I've got a definite ID.'

Chapter 9

Slumping into his office chair the next morning, Dan logged in and brought up his email account. There was still no response from James Wilton. He sat back and tapped his pen against his chin.

'Problem?' asked Ed.

'I've been trying to get hold of one of the planning officers, James Wilton, but he's not answering emails.'

Ed inhaled through his teeth. 'You're trying that again? Remember what happened last time.'

'This time he approached me.'

'You'll incur Daisy's wrath again.'

'Believe me, this time it's worth it.'

'Is it worth calling his office?'

'I've tried that and left messages. He should have responded before now, shouldn't he?'

'Who should?' asked Emma, hanging up the phone.

'James Wilton from the planning department.'

'You won't get hold of him today,' she remarked standing up, notebook in hand.

'Why not?' asked Dan, looking up at her.

'He's dead. He was the body in the car yesterday.'

Chapter 10

Dan stared at Emma.

'What?' he asked.

'James Wilton, he's dead. He was in the car the police found in the woods.' She turned away to brief Daisy. Dan stood up and watched her go. Ed stood up too.

'He's dead?' he asked, looking at Dan.

Dan felt his heart sink. He sat back down trying to think. He looked up to find Ed staring at him.

'What?' he asked.

'You OK?'

'Yeah, yeah, I'm fine,' he muttered under his breath. 'No wonder he wasn't at planning.'

'What?' Ed asked.

But Dan was looking at Emma, who was returning to her desk followed by Daisy.

'James Wilton is dead?' he asked.

'Yes, I told you that.' Emma sounded impatient.

'When? Wednesday night?'

Emma stared at him. 'Why would you say that?'

'He was supposed to be at the planning meeting, but he didn't show up.' He was about to mention that Wilton hadn't turned up to his meeting either, but stopped just in time.

'As it happens, they've not tied down the time of death yet. They're still waiting on some test results.' She was staring at Dan as if he were an exhibit in a museum and it wasn't a pleasant experience.

'Right, enough standing around chatting.' Daisy took charge. 'Let's get a couple of lines on the website and start chasing tribute pieces. Emma, you go to the police and see if we can talk to his family. Dan, if you're free, can you go to the council press office, and see if they want to make a statement.'

But Emma interrupted. 'Thanks, but it's my story.' She glared at Dan. 'I can handle it myself.'

Dan sat back down at his computer frowning. Had someone silenced Wilton to prevent him talking? But why would someone kill over a planning application?

Chapter 11

Several hours later, Burton found herself doing her least favourite job. She sat on the chintzy sofa in James Wilton's crowded little living room, trying to interview his grieving widow. A posting box game spilled its plastic shapes across the floor, wooden building blocks were strewn and in the middle sat a toddler, no more than a year old by Burton's best guess, blissfully unaware of the crisis unfolding in her life.

'Are you sure it's him?' Lila Wilton's voice was almost a whisper.

'I'm afraid so.'

'Will I have to do an identification?'

'No, we managed to get an ID from his dental records.'

Lila Wilton's fingers twisted around each other and her eyes never left the little girl on the floor. Tears leaked down her cheeks.

Burton looked helplessly at Shepherd. What she lacked in instinctive empathy, he more than made up for in dealing with the grief-stricken. After all, he'd had the practise. His wife Stacey had been killed in a hit-and-run the previous year. He knew exactly what it was like to get a knock on the door from the police bringing bad news. And Burton had been the one to deliver it. She wouldn't have had it any other way. He moved to sit beside Lila and handed her a tissue. She raised bloodshot eyes to smile a thank you at him.

'You can't think of anyone who would want to hurt your husband?' he asked.

Burton saw rather than heard the other woman's 'no' before the sobs overcame her again. She was a slender woman, whose pale complexion and blonde hair served to make her look entirely washed out. Her whole body shook with the weight of her grief.

'What are we going to do now?' she asked, flapping her hand towards the child. The little blonde girl looked up in surprise before using Shepherd's trouser leg to pull herself onto her feet.

'Mama,' she said toddling over to Lila. The woman scooped the child into a hug, but the girl was soon restless and demanding to be back on the floor.

'She knows there's something wrong, but she doesn't know what it is,' Lila explained.

Shepherd smiled. 'I know it's difficult, but can you tell us what happened on Tuesday?' he asked, handing her another tissue.

His comforting bulk seemed to calm the woman and, not for the first time, Burton was glad of her sergeant's presence.

Lila wiped her nose and took a deep breath, steadying herself.

'James rang me from work at about three asking if I'd meet him in town for dinner,' she said. 'He said we needed to talk.'

'Was that unusual?' asked Shepherd. Lila thought for a moment.

'It was. He liked to eat dinner at home so he could see Molly and help put her to bed. I was a bit surprised but he said that we deserved a treat, that we'd both been busy recently.'

'And is that true? You've been busy?'

Lila looked surprised at the question. 'Well, yes, James certainly was. He was working all hours.'

'But he was always home for dinner?'

Lila snuffled into a tissue. 'Yes, like I said, he liked to be home for bath time, unless he had to go to a committee meeting. They're usually only once a month. But then when Molly was in bed he'd often go to the office upstairs and do more work.'

'What did your husband do?' Shepherd asked.

'He worked for the local council, in the planning office. Planning applications and stuff like that.'

'Busy job?'

'It certainly had been recently. As I said, he'd been working more and more. When I asked why, he just said I'd understand in time.'

'And have you found out why?'

Lila looked up sharply. 'No, and I'm never going to now, am I?' Her face crumpled again and Shepherd supplied another tissue.

'What did he need to talk to you about?' Burton asked.

'When?'

'He asked to meet you for dinner and said he needed to talk to you. What did he say?'

'He said he'd got into trouble.'

'What kind of trouble?'

'He didn't really say, but I assumed it was financial.'

'Why?' asked Shepherd.

'What else could it be?' The slim shoulders shrugged.

Burton raised an eyebrow. She could think of a whole range of things before financial trouble.

But Shepherd was nodding. 'I suppose you're right. What did he say?'

'All he'd say was that he'd got into trouble but he was getting out of it and I didn't need to worry.' She frowned. 'I said that there were two of us in the relationship and to tell me the truth. He said he couldn't. That's when I yelled at him. I said that if he couldn't trust me enough to tell me the truth, maybe I'd reconsider our marriage.'

'Harsh words,' said Shepherd. 'What happened next?'

'I stormed off, expecting him to follow later.'

'Do you know where he went?'

Lila frowned. 'No. How would I know that?'

'And when he didn't come home?'

Lila hung her head and muttered something.

'I didn't catch that,' Burton said.

'I fell asleep!' Lila shouted. 'All right? I fell asleep and didn't notice he wasn't there until the next morning. I knew he hadn't been home but I assumed he'd gone to stay at his brother's because he knew I was angry.' She gave another sob. 'I was fast asleep and my husband was out there committing suicide.'

Burton looked at Shepherd. The sergeant finished scribbling in his notebook and looked up.

Burton took a deep breath. 'Mrs Wilton, we have evidence that shows your husband didn't commit suicide.'

The tear-stained face appeared quickly from behind the tissue. 'What? But I thought he'd ... the other police said ...'

'During the post-mortem wounds were discovered on the body which would suggest that your husband was killed and then put in the car which was set alight to conceal the injuries.'

Lila looked from one detective to the other. 'He didn't commit suicide?' she asked eagerly, sitting forward. 'That's definite?'

Burton and Shepherd looked at each other.

'Yes,' said Shepherd. 'It is.'

The woman sat back in the armchair and rested her head back, looking up towards the ceiling. 'Thank God.'

'Why?'

Lila looked back at him, surprised. 'I mean, I'm just so glad that it wasn't because of something I said, that he hadn't done it to himself. I thought I'd driven him to it.'

Shepherd was looking back at his notes.

'When he didn't come back, how did you find out that he wasn't at his brother's?'

'I called in the morning and Trev said he hadn't seen him since last week.'

'Then what did you do?'

'I called the office at the time he usually gets in but they'd not seen him and he hadn't called in. I tried again a bit later and he still wasn't there. That's when I called you. Well, I called the police, not you specifically. I can't describe how I felt when they knocked on the door to say he'd been found dead.'

'What time did you get home after you left your husband in town?'

'About half-past seven. Mum was here minding Molly.'

'Did you go out again?'

'No.'

'Anyone who can corroborate that?'

Lila indicated the little girl who chose that moment to wipe a very snotty nose on her hand and use the same hand to pull herself to standing aided by Shepherd's trousers. 'Ask her. She's the only proof I've got.'

Shepherd opened his mouth but Burton stood up suddenly, straightening her suit jacket.

'That's all for now, Mrs Wilton. We'll be in touch when we have more to tell you. If you think of anything.' She held out a business card.

Lila Wilton struggled out of the low sofa and got to her feet. She took the card.

'Thank you. I will.' She paused for a moment. 'You might want to speak to a Dan Sullivan.'

'Who?'

Lila shrugged. 'I don't know. I'd never heard the name before but James said he was involved.'

'Thanks, Mrs Wilton,' Shepherd said. 'That's really helpful. If you think of anything else …' He pointed to the card in her hand.

In the hallway, Burton beckoned to the family liaison officer.

'Angela, keep an eye on her. Let me know if anything happens.'

Angela raised an eyebrow. 'Yes, sir. I know the drill.'

'I don't know how you cope with all this,' Burton said shaking her head.

Angela smiled. 'Someone has to be there in the hour of need,' she said, then turned back into the living room.

The detectives walked to their car in silence. As Shepherd settled himself into the passenger seat of the car, he looked at Burton who was buckling her seat belt.

'Why did you stop me? It was just getting interesting.'

'That's exactly why I stopped you. We're going to need to question her again, but next time I want to be the one holding the cards, not her.' Burton checked her mirror, signalled and pulled away from the kerb.

'How do you mean?'

'Something doesn't feel right. She seemed more pleased that we'd decided it wasn't suicide, not that it wasn't suicide.'

'Maybe she's religious. Catholics think suicide is a sin and you can't get properly buried, or something, if you've done it.'

'And the fact she'd decided it was financial problems, and not an affair or something like that.'

'Maybe she wouldn't want to believe that he would have an affair.'

'I think it's more than that. I think she already knew it was financial problems, that's why she fired up and yelled at him so easily. I think it was her that asked for the meeting. Even more importantly she's got no alibi.'

Shepherd turned to face Burton. 'You think she took her daughter along while she murdered her husband?'

Burton frowned. 'No, not really. But I think there's a chance there's more to this than meets the eye. I think she's involved in the murder. It was supposed to look like murder, but something went wrong. For some reason she was worried that we'd think it was suicide.'

'Why would she be worried about that?'

'That's just it. I'm not sure.'

'What's next?'

'We need to find out everything about the Wiltons that we possibly can, particularly their finances. She's supposed to be a grieving widow. If we take another shot at her, I want us to be sure of our ground.'

Burton looked at Shepherd who was inspecting a string of toddler snot on his trousers. 'There's some baby wipes in the glove compartment,' she said. Shepherd pulled one out and began to dab at his trousers. The look of disgust on his face made her laugh. 'Were they expensive?' she asked.

Shepherd pulled a face. 'No, they're the only clean pair I have left.'

Burton smiled. 'You need a housekeeper.'

Burton stood in the middle of the council planning office, her latex-gloved hands on her hips, looking around with a frown on her face. Shepherd stood beside her also wearing gloves.

'It's very clean, isn't it?' Burton said.

'They have cleaners in every day, same as we do.'

'Our place never looks this clean though, does it?'

Shepherd shrugged. 'Maybe because we're always rushing about working.'

Burton's sideways glance caught the smirk on his face and she raised an eyebrow. 'Some more than others,' she remarked. Then she straightened her suit jacket. 'So, could Wilton have come back here after the row with his wife? Do we think that's what he did?'

'He could have done, but why? What was so urgent at work that it would keep him from solving the issues with his missus? She was pretty angry, wasn't she?' He moved towards one desk. 'This is his, isn't it?'

Burton nodded. At that moment there was a hesitant knock on the office door. Burton opened the door and came face to face with Richard Drimble. The mayor was anxiously running his hand over the two days' stubble on his chin.

'Can I help, Councillor Drimble?' asked Burton.

'How long will the planning office be closed?' he asked, peering over Burton's shoulder at Shepherd, who was bending over James Wilton's desk.

'We're just checking over the office and then you should have it back,' said Burton.

'The staff are all very upset. James was very popular.'

'I know; I sent them out for coffee while we got this out of the way. There's no need for them to be here. But if you want to help, you can keep them all in the canteen so we can do interviews. Now if you'll excuse me.'

'Yes, yes, I'll do that now.'

Burton shut the door on Drimble but she could sense the mayor was still standing outside. She shook her head and turned back to Shepherd who was now sitting in Wilton's chair.

'Any luck?'

'Possibly. The desk is all clean and tidied away, but this is odd.'

Burton moved to stand behind him. 'Odd in what way?'

'Sections of the computer have been wiped,' said Shepherd, gesturing to the screen in front of him. 'All the programs are still here but his documents have all been deleted and there's nothing in his inbox earlier than Wednesday. All the sent and deleted items are gone. The emails since then are mostly internal and planning related, but then there's this one.' He pointed to an email from daniel.sullivan@allensburypost.com. 'That's external.' He peered at the screen. 'James, I don't know why you didn't turn up last night but we need to talk. Whatever is going on, I don't want to lose this one. It's clearly big and I have to have it. Call me or respond to this email asap.' Shepherd sat back in the chair, frowning.

'Interesting,' remarked Burton. 'When did that come in?'

'Late on Wednesday night.'

'So Wilton may never have seen that? We need a definite time of death from Brody.'

'Right, let's take the computer with us.'

Shepherd shut down the computer and as he started to unplug it, he paused.

'What?' asked Burton.

'Stacey was pretty strict on cleaning but the leads on our computer were always dusty,' said Shepherd. 'Either the cleaners here are very thorough or someone has deliberately cleaned them.' He completed the unplugging process and lifted the computer. He juggled it in his hands as he freed it from the power lead. Then he stared at the underside of the computer. 'Sir,' he said. 'Look at this.'

Burton stared at the spots of a red substance that appeared on Shepherd's gloved fingers as he touched the underside of the computer tower.

'Is that blood?' she asked.

'Looks like it.'

Burton swiped the screen of her phone and dialled a number.

'Can we get SOCO down here, please?' she asked, when the call was answered. 'We've got a secondary crime scene.'

Chapter 12

Daisy and Emma both looked up in surprise as Ed came sprinting down the office. Daisy had a bemused expression on her face as he hung onto her desk, gasping for breath. He tried to speak but began coughing.

'What did you say?' she asked.

'They've cordoned off the town hall.' Ed coughed again heavily.

'Who have?' She peered at him. 'You haven't run very far. Should you be that colour in the face?'

Ed glared at her. He gulped once and spoke again. 'I really should give up smoking. The police. There's blue and white tape everywhere.'

Emma appeared next to Ed, pulling on her coat.

'Did he just say the police have cordoned off the town hall?'

'Yes, he did, but so far I've not been able to get any more information.'

Emma laughed. 'You're out of shape. Too much sitting on court benches.'

Ed grinned. 'I stopped and asked the officer on duty what was going on but he politely sent me packing. Looks like scene of crimes are up there too.'

'Did you see Burton?'

'No, didn't see Shepherd either, but they'll probably have been inside.'

'I'm on it,' Emma said, already halfway out of the door.

Ed walked back to his desk and sat down. On the other side of the computer monitors, Dan sat, his pen balanced between his first two fingers and tapping rapidly as if sending a Morse code message. Ed extracted two foil-wrapped packets of sandwiches from his bag and got up and walked round to Dan's desk.

'Here,' he said. 'You forgot to get these from the fridge this morning.' As he approached he saw words typed on Dan's screen, but with a click of the mouse, the file was minimised before he could look at it.

'Thanks.' Dan took the sandwiches without really looking at Ed.

'What's the matter?' Ed asked, sitting down in Emma's chair.

'Nothing. Why?'

'You're acting a bit strange.'

'Strange, how?'

'I don't know. There have been people we know through work who've died before but you've not acted like this before.'

'Like what?'

'You're being weird. What's so different about James Wilton?' When Dan said nothing, Ed asked quietly, 'What have you done?'

'What?'

'I said what have you done?'

'What do you mean?'

'Did you do something to him?'

'To James Wilton? No, why would you think that?'

'Why did you think he died on Wednesday? Did you see him on Wednesday?'

'No, I was—' Dan looked over his shoulder. Daisy was safely at her desk. 'I was supposed to,' he said in a low voice. 'Before the planning committee, but he didn't show up.'

Ed pursed his lips. 'You were meeting him, even though you've been told not to talk to council officers?'

'He approached me, he was going to tell me something.'

'Tell you what?'

Dan growled in exasperation. 'That's the problem. He didn't show and now he's dead I'll never find out.'

'But you have an idea, don't you? That's why you've been so frantic since the planning meeting.'

'I have a suspicion but I've no idea how to turn it into a story now.'

Ed stood up. 'You said it yourself that without Wilton there's no story. Be wary of trying to make a story where there isn't one.' He walked back to his desk, munching on a cheese and pickle sandwich.

Dan took a bite of his own sandwich. He had no idea where to start next. The letter that had been sent to the residents' association had given him no help at all. It was typed in block capitals and presumably printed on a normal computer printer. He couldn't approach any of the other council planning officers because they were likely to tell the head of planning and he'd be in it up to his neck with Daisy again. Should he try one of the councillors on the committee? Johanna Buttle was usually pretty nice but she'd seemed a bit wound up at the last meeting. That could be a sign that she knew something. He glanced around the office. 'Where's Emma?'

Ed stared at him. 'She left a couple of minutes ago. The police are up at the town hall now. They've got it taped off.'

'What?'

'Yeah, I just saw scene-of-crimes bods going in there when I was coming back from court.'

Dan stared at him for a moment and then grabbed his coat and bag. 'I'll be back,' he said, and dashed out of the office.

Daisy stared after him and turned to Ed.

'What's got into him?' she asked.

Dan elbowed his way through the crowd gathered on the pavement outside the town hall. It was not often they got this close to a crime scene and a small group stood like sheep gazing at the police officer guarding the tape. He shifted uncomfortably and managed not to meet anyone's eye. Then Dan spotted a familiar black-suited back. He shoved his way through the crowd to where Emma stood also eyeballing the police officer. She looked surprised when Dan appeared at her elbow.

'Did Daisy send you?' she asked, looking annoyed. 'I can manage on my own.'

'Are they not letting anyone in?'

'Nope. The staff have all been moved to other buildings or sent home. They were quite distressed apparently.' She glared at him. 'And if the police were letting anyone in it would be me, right?'

'I don't know what you mean.'

'This wouldn't be the first time you've tried to muscle in on my territory. Don't even think about it.' When Dan didn't reply, she narrowed her eyes. 'Are you OK? You look a bit funny.'

'I'm fine.'

Emma shrugged. 'Suit yourself, I was only asking.'

Someone poked Emma in the back. She turned to find Chris Fryer grinning down at her.

'Oh, great. Now I get Dumb and Dumber,' she growled, glaring from Dan to Fryer. Fryer continued to smile. With Teflon-coated skin, no insult affected him for long. Dan wasn't paying attention; he was straining to see inside the building.

'Ah, come on. You love the competition,' said Fryer, elbowing the woman on his other side away to leave him room to raise his camera.

The police officer on duty flinched away as Fryer's flash went off right in his face.

Suddenly there was activity on the steps in front of them. DI Burton appeared and raised the tape to allow a white jump-suited investigator to exit the building. Carrying a computer, he rustled past Dan and Emma and climbed into a waiting car, which sped away.

'Hey, Emma,' Burton said. 'Still here?'

'I'll be here until you tell me what's going on,' Emma replied.

Burton returned her smile. She'd always liked Emma for her tenacity, among other things, even if sometimes it made her job harder.

'Sorry, it's taking a bit longer than we thought. I'll be with you as soon as I can.' Then she spotted Fryer. 'You again.'

'Me again. You'll give me the same update as you give Emma then?'

'I'm tempted not to after the balls-up you made of the last story you were involved in. Maybe if you had some training?'

Fryer nudged Emma with his elbow. 'You'll tell me, won't you?'

'As if. I wouldn't even tell you the time.' Emma sniggered as the smile froze on Fryer's face.

'What's happening? Why is this a crime scene?' Dan interrupted. Burton looked at him and then raised her eyebrows inquiringly at Emma.

'This is my colleague, Dan Sullivan,' Emma said, glaring at Dan.

'Is it?' Burton stared at Dan.

'I've got to go.' Dan turned and started to walk away.

'I'll see you back at the office,' Emma called after him. He waved a hand without looking back. She shook her head and returned her attention to Burton. 'I'd like to say that he's not normally like that, but he's a bit of an idiot,' she said to Burton.

'Why is he an idiot?'

'He's just annoying and he tries to steal my stories.'

'A heinous crime,' Burton said with a smile. 'Apart from that, what else do you think of him?'

Emma frowned. 'He's quite smart and he's not a bad journalist when he tries, but he has o'er vaulting ambition.'

'Shakespeare?'

Emma grinned. 'Best describes it.'

'How o'er vaulting is he?'

'Enough that he's prepared to incur the wrath of other people to get what he wants.'

'I see.'

'And when I told him James Wilton was dead, he asked if it had happened on Wednesday.'

'He asked about Wednesday? Why Wednesday?'

'I don't know. It struck me as odd to try and second guess like that, but he's arrogant enough to attempt it, I suppose.'

'Do you know where he was on Wednesday night?'

'Council planning committee, I think. He was moaning about it during the day but then he left early to get there. Actually, now I come to think of it, he went way earlier than he needed to.'

Burton frowned. 'And Tuesday night?'

Emma shrugged. 'No idea. As far away from me as possible.'

'He's good looking though,' Burton said with a grin.

'If you like that sort of thing.' Emma glared at Burton's grin. 'What?'

'Methinks the lady doth protest too much.' Burton said with an arch look.

'Oh, whatever. When am I going to get an update?'

'As soon as I know something, you'll know something.' Burton turned and climbed the stairs into the building.

The doorbell chimed a fancy tune Emma didn't know. She waited so long for an answer that her hand was creeping towards the bell again when a shape grew up behind the frosted glass.

The door opened a crack and the pale face of Lila Wilton looked out at her.

'Yes?'

'I'm Emma Fletcher from the *Post*. We spoke on the phone?'

'Oh, yes, that's right. Come on in.' Lila led the way into the sitting room and gestured towards a chair. Stepping over various toys strewn on the floor, Emma sat down.

The police family liaison officer appeared in the doorway. Emma recognised her but didn't know her name. 'Would you like a coffee?' she asked.

Mrs Wilton rubbed a hand over her face and shook her head wordlessly.

'No, thanks,' Emma said, keen to get started. Tribute pieces were her least favourite bit of the crime beat.

'It's weird how people think a hot drink will make you feel better, isn't it?' Lila said. Emma looked up from her notebook at the sharp tone in the other woman's voice. 'Like it's going to fix things?'

'I suppose it's something to do, isn't it? In a situation like this, it's difficult for other people to know how to help you.'

Lila smiled. 'Everyone's treading on eggshells, worried that they're going to upset me. I wish they would just act normal.'

Emma struggled for the right words to answer her, but failed. She knew the frustration of incessant tea making as a stage of grief, along with being bitter and angry. In her case it had been accompanied by guilt and powerlessness.

'Are you OK to get started? Then I can get out of your hair.'

'It's as good a time as any. My mum is out with Molly, my daughter, at the moment. They should be back soon.' She leaned forward, hands clasped between her thighs, as if they were cold. 'Sorry, I don't really understand what a tribute piece is.'

'It's a chance to pay tribute to your husband and the kind of person he was. The people who know him, who read the paper, will want to know about what happened. This is your chance to show them what he was really like.'

Emma looked up to see a hard expression on Lila's face. Again she was struck by the widow's attitude.

'He was a good man.' But Lila Wilton's tone said something very different. It said the complete opposite, in Emma's opinion.

If the interview went on this slowly, she'd never get out of here, and the piece would be boring.

'Had you been married for long?'

'About six years.'

'And you have a daughter?'

'Yes, Molly. She's only just turned one.'

Emma was busily scribbling in her notebook.

'We'd been out for dinner that evening,' Lila continued. 'We went to a bar in town.'

'That's nice.'

'It's not something we often do. James liked to be home to put Molly to bed. He was working later and later after he got home recently so it was the least he could do for his only daughter.' Again the tone didn't fit that of a grieving widow.

'He sounds like he was dedicated to his job and his family,' Emma said, trying to leave Lila to create a more substantial answer.

'One more so than the other it would seem.' Then Lila seemed to remember who she was talking to. 'He was dedicated to our family. He looked after us very well. I can't imagine what me and Molly will do now.' She suddenly looked very sad. 'My little girl is going to grow up not knowing her father. She doesn't really understand what's going on.'

'That's usually the hardest bit.'

Lila looked up when Emma spoke. 'You seem like you understand, like you've been there.'

'In a manner of speaking.' Emma smiled. 'You sound like you've got a close family though.'

'Yes, my mum and sister don't live too far away and James's brother is helping too.'

'What did your husband do?' Emma already knew the answer but was trying to create some quotes.

'He worked for the council, in the planning office. Working on planning applications and that kind of thing.'

'It sounds like a very responsible job.'

'It was. He was good at it. Very meticulous and attentive to details.'

'I have a colleague who covers planning a lot, and he said the same thing, he always produced really detailed reports on the planning applications he worked on.' This was untrue. Emma had never, until recently, heard James Wilton's name mentioned. 'Is that why he was working more? Taking too much time over the details?'

'Who knows? All I know is that his workload had increased a lot recently.'

'The perils of being too good at what you do, I suppose?'

'Something like that.'

'Is there anything else you'd like people to know about him?'

'That he'd hate all this fuss? James was a private man, didn't like the limelight. He would have hated being in the news.'

Emma smiled. 'I think that's all I need, so I can leave you in peace.' She closed her notebook and stood up. Lila stood up too and followed her to the door.

'The colleague you mentioned,' Lila asked. 'Is that Dan Sullivan?'

'Yes. Why? Do you know him?'

'James mentioned him to me when we went out for dinner. He

said they had a meeting set up but he didn't say when it was. When James didn't come home I wondered whether that was because they were meeting.'

Emma said goodbye and walked back to her car. So Dan had been trying to meet James Wilton. What could he possibly want with the planning officer who had previously got him into trouble?

Chapter 13

It was the phone call Burton was expecting.

'DI Burton? It's Angela. I'm the FLO for Lila Wilton.'

Burton sat up straight. 'Angela? What's up? Where's Mrs Wilton?'

'She's upstairs, that's why I'm calling.'

'I don't follow.'

'You said to call if anything odd happened and, well, she's certainly odd.'

'How do you mean?'

'The grieving widow act seems to be just that. When you left she sat there for a moment looking stunned and upset. I went to answer a phone call and when I came back she was texting, the tears all dried up and a smile on her face. The smile disappeared when I came back into the room.'

Burton's brow furrowed. 'I did wonder if there was more to the situation than met the eye. What's she doing upstairs?'

'Sorting out her husband's things.'

'Already?'

'I thought she meant clothes and suchlike but when I went to offer to make tea she was in the office and told me not to come in. She sounded a bit tearful, but I'm not sure I believe it anymore.'

'OK, keep an eye on her. If you hear a shredder, get in there and stop her. Call me if that happens.'

'A shredder?'

'Yes, I've got a pretty good idea what's in that office. Has Emma Fletcher been yet?'

'Yes, she'd been and gone before Lila went upstairs. Talking to the media didn't seem to faze her at all.'

Burton hung up the phone just as Shepherd came through the door. She brought him up to speed with the details of the phone call and the corners of his mouth turned down.

'She's not upset at all?'

'I don't think the tears were entirely crocodile, but there was something else that upset her more than him being dead. I thought she seemed more deeply hurt.'

'Grief is pretty deep, sir.'

Burton looked up at Shepherd's sharp tone to find him with a clenched jaw.

'Sorry, Mark, I didn't mean it like that. I meant that she seemed angry rather than sad.'

'That's one of the stages of grief. Anger. That and guilt for not being there to stop it.'

'I know. I'm sorry. What did you think of her?'

Shepherd frowned and lowered himself into the chair opposite her desk. 'I thought she seemed genuinely upset, but your initial supposition may be right.' He handed her a cardboard folder.

'What's this?'

'Something that would, if she were that way inclined, ease the pain of a grieving woman whose husband didn't commit suicide.'

Burton gave him a puzzled look and flipped open the folder with a neatly manicured fingernail. Her eyes widened and a smile spread across her face.

'Gotcha.'

Lila Wilton answered the door and a fleeting look of annoyance crossed her face when she found Burton and Shepherd on the doorstep. She allowed them inside, bringing a ragged tissue to dab at eyes that were no longer red or tear-stained.

'Come through.'

As she led the way to the living room, Angela appeared in the kitchen doorway drying her hands on a tea towel.

'Shall I make some tea?'

'Oh, thanks, Angela.' Lila led the way into the living room.

Catching the expression on Burton's face, Angela came into the room and held out a hand to Molly. 'Shall we see if we can find some chocolate biscuits?'

The little girl pushed herself to her feet and took several tottering footsteps towards Angela. The woman stepped forward, took her hand and shut the kitchen door behind them.

'You both look serious,' said Lila, looking at the two detectives.

'Just a few more questions,' said Burton briskly, sitting down on the sofa.

'How are you doing?' Shepherd asked.

'I don't really know.'

'How do you mean?'

'Put it this way, I've learned a lot about James in the last day or so.'

'How do you mean?' Shepherd repeated.

'He was in a lot of trouble.'

'You've been sorting out his things.'

'I thought I'd better make a start. There are a lot of papers up there.'

'Mind if I take a look?' Shepherd was on his feet and halfway out of the door before Lila Wilton could react. She made to follow him but a sharp 'sit down, please' from Burton meant she kept her seat.

The floorboards creaked overhead as Shepherd moved about the small office.

He soon reappeared with a red cardboard folder in his and nodded at Burton. She stood up and turned to Lila Wilton. Lila stood too, staring at the folder and looking worried.

'I think we'd better continue this at the station,' Burton said.

'You've lied to me, Mrs Wilton,' Burton said as they sat opposite the woman across an interview room table. The tape recorder whirred.

'What you mean?' The woman sat bolt upright in her chair looking uncomfortable. Burton produced a piece of paper. It was printed with a telephone company logo on it. Lila looked at it without touching it. 'What's that?'

'Your mobile phone calls over the last few days.'

'You can't do that! That's invading my privacy.'

'We can do what we like in a murder inquiry. You lied to me about what happened on Wednesday.'

Lila slumped back in her chair looking very much like a sulky teenager. 'What are you saying happened?' she asked.

Burton smiled. It was not a cheerful smile. 'You said your husband called you, but that's not true, is it?' She tapped one particular call with a painted fingernail. 'You called him and you were on the phone for four minutes. You obviously spoke to him and it was important enough for you to then call your mum to come and babysit Molly while you went to meet him.'

'So? I wanted to have dinner with my husband. Is that a crime?'

'You could have done that at home. Why did you have to go out?'

Lila Wilton glared at her and said nothing.

'Shall I tell you what I think happened? I think you found this paperwork that afternoon. You broke the rules, went into his office and discovered that your joint credit cards had a total debt of around fifty grand and only the minimum payment is being made on each card. I don't know about you, but that would make me very angry.'

Lila stared back at her.

'I think you were angry, you went to meet him and you argued. Publicly, I understand. Enough that staff in the bar where you'd had drinks remember seeing you.' Lila still sat staring at Burton. 'And you know what I think happened next, I think you went with him to the office, you argued again and stabbed him in the back.'

'No!' Lila leapt to her feet, her chair scraping across the floor.

'Sit down, Mrs Wilton,' Shepherd said calmly. But Lila stayed on her feet.

'No! That's not how it happened!'

Shepherd rose to his feet, stared hard at her and repeated, 'Sit down.' Sensing his tone, she sat down again.

'How's the mortgage looking?' Burton asked. Lila stared. 'First thing I'd check,' Burton continued. She stared at Lila until the other woman broke the silence.

'I don't know. That's what I was looking for when your officer disturbed me this afternoon. I can't find it and I was scared.'

'You were scared? Past tense?'

'Like you said, I figured out if he was buying everything on credit, and couldn't pay that off, what else had fallen by the wayside.'

'Why was he using so much credit?'

Lila smiled sadly. 'We had such a nice life before Molly came along. Expensive holidays, meals out, the usual. We even managed to get a mortgage.' She paused. 'I don't for a moment regret having Molly, but I didn't adapt to life on a single income very well at first. I thought we should be able to continue having nice things. James was happy to buy them and I didn't realise we really couldn't afford them.'

'And you didn't think of getting a second income?'

'I suggested it, but James said it was a waste of time, that I'd only be earning enough to pay for childcare, and he was probably right. So I started to try and rein in the spending, but he couldn't stop.'

'He didn't gamble?'

'Not to my knowledge.' She indicated the financial paperwork. 'But what would I know?'

Burton paused and Shepherd spoke. 'You said you were scared. What changed?'

Lila said nothing. 'Is it because you killed him? Knowing he was worth more to you dead than alive?'

Lila stared at him and then looked at Burton. 'I don't understand. How would he pay them off if he was dead?'

Shepherd nodded to Burton. She slid a sheet of paper across the table towards Mrs Wilton.

Lila looked down at it and her eyes widened. 'You got this in the office at home, didn't you? How dare you?' Her eyes were filled with angry tears.

Shepherd shook his head. 'No, we got it through looking at your financial records. What is it?' he asked, pointing.

'Life insurance,' she whispered.

'Louder please, for the tape.'

'Life insurance. For James.'

'And that's why you were so worried when we said at first that it looked like suicide. You got that detail wrong, didn't you?'

'If I had killed him, how would I have got him to the woods? He wasn't a big guy, but he was far too heavy for me to lift and why would I have made it look like suicide?'

'Someone else did that for you, though, didn't they? You asked them to help get rid of the evidence, to hide the body, but they didn't do it how you wanted, did they? You relaxed when we said it was murder, because you knew you'd get the money from the insurance.'

Lila looked down at her hands clenched on the table top; two more tears plopped onto them but she didn't wipe them away. 'I was angry with him for running up all those debts and leaving me with them. You're right that the life insurance wouldn't pay out for suicide so I was angry with him. I felt awful for being relieved especially as all the money in the world wouldn't bring him back.' She paused. 'There was an irony in getting this bill the following day.'

Lila put her hand into her jeans pocket and pulled out a piece of paper, folded into quarters. 'It was in a sealed envelope addressed to James, but I opened it.' She smoothed out the sheet of paper and slid it across the table. Both detectives leaned in to look at it. There was a sharp intake of breath as they looked at the credit card statement. Shepherd looked up first.

'It's been paid off?' he asked.

The woman nodded. 'They all have. I phoned all the other companies and they said the same thing. In the last few days they've received payment in full.'

Burton was looking sceptical. 'Where did your husband suddenly get fifty grand?'

Lila shrugged. 'You tell me. When we argued, he said he'd done something wrong, but it was all for me and Molly, that he hoped I wouldn't hate him for it. He said he was done with all that and soon we'd be free and we could go away, wherever I liked.'

'He was planning to do a runner?'

'James wasn't a coward. He was fixing what he'd done wrong.' She stared at Burton and a single tear slid down her cheeks. 'What happened to him? Who killed my husband?'

'The grieving act is wearing a little thin,' Burton said. 'From where I'm sitting, you have a very good motive.'

'Why would I kill James? I love him.'

'Even when you found out the financial position he'd put you in?'

'I was angry, yes, but I didn't kill him. Why would I kill him?'

'You killed him for the insurance money and then realised that in actual fact you needn't have done that, that he was true to his word and had sorted it all out,' said Burton.

'I didn't know that he had.' The woman stopped suddenly as if realising what she'd said.

Burton smiled her crocodile smile and looked over at Shepherd.

'I don't think you meant to kill him, did you, Lila?' Burton leaned back in her chair. 'I think you were so angry that you followed him to the office, there was an argument. He tried to walk away and you stabbed him in the back.'

'No!' Lila interrupted thumping her fist on the table. 'I didn't, I wasn't there. James went off to his office at the town hall, and I went home. I had to get back to Molly.'

'We'll have to check up on that and get back to you.' Burton collected her papers together and stood up. Lila looked up at her eagerly.

'Can I go home now? I need to be with my daughter.'

'You're not under arrest yet, Mrs Wilton, so you're free to go, but be where we can find you.' Burton swept from the room, high heels clacking, leaving Shepherd to show Lila Wilton out and arrange a lift home.

When Shepherd returned to the office, he found Burton putting down the telephone receiver, a frown creasing her face.

'What's up?' he asked sitting down opposite her.

'I had a message to call Emma at the *Post*.'

Shepherd grinned. 'She's nothing if not tenacious.'

'She wasn't after information. She had information to share.'

Shepherd leaned forward, resting his forearms on his thighs. 'Such as?'

'When she interviewed Lila Wilton, Dan Sullivan's name came up.'

'The guy who sent the email on Wilton's computer?'

'The very same. His name has now come up three times, and Emma told me earlier that he was acting strangely after he found out Wilton was dead.' She paused. 'I suggest we pay Mr Sullivan a visit first thing tomorrow and see what he has to say for himself.'

Chapter 14

The sound of the flat's intercom buzzer roused Dan from sleep at seven o'clock on Saturday morning. He was just trying to work out where he was and what was happening, when he heard Ed banging on his bedroom door.

'What is it?' he mumbled sleepily.

Ed pushed open the door and stared at him. 'The police are here, they want to talk to you.'

Dan pushed himself up on his elbows. 'What? I don't do jokes this early in the day.'

But Ed's face was serious. 'I'm not joking. The police are here.'

'Where?'

'They're on their way up.'

'Why?'

'They want to talk to you.' He turned as there was a hammering at their door and then looked back at Dan. 'What have you done?' he asked.

'Nothing,' Dan protested.

'Really?'

'Yes. I don't know why they're here.' But Ed was already walking down the hall to answer the door.

Dan threw on a pair of tracksuit bottoms and a stained, creased

T-shirt over the boxer shorts he slept in. He stood in his bedroom doorway, rubbing his eyes, and trying to flatten his hair as Ed ushered Burton and Shepherd down the hall into the living room.

'Morning,' said Shepherd looking Dan up and down as he passed. His shoulders almost touched the walls of the narrow hallway.

'Cup of tea?' Ed asked as Dan followed them into the room, yawning.

'No, thanks, we'd just like a word.' Burton looked at Dan.

'Sure. Have a seat.' Dan sat in an armchair and faced the detectives. They both remained standing. 'What's this about?' Dan asked.

'Do you know James Wilton?'

'Not really. If you need information about what's running in the paper, you'd better ask Emma. She knows more about the case than I do.'

'Oh, I doubt that,' said Burton.

Dan raised his eyebrows.

'I think this would be better done at the station,' Shepherd put in, eyeing Ed who hovered in the doorway. Burton nodded.

'You'd better get dressed properly,' she said.

'What? Is he under arrest? What's this about?' Ed asked. Dan stood silent, looking from Burton to Shepherd, searching their faces for a clue as to what was going on.

'Why do you need to talk to me?' he asked.

'We'd like you to help with our inquiries into the death of James Wilton.'

'Me? Why? Emma's the one covering the case, as she keeps reminding me. She spoke to his wife yesterday.'

'We're just making inquiries,' Shepherd said.

'I think you should get some clothes on,' Burton said to Dan, who turned and left the room.

Back in his bedroom he began to pull on a pair of jeans. The police couldn't possibly know about the story so why did they want to speak to him?

'Comfortable?' asked Burton.

'Not exactly.' The interview room wasn't designed for comfort, but for boredom. The walls were blank beige and there was a wooden-topped, metal-legged table in the middle of the room with four blue plastic chairs, two each side, that were designed for no bottom in the world to be comfortable on them. The room was very warm and a fluorescent light buzzed overhead. Dan wondered whether this was part of the interrogation technique, making the criminal sweat physically as well as mentally. Shepherd switched on the voice recorder and introduced everyone at the table.

'What's this about?' Dan asked.

'James Wilton. How well did you know him?'

'I didn't. Not really. I'd seen him at meetings and stuff but then out of the blue on Tuesday he emailed me.'

Burton and Shepherd looked at each other.

'Did he?' Burton asked.

'Yes.'

'Why? If you didn't really know each other?'

'Like I said, I don't know. Last time I tried to work with him on something we both got a bollocking because reporters aren't supposed to contact the officers directly. It's got to go through the press office.' Dan put on a pompous voice, imitating the head of the planning department.

'He'd got you into trouble previously?'

'Yeah, but it was no real biggie.'

'You wouldn't say you were angry with him?'

'No, it's not his policy. He was eager enough to help. Besides, I'm always getting into trouble with my news editor about something.'

'Why did he email you?'

'He said he had something to tell me and asked me to meet him on Wednesday before the planning committee meeting.'

'What did he tell you?'

'That's just it, he didn't show up. I was a bit annoyed because it sounded like he had something pretty big to say.'

'Something big?' Shepherd asked, but Burton held up a hand to stop him.

'Then what happened?' she asked.

'When he didn't show I went into the planning meeting. There was a specific application I was interested in.'

Burton snorted. 'I wouldn't have thought planning applications were interesting.'

'They're not usually, but this one had got my attention. Something seemed really off with it. I wondered whether that was what Wilton wanted to talk about.'

'How do you mean "seemed a bit off"?'

'The numbers were wrong. On the application.'

'So? People make mistakes.'

'Not these guys. The applications are checked about six times, by different people. There's no way they'd got that wrong. It's too contentious an application for them to risk a mistake.'

'And the next day you emailed James Wilton to ask where he was and what had happened with the application?'

'Yes. I had no idea he was already dead.'

Burton pounced. 'How do you know when he died?'

Dan looked surprised. 'I assumed. You found the car the next day.'

'And you asked Emma whether he'd died on Wednesday night?'

Dan frowned. 'Been telling tales, has she?'

'Just answer the question. Why did you suggest Wednesday?'

'Like I said, I assumed he died on Wednesday. That was why he wasn't at the planning meeting.'

Shepherd leaned forward. 'Apart from that, we've only got your word that you went to the town hall to meet him.'

'Did anyone else know about the meeting?' Burton put in.

'No.' Dan's heart sank. 'No, I didn't tell anyone.'

'Did anyone see you going to meet James Wilton?'

'No. He said to make sure I wasn't seen.' Dan rubbed his hands across his face. How could he have been so stupid?

Burton leaned back and folded her arms. 'Convenient,' she said. 'Assuming that you did go to meet Mr Wilton and you say he didn't turn up, do you have any proof that he didn't?'

'Prove he wasn't there? How would I prove that?'

Burton stared at him and Dan had the horrible feeling that she could read his mind. Shepherd was staring at him too. The silence was deafening.

'Where were you on Tuesday night?' Shepherd asked, breaking the awkward silence.

'Why? Was that when he was killed?'

'Just answer the question.'

Dan thought for a moment. 'I was in work until six o'clock. I went home, had a shower, something to eat and then went out to meet a girl.'

'You had a date?' Shepherd asked.

'Yes.'

'Go well did it?'

Dan shrugged. 'Not really. I wasn't very attentive and she left early. She did the "have to get up early" excuse.'

Shepherd raised an eyebrow. 'Get that often, do you?'

'No, usually we leave together, if you know what I mean, and I get home the following morning.'

'Always stay at theirs, do you?'

'Yeah, Ed's girlfriend doesn't like finding strange women in the kitchen when she stays over. Plus it means I can leave when I want.'

'Classy,' remarked Burton.

'Maybe, but it doesn't make me a murderer.'

'What time did she leave?'

'About half-past eight, I think.'

'Wow, things really didn't go well,' Shepherd said. Dan shrugged.

'So from roughly half-past eight onwards, you don't have an alibi.'

'Well, I stayed on to finish my drink so people would have seen me in the pub. Then I walked home via the chippy.'

'Comfort eating?'

'No. I wasn't really hungry. I just fancied some chips.'

Shepherd smiled. 'Reckon they'll remember you in the shop?'

'Possibly. It was quite busy, but I've been in there a few times before.'

'And then?'

'I walked home. I wasn't late so Ed probably heard me come in.'

'James Wilton was out on the town too on Tuesday. Did you see him?' Burton asked, glancing down at some notes.

'No.'

'You sound pretty certain of that.'

'I don't remember seeing him.'

Burton and Shepherd both stared at him again. This time Dan bowed to the pressure and spoke first.

'I've told you everything I know. James Wilton was supposed to meet me on Wednesday, presumably to talk about a planning application. He didn't show so I went on to the planning meeting as I was supposed to. He didn't show up for that meeting either, and ...'

'You still wanted to meet him, despite the trouble you'd got into previously?'

Dan shrugged. 'He seemed so desperate to talk about something. When I saw the Elliot's Walk report later, I assumed that was what he wanted.

'The application I was interested in was one of his. I thought he must have been called to that meeting early and that's why he couldn't meet me.'

'But he wasn't there?'

'I've told you that already.'

'OK.' Burton stood up. 'That's all for now. Stay where we can reach you.' She moved towards the door.

'Any chance of a lift home?'

'We're not a taxi service,' she said.

Dan shrugged at Shepherd. 'Worth a try, eh?'

When Dan pushed open the front door, Ed came out of the sitting room with a frown on his face.

'What's going on?'

'At least let me get my coat off.'

'Dan, the police lift you from the flat at the crack of dawn on a Saturday morning and you're acting like it's nothing.'

'Any chance of a cuppa?'

'You don't deserve one. Are you going to answer my question? I have a right to know.'

'Why do you assume I've done something?' Dan pushed past Ed and walked through the living room into the kitchen.

Dan filled the kettle with water and flicked on the switch. He took a teabag from the box in the cupboard and dropped it into his favourite mug, shaped like a football.

'Don't snap at me. I'm concerned. Have you been at the police station all this time?'

'Yes.'

'Why?'

'Just helping with inquiries.'

'What inquiries?'

Dan turned to get milk from the fridge and found Ed blocking his path.

'What inquiries?' Ed paused. 'It's James Wilton, isn't it? They're interviewing you about his death, aren't they?'

'Yes.'

'And they think you did it?'

'They're are asking about Tuesday night, where I was and stuff.'

'They're checking whether you have an alibi?'

'I suppose so.'

'How can you be so blasé about this?'

'Because I was with that girl until half-eight, and then I went to the chippy and came home. I didn't see James Wilton and I wasn't seen with him.'

Ed frowned. 'What time did you come home?'

'I don't know but—' Dan frowned. 'Didn't you hear me?'

Ed looked at him. 'No, I changed my plans and I stayed at Lydia's. So I have no idea when you came home,' he said quietly, turning and leaving the kitchen.

Behind Dan the kettle boiled, hissing steam and clicked off. He stared at it. He'd been counting on Ed and now he really had no alibi at all.

Chapter 15

There was a light tap at Richard Drimble's office door. The mayor looked up to see Johanna Buttle's blonde head appear around it.

'You wanted to see me?' She was gripping the side of the door tightly as she looked into the room and seemed reluctant to step inside.

'Hi, Johanna. Come in.' Drimble stood and pulled up a chair for her. 'Have a seat.'

She perched on it, her slightly shaking hands clasped in her lap.

'What's this about?' she asked.

Drimble sat for a moment in silence, looking at her. 'This is a bit awkward. The police are investigating James Wilton's murder, but I'm afraid I'm going to have to start an investigation of my own.'

'Into James's death? Is that not a bit pointless?'

'No, I'm investigating the planning department and the committee.'

Buttle's eyes widened. 'What? Why?'

'I'm worried, Jo. That meeting on Wednesday, something was very wrong. That application was all over the place.'

'You're going to launch a full-scale investigation over one planning application? It was probably a mistake.'

'My investigation will be kept off the books for now, but most importantly, it's not just one application. I've been reading back through some papers, from before I joined the committee and something doesn't add up.'

'What do you mean?'

'I've come across several applications, well, five or six actually, which directly or indirectly breach the planning laws, amendments being tabled and made without any cross-checking.'

Buttle raised her eyebrows, opened her mouth to say something and then closed it again.

'James Wilton's name was on all of them,' Drimble continued, 'but I don't know how far this goes. Are there other planning officers involved? Does the head of planning know? What about the committee members, are they involved?' Drimble stopped to take a breath. 'I need to who is involved.' He emphasised his point by tapping his forefinger firmly on his desk.

'I don't know what I can do,' Buttle said.

'I think you do, Jo. People trust you; they'll talk to you. I can't get them to talk. Find out if anyone else in the council or on the committee has noticed something dodgy going on.'

'I can't. I wouldn't know how.'

'You have to, Jo; you have to. If I'm right, this is corruption at the heart of the council and I won't have it on my watch.' He leaned forward on his desk, clasping his hands like a newsreader. 'Will you help me?'

'What do you expect me to do?'

'Just ask a few questions. Even the applications that came to committee weren't questioned, so the members must be involved. Everyone knows I'm investigating and they're all avoiding me.'

'You want me to do your dirty work for you?' Her voice was sharp.

'Not dirty work – just ask a few questions and see if anyone knows anything.'

'I'll see what I can do.' Buttle stood up.

'Thanks, Jo. I'll remember this,' said Drimble. He waited until she was at the door. 'I'll be in touch for an update in a couple of days,' he added.

She nodded slightly and went out, closing the door quietly.

Councillor Johanna Buttle was summoned back to the mayor's parlour sooner than she'd hoped. She looked even smaller than her five-feet-two-inches height as she sat poised on the edge of the large leather armchair.

Drimble wasn't present, having been sent out by the council's chief executive so Burton and Shepherd had somewhere to conduct their interviews. Drimble wasn't happy, but the chief executive pulled rank and the mayor had to find somewhere else to work.

'We'll need to talk to you too, Councillor Drimble,' Burton had told him.

He'd seemed flustered but replied, 'Yes, yes of course. Just call me when you're ready.'

Now Buttle's legs were tightly crossed at the knee and her right foot was bouncing up and down. Whether she was nervous or it was a habitual tic, Burton wasn't sure, but she couldn't help being mesmerised by the pointed, patent leather, T-bar shoe jiggling about in front of her.

Shoes were her own personal weakness and she ached to ask where the other woman got them. But now was not the time. She opened her mouth to speak.

Suddenly Buttle burst out, 'I don't know why I'm here.' She crossed her arms tightly across her ample breasts as she spoke.

'We're speaking to anyone who had a connection to James Wilton.'

'I didn't have anything to do with him.' The words hurried out as if Buttle couldn't keep them back.

Shepherd frowned. 'You were both involved in the planning committee,' he said.

'Oh, yes, of course.' Buttle flushed.

'How well did you know Mr Wilton?' Shepherd continued. Burton leaned back in her chair, mirroring the other woman's body language.

'I didn't. I only really saw him at planning committee meetings or at pre-meeting briefings.'

'You didn't see each other outside work?'

'No, of course not. Why would I?' Her arms had unfolded and the hands were clasped in her lap.

'Did you never meet him to discuss applications?'

'We might have done, but it would always have been as a committee, to brief us on the applications, but never alone.'

'If we were to check on his emails we wouldn't find any contact between you?'

'No. Like I said, apart from group emails to the committee as a whole, I had no contact with him.'

Burton took a breath. 'Do you know much about computers, Councillor Buttle?'

Buttle blinked at the sudden change of conversational direction. 'I know how to use one, how to set up word processing documents and spreadsheets and do presentations, but nothing past that.' She looked at the detectives. 'Why?'

'James Wilton's computer had been wiped of all his files and emails. Can you think of anyone who would want to do that?'

'Would you have wanted to do that?' Shepherd asked. 'I mean, it can't be that difficult to delete files, can it?' He looked at Burton. 'Wouldn't you say?'

Buttle stared at him. 'Delete files from his work computer? Why would anyone do that?'

'We have a few theories,' Burton said. 'We're sure it was someone who works for the council because they would have needed access to his log-in details.'

'They might have made James tell them,' Buttle suggested. 'In which case it could be anyone.'

'But would an outsider know what they were looking for?' Shepherd asked.

'Maybe they didn't, maybe that's why they deleted everything.'

'You mean someone from inside the council would know what to look for?' Shepherd asked.

Buttle opened her mouth to speak but then closed it again, seeming to think better of what she was about to say.

Burton paused staring at Buttle who couldn't quite meet her eyes. 'Where were you on Tuesday night, Councillor?'

Buttle frowned. 'Where was I?'

'Yes. Mr Wilton died on Tuesday night. His body wasn't found in the woods until Thursday morning, but we're quite sure he died on Tuesday.'

'He was stabbed in the back,' Shepherd said. 'It wouldn't have been a quick death, either. We know he was dead when he went into the car, but a stab wound like that would have meant he bled to death and that takes some time.'

Buttle clapped her hands to her ears. 'Stop it, stop it. I don't want to hear this.'

'Wilton was your work colleague, a man you worked closely with on the planning committee. He had a wife and a daughter.' Shepherd was speaking in a low voice, but his tone was urgent. 'Please, Councillor, if you know anything you have to tell us.'

Buttle looked at him, tears welling in her blue eyes. 'I don't know anything,' she whispered. 'I don't.'

'Did anyone get angry with Mr Wilton? Did he have any

enemies?' Shepherd continued to speak in the same tone.

'I don't know.' Buttle's voice had dropped to a whisper.

'I don't believe you.'

They were the wrong words. Buttle sat back, wiped her hands across her face and got to her feet. 'I'm sorry that I can't be of more help, but I simply don't know anything. Can I go? I need to get back to work.'

Burton looked like she wanted to refuse permission but instead got to her feet, thanked the other woman, and allowed her to depart.

'Shit,' said Shepherd. 'I went too far.'

Burton sat down again. 'No, you nearly had her. She's definitely involved. She knows something and hopefully she's the weak link in the chain. Once we know a bit more, she'll break easily.'

'Now we just need that little bit more.'

'We've got more than enough people to work on. DC Toms and DC Williams are interviewing the other staff and we've still got a considerable list. Someone in the council knows exactly why Wilton was killed. We just need to find the right button to press.'

Chapter 16

Burton entered the CID office and was walking towards her own glass-fronted corner when she saw Shepherd waving an arm to attract her attention. The detective sergeant was peering at a television screen and had paused what he was watching.

'What is it?'

'I've just found something interesting on this CCTV footage.' He skipped the DVD back a few scenes as he spoke. 'We called in the CCTV from the night Wilton died from the High Street outside the town hall.'

'And?'

Shepherd began to roll the recording. 'Here comes Wilton now.' He pointed a stubby finger at the screen. 'He's not looking around and he goes straight into the town hall.'

'So? We know that already, although I suppose it tallies up with the time of death that Brody gave us.'

'This is where it gets very interesting. He's talking on the phone as he's walking along.'

'Why is that interesting?'

'Not the phone, the fact that there's no sign of Lila Wilton in it anywhere.'

'Damn it, so she was telling the truth?'

'It would seem so.'

'Could she have got in another way?'

'It's possible but the back entrances are locked at night and the security guard didn't see or hear anything.'

Burton was about to turn away when Shepherd raised a hand. 'Keep watching.' The recording continued to roll and Burton inhaled sharply as another figure stepped into shot.

'Mr Sullivan,' she said.

Shepherd grinned. 'Mr Sullivan. He told us he was in a bar and didn't see Wilton that night.'

'How could he have missed him when Wilton is right in front of him down the street?'

'Maybe he's just unlucky and is in the wrong place at the wrong time but watch this next angle.' Shepherd skipped forward until the camera switched to the other end of the High Street. 'Wilton's disappeared because the town hall is here.' He pointed to the left-hand side of the screen just out of sight. If Mr Sullivan is just walking along he should appear in the next minute or two.'

'But he doesn't,' said Burton slowly as the recording ran on. 'So where did he go?'

'Exactly.'

Burton shook his head. 'I knew he wasn't being straight with us. Time we had a more official chat with him.'

'The police had someone in over the weekend,' Emma said to Daisy, hanging up the phone.

'Any details?' asked Daisy. Dan and Ed looked at each other.

'They're playing their cards close,' said Emma. 'All the press office would say is they had someone in helping with inquiries, but we all know what that means. The person they've grabbed is guilty as sin and they're just waiting for the evidence to prove it. It stands to reason that they must know who did it if they've had someone in this early on.'

Dan stared at his computer screen, trying to look like he wasn't listening to what Emma was saying. He could feel Ed peering at him down the side of their computer screens, trying to catch his eye.

Then the editor appeared, walking down the office flanked by Burton and Shepherd and two uniformed officers. Emma stood up.

'Aha, I knew you had more information for me than the press office was letting on, but if you wanted to see me you should have phoned and I would have come to the station.'

'Sorry, Emma. It isn't that kind of call.' Burton approached Dan, who stood up as well. 'Daniel Sullivan, I'm arresting you on suspicion of the murder of James Wilton.'

Chapter 17

Emma turned slowly on the spot. She was staring at Dan as if she'd never seen him before. Dan couldn't breathe and thought he might faint. He could hear Burton's voice talking but he couldn't take in a word. Then Daisy's voice broke into his thoughts.

'What's this about? Why are you arresting Dan?'

'We have reason to believe Mr Sullivan may be involved in the death of James Wilton.' Burton motioned for Dan to step forward.

'But that's ridiculous. Dan wouldn't have done it. He couldn't.'

Burton and Shepherd looked at each other, at her and then at Dan. He stood, staring at the ground in shock.

'Dan?' Daisy said. He looked up at her but without seeing. 'Dan? What's going on?'

'I didn't … I don't …' he started to say.

'Let's continue with this down at the station,' said Burton. A uniformed officer stepped forward with a pair of handcuffs and Dan held out his wrists without protest.

'Do you really need to cuff him?' Emma asked, eyes wide. Dan didn't look like he was planning to put up any kind of a fight.

'It's procedure, Em,' said Burton.

As Dan was led away, he looked back over his shoulder, meeting Daisy's eyes but couldn't say anything.

'Call me if you need anything,' she said.

He nodded.

'Do you want a solicitor present?' Burton asked as Dan was led into the custody suite.

'Yes, I suppose so.'

'OK, I'll have the duty solicitor paged and then we can talk.'

Sitting on the narrow bed in his six-foot square cell, Dan stared at the grey stone wall in front of him. How had he ended up here? One minute he was chasing what he'd hoped was a big story, the next his potential source was dead and he was prime suspect. But why did the police think he'd done it? Surely there were more obvious people.

He sighed and flopped back onto the bed but sat up again very quickly. You never knew how often they changed the beds in here and God only knew who had laid on it last.

The flap on his cell door opened and an officer peered in at him.

'Duty solicitor's here,' he said.

'That was quick.'

'We're not busy,' came the matter-of-fact response. The door opened and the duty solicitor appeared. Dan's heart sank. It was Monica Wells. She lounged elegantly in the doorway, a smug smirk on her face.

'I always hoped I'd be the one in this position, but I never thought it would happen,' she said.

'That sounds like something from a film.'

'How about "Of all the police cells in the all the world …"?'

Dan rubbed his nose. 'Be gentle with me.'

'The way you were with Katy Baines, you mean?'

Dan winced. He'd been covering court a few months previously while Ed was on holiday. He'd persuaded Katy Baines, one of Monica's clients, to speak to the paper when she was acquitted after attacking her ex-partner who had been abusing her. The woman had told him everything, but right at the last minute got cold feet because the story included details not given out in open court.

Dan had refused to pull the story and two days later the woman had been rushed to hospital, attacked by her ex-partner's sister and cousin. Monica blamed Dan, and the woman had tried to sue the paper. Only the prohibitive cost of a legal suit had put her off and the paper had been advised to give her money quietly as a 'goodwill gesture'.

The next time he came face-to-face with Monica she had come close to punching him in the face, only stopping herself because they were in court at the time, and Daisy had relegated him to the flower show beat. Even Ed had needed serious coaxing to speak to him again. The atmosphere in the flat had been awful for weeks afterwards.

This was the first time he'd seen Monica since the encounter in court and it was not the ideal situation.

'OK,' she said, cutting across his train of thought. 'We're both professionals and I've got a job to do. It's my job to defend you, regardless of what I think of you, and that's what I'm going to do.'

'Thanks. Look, I'm really sorry for what happened.'

'No, you're not. You're just sorry you're in this position and I have power over you but you're going to have to trust me.'

'OK. Where do we start?'

'You've got yourself in some serious trouble and we have to get you out of it. So, begin at the beginning.' She sat down next to him on the bed and took out a pen and notebook. 'I need to know everything.'

Twenty minutes later Monica was looking at several pages of notes in her precise handwriting.

'You're saying you never went to the town hall that night?' she said.

'No, I didn't even see Wilton. I'd been on a date but it didn't go very well and she left early.'

'I don't blame her. Any idea what her name was?'

Dan screwed up his forehead and Monica tutted at him. 'Elana. Don't know her surname.'

'Get her number?'

'Yes, but I can't imagine she'll help.'

'You need an alibi and she's a good start.'

'The number is saved in my phone, but the police have got that.'

'OK, I'll get that later.'

There was a knock on the door and Burton appeared.

'It's show time,' said Monica standing up. 'Let's go.'

Burton leaned forward and rested her chin on her hand staring at Dan.

'Your defence is that you weren't there? I thought you'd have come up with something better than that,' she said, looking at Monica.

The solicitor smiled. 'Makes you think it might be true then, doesn't it?' she said.

'I was in the bar and I didn't see James Wilton,' Dan said.

'And how do you explain this?' Burton pushed a still photograph from the CCTV towards him. Dan stared at it.

'Where did you get that?'

'Just answer the question. You told us you were in a bar with a girl and then went to the chippy, so how did you get onto the High Street CCTV camera behind James Wilton?'

'I don't know. I didn't see him.' Dan was peering at the date stamp on the picture.

'Why were you following him?'

'I wasn't. I told you I didn't see him.'

'Apparently he'd met his wife in a bar for dinner. It wasn't the same bar that you were in, was it?'

'I don't know. I was only in there for an hour, maybe an hour and a half, and I wasn't really looking around.'

'That's not why you were inattentive to your lady friend?'

'No. I'm telling you, I didn't see him.'

Burton tapped the CCTV image with a forefinger. 'How could you be that close and not see him?'

'I've only ever seen him across the council chamber. I wouldn't know what he looks like from the back.'

Monica nudged him. 'Don't be facetious,' she whispered in his ear.

'Would you say you knew James Wilton well?' Shepherd asked.

'No. Like I told you before, we've spoken a few times in the past and then he emailed me on Tuesday. You've got the email.'

'Any idea why that email was only one of a dozen left on his account when we seized his computer?' Burton asked. 'All his sent items, inbox and deleted items were gone. Permanently wiped.'

'They were deleted?' Dan's eyebrows shot up and his stomach did its flickering thing.

'You were alone in his office for roughly half an hour on Tuesday night. How do we know you didn't wipe them and then email later pretending you didn't know he was dead?' Shepherd asked.

Dan stared at him. 'Completely deleted all his emails? I wouldn't know how to do that. I would just send them to the recycling bin. I wouldn't know how to go any further.'

'Don't say any more,' Monica advised. She looked at Burton. 'You're fishing, DI Burton. This is circumstantial. I want justification for why you arrested my client on such a flimsy pretext.'

'And I'm waiting to hear good reason why your client was meeting in secret – if that's even true – with someone who was later murdered.'

'I've told you,' Dan interrupted. 'It was the planning application.'

'What planning application?'

'Elliot's Walk. It's an application for a housing estate. A detailed planning application to be exact.'

'And this is the one you mentioned before?'

'Yes. There was something weird going on for a start.'

'What do you mean?'

'The numbers were wrong. The council sent out an agenda and papers before the meeting. When I got there, there was a new bundle on the reporter's desk and the numbers were different.'

'What numbers?'

'The number of houses the construction company was asking to build. I hadn't noticed at first but the mayor asked if they were the right papers. Then when the builder's representative spoke; he said one hundred and forty-six houses but the papers said two hundred, which would be massive overdevelopment.' He took a breath, his stomach flickering again just talking about the story.

Burton interrupted. 'You're telling me that you think James Wilton was killed because a planning application was wrong?'

'What other reason is there? He was going to tell me what it was about but they killed him.'

Burton raised an eyebrow. 'Who's they?'

'Whoever knew those numbers were wrong.' Dan frowned.

'What else?' Burton asked.

'Something else was going on. The residents who live nearby formed an action group to campaign against any development. They were all at the meeting, but they nearly weren't.'

Burton and Shepherd were both staring at him.

'What do you mean "nearly weren't"?'

'They hadn't had prior notice. They only found out the application was up for consideration the day before the meeting.

Someone put an anonymous note through the door of the chairman of the group.'

Shepherd's face wrinkled into an expression of disbelief.

'Why would someone kill over a planning application?' he asked.

'It could be worth a lot of money,' Dan said. 'Think about how much the builder could have made selling off all those flats and houses. By not getting the application passed, they've potentially lost millions, not to mention the money they've spent upfront fighting to get the application past the committee.'

Burton sat back with her arms folded, stony faced. Dan couldn't work out whether the stare was because he'd upset her theory or about something else. She nodded to Shepherd who pulled out a plastic evidence bag and placed it on the table. Inside was a wooden handled letter opener.

'Seen this before?' she asked.

'No,' said Dan.

'Look at it properly.'

Dan picked up the bag and turned it over in his hands. Then he shook his head. 'It looks vaguely familiar but couldn't say for certain where I've seen it before.'

Shepherd leaned forward. 'We think it was used to stab James Wilton in the back in his own office. Care to explain how your fingerprints are on it?'

Chapter 18

Dan stared at him. 'What?'

Monica raised a hand. 'Don't say anything else,' she snapped. 'Dirty tricks aren't your style, DI Burton, so why you playing this one now?'

'What you mean?'

'You said nothing about how James Wilton was killed up to this point and the sudden production of the murder weapon is a bit below the belt.'

'I wanted to see Mr Sullivan's reaction.'

'And fingerprints?'

'We took them from Mr Sullivan at our last interview.'

'Was he under arrest?'

'No, we asked and he gave them.'

Monica gave Dan a withering look, which told him he'd made a rookie mistake.

'I had no reason to refuse,' he said. 'I thought it would help clear my name.'

Monica glared at Burton.

'Are we safe to resume questions?' Burton asked.

Monica looked at Dan and he nodded.

'Fine, but don't expect an answer for everything.'

'So,' Shepherd began, 'you say you've never seen it before, but you've obviously touched it at some point.'

'I don't know, I don't remember ever—' Dan paused.

'Yes?' Shepherd asked.

'I remember now. It was in James Wilton's office. I knocked it on the floor while I was waiting for him and then put it back on his desk.'

Dan looked from Burton to Shepherd and back again. They remained impassive.

Monica put a hand on Dan's arm warning him not to say anything further.

'Who else's prints are on it?' she asked.

'His are the only ones.'

Monica's face twisted in disbelief.

'James Wilton's fingerprints weren't on an object that belonged to him? Isn't that a bit odd?' Burton said nothing. 'And do you really think that Dan would leave it behind with his fingerprints on it if he'd killed someone with it?'

'It wasn't found in the office.'

Monica raised an eyebrow. 'Where was it found?' she asked.

'In a bin on the High Street not far from the town hall.'

'Why was it in a bin?'

'There's blood on it,' Shepherd indicated where the metal blade met the wooden handle. 'Clearly the killer dumped it to get rid.'

'How did you find it?'

'We had a tip-off.'

'Anonymous, I bet,' Monica said. Burton nodded. 'Do you really think my client would be stupid enough to dump the murder weapon in the first bin he found? And, if you have CCTV of the High Street presumably you have footage of my client dumping the letter opener?'

Burton remained silent.

'I thought not. So far all you have is circumstantial evidence. My client has explained how his fingerprints came to be on what you claim is the murder weapon and you have no proof that he followed Mr Wilton into the town hall on the night of the murder. To my mind, you're a long way from having enough evidence to charge him. I suggest you carry out more investigations before you speak to my client again. We're done here.' She stood up. Burton stood too.

'I'm prepared to bail Mr Sullivan, but he will be reporting to the station every day at noon and surrendering his passport.'

'Fair enough,' Monica replied.

'What about work?' Dan asked, standing up. 'I might not be able to attend at noon.'

'I said, fair enough,' Monica gave a stern look.

'OK, you can go,' Burton said.

Once they'd been through the process of being bailed, Dan and Monica stepped into the fresh air.

Dan breathed deeply. 'Thanks,' he said. 'That was hard going.'

'They were tough, but you held up well. Is there anything else I need to know?' She lit a cigarette.

'Not that I can think of.'

'OK. Don't go near the bar you were in, or the chip shop, until you've been interviewed again. Let Burton and Shepherd find out for themselves that you were there without any interference from you.'

'OK.'

'And call me as soon as you hear anything from them.'

She turned and walked away, smoke billowing behind her.

As Dan put his key into the front door, Ed yanked it open.

'What the hell is going on? Have you been at the police station all this time?'

'Hi, honey, I'm home,' Dan said, hanging his coat up in the hall.

'Don't be a smart arse. You said they had nothing on you. Next thing you're being arrested. What did they want?'

'They wanted me to— what's she doing here?' He had just walked into the living room and spotted Emma sitting on the sofa with a mug of tea in front of her.

'Never mind Emma, what's going on? What happened?' Ed demanded.

'What's she doing here?' Dan repeated.

'That's friendly,' Emma said.

Dan looked at her. 'Come to gloat have you?'

'She's come to help you,' Ed said. 'For some reason she doesn't think you're an ungrateful shit who would rather end up in a police cell than ask for help.'

Dan returned from the kitchen with a bottle of beer from the fridge and flopped down on the sofa. He took a long swig. 'They had more questions.'

'About?' Ed asked.

'Where I was the night Wilton died, and whether I saw him in town.'

Ed frowned. 'That's weird. Did you see him?'

'No. That's what I told them. I went to the bar with that girl. She left early, I got chips and came home. Which you would know if you hadn't gone off to Lydia's.'

'So it's my fault that you don't have an alibi? If only I'd known you were going to be accused of murder, I'd have stayed at home.'

'No, that's not what I meant.'

'Well, that's what it sounded like.'

Emma raised a hand. 'It's no good arguing with each other. That's not going to help.'

Dan slumped back against his chair's cushions, swigging more beer.

'What are you going to do?' Ed asked.

'I'm on bail so that's one thing.'

'But they obviously think they've got good evidence against you or they'd have released you without needing bail,' Emma said.

'I had thought of that.'

'There's no need to snap at me either.' Emma's tone was moderate.

'You haven't come to gloat?'

'No, I've come to help.'

Dan made a snorting noise, in the absence of thinking of anything to say.

Ed was looking at him expectantly. 'What are you going to do?'

'I need to find out what's going on at the council.'

'What?'

'There's something going on, I just know it. I need to find a way in.'

Ed shook his head and looked at Emma. 'Here he is facing a murder charge and all he can think about is some poxy story.'

'It's not poxy, it's a good story.'

'How can you know that? You didn't get anything out of Wilton—' Ed's words died away as he realised what he'd said.

Emma was looking from one to the other like a tennis spectator and at the mention of Wilton her eyes widened. 'You were speaking to James Wilton? After what happened last time?'

'But this time I know he had something big,' Dan said.

Ed rolled his eyes. 'That is so typical. Instead of keeping your nose clean and avoiding a murder charge, you're going to stick your nose in where it doesn't belong?'

'Someone killed Wilton and I'm sure it's to do with what's going on in the council planning department.'

Ed scrubbed both hands across his face in frustration. 'You don't know that there is anything going on in the planning department.'

'Even if you do find something out,' Emma said, 'all it'll take is one foot out of place and Burton will hammer you. It'll look like you're trying to cover your tracks.'

Dan shook his head. 'I've got to do it.'

'He's all yours, Em,' Ed said, walking towards the living room door. 'See if you can knock some sense into him. I'll be at Lydia's if you need me.'

They heard the door close behind Ed and then Emma looked at Dan.

'You were the person they had in at the weekend.'

'Yes, of course I was,' Dan snapped. He saw Emma's raised eyebrow. 'Sorry, I'm a bit wound up.'

'I am trying to help. Ed said you were confident you'd explained it all away on Saturday. What's changed?'

Dan sighed. 'CCTV evidence.'

'Of what?' Emma asked. Dan looked at her. 'What?' she asked.

'You're not just here to dig for dirt, are you?'

'No, I want to help.'

'Help with what?'

'I know Burton and I know the case. It's not like I can report anything anyway.'

'So you are after the story.'

But Emma was already laughing at the outraged expression on Dan's face. 'No, I'm genuinely trying to help.' She paused. 'What was the CCTV of?'

'It's footage of James Wilton going into the town hall late on Tuesday night and it appears to show me following him.'

'Appears? Why were you following him?' Emma asked, leaning forward with her elbows on her knees.

'That's what I don't understand. I wasn't following him. I didn't even see him. I'd been for a drink with a girl.'

'Which one this time? You seem to change women like other people change socks.'

Dan smiled. 'It's no one you've heard about. I'd left the bar and was walking home. I don't even remember seeing him, or in fact seeing anyone, but there it is, date and time-stamped, so I must have been there.'

'I can see that giving them a reason to pull you in again, but to arrest you? They must have more than that,' Emma said.

'Like my fingerprints on the murder weapon, you mean?'

'What? What's the murder weapon?' Emma demanded.

'A letter opener, apparently. The police were obviously keeping something back, maybe so you wouldn't tip me off about what they were thinking.' He pulled a face.

'They just told me a stab wound.'

Dan took a sip of his beer and nodded. 'He was stabbed in the back with a letter opener in the town hall.'

'How did he get to Coppin Woods?'

'I reckon whoever stabbed him thought they would cover the evidence by setting it up to look like suicide and hoping the police wouldn't spot the stab wound.'

'Something clearly went wrong then. The police weren't fooled at all. It would have made more sense to set fire to the car.'

'There's nothing connecting me to the car as far as I know.'

'But how did your fingerprints get on the murder weapon? You've never been in any of the offices, have you?' Emma asked. Dan hung his head and peered up at her through his eyelashes. Emma groaned. 'Oh God, whose office had you been in?'

'Wilton's.'

Emma groaned again. 'When? And why?'

'I was supposed to meet him there before the planning meeting, but he didn't show, and now it's obvious why. I picked it up while I was there, after I knocked it off the desk accidentally.'

'OK, that's fairly self-explanatory,' Emma said.

'I don't think Burton sees it that way.'

'You didn't try that look on her that you just pulled on me? She's a suspicious old bugger and that made you look like you're up to something.'

'I'd prefer it if she left me alone.'

'She won't until she's completely convinced that you're telling the truth. We need to work out what's going on.'

'We?'

'Yes, you won't get very far on your own. Two heads are better than one etc.'

'I suppose so.'

'Look, I know we don't always see eye to eye—'

'Try never.'

Emma grinned. 'OK, maybe you're right, but I think we can agree that someone is setting you up.'

'But that's what I don't understand. Why would someone do that?'

'Convenience? They found out you'd been in touch with Wilton and decided to make it look like you did it to cover their tracks.'

'In other words, I played right into their hands.'

'Not necessarily. They wanted to stop Wilton from talking to you and realised they would implicate you at the same time.'

'So if I hadn't gone after the story, Wilton would still be alive.'

'It was him deciding to come to you that got him killed, not the other way around.' Emma paused and sipped her drink. 'What was the story?' she asked casually.

Dan paused but then gave her a precis of what he knew.

Emma frowned. 'That's all you've got? Some planning

applications might be wrong? And Wilton was coming to you about it?'

'He was taking more of a risk than last time. We both just got blasted then, not killed.'

'I think Daisy would have liked to murder you.' They both laughed.

'I figured it must have been something important for him to take a risk.'

'If we're going to prove that you didn't do it, then we need to find out exactly what Wilton was planning on telling you and who would want to stop him.'

Chapter 19

The next morning the shit really hit the fan. The moment Dan's bag landed on his desk his phone began to ring. An internal call.

'You! In my office! Now!' barked the editor and the line went dead. Pulling a pained face at Emma, Dan trudged down to the glass-walled office where the editor sat glaring out like a disgruntled goldfish. He was aware of heads turning as he walked through the subeditors' section of the office.

'What the hell was that yesterday?' the editor asked when Dan entered the room and closed the door. 'Sit down,' he added indicating a chair. Daisy was already seated in the office, looking uncomfortable. She didn't meet Dan's eye even when he sat down next to her. 'Well?' asked the editor when Dan did not reply.

'I'm not sure where to start,' Dan said. 'The police found out I'd been talking to James Wilton.'

'The council officer who was killed?'

'Yes. They had some CCTV footage and some other stuff to talk to me about. But they've bailed me and I just need to report in to the station at lunchtime.'

'What the hell were you doing talking to an officer? You've been warned for that before.'

Dan peered at the man, feeling that he was focusing on the smaller issue. 'But this time he came to me. It's a good story—'

'How do you know that?'

'Well, I don't know for sure but if you give me time to—'

But the editor was already flapping a hand to stop him. 'Sorry, Dan, but this is the last straw. I can't have staff members being arrested in the office, interviewed as a murder suspect and then being back on the job the next day. You can't do your job while you're on bail.'

Dan felt himself go cold. This couldn't be happening. 'Wait, what do you mean?'

The editor got to his feet. 'You're suspended.'

'What?'

'You heard me. You're suspended on full pay until further notice.'

'But why—'

Daisy interrupted. 'Dan, it won't be long before other people hear rumours that you're involved and then we lose our objectivity. We need to be able to report this story. We can't do that with you here.'

'But I'm not on the story, Emma is—'

'Do you really think she can be impartial with a colleague on bail for murder? And sitting next to her?' the editor barked. 'No, no, Dan, it's got to be this way. When this is all done—'

'I'll be reinstated if I don't go to jail?'

The editor glared. 'I'm sure it won't come to that, but yes, when the case is resolved we'll talk again.'

'And I'll be reinstated?'

The editor paused. Then he said, 'We'll see.'

Dan snorted. 'So regardless, my job is on the line?'

'We'll see.'

'And you agree to this?' Dan turned on Daisy.

She looked down at her notebook clutched in her hand.

'Daisy doesn't get a say in this. We have to consider what's best for the team.'

'What if … what if I brought you a better story?'

'What?'

'What if I brought you a better story? What happens then?'

'Oh, Dan. Not the planning story.' Daisy closed her eyes, a pained expression on her face.

'Yes. I'm sure there's something in it. There's—'

But the editor was shaking his head. 'No, Dan, that's my final word. You leave now and we'll revisit the situation when it's appropriate.'

Dan turned on his heel and stormed out of the room.

At his desk he grabbed his bag.

Emma looked up.

'What's going on?' she asked.

'I'm out until this is all over in case it damages the company's reputation,' Dan growled. 'I'll see you later.' He marched out of the building without looking back, slamming the door.

Dan stormed into the flat and threw his bag across the living room. He felt like screaming or punching something.

'Why am I being punished?' he asked a dying pot plant. 'I've done nothing wrong.' But the pot plant just sat there. 'Hmmm, maybe you need some water.'

He slumped on the sofa and put his head into his hands, rubbing his eyes. The police were watching his every move and trying to find evidence against him and Daisy expected him to sit at home, doing nothing. There was only one thing for it. He was going to have to find out for himself who killed James Wilton and, more importantly, why.

His mobile phone began to ring in his trouser pocket. The screen said number withheld.

'Hello?'

'Dan, hi. Chris Fryer here.'

'What do you want?'

'That's not very friendly.'

'It wasn't meant to be.'

'So I hear the police have arrested someone in the James Wilton murder case.'

'I don't know. You'd have to ask Emma.'

'Oh, come on, Dan. It's common knowledge that it's you. Why not give me your story? That way at least you'll get paid for it. I could sell it to one of the nationals.' Dan could almost hear the pound signs ratcheting into Fryer's eyes like a cartoon character.

'No, thanks.'

'You're not going to be dull and give it to Emma, are you?'

'I won't be giving anyone anything because there's no story.'

'Ah, rookie mistake, Daniel. Never tell a journalist that there's no story. It immediately makes us suspicious that there is something there.'

'You're calling yourself a journalist now, are you?'

Fryer's voice became harsh. 'Don't mess with me, Sullivan. I'll make you pay for it.'

'Fuck off, Fryer.' Dan ended the call and threw his phone onto the sofa.

He changed his clothes, loaded up his laptop on the living room coffee table and clicked onto the council's website. In the planning section the latest committee agenda was online. FGB Contracting was behind the Elliot's Walk plan, so he needed to find out what other plans they'd had passed. A quick search yielded nothing. That was odd. He'd been sure there were more applications under their name. Instead he searched for large housing applications.

'That's more like it,' he muttered as fifteen applications popped up on his screen. There were six where changes had been passed by the officers under their delegated powers. In all six cases the officer was James Wilton. Dan sat back on the sofa.

'What was Wilton playing at?' he asked. All the applications were too big for the area they were in. He clicked on one. It was for sixty houses in an area that was already considered overpopulated, but he couldn't remember the paper covering it at all. Dan read through the conditions Wilton had put on the application and gave a low whistle. On the surface the conditions looked onerous, but in fact they were cleverly worded to simply plug the loopholes caused by objections from the environmental health and highways departments.

'Hang on,' said Dan frowning. 'If there were any objections, this should have come before the committee.'

The objections were legitimate. Dan remembered now that he'd been to the new housing estate when people started to move in. They'd contacted the *Post* when they'd realised the roads weren't wide enough.

'These are supposed to be family homes,' one resident had told Dan. 'My wife and I have a car each because we need to get to work and ferry the kids around. We have to park one car on the road because our drive only has room for one. That's the damage the bin wagon did getting past and I'm parked almost entirely on the pavement.' The man had shown him the scratched and dented side of his Ford Focus, while Brendan the photographer snapped away.

'I see what you mean,' Dan had said.

'What would happen if an ambulance or a fire engine needed to get down here?' the man had continued.

Brendan had set up a picture of Dan and the man measuring the width of the street, which had appeared in the paper.

'It's not even wide enough for two cars to pass each other,' Dan had said to the press officer of the building company. 'How did you get that past the planning department?'

Now things were becoming clearer. All these applications had James Wilton in common. Suddenly his mobile rang.

'Are you alright?' Emma asked.

'Yeah, I'm OK. I've cooled off a bit. Listen, I think I'm onto something.'

'What do you mean?'

'I've been going through some old planning applications that James Wilton was involved in and there's something not right.'

'Like what?'

'There's one housing estate that we wrote about where there seem to have been more houses on the plan than in the papers, and the roads weren't wide enough.'

'Would that not have been investigated?'

'It should have been, but I've not heard anything about it. What if the council covered it up?'

'Could they get away with that?'

'Who knows, but it's a good place to start.' He was silent for a moment.

'Hey, are you still there?'

'Yes, just thinking.'

'Hmmm, first time for everything.'

He could hear the smile in Emma's voice but still responded, 'Oh shut up.' He could hear her sniggering down the line.

'Thinking about what?'

'With this application, it's really obvious that something is going on. The fact there were two sets of papers, two different sets of figures.'

'Someone was trying to draw attention to it, you mean?'

'Yes, but who knew? Who found out about it?'

'What are you going to do?'

'I'm going to have a word with Richard Drimble. He voted against the application, maybe he knows what's going on.'

Pushing open the door to the town hall Dan smiled at the security guard on duty.

'Is the mayor around?' he asked. The man looked up from his CCTV screens.

'Sorry, he's out at an engagement,' he said. 'Can I pass him a message?'

Dan thought for a moment. 'No. I'll come back later.'

'Can I tell him who called?'

But Dan was already pushing open the door. He paused at the top of the steps. He needed to think about what he'd found out.

Councillor David Edmonds stood at the bottom of the town hall's staircase staring after Dan.

'What did he want?' he asked the security guard.

'He was asking for the mayor, but he's out, ain't he? Said he'd call back later.' He indicated the door Dan had just walked through.

Edmonds stared at the reporter's back as he stood outside the door. Then Dan zipped up his jacket and marched away down the High Street. Edmonds paused a second and then slipped out of the door, following at a safe distance.

The councillor watched the reporter dodge through the crowds of shoppers, trying to stay at a safe distance without losing his prey.

Suddenly Dan disappeared down a side alley. Edmonds quickened his pace and was just in time to see him turning the corner at the other end. Where on earth was he going? His office was in the opposite direction. Peering around the corner he watched Dan push open the front door of a large ornate building. Edmonds' brow furrowed. Why was he going to the public library?

'Everything you want should be in here,' the librarian said, indicating two bookshelves. Dan smiled at her. 'If you need anything else just give me a shout,' she said, turning away. Dan looked around him and hung his coat on the back of a chair. He selected several volumes from the shelf and sat down.

Digging into the first book he found the planning application he was looking for. Again it was another housing development that seemed to be overkill and James Wilton was the officer named on the application. Dan made a note of it and moved to the next application.

Soon he had six pages of notes with a list of company names. Each one appeared twice but Dan didn't recognise any of the names. He tracked down the librarian.

'If I wanted to check on some companies, their names, addresses and directors that kind of thing, where would I look?' he asked.

'You can check online at Companies House, that's a good place to start. What sort of companies?'

'Building contractors.'

'Hmmm, we've got a book on local building contractors but it'll probably be out of date by now.'

'I'll take it as a starting point.'

The librarian disappeared among the shelves for a moment and returned with a triumphant grin. 'Here you go.'

Dan smiled and took the volume. As she walked away he shook his head. It was slightly sad to be so excited about finding a book in a library. But as he sat back down at the table and flicked open the book, he began to feel very grateful.

Suddenly a bell began to clang loudly and Dan started, his pen shooting across the page. The librarian appeared.

'Sorry, that's the fire alarm. Can you go outside?' She sounded weary.

Dan grabbed his jacket.

'Is it a drill?' he asked stuffing his notebook into his pocket. She shook her head.

'They usually tell us if there's a drill but we have had a spate of false alarms recently. Maybe there's a fault in the wiring.'

'Don't you worry about the books going up in flames?'

She laughed. 'They're all insured and the fire brigade usually get here pretty fast. Although if the healthy living section went up, I wouldn't lose sleep.' She patted her rounded waist.

Dan grinned and followed the other library customers out of the emergency exit. They stood in a gaggle at the meeting point on the corner. The librarian went to check in with her boss and Dan stood alone, his brain whirring. He felt he was very close to finding something important and he was sure that book could be a helpful starting point.

As he stood lost in thought, his mobile phone burbled in his pocket. It was Ed.

'Hey, mate.'

'Dan? Where are you? I went to the flat and you weren't there.'

'I'm at the library.'

'What are you at the library for?'

Dan laughed. 'I was looking for the new Rebus book. I could do with some help.'

'Help with what? Why would Rebus help?'

'It's nothing. Look, there was a fire alarm at the library but I think we're allowed back in now. I'll talk to you tonight.'

'But you're OK?'

'Yeah, of course.'

'OK. Laters.' Ed hung up. The librarian appeared at Dan's left hand.

'You can go back in now.'

'Thanks.'

Dan pounded up the stairs. Turning the corner around the end of the bookcase he stopped and stared. His table was completely empty. All the books were gone.

He clutched at his pocket, his body flooding with cold, but his notebook was still there. He looked on the floor under the table and walked to the next section in case he was at the wrong table.

'Lost something?' The librarian appeared behind him as he turned in a circle.

'You didn't move the books that were on that table, did you?'

'No, I went outside when you did. Maybe someone else put them back. Do you want all of them again?'

'Just the companies' one.' She disappeared and returned two minutes later.

'Nope, not on the shelf. Maybe someone else has borrowed it.'

'Could they have taken it out of the library?'

'No, it's reference only. Although with the fire alarm going on we wouldn't have noticed the book alarm going off as well.' Dan stared. 'The stuff should be online if you do a search.'

Dan stood for a moment thinking. He was even more convinced he was onto something now the book was gone. But who would have wanted to stop him getting to that information?

Chapter 20

'I'm glad you called this meeting. I was about to ring you myself,' said Richard Drimble.

Burton and Shepherd sat down in the seats he indicated. Drimble looked a lot calmer and better rested than he had two days ago.

'You wanted to see us?' Burton raised her eyebrows.

'Well, yes. I'm a leader around here and it would be nice to be able to tell people what was going on,' replied the mayor. He leaned back in his chair, elbows on the armrests, and hands clasped across his stomach. 'How are things progressing?'

'Slowly, but we are moving forward,' said Burton.

'Have you had someone in for questioning?'

Shepherd looked at Burton, taken aback by the remark, but if the DI was surprised, she certainly wasn't showing it.

'What makes you say that?'

'I know someone who works at the police station. He told me.'

'We're not officially releasing any information yet, but yes, someone has been helping us with our inquiries,' she said.

'Good. I'm glad you've got him. James was popular and everyone in his team is suffering. It'll be good to tell them you've caught him.'

Burton raised a hand to stem the tide of Drimble's words. 'I didn't say we'd arrested or charged anyone and I'd prefer it if you didn't go around telling anyone we have.'

Drimble looked stunned for a moment. 'Oh, so he isn't the person?'

'We don't know yet. We have a lot of people still to interview.' Burton smiled. 'For instance, we haven't spoken to you yet, Councillor Drimble.'

'Me? But why would you want to speak to me?'

'You were on the planning committee. You must know Mr Wilton quite well?'

'Only as much as you know someone who is a colleague. Even then we didn't work very closely.'

'It's strange how all the councillors on the committee have said that,' Shepherd put in. 'I'd have thought you'd need to see him quite regularly to be briefed on planning applications.'

Drimble looked at him. 'No, not really. In fact, we barely spoke from one month to the next.' Shepherd frowned and scribbled for a moment in his notebook.

'What did you think of Mr Wilton?' Burton asked.

'He was a thoroughly nice man. Very capable.'

'You'd never had a problem with his work before?'

'Before?'

'I understand there was a problem with one of his applications recently.'

'Yes, well, everyone makes mistakes.'

'More than that from what we've heard.'

Drimble sighed. 'This is difficult.' Burton and Shepherd waited in silence. 'Yes, I had noticed some errors in James's work. Applications that didn't add up.'

'And you shot one down at the last committee meeting.'

'Yes. James wasn't there but ... wait a moment, who told you about that? I didn't see you at the meeting.'

Shepherd smiled. 'Let's just say that we found out. What was the problem?'

'It was a housing application and the numbers didn't add up. It could have been an honest mistake but I couldn't go into it publicly.'

'Meaning that you're going to look into it privately?'

'I'm relatively new to the planning committee. I took over as chairman when Alan Horgan had a heart attack just over a year ago. I hadn't really paid much attention to planning when I was just a councillor but my party encouraged me to step up to the role. Once I was in charge I started noticing there were some dubious applications coming before the committee. Now I have good reason to look into it and I'll be investigating the planning department. I need to know what's going on.'

'Where were you the night before the planning committee?' Shepherd asked.

Drimble stopped and stared at him. 'Tuesday night? Is that when you think ...?'

'That's our pathologist's timetable, yes.'

'And you want to know where I was?'

'Yes please.'

'Well, erm, let's see.' He paused to flick through the diary on his desk. 'No, no official engagements. Erm, let me see.' He gave a little laugh. 'This is why I keep a detailed diary, otherwise I forget where I'm supposed to be.' But Burton and Shepherd didn't join in the laughter. He seemed to sense their disapproval and quickly said, 'If I wasn't at an engagement, I must have been at home.'

'Alone?'

'Yes, no wife or family unfortunately.'

'Is there anyone who might have seen you?'

'I don't know. The neighbours might have seen me come home but we're only really on nodding terms.'

Burton looked at Shepherd waiting for him to finish scribbling in his notebook.

'Do you have a suspicion of what Mr Wilton was doing with those applications?' she asked.

Drimble shook his head. 'No, at the moment I have no idea. I have to ask some difficult questions of people who knew James well, people who have worked with him for years. It's a terrible time.' He looked at Burton and Shepherd. 'I'll keep you posted how I get on.'

His tone sounded final and Burton and Shepherd took the hint. They got to their feet.

'We may need to ask you more questions, Councillor Drimble, so don't go anywhere,' Burton said.

'I have nowhere else to be.' Drimble smiled and then his face fell. 'Not at least until I get some answers.'

'Be sure to share them with us,' Burton warned him as the detectives left the room.

Chapter 21

'Jo, stop panicking.'

'How can you say that?' Johanna Buttle paced Edmonds' office. 'He knows.'

'He knows nothing,' Edmonds said dismissively. 'All we have to do is keep our heads—'

'I can't believe I let you talk me into this,' she interrupted. 'I feel so bad about what we're doing.'

Edmonds smiled smugly. 'You know exactly how I talked you into this, and I don't hear you complaining about the benefits it brings.'

There was a knock at the door and Councillor Paul Sanderson appeared.

'You wanted to see me,' he said, looking from Edmonds to Buttle and smiling at her.

'Jo's panicking. Drimble called her in to ask for her help in investigating the planning department.'

Sanderson stared. 'What? You said he didn't know anything,' he said, moving to stand by Buttle.

'He doesn't. That's why he's asking for help,' Edmonds said.

'So why did he ask Jo if he knows nothing?'

'I don't know. He probably thinks she'll be the best person for getting information out of people.'

'You don't think it's because he knows exactly what's going on?'

'If he knew already, he would have launched a full-scale enquiry, or called the police,' Sanderson said.

'He's looking for proof!' Buttle sank into a chair. 'And if he gets it we're in big trouble.'

'Jo, you have to toughen up,' said Edmonds. 'Any proof has been destroyed.'

'What about the minutes of the meetings?'

'They prove nothing. What's the problem?'

'You didn't see Drimble earlier. I'm sure he knows. I could see it in his eyes.'

'No, he doesn't,' said Sanderson, kneeling in front of her and taking her hands. 'You have to believe that. Like David says, he's bluffing.'

'He must have been hoping I'd give something away,' she said, tears glistening in her eyes. 'The weak link.'

'Jo, he doesn't know you're involved. He doesn't even know for sure there's something going on.' Sanderson's voice was soothing but the glare he shot at Edmonds over her shoulder was not.

'What if I give something away? I'm a hopeless liar and I've already got too many secrets.' She clutched at his hand. He smiled warmly.

'I'll help you keep that one,' he said in a low voice. She smiled at him through her tears. Squeezing her hand he stood up and faced Edmonds. 'What do we do about Drimble?'

'You two do nothing,' said Edmonds. 'I'll keep an eye on him and make sure he's getting nowhere.'

'And what should Jo tell him?'

Edmonds thought for a moment. 'Just stay away from him. With any luck, if he gets stone-walled, it'll slow him down.'

'And if he comes looking for me?' She dried her face on a tissue.

'Make something up. Tell him you think you're onto something but you need more time. Leave him to me,' Edmonds said. 'Just carry on as if there's nothing to know.'

At the door Sanderson squeezed Buttle's arm.

'Don't worry. I'll help you,' he said quietly.

Edmonds cleared his throat and they both looked back at him. 'Remember, I know your secret,' he said. 'You can't let me down now.'

Chapter 22

'Someone stole the companies' book while the fire alarm was ringing?' Emma stared at Dan.

'Yes.'

'But why would they do that?'

They were sitting on a bench in the park near to Dan's flat, each drinking a can of Coke. Emma shivered slightly in the late afternoon air despite her jacket.

'I think it was to stop me from seeing whatever was in there.'

'Which is?'

'I don't know. I didn't even get a chance to look at it.'

'But why were you looking at it in the first place?'

'Those planning applications had different company names on them, but they were similar applications. Plus they were names I didn't recognise and I don't think there can be that many construction companies in the area, not that do housing estates on that scale. I thought there might be a connection.'

'The fact that the book is now missing does suggest there was something in there that someone didn't want you to see.'

'Exactly.'

'What are you going to do next?'

'I need to speak to Richard Drimble. He was out earlier when I called in but he must have noticed something was going on in his committee. I want to see what he knows.' Emma didn't reply for a moment. 'What's up?' Dan asked.

She was frowning. 'Who did you tell that you were going to the library?'

'No one. The only person who knew was Ed, and I only told him once I was already there and outside for the fire drill. What's your point?'

'It's not like you to go to the library randomly in the middle of the day. In fact, I didn't know you knew where the library was.'

'Ha ha, enough of the insults. What are you getting at?'

'How did they know you were there?'

'What?'

'How did the person who took the book know you were there and where you were sitting? How did they know what book you were reading and which one to take?'

Dan stared at her. 'Do you mean what I think you mean?'

'I think someone followed you to the library and was watching you.' Emma paused. 'And the worst bit is, we have no idea who or why they wanted that book.'

When Dan went back into the flat he could feel a cold draught. He entered the living room to find Ed standing on the balcony smoking. Hearing footsteps, Ed turned with a sly grin on his face.

'What?' Dan asked.

'Had a nice trip to the park?'

Dan frowned. 'Yes, thanks. Why?'

'Oh, just that I saw who you were meeting.'

Dan looked at him, but said nothing.

'Don't worry, your dirty little secret is safe with me. I am surprised though. I thought you guys hated each other.'

Ed stubbed out his cigarette in the ashtray out on the balcony and stepped back inside, shutting the door behind him. He didn't mention Emma again, but contented himself with giving Dan knowing looks for the rest of the evening.

Chapter 23

David Edmonds was pacing his office in the town hall when the call came. Ten paces were enough to get him across the room and ten paces back. He'd lost count of the number of steps he'd taken but he knew it would never be enough. The theme from *Jaws* brought him out of his thoughts and he snatched up his mobile phone.

'I got your text,' said the voice.

'What do we do now?' Edmonds' voice was tight with anxiety.

'Calm down. You only stole a library book. Considering what else you've done it's small fry.'

'Not the bloody book. What about Sullivan?'

'What about him?'

'He's clearly onto something and we have to stop him investigating.'

'You said you'd taken the book. He can't use that.'

'Yes, but that was a short-term measure. He can get that information from other sources. It's only slowed him down.'

There was a deep sigh. 'Leave him to me.'

The line went dead.

Chapter 24

Burton looked up at the technician standing in front of her desk.

'What you're telling me is that we still don't know whose email address it is?' she said. The tech nodded.

'Sorry, sir. Whoever it is they're very good at what they do.'

Burton leaned back in her chair. 'Better than you?'

The tech smiled. 'Not quite.'

'How do you mean?'

'They've covered their tracks pretty well. I managed to decode some of the messages to find out their ISP but …'

'ISP?'

'Internet service provider, sir. You need that to access the Internet and send emails.'

'Right, so you traced that?'

'That's just it. I couldn't find the number it came from.'

'Couldn't find it?'

'It just doesn't exist. I tried contacting Hotmail but all they could give me was the name on the account.'

'Which was?' Burton half hoped it would be this simple.

'Owen Dunn. There was no postal address because you don't need that for a remote account.'

There was a knock and Shepherd entered. Burton nodded to him.

'Is the name real?' Burton asked the techie.

'I think that's a bit too much to ask, sir,' said the man grinning. 'He's made such a good job of covering his tracks, I doubt he'd be stupid enough to use his own name. Anyway, I've put all the details in here for you.' He handed Burton a flimsy cardboard folder.

'Thanks, Steve,' said Burton and the man left. Burton handed the folder to Shepherd and gave him a chance to peruse its contents.

'The emails are effectively untraceable then?' said Shepherd.

'So it would appear.' They sat in silence for a moment. 'Reckon Sullivan is smart enough to know all this?' asked Burton.

Shepherd frowned. 'I reckon some computing qualifications would teach you about it.'

'Do you think he could do it?'

Shepherd paused a moment. 'I don't know, sir. It depends on what he studied at college or university. But this seems very premeditated and Sullivan doesn't strike me as that type. He doesn't seem calculating enough.'

Burton rubbed his eyes. 'We don't seem to be getting anywhere, do we?'

'There is one way to find out if Sullivan did do it.'

'What's that?'

'Seize his computer. If he's used it to send those emails then our guys will find them.'

Burton smiled. 'Good plan.'

Monica Wells answered her phone. 'Hello?'

'It's Dan Sullivan.'

'Keeping out of trouble, are we?'

'Trying to.' She could hear a slight smile in his voice.

'What can I do for you?'

'The police are asking for my laptop. They want me to bring it to the station and answer some more questions.'

'When?' Monica was already flicking through her diary.

'At lunchtime. They said to bring it when I answer my bail.'

'I'll meet you at the police station at noon.'

'Thank you. See you there.'

'How long will you be keeping it for?' Dan looked up with the pen poised above the receipt for his computer.

'As long as it takes. You don't need it for anything do you?' Shepherd asked. 'I hear you're not working at the moment.'

'It's my personal laptop, it was expensive and I like to keep it where I can see it.'

Shepherd grinned. 'Got private stuff on it, has it?'

'It's got work on it as well. I'd rather that's not lost.'

'Don't worry, we'll look after it.'

Dan signed the form and Shepherd packed the computer into an evidence bag. He handed it to the waiting technician.

'Do your stuff, Steve. Let me know if you get anything.'

'Yes, sir.' The man disappeared.

'Are you looking for something specific?' Monica asked Shepherd.

'Just making inquiries,' he said.

Monica eyed him. 'What sort of inquiries?' she asked.

'Just inquiries. We'd like another word,' he replied, herding them towards the interview room where Burton was waiting.

'Thanks for coming in,' Burton said when they were all seated.

'He didn't really have much choice,' Monica said.

'We just need to clear up a few things.'

'And the laptop?'

'Just part of our inquiries.'

'Any progress on the investigation?' Monica asked.

Burton shrugged again. 'It's moving along slowly.'

'Do you have any other suspects?' Monica's tone was aggressive.

'We're pursuing a number of lines of inquiry.'

'That doesn't answer my question. Is my client the only suspect?'

'He's the only person we've arrested so far but he's not the only suspect,' said Burton.

'Dan has been making some inquiries of his own,' said Monica, indicating for him to begin.

Burton leaned back in her chair as Dan told them about his Internet research and the library.

'You think there must be something important about a stolen library book?' said Burton, her nose wrinkled and her eyebrows raised.

'There must be. Why else set off the fire alarm so you can steal a book?'

'Maybe the two aren't connected?'

'How can they not be? The book was there when the fire alarm went off and it had gone when I came back. It didn't just walk off on its own.' Dan leaned forward with his palms flat on the table.

Burton looked at Shepherd who was scribbling in his notebook. She frowned.

'Did you see anyone around in the library before the alarm went off?'

'No. I was at a table in the reference section. It was surrounded by bookcases so I couldn't see anything. The librarian had shown me where everything was and then she wandered off. I was just getting settled when the fire alarm went off.'

'You got sent outside?'

'Yes.'

'How long were you outside for?'

'Five minutes or so.'

'And it wasn't a drill?'

'The librarian said they usually get a warning if there's going to be a drill.'

Burton frowned. 'It certainly seems odd. And it was only the book about local companies that went missing?'

'Yes, the librarian found the other books on the recently-returned shelf so they must have just dumped the others and run off.'

'And the library staff didn't see anything?'

Dan shook his head. 'They were focusing on getting everyone accounted for outside. Emma thinks someone was following me.'

'Following you? Why?'

'I don't normally go to the library during the day, so how would they know I was going to be there and what books I was using?'

'You keep saying "they" … who's they?'

'Whoever is behind the planning stuff.'

'Planning stuff?'

'I think this is connected to planning.'

'Sorry?'

'I don't mean planning as in planning the murder; I mean the council planning committee, applications and stuff.'

Burton frowned. 'You mentioned planning before.'

'Yes, but now I've done more research I'm convinced that the planning committee is involved. Wilton was on planning and he was murdered. What if he was killed because he was involved in changing planning applications or whatever is going on?'

'Changing applications?'

'Yes. There has to be a reason why there were two different sets of papers at that meeting. I think he changed them.'

Shepherd looked up from his notebook. 'Changed the paperwork? Why?'

'I don't know, maybe so that someone would notice the discrepancy and investigate, which is exactly what's happened.'

Burton looked at him. 'And you think that's what Wilton was going to tell you about?'

'Yes, and someone killed him to stop him talking.'

'And this is the story you mentioned to us before?'

'It is. I didn't kill him. Now he's dead, I've lost my source. Everything I found and surmised isn't enough to stand up my story. I still need proof.' His stomach was flickering again.

Burton leaned forward, hands flat against the table top, her wedding and engagement rings flashing in the overhead light. 'When did you start working on this story?'

'After the planning meeting.'

'You hadn't done anything before?'

'Apart from read Wilton's email and set up to meet him, no.'

Burton paused for a moment and then said, 'OK, thanks for coming in. It clears a few things up. But I'd advise that you stay away from the story until this is all sorted out.'

'I can't. I need to get the story written before anyone else get onto it.'

'Who else knows about it?'

'Just Emma. I've told her what I know.'

Burton sighed. 'I might have known she be in the middle of this. Tell her it'll affect what we can tell her off-the-record so she can't pass that on to you.'

'I'm sure she won't mind.' Dan knew that wasn't true. Emma was very proud of the fact that the police often tipped her off in those kind of chats.

Burton raised an eyebrow. She knew that wasn't true as well. 'Just make sure you tell her that.'

As Burton walked back to the front of the building, Dan asked, 'When can I have my laptop back?'

'It will be a couple of days. We'll call you, OK?'

'The sooner I get it back the better.'

Burton eyed him. 'Remember what I said about leaving it alone.'

She said goodbye and headed back inside the building.

Shepherd was standing at the window of the CID office looking at Dan walking away when Burton returned to the room.

'What you think?' he asked turning to look at her.

'Food for thought,' she replied. 'Still feels like he knows a bit too much about this.'

'We don't have a good theory for why he would kill Wilton and you said it yourself that the wife is not out of the frame either.'

'But would you really kill someone for a planning application?'

'Sullivan said it could be worth hundreds of thousands.'

'They always say follow the money,' she said.

'Exactly.'

'OK, let's look into the planning angle and speak to the committee members again. If Wilton was changing the plans, he can't have been working alone. It'll be interesting to find out how many committee members knew about it. Let's also see if Sullivan is telling truth about when he started working on the story. That'll help us clear him up.'

Chapter 25

'It's a nice tribute piece but it doesn't help us much, does it?' said Dan. He and Emma were drinking beer in the flat and Dan was reading Emma's interview with Lila Wilton in that day's edition of the *Post*.

'It tells us one thing,' said Emma. 'She didn't know anything about his work.'

Dan looked up from the newspaper. 'Why does that matter?' he asked.

'You think this is all connected to planning. She clearly knows nothing about it so it suggests she's not involved.'

Dan got up and started pacing. 'You thought she was involved?'

'I did at first, because she was acting weird when I interviewed her. Almost like she didn't care. Plus the spouse is always the first place the police look. I imagine Burton and Shepherd will already be onto her.' She paused. 'She asked if I knew you.'

At the far end of the room, Dan turned slowly to look at her. 'Why did she ask that?'

'She said he talked about you at their last dinner.'

'You still think I'm involved in this, don't you?'

'Not really, but she said he'd said he needed to speak to you and that you were the key to the whole thing.'

'What?' Dan stared at her open mouthed. 'She said that?'

'Yes. I'm wondering whether she told the police about it as well. It would certainly explain why they were coming after you.'

Dan sat down and stared at the table top, covered in papers.

'And you think I did this, that I was involved in whatever's going on in planning and that I killed Wilton?'

Emma paused. 'I don't know what I thought. You've been so desperate to prove yourself that I thought maybe you'd pushed too hard on a story, but I couldn't get my head around that.'

Dan stared at her. 'You really thought I was capable of killing someone? Just for a story?'

'It looked bad. You were acting all weird about him being found dead and then the police turn up and arrest you. I didn't know that he'd asked to meet you.'

There was an awkward silence

'All we really know is Wilton was making mistakes in his applications and was stressed at work.' Dan jumped up and started pacing again, raking his hands through his hair. 'Is that why he called me?'

'He called you because of work-based stress?'

'No, about the thing that was stressing him out. There were a lot of dodgy applications and they all had his name on them.'

'You think he'd been doing this for a long time?'

'So far I've found fifteen applications that look like they're iffy, and he couldn't have done it for every meeting because that would be noticed. So, he could have been doing it for months.'

'I still don't get why someone would do that, falsify planning applications. It seems like an odd thing to do when you're a nobody.'

'You think it's more likely to be someone in a more senior position?'

'James Wilton's work would get checked, wouldn't it? Before it went to the committee?'

'I suppose so.'

'So why weren't the mistakes picked up? Why didn't his line manager notice what was going on? Daisy would spot it from a mile away and be on us in a minute.'

'You think there were other people involved? That he was working to order?'

'There must have been. He couldn't orchestrate something this elaborate on his own.' Emma leaned back against the sofa cushions. 'Why hadn't he been caught? Why no investigations?'

'Someone above him is covering for him?'

'Exactly.'

Dan stood at the other end of the living room, hands on hips. 'I've been looking at this all wrong. I told the police that the builders would make money from having bigger housing estates built, but what I hadn't thought of was how they were getting them passed.'

'They were paying him,' Emma said, staring at him.

'Exactly.'

'But who would be doing that?'

'It would have to be someone close enough to him to know that he would take a bribe.'

'Wouldn't anyone want more money? I know I do.'

'But would you take a bribe?'

'Well, no, but—'

'There you go. Someone from the housing company must have picked him out.'

'Dan, these are applications for lots of different companies. There's no way one person from each company knew him well enough to know he was corruptible.' Dan opened his mouth to speak, but she carried on. 'How would they know before they started that he would also be the officer on their case?'

'They could have met him, or had contact with him, while he was putting the report on the application together.'

'But that sort of meeting wouldn't be enough for you to offer a bribe, would it? When you know nothing about him? He might just report you.'

'Can't scam an honest man, you mean?'

'Exactly.'

'So you're saying that we're looking for someone who knew him and knew what applications he was working on?'

'Yes. Find out who had the most access to him as a planning officer and that will most likely give you the killer.'

Dan frowned. 'Had they found out he was going to talk to me?' Then he slapped a hand to his forehead. 'No, he must have said he wanted out and thought the plans with the blatant mistakes in it would be enough to blow the thing wide open.'

Emma looked serious. 'They must have realised he was getting edgy and killed him, not realising he'd already put his plan into action. His plan to talk to you must have been a final straw.'

Dan looked at her. 'We need to find out who lost the most from that application being rejected. That'll give us our killer.'

There was a rattle of keys at the door.

'Quick, it's Ed.' Dan began to gather the pages together roughly and shoved them into his bag, which he stuffed down the side of the sofa. When Ed entered the room he found Dan and Emma sitting awkwardly on the sofa, each clutching a beer. A sly smirk slid across his face.

'Oh, I'm sorry. Am I interrupting?'

'No, no, we were just … um …' Dan didn't know how he was planning to finish the sentence. Ed stood there grinning, enjoying his discomfort.

Emma ended things by standing up. 'I'd better go.'

Ed looking surprised. 'No, don't. I was just—' but she was draining her beer.

'No, I've got to be somewhere. See you later.'

Dan showed her to the door of the flat and returned to find Ed looking contrite.

'Sorry, mate. I didn't mean to scare her off.'

'Nothing's going on.'

The smug grin returned to Ed's face. 'I believe you. Thousands wouldn't.'

Chapter 26

After Ed had got changed out of his work clothes he decided he wanted sweet and sour chicken for dinner, but couldn't be bothered to fetch it. Grumbling, but with Ed's £20 in his pocket, Dan headed out.

He paused at the side of the road as his mobile beeped. It was a message from Emma saying she'd heard from Burton about the off-the-record chats and wasn't happy. He rubbed his forehead and tried to form a suitable response that wouldn't earn him a slap. A string of cars passed, their headlights dazzling him in the gloomy early evening light. Glancing up he spotted a gap in the traffic and stepped into the road, eyes still on his mobile.

Suddenly an engine revved and a pair of extremely bright headlights illuminated the road. Dan froze for a moment as the car hurtled towards him and then dived onto the pavement.

He landed with a bone-shaking thud, his head hitting the pavement. The car missed him by inches, colliding with some black plastic rubbish bags piled on the kerb and sending litter flying across the road. It roared away down the High Street as Dan struggled into a sitting position.

He put his hand to his head and it came away red and sticky. His vision spun for a moment and he sat back stunned.

He hadn't even seen the colour of the vehicle.

The young police officer looked sceptical.

'The car tried to run you over?' he asked for about the fifth time looking back at his notes.

'Yes,' said Dan wearily. His head was still spinning although the bleeding had stopped. A dull ache was developing.

'And you say it swerved towards you?'

'Yes,' Ed said, leaning forward towards the officer. 'God, how many times does he have to tell you? The car even hit some rubbish bags on the pavement.'

Dan elbowed Ed in a bid to calm him down.

'The car hit some rubbish bags?' the constable repeated, writing it all down.

'Yes, there were some rubbish bags. The car hit them and the rubbish sprayed across the road and the pavement.'

The police officer nodded shortly and looked at his partner.

'But you didn't see the driver?' said the second officer.

'No, I didn't. It was dark, the headlights were too bright and I was too busy diving out of the way.'

'The headlights were bright, you say?' asked the police officer shaking his pen, which seemed to be running out.

Ed snorted in frustration.

Dan took a deep breath. 'Yes, I think they were on full beam or something. They dazzled me.'

'And you say the road was clear?'

'There were a few cars passing me but when I glanced up the road was clear.'

'You glanced?'

'I was replying to a text message.' The officers exchanged a look.

'Oh, now, come on,' Ed's voice was raised. 'Dan isn't stupid enough to just step into the path of an oncoming car.' The officer looked up from his notebook and raised his eyebrows.

'I waited until the road was clear,' Dan said. 'There were no more cars coming. I was in the middle of the road when the engine revved and the car came flying towards me. I dived out of the way. It swerved towards me and then drove off.'

'And you didn't see what kind of car it was? Or even what colour?'

'No.'

The constable snapped his notebook shut. 'Well, Mr, er,' he paused.

'Sullivan.'

'Mr Sullivan, there's not much more we can do tonight. If you remember anything be sure to call us.' The officer handed Dan his card. They both stood up.

'Can you tell DI Burton what happened?' Dan stood up quickly but his head spun and he quickly sat back down.

'DI Burton?'

'She needs to know,' Dan insisted.

'OK, sir. We'll tell her.' The two officers left. Ed came back into the room, having shown them to the door.

'They didn't believe me, did they?' Dan asked rubbing his face.

'Are you sure you shouldn't go to hospital and get checked out?'

Dan shook his head. 'No, I'm OK. It's only a scratch. That's not important. As long as they tell Burton and Shepherd.'

Ed looked at Dan, his face serious. 'Now do you want to tell me what's been going on?'

Dan took a deep breath. 'Not really.'

'Why not?'

'You'll get angry with me.'

Ed pulled a face. 'So what's new?' But when he saw the look on

Dan's face, he asked, 'What have you got yourself into?'

'That story, the planning one.'

'The one with James Wilton?'

'Yes, that one. I think there's more to it than I originally thought.'

'You mean it's dangerous?'

'I think so.' Dan hung his head.

Ed sighed deeply. 'I told you to leave it alone.'

'But if I'm right, and there's corruption in the planning committee, people need to know.'

'And you need the big story? The one that will "get you out of this dump", as you so eloquently put it?'

'No, it's not that …'

'I've told you before about trying to force a story.'

'But I don't really know anything yet.'

'Someone obviously thinks you do.' Ed paused for a moment. 'So this is why you've been spending so much time with Emma?'

'She has the crime connections, the links with the police. She's going to be able to keep me up to speed with what they're up to.'

'You and Emma aren't an item then?'

'Sorry, but your romantic theories are all wrong on this occasion.' Dan rubbed his face again. 'I just don't understand why someone would try to run me over. It just seems so random.'

'What worries me more is someone knew to find you in the High Street tonight. It's not like you go there every night.'

'What do you mean?'

'Someone is keeping tabs on you. You must know more than you think you know, and they're prepared to stop you by any means necessary.'

The following day Burton faced the police's top technician Steve Proctor across her desk.

'What have you got for me?'

'It was a bit of a rush job because I know you wanted it quickly so it's not very detailed.'

'Never mind that. Did you find anything?'

'Nothing.'

'Nothing?'

'Nothing criminal, apart from some rather dodgy photographs of him and his mates at a fancy dress party. Not entirely sure what he was supposed to be.' Proctor sniggered.

Burton didn't smile. 'But there's no sign of any email accounts?'

'He's got two of those, sir. One is from his ISP and one is a remote one. It's a Hotmail account, but it's not got what you're looking for.'

'No sign of any other emails between him and James Wilton?'

'No, sir.'

'Any notes about planning applications?'

'Some, but they start a couple of days ago.'

'He didn't know about the planning applications before,' Burton muttered to herself.

'He could have flash drives for files and photographs but it doesn't work like that with email accounts that are in the cloud. Plus there was nothing deleted or we would have found that. The only other alternative,' said Proctor, 'is that he did it from an entirely different computer. But it would have to be somewhere pretty secure or anyone could see it.'

Burton thanked the man and he left with a jovial wave. These techies were all too cheerful, she thought. She had too much to worry about, including whether her youngest daughter had caught measles after a recent afternoon at another child's birthday party. She stared at the wall for a minute, lost in thought. Then she seized the phone.

'Hello, newsroom,' came Emma's voice.

'Emma? Jude Burton.'

'Hey, a call from the horse's mouth. I'm honoured.'

'Less of the insults.'

'Sorry.' Emma laughed. 'How's the investigation going? Your press officer is being very coy.'

'She's good like that, is Suzy. It's progressing. That's all I can say at the moment. I'm surprised that you've got involved with Mr Sullivan's investigation.'

'You know me, can't resist a mystery. Come on, you usually give me more than "it's progressing". What's the off-the-record story?'

'I told Mr Sullivan and now I'm reminding you, I can't give you anything given your connection to the person we arrested.' Burton's voice was sharp.

'Oh, OK.' Emma's voice was disappointed.

'I actually wanted to ask you a favour,' said Burton.

'Go on.'

'Your computer systems at work. Can you access remote email accounts from there?'

'What, like Hotmail or Yahoo, you mean?'

'Yes.'

'No, you can't. The server won't let you even get on the site, never mind actually log in. They want to make sure we can't do anything but work.' She laughed wryly.

'Are you sure? There's no way to override it?'

'I've no idea. I've never tried. I presume you would have to get access to the server and change it but that's all run centrally.'

'An individual couldn't do it themselves?'

'I doubt it. Someone from the IT department might have the access and permissions but this place is pretty tight on computer security. They wouldn't just give that information to anyone.'

Burton thought for a moment.

'Hey, you still there?' Emma's voice cut in. 'When do I get an update?'

'I'll give you something as soon as I have it.' Burton hung up.

Just then there was a tap on the door. Shepherd appeared with a coffee in each hand and a bemused expression on his face.

'What's up with you?' Burton asked.

'Something very bizarre, sir. Two uniforms who were on duty last night just collared me in the canteen.'

'And?'

'Apparently someone tried to run Mr Sullivan over last night in the middle of the High Street.'

Ten minutes later Burton and Shepherd were in the town centre CCTV control room.

'These are the tapes from last night,' said the operator scrolling through, eyes fixed on the screen. 'What time are we looking for?'

'Seven o'clock,' said Shepherd, looking quickly at his notebook.

'OK,' said the man scrolling quickly until the clock read eighteen fifty-five. 'Here we go.'

'And here's our boy,' said Shepherd after a couple of minutes, pointing as Dan paused on the screen, looking into the palm of his hand.

'Dangerous things, mobile phones,' Burton said to Shepherd with a grin. The latter smirked as a line of cars passed Dan where he stood. After pausing for a couple of seconds, he looked up and stepped into the road.

'And here comes the car,' said Shepherd as the vehicle roared into view.

'Quite dramatic that,' said the operator dispassionately. They watched Dan roll across the pavement and try to get up.

'Can you even tell what colour it is?' Burton muttered. Shepherd squinted at the screen.

'I'd say dark.'

'That's helpful.'

'It's awkward lighting. It's caught the number plate wrong too. You can't see what it says.'

'Wind it back,' said Burton. 'And stop it there.' The man paused the tape with the car in the middle of the screen.

'What is it?' asked Shepherd.

'Well,' said Burton pointing. Her finger indicated where the light had caught on the car's badge. 'We know we're looking for an Audi.'

Chapter 27

Johanna Buttle looked up from the desk in her open-plan office in the town hall.

'A package? For me?'

'Yes,' said the council mail woman. 'It's not got a date stamp on it or anything so I'm not sure when it came in. I've been off for a few days and I just spotted it this morning.'

'Oh, thanks.' Buttle looked at the brown paper-wrapped package turning it over in her hands. It was an A4-sized expandable envelope with no stamps or postmarks on it. The name and address were handwritten but she did not recognise the irregularly formed capitals. It seemed to have been written in a hurry.

'Oooh, have you got a secret admirer?' asked Edwin Farmer, one of the project managers, looking over from his desk.

She laughed. 'It doesn't look much like a secret admirer package, does it?' But she wouldn't put it past Paul to send her something romantic and disguise it. It was meant to be a secret after all. She turned her attention back to the address label. She didn't think it was Paul's writing but if it was from him she didn't want to open it publicly. She waited until Edwin was immersed in a phone call before she quietly slit the envelope open. Peering inside, her heart pounded and her body went cold. Someone knew.

She stared in horror and then leapt to her feet.

Hanging up the phone Edwin Farmer looked up.

'You OK?' he asked. 'You're white as a sheet. There wasn't a ghost in there, was there?' He laughed heartily at his own joke.

'I've ... I've just got to ...' stammered Buttle. 'I'm just popping out.' She grabbed her handbag and the envelope. She needed space to think.

Downstairs in the empty councillors' coffee room, she opened the envelope again and took out its contents. Her hands shook. The papers which had spilled out onto the table contained two copies each of twenty planning applications, the dates going back two years. The applications had subtle differences, just the number of houses in each development were changed. In each case the initially dated application had fewer houses than the one that had been amended later. She sank into her chair, a hand rising to cover her mouth. Someone knew; someone knew what they had been doing. There was no way anyone would believe that the committee had been kept in the dark. An investigation could ruin them all.

But a printed note also threatened to tell her husband everything if she didn't come clean and go to the police. Buttle's heart thudded against her chest and the room swam before her eyes. Where had this come from?

Digging feverishly in her handbag she seized her mobile phone and dialled the familiar number.

'Paul? Paul?'

'Jo? Darling, are you OK? You sound awful.' His voice was soft and warm.

'Someone knows.'

There was a pause. 'Someone knows what?'

'They know everything. I got a package in the post this morning. They know about the planning department and they know about us.'

'A package of what?'

'Loads of planning applications. All the ones that got changed once we'd agreed them. There's a note saying they'll tell Peter everything unless I put a stop to what's been going on.'

'Who sent it?'

'That's just it, I don't know. The package is anonymous. There wasn't even a postmark on it.'

There was another pause.

'Paul? What are we going to do?' Her voice was high and scared.

'Just calm down. They might be bluffing.'

'I can't take that chance. I still love Peter and I don't want to do anything to hurt him. It would kill him to find out.'

'What are you going to do?'

'I don't know. I need to think.'

'Jo, don't do anything rash.' His voice was urgent. 'We'll all end up in prison.'

'I'll have to go to the police. It's the only way out I can think of that protects Peter. I'm sorry, Paul. I'm just so sorry.' The last thing he heard were her sobs before the phone disconnected.

In the ladies toilet, Jo Buttle pulled herself together with an effort. She splashed cold water on her face and repaired her make-up. It didn't solve her problem but it made her feel slightly better.

Squaring her small shoulders she scooped up the envelope and opened the toilet door a crack, making sure the coast was clear. No sign of anyone in the corridor.

She walked quickly down the hall and down the stairs, heels clacking. She winced at the sound. Why hadn't she worn quieter shoes? She didn't want to attract attention.

She'd reached the lobby and was heading towards the front door when she spotted someone standing at the reception desk. It was that

Post reporter who was at the last planning meeting – Dan something.

She paused for a moment and decided on a plan. Stepping forward she grabbed his arm. He stopped, starting back down a step in surprise.

'It's Dan, isn't it?'

'Yes?' His voice was cautious. 'And you're Councillor Buttle.'

'I need a word. I need your help quite urgently.'

Dan didn't resist as Buttle towed him outside and round the corner into an alleyway beside the town hall. She turned to face him, eyes wide and frightened.

'I have a good story for you,' she said.

Dan raised an eyebrow trying to look cool and calm despite the flicker in his stomach.

'But I need to be anonymous,' she continued.

'Why?' Dan asked.

'What I'm about to give you is very sensitive and I need to know that it won't come back to me.'

'I always protect my sources. Go on.'

'The mayor is investigating the planning department.'

This was news to Dan. He got that feeling in his stomach again, but he didn't want to give away his lack of knowledge. 'I'd heard something about it,' he lied.

'I have some information for you.'

'Such as?'

'But first I want your assurance that you'll protect my identity.'

'As I said, we never reveal sources.'

'What I'm about to show you could get me into a lot of trouble.' Dan nodded his assent and she handed him the envelope.

'What is it?'

An alarm sounded on Buttle's phone. She dug it out of her bag, looked at the screen and killed the alarm. 'I have to go. I need to keep things looking normal,' she muttered under her breath. To Dan she said, 'My number is in there. Call me when you've had a chance to look at it.'

And she scuttled away, her bottom swinging in her tight skirt. Dan stared after her, weighed the envelope in his hands and headed for home.

Back at the flat Dan laid out the papers on the living room floor. He was sitting cross-legged staring at them when Ed came home.

'What have you got there?' Ed asked, pulling off his shoes with the toes of his other foot.

'I think it's the story.'

'What?'

'I think it's what James Wilton wanted to tell me about.'

Ed peered over Dan's shoulders. 'From Drimble?'

'No, I barely got into the town hall. I got a bit more than I bargained for.'

'How so?'

'I ran into Councillor Johanna Buttle.'

'Yum. What did she have to say for her gorgeously pointy-shoed self?'

Dan grinned.

'Don't let Lydia hear you say that!'

'Good point.' Ed checked behind the long window curtains. 'Nope, she didn't hear me, phew,' he said wiping his brow and grinning. Dan laughed too.

'What did Buttle have to say?' Ed asked.

'Not much, really. She seemed really stressed.'

Ed sighed. 'You're still going to keep this from me?'

'She gave me this.' Dan pointed at the pages lying in the floor.

Ed knelt next to him and leaned down to look at them. 'What is it?'

Dan pulled the papers into a neat pile. 'It's planning applications.'

'I still I don't understand how you can get excited about planning applications.'

'It's not planning applications in general, it's these specific applications.'

'What about them?'

'It's like the application from the other night. The numbers don't match up.'

'But Buttle didn't really tell you anything?' Ed asked, getting to his feet and pulling off his tie.

'No. She'd had an appointment and had to rush off. I don't think she'd planned on telling me about it.' He glanced at his watch. 'I need to speak to Em. Was she still in the office when you left?'

Ed scowled. 'You'll talk to her but not to me?'

Dan pulled an apologetic face.

'You know Daisy won't take a story from a leaked document without evidence to back it up.'

But Dan wasn't listening. 'I'll have to give Buttle a ring and get her to meet me tomorrow. See if I can find a way to persuade her to tell me what's going on.'

'Just remember what happened last time you pushed someone into talking to you,' Ed said as he walked out of the living room door.

But Dan was already grabbing his phone and dialling the number on Buttle's business card. After six rings her voice cut in asking him to please leave a message after the tone.

'Councillor Buttle? It's Dan Sullivan. Look, I need to speak to you urgently about that stuff you gave me earlier. Can you give me a ring as soon as possible so we can discuss it?' After leaving his number, he hung up.

Chapter 28

Johanna Buttle straightened the neckline of her top. It was low cut enough to show off her ample cleavage. Paul always liked that, although her husband didn't. Peter preferred her to dress more modestly.

She exited the lift on the first floor of the Turpin Hotel and walked to room 16. She was glad he'd picked somewhere quiet for their meeting. The email arranging the meeting had told her where to come and to bring the envelope so they could discuss it. She wasn't sure they would be able to agree on a course of action, but she'd have to tell him what she'd done with the envelope. Maybe they could talk to the paper together, present a united front. Nothing could happen to them then.

She raised a hand and knocked on the door.

'Come in,' a voice called. She saw that the door wasn't latched and pushed it open.

'Paul?' she called, allowing the door to close and lock with a soft click behind her. He must be in the bathroom, she thought, dropping her bag on the bed and taking off her coat. She looked up at the sound of the bathroom door opening but the welcoming smile froze on her face. It wasn't Paul.

'You?'

The man smiled. 'Me.'

'But you said … you said? Where's Paul?'

'You've let us down, Jo, I'm very disappointed.'

'But I don't understand—' Her mobile phone beeped the depths of her handbag.

'Leave it,' the man ordered.

She stood, hands limp by her sides. 'What do you want from me?'

The mobile beeped again and the man pushed roughly past her to reach the bed. He dug in her bag and removed the phone. Buttle started to edge towards the door but the man grabbed her arm and threw her onto the bed. She hadn't realised how strong he was. The duvet cover slid under her as she sat up and perched on the side of the bed, her feet barely touching the floor. Her eyes were wide and frightened as the man jabbed a few buttons and started to listen to the message the caller had left earlier that evening. His face darkened as he listened to Dan Sullivan asking her to call.

'You've been talking to that journalist, haven't you? Haven't you?' He threw the phone against the wall. The cover flew off and the battery popped out falling to the floor. 'Why, Jo? When we had so much going for us? We were making money, making nice new homes for the people of Allensbury.'

'I see that you put money before everything else. That's all that matters to people these days,' she retorted.

'Don't give me that crap,' the man sneered. 'What else were you in it for if not for the money?'

'You're mad. I had no choice. I had to protect Peter.'

The man snorted. He turned away and Buttle took a chance. She scrambled across the bed and ran for the door but the man was too quick for her. He grabbed her around the neck and dragged her back across the room.

'You don't just walk away from this, Jo,' he hissed, pushing his face so close to hers that she could see sweat beading on his upper lip. 'I'm going to show you what happens to naughty girls who don't do what they're told.'

With his free hand, he dragged the duvet and top sheet from the bed. He threw Buttle onto the bed and straddled her, pinning her arms to the mattress. Oh God, he was going to rape her.

'Please, no please,' she begged.

'I'm sorry, Jo, but you brought this on yourself.' He began to wind the sheet into a rope. 'You see, if you'd just done what you were told I wouldn't have to do this.' Her eyes were fixed on his face, desperate for a way to make him stop. 'If you hadn't spoken to that reporter, we could have fixed this. You could have come and talked to me. I could have made you see … but it's too late now.'

'I didn't know. I was trying to protect my husband.'

'You should have thought of that before you took up with Paul Sanderson.' He grinned at her tear-stained face.

'We could have continued with our plan. But now I've got to make sure you don't tell that reporter anything.'

'It's too late, he already knows.'

The man shook his head in mock sorrow. 'I'm sad to hear that, Jo. But it won't save you.'

He began to wind the sheet around her neck. Buttle bucked and struggled but she was no match for his weight. Her fingernails tore red scratches in his hands and he slapped her. She clawed towards his face but was unable to make contact.

He laughed. 'Not enough, I'm afraid, Councillor Buttle. Remember you brought this on yourself.'

He began to tighten the sheet. She struggled, eyes bulging as she fought for breath, the room started to go dim around her. Her last thought was of Paul and whether he was due for the same treatment. The sheet was tightened until she stopped struggling.

The man climbed off the bed looking down with contempt at the small body. Then he crossed to the pieces of mobile phone, and fitted them back together. Fortunately it still worked. He sat down on the corner of the bed and started to tap out a text message.

Chapter 29

'It's about time you two came back. I've been waiting ages.'

Burton and Shepherd jumped as Eleanor Brody's voice rang out across the empty CID office. She was standing in the doorway of Burton's office and turned back inside to sit down as they approached. She sat neatly in the chair opposite Burton's desk, clutching a cardboard folder.

'You don't normally come here,' Burton said, looking suspicious. 'Usually we have to come to you.'

Brody gave a slight smile. 'I was passing and thought it best to deliver the bad news quickly.'

Burton sat back in her creaky chair and eyed the pathologist. 'Bad news? We don't need any more of that.' She paused and then said, 'Come on, hit me with it.'

Brody handed over the cardboard folder. 'The letter opener definitely isn't the murder weapon.'

Burton looked up in dismay. 'What? I thought you said there was blood on it.'

'There is, but there's no skin or tissue or anything like that. You couldn't stab someone, even with a smooth blade like that, without getting tissue on it.'

Burton looked at Shepherd, who had thrust his hands into his trouser pockets and sighed heavily.

'What did stab James Wilton?'

'Something longer and thicker than that.' Brody pointed at the folder. 'As you'll see from my report, I've tested the wound and it's too deep for that blade.'

Burton swore under her breath.

'How did blood get on the letter opener?' Shepherd asked.

'After you found blood on his desk, we examined it under ultra-violet light. Someone had tried to clear it up, but it's harder to do than people think and there were other patches. My guess is that the letter opener was on the desk and Wilton could have fallen on it after he'd been stabbed and that's how the blood got transferred. Something like that.'

'And we're now looking for an entirely different murder weapon?' Shepherd asked.

'That's the long and the short of it.'

'Where do we start?' Shepherd looked from Brody to Burton and back again.

'That's your department.' Brody stood up. As she retrieved her bag from the floor, her coat fell open to reveal a dark red knee-length dress.

'Going somewhere nice?' Shepherd asked, arching an eyebrow.

'Meeting a friend for a drink, if you must know.'

'I didn't know you had a life outside the morgue.' His cheeky grin was rewarded with a glare from Brody as she sailed from the room.

Shepherd closed the door and turned back. Burton was staring at the pages in the folder, flicking through them in a dispirited manner.

'I was so sure it was the letter opener,' she said.

'That's because we didn't think to look for anything else. The letter opener seemed the most likely.'

'Now we're back to almost square bloody one with no murder weapon.'

'The SOCOs didn't find anything else in the bins so the killer must have taken the murder weapon away with him.'

'He came prepared,' Burton said. 'It was premeditated.'

'I doubt his wife had something like that concealed in her handbag,' Shepherd said. 'It says here the knife was twisted when Wilton was stabbed. Someone was making damn sure it was fatal.' Shepherd sat in the chair recently vacated by Brody, resting his elbow on the armrest and massaging his jaw with his fingertips. 'Who among our suspects has that kind of training?'

Burton frowned. 'Can you look into that? Maybe one of them is ex-army?'

'It might take a while getting something out of the MoD but I'll give it a shot.'

'And there's no other way someone could learn to do that?'

'Whoever did this looks like a pro, based on the wound. It was tidy but fatal, fatal in one stroke. That's someone who's done this before and more than once.'

'Great. Even more back to square one.'

Chapter 30

The following morning Dan and Ed were tripping over each other in the kitchen making breakfast.

'I don't understand why you need to be up so early,' Ed yawned. 'It's not like you have anywhere to go.'

'I had a text message from Buttle last night. She wants to meet at the Turpin Hotel in about twenty minutes.'

He slurped his coffee, burning his mouth.

Ed looked at his watch. 'You're cutting it fine.'

Dan patted his bag. 'I've been up for hours rereading this to make sense of it.'

'You think that she'll just tell you what you want to know?'

'She's given me this information so far. She's clearly keen to get something off her chest.'

Ed snorted into his coffee. 'With a chest like that, I'm not surprised she needs to get something off it.'

Dan rolled his eyes. 'That's a bit harsh.' But Ed grinned.

'All I'll say is be ready for the fact she might have had a change of heart. If it is allegations of fraud and corruption, she'll have to be sure of her position before she goes public with it.'

'I think she's already gone public by giving it to the media.'

'She might want it back. Be prepared for that. You don't know where she got it from.'

'She's on planning. She'll have got it from their records. She's clearly noticed what's going on and wants to blow the whistle.'

'Don't go overboard. You can't force it. When you push it, that's when you end up making mistakes.'

'Thanks for reminding me.'

'Sorry, mate, but I think you need to keep your feet on the ground.'

'But this has got to lead somewhere, hasn't it?'

'Just be careful. James Wilton got killed remember, and you said Buttle seemed scared. Don't jump in with both feet.'

'I'm only going to feel her out. See what she has to say.'

'Don't push too hard or you'll spook her.'

'I know what I'm doing.'

'Do you?'

Ed's final words rang in Dan's ears as the flat door banged shut behind him. But his stomach was flickering and nothing Ed could say would change that.

The lobby and lounge of the Turpin Hotel were crowded but a quick scan of the room showed Johanna Buttle was not there. A waitress approached Dan.

'Table for one?'

'I'm supposed to be meeting someone. A councillor. Johanna Buttle?' The woman looked puzzled.

'I don't know her. I'll ask at reception.' She led Dan to the front desk and spoke with the receptionist.

'Is it Dan Sullivan?' asked the receptionist.

'Yes.'

'Here. This was left for you.' She handed him an envelope. He ripped it open, praying that it wasn't Buttle bailing on him. Inside was a note.

'I don't want to do this publicly. Meet me in room 16.' Dan read the note again and shrugged. If she wanted to meet privately, that was fine with him.

'Where is room 16?' he asked the receptionist.

'It's on the first floor. Take the lift just there and turn down the corridor on the right,' the woman said, pointing.

Dan rode the lift to the first floor and stepped out into the corridor looking around him. It was empty and quiet. Turning right, he walked quickly down the corridor and knocked on the door of room 16. There was no answer and he knocked again. Putting his ear to the door Dan listened for a moment. There was no sound from inside the room, not even someone coming to answer the door. Then he realised the door was open. He pushed it gently and paused on the threshold.

'Hello?'

At first the room seemed empty, the bed unmade. Then he saw Johanna Buttle, sprawled across the bed fully clothed. Her arm hung limply off the side of the mattress and her head lolled to one side. A step forward into the room told Dan something was very, very wrong. Her eyes bulged with shock at the bed sheets wound tightly around her neck and she stared glassily at him.

Dan had taken a step back in horror when a strong arm grabbed him around the neck from behind. There was a sharp prick to his neck behind his right ear and everything went black.

Dan's eyes flickered open and he squinted against the bright sunlight pouring through the window. His head was pounding and felt swollen. He looked around. What was he doing lying face down on a bed?

He moved slightly and his arm touched the woman lying next to him. She was ice cold, making him jump.

He raised his head and looked at her. This wasn't his bedroom. He tried to stand up and tumbled onto his hands and knees on the floor.

Jo Buttle's cold, dead arm hung almost in his face. He couldn't stop staring at her. Hands shaking, Dan got gingerly to his feet and reached into his pocket for his mobile phone.

Suddenly there was a heavy bang on the door. He had no time to react before the door flew open and armed police stormed into the room. Dan automatically raised his hands in surrender, his mobile falling to the floor. The first officer kicked it away and shoved Dan's face against the wall. A second officer raced to the bed, bending over Johanna Buttle.

'She's dead,' he said, two fingers searching her neck for a pulse. Rough hands patted all over Dan's body.

'Clear!' a voice shouted.

Suddenly the room was full of burly police officers, all wearing body armour and carrying guns. There seemed to be more police officers than air and Dan's head started to spin again.

He tried to speak to the officer but the man held up a hand to stop him.

His head felt fuzzy but when he shook it to try and clear the ringing, it simply made his legs turn to jelly. DS Shepherd appeared next to him.

'Fancy meeting you here,' he said, raising an eyebrow. Dan stared stupidly at the detective for a moment as if not recognising him and sagged against the wall. Shepherd peered at him.

'What did you do to him?' he asked the nearest officer.

'Nothing,' came the reply. 'Maybe he's just not very bright?'

Shepherd laughed. 'Nah, he's usually got plenty to say for himself.'

'How did— did— how did you know?' Dan stuttered.

'Anonymous tip-off,' said Shepherd, picking up Dan's mobile in gloved hands.

'He was using it when we came in,' said the officer.

'It's mine,' said Dan defensively. 'I was trying to call you guys. How did you know where to find us?'

'Like I said, an anonymous call told us to come here to this room because there was a man with a gun,' said Shepherd. 'Funny, it didn't mention you.' He looked down at Buttle. 'I wouldn't have thought she was your type.'

'She's not. She asked me to meet her because she had information about the planning story I told you about. She's on the planning committee. She had applications to give to me.'

'Hmm, wasn't James Wilton going to do the same? Isn't it odd how people who help you seem to end up dead?' He nodded to the police officer, who stowed his gun and jerked Dan's arms behind his back to snap on handcuffs.

'What are you doing? I've told you she was dead when I got here.' Dan tried to struggle against the burly policeman. The man waited patiently for his efforts to be over before completing his action.

'You were found in a hotel room standing over a dead body. Do you really expect us to believe you had nothing to do with it?'

'Yes,' Dan said, willing them to believe him. Suddenly his stomach rolled and he leaned over and vomited onto the floor. The police officer wrinkled his nose.

'Nice,' he commented. Shepherd waited until Dan was finished and fetched him a glass of water from the bathroom.

'Thanks,' Dan said. Shepherd peered at him for a moment.

'Not going to be sick again, are you?' he asked. Dan gently shook his head and Shepherd seized his arm and led him towards the door.

'She asked me to meet her here,' Dan continued.

'And then spontaneously dropped dead, did she?'

'She was already dead when I got here.'

'Whatever you say. DI Burton will want another word with you. Consider yourself under arrest on suspicion of the murder of Johanna Buttle.'

Chapter 31

'And here we are again,' Burton said, looking at Dan across the interview room table. Dan looked back at her, not saying a word, fearing that if he opened his mouth he might be sick again.

Burton peered at him. 'Are you OK?'

Dan blinked and looked at her.

'Something is definitely not right,' she said. 'He looks really vacant.'

'He was sick on the floor at the hotel,' Shepherd said.

'I feel funny, sort of like being drunk,' Dan put in. 'My head feels all swimming. It must have been the injection.'

'Injection? What injection?'

'The man who grabbed me. He injected me in the neck. I passed out.'

Burton stared at him for a moment. Then she turned to Shepherd. 'Go and fetch a doctor will you.'

Burton and Dan waited in silence in the interview room until Shepherd returned with the doctor.

'You're lucky to catch me,' said the doctor. 'I was about to leave to go to another job.' He placed his medical bag on the interview room table. Then he looked at Dan, taking in his pale face. 'What have we got?'

'He says he's had an injection in his neck. We don't know what it was,' Burton said.

The doctor took out a small torch and leaned over Dan flicking the torch over his eyes. Dan squinted and tried to move away.

'Any vomiting?' asked the doctor.

'Just once,' Dan said.

'Feeling dizzy?'

'Very.'

The doctor had switched off the torch and was testing Dan's pulse. After a couple of minutes he looked at Burton.

'He's definitely had a very powerful sedative. I don't know how big a dose, but his pulse is slow and his eyes aren't reacting the way they should. The vomiting is probably a reaction to feeling dizzy.'

'So he's not fit to be interviewed?' Burton asked.

'Definitely not, he won't know what he's saying. I'd say let him rest for at least half an hour, and then see how he's feeling.'

'Will you be able to come back and look at him again?'

'Yes, if he's no better in half an hour give me a call and I'll come back.'

The man left the room with a cheery smile. Shepherd looked at Burton.

'The only thing we can do is put him in a cell where he can lie down,' she said. 'And get Monica Wells down here. She needs to see him.'

Shepherd walked round the table and put a large hand under Dan's armpit. He gently pulled Dan upright and walked him out of the room and along the corridor to the custody suite. It was fortunate there was a cell free and he settled Dan on the bed and gave the custody sergeant instructions to keep an eye on him.

Shepherd found Burton in her office staring off into space.

'How is he?'

'Settled in a cell. He was almost asleep by the time I left the room.' He stood silently for a moment. Then he said, 'Do you believe his story, that he was injected?'

'How else could he have been sedated? And you could tell there was something wrong, even before the doctor came in.' She paused and rubbed the bridge of her nose. 'Something feels wrong. It's all a bit too convenient that he was at the scene of the murder of another person helping him with a story.'

'You think it's a setup?'

'Normally I'd say when you find someone standing over a dead body with a smoking gun they're usually the person who did it, but it feels wrong that he's so keen on this story and now both the sources he was using have been murdered. He wouldn't do that.'

'Unless the story is a cover.'

'If it is, then there would be a reason why he's killed two people he's not connected to in any way but I struggle to believe that.'

'You think someone else killed Councillor Buttle and Sullivan just walked into the middle of it?'

'It's the only solution that make sense. Do you remember how agitated she got when we interviewed her? There was obviously something bothering her.'

Shepherd nodded. 'I'll speak to the councillors again, see if anyone knew what was upsetting her. They might have some insights.'

'Check alibis as well. Find out who was where and when and whether any of them would have wanted her dead.' She paused. 'Who booked the hotel room?'

Shepherd pulled a face. 'Raymond Chandler,' he said.

Burton stared. 'The novelist?' she asked. 'The one that died in nineteen fifty-nine?'

'That's him.'

'I suppose it was too much to hope for that the killer booked under his own name.'

Shepherd paused on his way to the door. 'What I really want to know is why and how Sullivan came to be at the murder scene.'

'Hopefully he'll be able to tell us that. Actually, hold on a minute, speaking of guns, that tip-off that took us to the hotel, what's happening there?'

'The staff seemed to know nothing about the phone call. They were surprised to see us but the manager was keen for us to sort it out.'

'Was there a man with a gun?'

'Not when we got there, sir, and I've got someone looking at the hotel CCTV, but my thinking is that there never was one.'

'Someone wanted us to go down there and find Johanna Buttle murdered. More than that, I think they wanted us to find Sullivan there,' Burton said. 'What was the cause of death?'

'It looks like she was strangled, but Brody and her team are still at the scene.'

Burton wrinkled her nose. 'It's just too simple that it was Sullivan who did it. But now we have a problem.'

'That someone else murdered Wilton and Buttle and tried to frame Sullivan?'

'Exactly. Wilton's wife had no reason to kill Buttle, let alone try to pin it on Sullivan.'

Shepherd took a deep breath. 'So who does benefit from Wilton and Buttle being dead and Sullivan being suspected?'

'That's the problem … I have no idea.'

'Can't you tell me anything?' Burton was pleading into the phone when Shepherd rustled into the room carrying a paper bag containing two doughnuts. She mouthed a thank you.

'I'm still at the scene.' Pathologist Eleanor Brody's voice was sharp even through the speakerphone. 'All I can tell you is that she was strangled, probably sometime after midnight.'

'Is that all?'

'All?' Brody's voice rose angrily. 'You're bloody lucky to get anything after only an hour. I can't work miracles and I won't be rushed. That's how mistakes happen and then where would you be?'

'OK, OK,' Burton quickly interrupted the rant. 'Just call me when you get something.' She thumped the end-call button and looked up. 'How is Mr Sullivan?'

'Seems to be OK. I just looked in on him and he says he's feeling better. Julianna in the custody suite had just made him a cup of tea.'

'Blimey, she never makes tea for anyone.'

'And the solicitor?'

'Monica Wells has been contacted. She's in court this morning but has said she'll get here as soon as she's finished.'

'What do we know about the emergency call?'

'Control is busy checking if they have a record of where the call came from, but the operator who took the call said the man wasn't on the line very long.'

'It was definitely a man?'

'Yes, sir. She was really sure about it. She said it sounded like he was disguising his voice but it was definitely a man. They're looking for the recording of it now so it can be checked.'

'Right, let me know as soon as we hear anything.'

Dan and Monica faced Burton and Shepherd across the interview room table.

'Tell us what happened,' Burton said.

'Where do I start?'

'Why were you meeting Councillor Buttle?'

'She asked me to.'

'It was that simple?'

'Yes, she texted me this morning and asked me to meet her at the hotel.'

'You were close enough to have each other's mobile numbers?'

'She gave me hers yesterday. She wanted to talk to me about some old applications that had been sent to her. They're similar to the one that got rejected at that committee meeting, the numbers were wrong. I think that Wilton wanted to tell me about it as well. I rang her last night and left a message so that's how she had my number.'

'Then what happened?'

'I went to the hotel. She'd left me a message at reception saying to come up to the room.' He paused. 'I went up and when I knocked there was no answer. So I pushed the door open.'

'It wasn't locked?' interrupted Burton.

'No. I was surprised by that too. I thought the room was empty at first but then I saw her lying there dead.' He shuddered. 'I've never seen a dead body before.' He looked down at his hands.

'What did you do?'

'Someone grabbed me from behind and knocked me out. When I woke up she was still there and then your guys burst in.'

Shepherd spoke. 'You said she gave you some old planning applications. Why would she have done that?'

'The plans went back at least a year. They're all housing applications and there were two copies of each one, the official one on file and then a second one. The second one had different numbers, a larger number of houses or flats than in the official one.'

'Meaning?'

'They've been doctoring plans, making them look legal when in actual fact they were over the maximum amount of houses allowed.

Then it looks like someone – probably Wilton – allows an appeal to be made and changes the number back to the initial proposal and swaps the two applications so the file now says permission was given for the higher number of houses.'

'And no one can check back on it?'

'If they looked back at the file, it would have the one version in it and there could be no questions.'

'It's real, then? This scam?'

'Did you think I'd made it up?' Dan asked.

Burton raised an eyebrow but said nothing.

'Where had she got this information from?' Shepherd asked.

'She didn't say, but the envelope was addressed to her and it had been hand delivered. She was really worried about it.'

'And she came to you?'

'I just sort of bumped into her at the town hall. She kept saying she wanted the truth to come out. She didn't want it covered up but she had to be anonymous. I figured she'd found out about the corruption and decided to blow the whistle on it.'

'You think it's more likely that she was a whistle-blower than being involved in it?'

'I would say so. She's a pretty straight arrow and why would she tell me if she was involved in it? Surely she would want to keep it secret if that was the case.'

'How did someone know you were going to be at the hotel?'

'I don't know. I just got a text message from her and went there.'

'Could that text message have come from someone else?'

'It came from her number. The message should still be on my phone.'

Monica interrupted. 'My client has more than explained how he came to be there. What are you thinking?'

Burton ignored her. 'Dan, have you upset anybody recently?'

'Not that I know of. Why are you asking?'

'I think it's too convenient that two people who volunteered information to you have since turned up dead, and you were found at the scene of one of them and have no alibi for the other.'

'You think someone is setting me up?'

'If they are, who would do that?'

'I don't know. I suppose it could be someone connected with the planning scam, who didn't want me investigating. Maybe they found out she had spoken to me. Did you find my bag?' Dan asked.

'Yes. It's been logged as evidence,' Shepherd said. 'What I don't understand is why you emptied it out onto the floor.'

Dan looked baffled. 'Empty my bag? It was still slung across my body, I hadn't even taken it off. All I'd done was push open the door and step into the room when I saw her lying there. Someone grabbed me, injected me in the neck and I blacked out.'

'Could you tell if it was a man or woman who attacked you?'

'A man. He was strong enough to grab me and hold me still while he injected me. I didn't get a chance to struggle.'

'How tall?'

Dan thought for a moment. 'Slightly taller than me, I think,' he said. 'He seemed to be reaching down a bit and he pushed my head forward.'

'Not much to go on,' said Shepherd.

'He seemed familiar in some way. Actually, he smelled familiar,' Dan said. Burton and Shepherd raised their eyebrows and exchanged a glance.

'Smelled familiar?' asked Burton.

'I can't explain it. He smelled familiar.'

'So you might know him?'

'I suppose, or it could just be a really popular aftershave.'

'What happens now?' Monica asked.

'I think Mr Sullivan should go home and rest,' Burton said. 'Is there someone who could keep an eye on you?'

'Ed is at work at the moment, but I'll be fine.'

'You're still on bail, so you still have to abide by all the conditions. That means report into the station every day.

'Yes, of course.'

After Dan and Monica had left, Shepherd looked at Burton.

'You're keeping him on bail? I thought you decided he hadn't done it.'

'It's for his own safety. We know when he is due to be here and if he doesn't turn up, we know something is wrong.'

'In other words you're protecting him?'

'I certainly am. Like I said, someone is setting him up, and I think we need to keep an eye on him until this is all sorted out.'

Chapter 32

Pain was etched on Paul Sanderson's face. He stared bleakly at Richard Drimble, his eyes filling with tears.

'Dead?' he whispered, his voice failing. 'She can't be dead, she just can't be.'

Drimble stood behind the younger man as he buried his face in his hands and placed a comforting hand on his shoulder.

'I'm sorry, Paul, I'm just so sorry. The police came to see me after they'd spoken to Jo's husband.' Drimble paused. 'I thought it was best to give you the news in private, give you a chance to pull yourself together.'

'Why would anyone want to kill her?'

Drimble took a deep breath. 'I hoped you might be able to tell me that.'

'Me?' Sanderson jumped to his feet.

'I know you and Jo were more than just friends,' said Drimble quietly.

The statement seemed to take all the life out of Sanderson and he sank back into his chair. Taking a tissue from a box on Drimble's desk he wiped his face and looked up at the mayor.

'How long have you known?'

'Long enough.' Drimble walked behind his desk and sat down. 'I feel responsible for this.'

'For her death? Why?'

'I'd asked her to help me investigate what's going on in the planning department.'

'The planning department?'

'She didn't tell you?'

Sanderson picked at a cuticle. 'She may have mentioned it. You think someone killed her because she was asking questions?' His face was white and scared.

'Yes. What other reason would there be to kill her? She was helping me by asking around and seeing who knew what. Now she's dead. It must be connected.'

'Have you told the police?'

'I've fobbed them off for now, pretended I didn't know anything because I want to find out how far this goes in the council.'

Sanderson was silent and looked at the floor. Drimble leaned back in his chair, his eyes fixed on Sanderson.

'I need your help, Paul.'

Sanderson looked up quickly. 'My help? What good would that do?'

'I need to find out what's going on. I need to protect the reputation of this council. If we work it out we can save ourselves some embarrassment by deciding how much information to release.'

'I don't understand.'

'I need you to find out what Jo knew. Did she tell you anything, anything that would lead us to who is behind this?'

'I ... I don't know.'

'Come on, Paul, think. She must have said something. Do it for Jo. Help me to catch whoever killed her.'

Sanderson put his head in his hands again. 'I just can't believe this has happened,' he said. 'I can't believe she's gone.'

'Paul, we must do something about this. I need to find out what is going on before more people get hurt. I can't do it on my own so will you help me?'

Sanderson took a deep shaky breath. 'I don't know, Richard. I really don't know. I need to think.' He got to his feet, wiping the tears off his face. He took a deep shuddering breath and then exhaled. He paused with one hand on the door handle as Drimble spoke again.

'We don't have long, Paul. We need to get to the bottom of this as soon as possible.'

Sanderson looked back at him. 'I don't know if I can help. I'll think about it.'

He left the room wiping his eyes.

'It always makes me sad to see a healthy body like this on my table,' said Dr Eleanor Brody, drying her hands on the paper towel. She looked almost affectionately down at Johanna Buttle's body lying naked before her. The councillor was in excellent shape, but her face was horribly disfigured. The horror of her death showed in her face, her eyes staring and her mouth still slightly open in shock at the attack. Livid purple bruises stood out on her neck and the skin on her face was mottled.

'What do we know?' Burton asked, trying not to look into the lifeless eyes, which seemed to be questioning her. A dripping tap in the back of the room added to the chilly feeling of the air and made her shiver.

'She was strangled using the sheets from the bed.'

'Sheets from the bed?'

Brody shrugged. 'I assume the killer just used what was to hand.'

'It was on impulse then, a crime of passion?' Burton asked.

Shepherd frowned. 'It suggests that this time it wasn't premediated. If it's the same killer, maybe he wasn't planning on killing her. She could have tried to walk away and he just attacked her.'

He was standing back from the morgue table, avoiding looking directly at the body.

'There's very little damage to the rest of her but there's a couple of damaged fingernails.' She held up Buttle's right hand. 'She put up a fight.'

'Any idea which bit of him she might have scratched?'

Brody glared at her. 'How am I supposed to know that?'

'It was worth asking. Got a time of death?'

'Sometime between eleven o clock last night and three o clock this morning judging by body temperature and rigor mortis. But the heating was turned right up. It's fudged things slightly so that's as sure as I can be.'

'What?'

Brody sighed. 'Don't blame me if the facts don't fit your theory. I just tell you what the evidence tells me.'

'It couldn't be any later?'

'No.'

'Anything else?'

'Yes, actually.' The pathologist was becoming annoyed at Burton's attitude.

'Her attacker is right-handed.'

'How can you tell?' Shepherd asked.

Brody indicated the knotted sheets, which had been cut away from Buttle's swollen neck. 'You can see the sheets have been knotted to the right, meaning he had to use his right hand to pull it tight and hold it in place.'

'Very perceptive.'

'That is what I'm paid for.' Brody leaned against the counter and folded her arms with a smug air.

'Any sign of drugs in her system?' Shepherd asked.

'No signs of anything that would have rendered her unconscious.'

'But there are drugs that don't show up in the system, aren't there?' Shepherd asked frowning.

Brody shrugged. 'I suppose something like Rohypnol, which would have made her easy to subdue, but then we wouldn't have had the broken nails because she wouldn't have fought back.'

'Any DNA?' asked Burton.

'No. She'd not had sex recently and she was left fully dressed, no disturbance to her clothes. There were some fibres on the knotted bed sheets but I've not managed to identify them yet. The rest of the room was completely clean so my guess is the guy wasn't staying there.'

'If she didn't go there to meet someone for sex – why else would you meet in a hotel room?'

'Maybe she *thought* she was going there for sex,' Shepherd said.

'Lured to the room, you mean?'

'Possibly.'

'She obviously knew him,' Brody put in. 'She was meeting someone she knew and knew quite well.'

'I agree. She put up a bit of a fight once she realised what was going on but you wouldn't allow yourself to be locked in the room by a stranger.'

'Unless she was coerced into the room. There's no indication she tried to escape from the room?' asked Shepherd.

'No, it seems she went blindly to her fate.' Brody sighed.

'Very poetic,' said Burton. 'Thanks for your help. Get in touch if you find anything else.'

Burton pushed open the door to exit the morgue building, Shepherd following behind.

'We're looking for an average height, right-handed man who

Buttle knew,' Burton summed up as he returned to join her. She sighed. 'Couldn't be more vague could it?'

When they arrived back at the office, there was a sticky note on Burton's computer screen. She pulled it away and looked at the only just legible scribble on it.

'Ah, uniforms have just got Councillor Buttle's husband back home after formally identifying her body. We must have just missed him at the morgue.' She frowned. 'Let's get round and see him. See what he knows about what's been going on.'

As Shepherd pulled the car in by the kerb, Burton looked up and down the quiet suburban street. It was a wide road with trees running at intervals down either side. Cars would be parked along both sides once the occupants got home from work. She frowned.

'Nice houses.'

'It's a popular part of town.' Shepherd undid his seat belt and climbed out of the car. Burton followed suit, still frowning.

'How does a councillor afford somewhere like this?'

'Most councillors are fairly wealthy. That's how they can afford to be councillors. She has another job too, as some sort of project manager, and her husband runs his own business in landscape gardening.'

'He'd be fairly strong then?'

Shepherd looked at her as they walked up the driveway. 'You think he killed her?'

'I don't see why not.'

'Motive?' Shepherd's index finger hovered over the doorbell.

'We'll soon find out if there is one.'

Peter Buttle answered the door, red-eyed and listless, and led them down a short hallway into a modern minimalist living room, which seemed out of place in the pre-war semi-detached house. Burton was almost worried that she'd untidy the place by sitting down when Peter indicated the sofa. Shepherd clearly felt the same and perched on the edge of a square-edged armchair.

'Jo liked everything clean and uncluttered,' said Peter, seeing the look on their faces. 'My office is the exact opposite. She always went mad at me about that. Said I'd never be able to find anything but I could.'

'We're very sorry for your loss, Mr Buttle,' began Shepherd.

'Please, call me Peter. And thank you.'

'OK, Peter.' Burton looked around. 'Weren't you assigned a family liaison officer?'

'He's gone to the corner shop for some milk and coffee. We'd, I mean I'd completely run out.'

'OK. I'm sorry about this but we need to ask you some questions. They may seem intrusive.'

'That's OK. You've got your job to do.'

'Do you have any idea why your wife would have been at the Turpin Hotel last night?'

'No, she said she was staying over with a friend. They were going to have a night in with a bottle of wine and a DVD. She said the friend had recently split up with her boyfriend.' Peter frowned. 'I thought I knew all her friends and she's never mentioned anyone breaking up until just the other day. Maybe it was someone new.'

'Were you and your wife close?'

'Emotionally yes, but we didn't live in each other's pockets. Jo had a lot of duties through her role as a councillor. I was so proud of her when she got elected.'

'When was that?'

'About four years ago. She's one of the youngest ones. She wasn't happy with how people were being treated in this area. This ward borders onto the crappy council estates at the south of the town and the residents on that side get fed up with the crime and antisocial behaviour. Jo always liked to help people.'

Shepherd nodded. He'd spent more than his fair share of time in that neck of the woods rounding up scumbags.

Burton now spoke. 'Did your wife have any enemies?'

Peter Buttle looked stunned. 'No. Why on earth—? Why would you think she had enemies?'

'Mr Buttle, someone killed your wife. We need to work out who that was and why they did it.'

'I can't think of any reason.' Peter Buttle had a stubborn look on his face.

'There were no disgruntled residents, or people unhappy about council decisions?'

Peter Buttle frowned. 'It's funny you mentioned that. She said after the last council meeting that they'd had to turn down an application because there were some irregularities, and she seemed jumpy afterwards.'

'Jumpy?'

'Yeah. Her mobile kept ringing and she wouldn't answer it. When I asked her who it was she said it was no one.' He shrugged.

'Did she have any particular friends at the council?'

'She got on well with everyone, but she was quite close to Paul Sanderson.'

Shepherd looked up from his notebook. 'Councillor Sanderson?' He gave a slight sideways glance at Burton whose eyes were fixed on Peter Buttle.

'He very much took her under his wing when she first joined the council. They were both very idealistic about being a councillor.' Buttle smiled fondly again. 'Even after so many years they still kept true to their ideals, stuck to what they believed in and refused to become party politicians. I hardly ever heard her mention her party – it was always about the local people and what she could do for the area.'

Burton paused. 'I have to ask this, Peter, but where were you last night?'

Buttle's face reddened. 'Are you asking if I killed my wife?'

'I'm asking where you were last night after your wife went out. We have to ask everyone the same question.'

'I … I was here. All night.'

'Can anyone vouch for that?'

'No, I was alone. I can't believe you're insinuating this crap. Is this how you treat all grieving families?'

'I wouldn't be doing my job if I didn't ask the question.'

'Now you've asked and had your answer and you can get out of my house.'

Burton opened her mouth to speak but he cut her off. 'Just get out!'

As the front door slammed behind them, Shepherd said, 'That's one rattled husband.'

'I had to push him.'

'I'm not questioning that. He got angry very quickly though, didn't he?'

'Let's start knocking on doors and see if we can find any neighbours who saw him last night.' As she spoke her mobile buzzed. She swiped the screen and read the email. 'And then we're off to the town hall. Someone wants a word with us.'

Councillor David Edmonds paced the length of the committee room. It took him just twelve paces to cover the floor. Normally it was fifteen. There was a knock on the door. They were here already.

'Come in,' he called.

A woman appeared. 'The police are here for you,' she said.

'Thanks, Harriet. DI Burton, DS Shepherd, do come in.' He stepped forward and offered a hand to Burton and Shepherd and then motioned them to sit down at the solid wood table that occupied the centre of the room.

The detectives sat opposite him and waited in silence for him to begin.

Edmonds paced the room once more and took a deep breath.

'I feel disloyal even calling you here but there are some things you really need to know. About Councillor Buttle.' He paused and looked up at the two officers, as if to gauge their reaction. Neither flickered.

'Go ahead,' said Burton. Edmonds paced the length of the room and back again rubbing his palms together.

'She was having an affair,' he said shortly. Burton and Shepherd both raised their eyebrows.

'With whom?' Burton asked.

'Paul Sanderson, one of our other councillors. He's on the planning committee too.'

'Does her husband know?'

Edmonds shook his head. 'I don't think so. I don't think many people know for sure but there have been rumours for a long time.'

'Why is this important?'

'I think he had something to do with her death,' Edmonds said quickly.

'Really? Why?' asked Shepherd.

'I heard them arguing. I think he wanted her to leave her husband but Jo was refusing. She kept saying that she couldn't do that to Peter, that it would break his heart and she still loved him.'

'And?'

'Paul kept saying, "you owe it to me, you said you loved me".

Then he said, "you have to make a choice, it's either him or me".'

'And what did she choose?'

'I couldn't hear properly but I'm guessing it was her husband because the next thing Paul stormed out of the room and shouted, "You'll be sorry. If I can't have you no one will".' Edmonds paused. 'And now she's dead. I only wish I'd said something sooner. I might have been able to save her.' He dropped into a chair and pulled at the skin on his chin.

Burton and Shepherd looked at each other.

'Is there anything else?'

Edmonds looked up. 'What more do you want?'

'You're not connected to the planning committee, are you?' asked Burton.

'No, why?' asked Edmonds sharply.

'I just wondered.'

'Everyone we speak to seems to be involved with planning,' said Shepherd with a smile that didn't quite reach his eyes.

'No, I'm not. I take an interest if it involves my ward.'

Burton stood up. 'If that's all, sir, we have to be getting on.'

'Oh, one more thing.' Shepherd handed Edmonds his notebook. 'Could you write down a contact number just in case we need to get hold of you?'

'Certainly.' Edmonds scribbled on the pad and then stood up. 'Thanks for seeing me.'

As soon as the door closed he whipped out his mobile and dialled the familiar number.

'I fed them the story and they bought it,' he said. 'They'll be talking to Paul soon. We're in the clear.'

Chapter 33

Dan was waiting by the steps of the *Post's* offices when Emma emerged at the end of the day.

'Hi,' she said. Then she peered at him. 'Are you OK?'

'Yeah, I'm fine.'

'You don't look fine.'

'I'm OK.'

'I tried to get hold of you earlier. There's been another murder.'

'Jo Buttle. I know.'

'How did you …?' She broke off but then sighed. 'You went to meet her, didn't you? That's why Ed was acting funny when we found out. He knew you'd gone.'

'I wish I hadn't gone. I found her dead and then the police burst in and arrested me.'

'That's why Burton hasn't been giving updates today.'

'Too busy interviewing me.'

They began to walk down the hill.

'Are you off bail then?'

'Nope, still reporting in daily at noon.' His stomach rumbled loudly. 'Was Ed still in there?' He pointed back towards the office.

'No, he left a while ago. Muttering something about Sainsbury's.'

'Excellent. That must mean he's cooking dinner.'

Emma looked at him awkwardly and Dan raised an eyebrow.

'What's wrong?'

'Is it weird that you find a second source for your story and they get murdered? And you just happen to be there when the police arrive?'

'No, I think someone is trying to cover up whatever is going on by silencing people who know about it and stopping me from writing the story.'

'And making you the scapegoat?'

'The longer the police spent on me, the less time they're looking for the real killer.'

'And now they're looking elsewhere?'

'They must be if they're not after me anymore.' He paused. 'Shall we head back to the flat? We'll have a bit of time to chat before Ed gets back.'

Emma grinned. 'So long as there's a cup of tea on offer. I've not had time for one all afternoon.'

They crossed the road at the traffic lights and began to walk down the hill towards the development where Dan and Ed's flat was.

'Are you worried?'

'Worried about what?'

'That someone is trying to make you look guilty and they're doing a bloody good job.'

'I just need to get stuck into this story. It's at the heart of everything.'

Their hope of a quiet chat before Ed got back ended when they met him in the street swinging a couple of supermarket carrier bags.

'Why haven't you been answering your phone?' he asked Dan. 'I've been trying to call you all day.'

Dan brought him up to speed about Johanna Buttle's murder.

Ed puffed out his cheeks. 'Bloody hell, mate. This is all getting a bit crazy, isn't it? Maybe you should drop the story and go away on holiday until it's all over.'

'Don't be daft. This is the story of a lifetime. I can't quit now.'

Ed frowned. He nodded to Emma. 'You can't possibly think this is a good idea.'

She shrugged. 'It's not a bad idea,' she said to Dan.

He shook his head and Ed tutted. 'You're going to have to stay for dinner, Em. Help me talk some sense into him.'

As they came out of the lift on the second floor into the corridor near the flat, Ed grabbed Dan's arm, pointing to their front door.

It stood ajar, splinters of wood standing away from the frame where the lock should have been. Dan crept towards it and pushed the door open with his elbow.

'Careful, don't disturb anything,' Emma whispered.

'Why are you whispering?' Dan asked looking over his shoulder at her.

'I don't know, sorry. I suppose I thought they might still be in there.'

They began to walk softly down the hall and Emma gasped as they turned into the living room. Books lay torn and battered on the floor, sheets of newspaper had been scattered around, DVDs and CDs littered the floor. In the kitchen, teabags, sugar and a bottle of milk had been spilt across the counter.

'Either you boys are pigs or someone was looking for something,' Emma said.

'What would they possibly be looking for?' asked Ed, his mouth turning down at the corners. 'Look at my poor sofa.' Stuffing poked out of slashes in the upholstery and the cushions had been thrown to the floor. Dan suddenly turned and sprinted from the room. Someone had searched his bedroom too, throwing clothes and shoes around the room and tearing the duvet and sheets from his bed.

Digging into the bottom of his wardrobe, he found his other satchel. Inside it was the package from Jo Buttle. He breathed a deep sigh.

'They didn't get it,' he said waving the package as he went back into the living room.

'That's what they were after?' asked Ed.

'I reckon so. Whoever knocked me out searched my bag. It wasn't in there so they must have assumed it would be here.'

'But you'd hidden it?' asked Emma.

'It wasn't so much deliberately hidden, as just put out of sight. I'm bloody glad I did that now. I only decided at the last minute not to take it with me. I figured that Buttle and I both knew what was in it.' They stared at each other for a moment, and at the package.

'We'd better call the police,' said Emma taking out her mobile phone.

Chapter 34

Burton was staring gloomily at the pub table. She stared even more gloomily at the pint of ale Shepherd set down in front of her.

'Penny for them,' said the sergeant pulling up a chair. They'd deliberately chosen an old-man pub to give them some peace and quiet to talk. Shepherd loved the stares they got as Burton's slender hand wrapped around the pint glass.

'I just can't get my head around all this.'

'In what way?'

'I was so sure Sullivan was our man. He had the means and the opportunity.'

'But no motive. He's actually lost out by Buttle and Wilton being killed.'

'Did he though?'

'If you believe that he thinks he missed out on a good story.'

Burton shook his head. 'I feel as if we're missing something really obvious but I can't put my finger on it.'

Shepherd paused to take a slurp of his pint. 'The only explanation is that Sullivan is being set up,' he said.

'What do you mean?'

Shepherd raised an eyebrow. 'I thought that was your theory?'

'I'm playing devil's advocate.'

'Oh, I see. Well, in both murders, the evidence is circumstantial. Apart from Sullivan being found at the second murder scene, there's no actual evidence that he did anything.'

Burton looked at Shepherd. 'True.'

'Lila Wilton is out of the frame for killing her husband because she wasn't on the CCTV footage from the night he died, and there isn't a good reason why she'd want to kill Jo Buttle.' Shepherd took a deep drink from his pint. 'By the way, before I left the office I had a call from one of the Buttles' neighbours. She was out at work earlier and she'd only just got in, so she phoned.'

'What did she see?'

'She's one of those busy-body neighbours, out walking her dog and just happened to peer in through the living-room windows where the curtains are open as she passed. She saw Peter Buttle sitting on the sofa drinking a can of lager and watching a film on DVD.'

'Hmmm, a very noticing witness.'

'Like I said, busy-body.'

'It's a weak alibi. She was killed late at night and he could have gone out later.'

'No one seems to have heard a door slamming or a car pulling away or anything like that.'

'I think we still keep an eye on him for now.'

'Who's next?'

Shepherd took a couple of swallows of his pint before he answered. 'We have Paul Sanderson.'

'Ah, yes, Councillor Sanderson. Supposedly having an affair with Mrs Buttle. Why would he kill James Wilton? Was Wilton also messing around with Mrs Buttle? A crime of passion?'

'Kills Wilton to stop the affair, then she says she's going back to her husband so he kills her?'

'That's what I was thinking.'

'If it's the same killer.'

'Isn't it?'

'It's a different MO. Usually a killer sticks with one. Stabbing and strangulation don't seem like a natural progression.'

'Hmmm, we know the stabbing was a planned attack. The killer brought the knife with him. Strangulation with bed sheets seems much more spur-of-the-moment.'

'If it's not Sanderson, who else could it be?'

'There's David Edmonds.'

Burton took a drink from her pint glass. More than half of it had disappeared and she stared at it as if disappointed.

'What did you think of Councillor Edmonds?' she asked.

Shepherd thought for a moment. 'He seems to know an awful lot about what goes on in the council,' he said slowly.

'Sullivan thinks he might be mixed up in the planning stuff.'

Shepherd snorted. 'You could say the same thing about Sullivan himself. Edmonds is a councillor. Isn't he supposed to be involved in local affairs?'

'I suppose so. But he admitted he doesn't have any connection to the planning department, so you might wonder why he's so interested in it.'

'He does seem like a "fingers in every pie" kind of bloke though, doesn't he? Likes to be in a position of power. What was Sullivan's reason for thinking he's up to something?'

'It was something to do with Councillor Edmonds' reaction to a decision at a planning committee meeting. I think it's more a suspicion than anything concrete. But it might be worth checking out his background. Get onto that first thing tomorrow.'

'OK. What're you going to be doing?'

'I think we need to have a word with Councillor Drimble and see how his investigation is going.'

Chapter 35

The next morning Dan was at the library photocopier when Ed joined him. He glanced at his watch before looking at Dan.

'What was so important that you're making me late for court?' He peered at Dan. 'You look terrible.'

'I didn't sleep much.' Both had stayed up late waiting for the front door to be repaired.

'Me neither. I kept thinking I heard noises in the hall.'

'Did you get up to check?'

'No.'

'So much for worrying about our safety.'

Ed grinned. 'I'm a rubbish guard dog.'

Dan collected together a sheaf of pages and pushed them into a brown A4 envelope. He sealed it and offered it to Ed. 'Here, take this for me.'

Ed took it and weighed it in his hands. 'What is it?'

'It's the stuff Jo Buttle gave me. Well, it's a copy of it. I'm going to turn the original in to the police.'

'Why?'

'The more I think of it the more I think the murders are tied up with planning.'

'Neither of them died of boredom.'

'Ed, for once you're the one being flippant. I'm serious. I think the committee was being paid to pass applications that shouldn't have been passed.'

'Really?'

'Yes. I don't think the police are taking that angle seriously but I reckon this will give them a kick-start.'

'Meanwhile you keep a copy for your story.'

'Yes. I don't know when the police will give it back – if they ever do – and I need it.'

'You really think two people have been killed because of what's in here? Surely then you should just get it off your hands.'

Dan stopped and looked at him. 'Once I've handed this over –' he waved the envelope '– I'm going to let the police get on with investigating the murder and I'm focusing totally on the story.'

'How are you going to do that when your two leads are dead?'

Dan frowned. 'I'm not sure. I think Richard Drimble is my next best shot.'

They separated at the entrance to the library, Ed heading towards the magistrates court and Dan turning in the direction of the police station.

As he walked along, his brain hummed with information. Everything he found out seemed to raise more questions. Why had James Wilton decided to blow the whistle on a scam he was up to his neck in? Who had sent the envelope to Jo Buttle? Why had she decided to tell him about it rather than go to the standards board? He found himself at the top of the steps to the underpass leading to the police station. He glanced around. He hadn't meant to come this way. He'd meant to cross the main road at the traffic lights. Maybe he should have taken a taxi straight from the doors of the library to the cop shop. Well, it was too late now and he was clearly getting paranoid. It was broad daylight after all.

But as he turned to retrace his steps and head for the pedestrian crossing, a hand grabbed hold of his jacket.

'Give it to me,' said a harsh voice.

'Give what? I don't understand.' Dan tried to turn and look at his attacker.

'The envelope. Give it to me.'

Dan tried to shake the man off, but his grip was like iron. 'I don't know what you're talking about.'

'Give me the bag.' His satchel was ripped from his shoulder and the man gave him a shove.

'Hey!' Dan took a step to steady himself, except there was nothing behind him but fresh air. He tumbled down the steps, his head hitting the ground with a dull thump. He felt his bag landing next to him and his vision swam in and out of focus. The sunlight hurt his eyes. A female voice said, 'Don't try to move. An ambulance is coming.' A cool hand squeezed his.

'Lucy?' he whispered. 'Lucy.' Everything would be fine now she was here and he faded into blackness again.

Emma was on the phone to the fire brigade when Ed strolled back into the office clutching a takeaway coffee cup.

'Shouldn't you be in court?'

'They had a burst water pipe overnight so it's closed until tomorrow. The scum of Allensbury aren't going to be happy that their cases will be delayed.'

Emma stood up and pulled on her coat. 'Right, I'm off to the police station. Burton is going to do a media briefing on the latest in the case.'

'You might see Boy Wonder at the cop shop because that was where he was headed to hand over that envelope.'

'OK. See you later.'

Glancing at her watch as she walked up the hill away from the office she saw that the morning round of calls to the police, fire and ambulance services checking for stories had taken longer than she thought. She'd better hurry. But there was a horrible sight waiting for her when she got to the top of the steps down to the underpass. Spread-eagled at the bottom lay Dan, completely still with his head bent at an angle. Blood was spreading from beneath it.

'Oh Jesus, Dan!' she cried.

In seconds she was on her knees beside him.

'Dan? Dan?' she yelled, shaking his shoulder. A tap to the face elicited no reaction either. She grabbed her mobile phone. 'Please, please be alright,' she pleaded as she jabbed the nine key three times. As the call was answered, Dan tried to stir. 'Just stay still,' she told him clutching his hand. 'Help's coming.' She was still shaking when the ambulance screeched to a halt, sirens wailing.

Chapter 36

When Dan opened his eyes again a bright fluorescent light dazzled him. He tried to sit up but his head gave a sickening throb. He quickly lay back down and breathed deeply, not wanting to throw up. His head was tightly bandaged and hurt a lot.

'Lucy?' he asked.

'Welcome back,' replied a voice. But it wasn't Lucy. It was Emma.

'How do you feel?' she asked, standing up and peering at him.

'Sick. What happened? Where did you come from? I remember … the underpass.'

'I found you. You'd fallen.'

'You brought me here?' Dan looked around. 'Where am I?'

'You're in hospital and technically the ambulance brought you.'

'Thank you for calling the ambulance then.'

'Who's Lucy?' Emma asked. An awkward silence descended.

Dan stiffened. 'Lucy? How do you know about her?'

'When you were lying at the bottom of the steps you kept muttering about Lucy.'

'Oh. Did I?'

'Yeah. Who is she?'

'Nobody special.' Silence descended again and Emma desperately tried to think of something to say. Dan looked so woebegone.

'What happened?' she asked.

'I went stair-diving without protective equipment,' Dan said smiling ruefully.

'No, seriously, what happened?'

'Someone pushed me down the steps.'

'What?' Emma asked. 'Who pushed you?'

Dan was about to reply when they were interrupted by a nurse appearing through the curtains drawn around Dan's cubicle.

'Hey, you're looking more with it,' she said. 'How're you feeling?'

'Awful.'

'You will do. You gave yourself a nasty knock to the head.' The nurse bustled around the bed straightening Dan's pillows. 'We're just waiting on the X-rays to come back to see if you have a skull fracture.'

'Thanks.' Dan couldn't even summon up the energy to smile at her. As the nurse pushed back through the curtains, Emma stood up.

'Where are you going?' he asked.

'I'll give Ed a call and let him know where we are. He'll be worried if he doesn't hear from either of us. I won't be long.'

'Don't be.'

Five minutes later she was back.

'Ed sends his regards,' she said slipping inside the curtain with two cans of Coke. 'Want one?' she offered. Dan shook his head very gently.

'No, thanks,' he said, his face still pale. 'I've already bled all over you today. I don't want to risk throwing up on you as well.'

Emma laughed and popped open the second can. A couple of mouthfuls later she still hadn't thought of a way to restart the conversation.

'Lucy was an ex-girlfriend,' Dan began suddenly.

'You don't need to tell me.'

'No, I do. I don't really like to talk about it. Everyone's had that kind of relationship, I suppose. I thought I was in love with her but it turned out I loved my job more.'

'I've been there. How did it end?' Emma took another sip from her can.

'Badly. She got fed up of waiting around for me and finished it. I didn't realise how bad a boyfriend I'd been until she started listing all the stuff I'd done – or rather not done.'

Emma smiled. 'How bad were you?'

'Work just got in the way a few dozen times. You know how it is when you're working on something or you have to suddenly cover a meeting.'

Emma nodded.

'Anyway,' Dan continued, 'things came to a head when it was Lucy's birthday. I'd booked a table at a restaurant, told her to meet me there and then forgot to turn up because I was working on something.'

Emma spluttered into her Coke. 'What? You booked something special for her birthday and then didn't show?'

'I know, I told you I was bad.'

'I'm not surprised she dumped you. You're lucky to be alive.'

'But I was really onto something with the story. I had to get it finished. I was just starting out and I needed to make my mark.'

'I can see that, but still …'

'Lucy couldn't see it at all. When we split up I decided no more relationships, because it was just easier that way.'

'Strangely, that's something we both share. It's easier to be alone than risk hurting yourself or someone else.'

'Sounds pathetic when you put it like that, but yes.' Dan sighed and then laughed. 'Sorry for depressing you.'

Emma smiled. 'You obviously needed to get it off your chest.'

'I must have had a good whack on the head to spill everything.' Dan smiled again, but this time he stared off into the distance.

'Sometimes it's better not to get involved, eh?' Emma asked, trying to cajole him out of the mood.

'I suppose. It's just sad at times like this when they ask if there's someone they can call for you and the answer is no.' He gestured towards a passing nurse. Emma smiled.

'It's a good job I found you then, isn't it,' she said brightly. 'I checked with Daisy and I don't have to go back to the office so I can stay and keep you company.' She patted his hand awkwardly.

'Thanks,' Dan said, gently catching hold of her fingers and giving them a squeeze.

Another nurse peeped around the curtain and then pushed it open to allow Burton inside. Dan started to sit up but Burton waved for him to sit still.

'How are you?'

'Sore.'

There was a moment of silence and then Burton asked, 'Are you going to tell me what happened?'

Dan opened his mouth to speak but then froze. He sat up, swaying in the bed. Emma jumped to her feet.

'What's the matter? Do you feel ill?' she asked.

'Where's my bag?'

'Your bag?'

'My bag. The guy dragged it off my shoulder but then I remember it landing beside me after I fell.'

'What guy?' Burton asked.

'The guy who grabbed me and pushed me down the stairs. I think he wanted the envelope and he took my bag.'

'Just sit still and I'll find it.' Emma looked under the bed and pulled a grey canvas bag from the shelf underneath. Dan immediately snatched it from her and yanked the zip open. He froze.

'Shit. It's gone.'

Chapter 37

David Edmonds' phone was playing the theme tune to *Jaws*. He snatched it up.

'We have the package,' said the voice. Edmonds sighed.

'Good. Destroy it.'

'I plan to. But first we have to find out where it came from. It was sent to Johanna Buttle and she admitted passing it on, but she didn't know the source.'

'What about Sullivan?'

'He's been dealt with.'

'He's dead?'

There was a silence on the other end of the phone and Edmonds shivered.

'What about the other man? The information was in their flat. Has he seen it?' he asked. There was a sigh on the other end.

'I've already thought of that. I have someone watching him and as soon as there's an opportunity we'll make sure he can't tell anyone about it either.'

The call was terminated and Edmonds found himself listening to the dialling tone.

Chapter 38

Burton stared at Dan.

'What?' she asked.

'The envelope. It's gone. He took it.'

'Who did?'

'The man who pushed me down the steps. Oh, shit … Ed. We've got to warn Ed.' Dan was trying to get up again but Emma stood in his way.

'Calm down. You'll make yourself worse,' she said.

Burton was looking confused. 'What's going on? Start at the beginning.'

'Johanna Buttle's envelope. I was bringing it to you to prove that I was right about the planning angle but I got pushed down the stairs and now it's gone.'

'You were pushed down the stairs for this envelope?'

'It was the papers that Buttle gave me. I made a copy of it this morning so I'd be able to keep it and—' His voice trailed away when he saw the stony expression on Burton's face.

'And you did what with it?' she asked.

'I gave it to Ed for safekeeping.'

'When I told you to stay out of this, what did you think I meant?' Dan looked at her without speaking. 'I told you to stay out of it

202

because two people have already been killed. Does anyone know that Ed has a copy?'

'I don't know. We did it at the library this morning but if someone followed me from there, there might have been someone after Ed as well.'

Emma put a hand on his arm. 'He was fine when I spoke to him earlier.'

'But if he's gone to court, he'll be out there on his own.'

'He hasn't gone to court. It's closed because of a burst water pipe, so he's in the office.'

Burton shook her head and left the cubicle, quickly pulling out her mobile phone. They heard her dial and pause while the call connected.

'He'll be fine,' Emma said, not sounding convinced by her own words. They heard Burton's voice.

'Mark, get down to the *Post's* office and pick up Mr Walker. Tell him to get all his belongings and bring them to the station. Don't make it obvious but we need to keep an eye on him. Call me when you've got him.'

She reappeared through the curtain and looked at Dan and Emma. 'OK, Shepherd is going to ring me when he's got Ed.'

They sat in silence for what felt like hours, but was probably only fifteen minutes, before Burton's phone burbled and she answered immediately. She listened for a couple of minutes during which time Emma wondered whether Dan would actually break her fingers he was squeezing them so hard.

'We've got him and he's in one piece,' Burton said, hanging up the call. Dan sighed and released Emma's hand. She flexed her fingers tentatively and looked at Burton.

'Where is he?'

'They're on their way to the station until we can make a plan. How long have you guys had this information?'

'Since the day before Buttle was murdered.'

'For now, let's just hope they haven't found out there's a copy or that it's still in your possession.'

Shepherd put the bar of chocolate in front of Ed, who eyed it suspiciously.

'Am I under arrest for something?' he asked.

'My governor just rang and told me to fetch you here.'

'How's Dan? Can we not go to the hospital?'

'I think it's best to sit tight for now and wait for instructions. Eat your Yorkie.' Shepherd gestured towards the chocolate bar.

Ed tore open the wrapper and put a chunk of chocolate in his mouth without really tasting it. 'This is serious, isn't it?' he said.

The detective looked up. 'Yes.'

Ed took a deep breath and tried to relax but his left leg jiggled constantly making the table squeak. Shepherd looked up from his paperwork and tapped his forefinger sharply on the table.

'Stop it.'

'Sorry, I can't help it. I fidget when I'm nervous.' Ed jumped up and started to pace the floor.

He had felt distinctly queasy when he'd answered his phone to find Shepherd on the other end.

'Bring my stuff?' he'd asked. 'Where are we going?'

'I'm in a black BMW parked outside your office. Bring all your stuff and leave the office as if nothing is wrong. Walk straight to the car and get in.'

'But …'

'Don't argue, just do it. It's important.'

'Why?'

'Just do it.' Shepherd had hung up. Clearly he was used to being obeyed.

Standing up, Ed had thought quickly. Pulling the envelope from his bag he'd glanced around. No one had been watching him. He'd quickly tucked the envelope away inside his desk and locked the drawer, pocketing the key. Dan had said they needed to keep the copy safe.

'Daisy,' he'd said stopping at the news desk. 'I'm just popping out.'

'Story?'

'Sort of. I'll be in touch.'

Legs shaking, he had managed to walk the length of the office and down the front steps of the building. A man on the opposite site of the street was talking on his mobile and seemed to be trying to cross the road. Ed spotted Shepherd's car and quickly walked over to it and got into the passenger seat.

'Alright,' Shepherd had said, immediately peeling away into the traffic. 'Back to the nick.'

'Why?'

Shepherd had shrugged. 'I was told to pick you up.' Using his hands-free kit Shepherd had speed-dialled a number. 'Sir, I've got him. Right, right.' Shepherd had listened a moment. 'OK, sir, I'll keep him there.'

They had been at the station for over an hour now, according to Ed's watch, and Shepherd hadn't spoken again. He pecked away at the computer keyboard with two fingers, sighing every now and then as he squinted at his notebook. The phone call to Daisy saying he wasn't coming back to the office that day had not been fun.

'What do you mean you're with the police?' she had demanded. 'What have you done?'

'Shhhh, no one is supposed to know I'm here,' Ed hissed.

'Sorry, but what is going on? Emma's already phoned to say she's at the hospital with Dan and he might have concussion. Now you're telling me you've been picked up by the police. What have you go into?'

'I'll explain later when I fully understand what's going on.'

'Does that mean you're not coming back today?'

'I don't know. At the moment it looks like I'm in protective custody.' Ed looked at Shepherd who nodded.

'So now I'm down all three senior reporters?'

'Three?'

'I already said Emma could stay with Dan so she isn't going to be doing any work.'

'Oh, right,' said Ed slowly.

'Don't worry I'll sort it out, as usual,' said Daisy irritably, hanging up.

'Everything OK?' asked Shepherd mildly.

'I've just pissed off my boss, my best mate has concussion and I'm in police custody without really knowing why I'm here so, no, things are not OK,' Ed retorted.

Back at the hospital Burton was getting frustrated.

'So you're telling me he's OK, but you won't let me take him away?' she demanded. The nurse stood her ground, hands planted on her hips.

'I'm sorry but he might have a concussion. We need the doctor to take another look at him before we can discharge him. We should really be keeping him in overnight.' Clearly she was not happy about breaking the rules.

'I'm a detective inspector with Allensbury police,' said Burton in a patronising tone. 'We can look after him.'

'You're not a medical professional,' the nurse replied. 'We need Dr French to give him the all-clear.' She faced Burton, both with hands on hips neither willing to give ground.

'It's like watching tennis, isn't it,' said Dan as his and Emma's heads swivelled from one side to the other. Emma laughed.

'You just like having people fight over you. Are you feeling any better?'

Dan grinned and then winced. 'Not entirely, although I think I could stand up without fainting now.' He ran a hand gingerly over his head, wincing as it hit piece of gauze covering the wound.

'Not quite back to full strength?'

'Not quite, no.'

'I kind of like you when you're like this,' Emma said softly, meeting Dan's eyes. There was a moment of silence, which was broken by Burton. She stomped back through the curtain.

'Bloody nurses. Don't know what they're doing,' she said. Dan and Emma both laughed awkwardly. 'You would think I didn't have your best interests at heart. It's typical that it's a man we're waiting around for.' There was a cough behind her. She turned to see a tall woman wearing a stethoscope around her neck, her blonde hair caught up into an untidy bun. Her eyebrows arched.

'Hello, I'm Dr Christine French,' she said, eyeing Burton with dislike. 'How's the patient? Mr Sullivan?' She walked over to Dan. Burton cleared her throat.

'Sorry ... I ... er ... didn't mean,' she stuttered.

Dan and Emma exchanged a sly grin.

Dr French regarded her coolly.

'If you could step outside the curtain I'll conduct my examination.'

'I'd rather not. He's under my protection.'

Dr French frowned. 'Right now he's under my protection and you need to be outside the curtain. Otherwise it'll be you who needs protection.' She turned towards Burton who quickly stepped outside and closed the curtain, muttering under her breath.

French turned to Emma. 'You'd better go too,' she said. Emma picked up her bag but Dan grabbed her hand.

'No, I want her to stay.'

'It's OK,' Emma whispered. 'You'll be fine. I'll just be outside.' She left, smiling at the doctor who turned to Dan.

'That was a nasty tumble you took,' she said, shining a pen light into his eyes.

'I know,' Dan said, trying not to screw up his eyes.

'Hmm.' She had peeled away the gauze and was examining the cut on his head. Dan winced as she touched the swollen area. 'You've got dissolvable stitches so they'll come away in the next week or so. I'll put a small dressing on it for now just to keep it clean, and I'll get you some information on taking care of your wound. If you look after it, you shouldn't be left with a scar.'

'Shame, I've heard girls love a scar.' He grinned but the doctor simply eyed him doubtfully and carried on putting a white plaster across the stitched area.

'How does your head feel?'

'A lot better. The swimming feeling has stopped.'

'Any double vision or nausea?'

'No.'

'That's a good sign. Right –' she made some notes on her clipboard '– much as I'm loathed to help her out –' she jerked her head towards where Burton waited '– I'm prepared to let you go home. But you must have complete rest for at least two days. No excitement and, if you feel sick or dizzy, then you come straight back and get checked out.'

'Excitement seems to be doing a good job of finding me at the moment,' Dan said, gently climbing off the bed.

'Dan!' Ed jumped to his feet, the wheeled chair he was sitting on shooting across the floor, as Burton pushed open the door to the CID office, leading Dan and Emma inside. 'You're OK?'

'More or less. Fewer brain cells perhaps,' said Dan, sitting down gingerly. He didn't want to admit it but he suddenly felt very tired. 'But at least you're OK. I was worried he would get to you.'

'Who?'

'The man who pushed me down the stairs. But you and the envelope are safe.'

'Oh, it's definitely safe.' Ed grinned.

'What do you mean?'

'They won't get it,' Ed said in a hushed voice, giving a slight nod towards Burton and Shepherd.

'What do you mean?' Dan repeated, the churning feeling returning to his stomach.

'I've not got it with me.'

'What?' Dan and Emma shouted together. Burton and Shepherd looked up.

Dan stepped forward. 'Why haven't you got it? Where is it?'

'I ... I left it in my desk in the office.'

'What? Ed, we need that envelope. It's really important. The guy who pushed me took my copy.'

'But you said it needed to be kept safe.'

Dan put his head in his hands. 'The safest place would be here where we can keep an eye on it. Why did you leave it behind?'

'I thought they already had your copy. Emma didn't say it had been stolen.'

'What's the problem?' interrupted Burton.

'Ed doesn't have the envelope with him.'

'We have to go back for it.' Burton glared at Ed and then turned on Shepherd. 'Didn't you check if he had it?'

Shepherd shook his head. 'I assumed he had it because I told him to bring all his stuff.' He also glared at Ed. Burton gave a snort of frustration.

'You three, stay here and don't touch anything. You –' she jabbed a finger at Shepherd '– with me.' She stormed out of the room.

210

Chapter 39

Burton marched up the steps outside the *Post's* offices and, flashing her warrant card, ordered the receptionist to open the door. The woman did so, staring in surprise at Burton's manner, but by the time Burton and Shepherd arrived in the newsroom the editor was waiting for them.

'More questions?' he asked. 'Daniel Sullivan isn't here.'

'We're not here to see Dan Sullivan.' Burton strode down the newsroom with the editor hurrying in her wake. Shepherd followed at a more leisurely pace. Daisy stood up, looking worried, as Burton approached.

Burton pointed to a desk. 'He said that one's his.' Shepherd walked over and began to rifle through the papers on the top.

Burton followed and looked down at it disdainfully. 'How does he find anything?'

Daisy, who now stood behind her, shrugged. 'Somehow he always does. It's a mystery to us all.'

Shepherd was now on his hands and knees wrestling with the drawers of the filing cabinet under the desk. The three junior reporters had crowded round to watch and were quietly debating whether they ought to tweet about it. One look from Daisy silenced them.

'What's taking so long?' Burton asked as the sergeant stabbed roughly at the lock with the key Ed had given him.

'More haste, less speed,' Shepherd replied. They heard a loud crack.

'Tell me you've not broken that key,' the editor said. 'We'll have to replace the whole unit.'

Shepherd looked over his shoulder. 'Not the key, but the lock seems to have given way.' He pulled open a drawer and wrinkled his nose as he looked inside.

'It's probably just full of crisps and cans of Coke,' said one of the junior reporters, in a stage whisper and the others sniggered. Daisy glared at him.

Shepherd pushed aside the packet of Mars bars and made a triumphant sound as he pulled out an envelope addressed to Councillor Johanna Buttle.

'Got it,' he said, holding it out to Burton. She took it under the watchful eye of the junior reporters, who were discreetly trying to look over her shoulder.

'You'll have to pay for that,' the editor said, pointing to the cabinet.

'Send me an invoice,' Burton said and then strode back down the newsroom, leaving the editor open-mouthed.

Chapter 40

Burton threw the envelope down on the desk in front of Dan, who pounced on it like a starving man on his next meal.

'It's safe,' he breathed.

'Your editor's not a happy man,' Shepherd said.

'He's never a happy man.'

'We broke your filing cabinet to get that out,' Shepherd said to Ed.

'But I gave you the key?' Ed moaned.

'Sorry,' said Shepherd. 'It must have been an old lock.'

'I bet he'll try to take it out of my wages.'

Dan shrugged. 'We'll deal with him later,' he said flicking through the sheets of paper.

'I can't believe I was so stupid as to leave it behind,' Ed said.

'No harm done, it's all here.' Dan was flicking through the pages.

Burton reached over and took the pages out of Dan's hands. They all waited while she flicked through them. Then she stood up.

'Right, we'll keep this. There must be something in it that made it worth killing Jo Buttle.'

'You'll tell us what you find out though, won't you?' Emma asked.

'If and when we find something, we'll notify the press in the usual way.'

Emma's face fell. 'You meant it about the tip-offs?' she asked.

'Yes. No tips on this case.' Then she looked at Dan and Ed. 'Have you two got somewhere to stay? I don't think it's wise to go back to your flat.'

'You can stay with me,' Emma said.

'We'll get the patrols to swing by to keep an eye on you.'

Shepherd stood up and gestured to Dan, Ed and Emma. 'I'll show you out.' He moved towards the office door and held it open. They followed him downstairs and out of the reception area. The flag-stoned area outside was empty.

'Thank God the vultures have gone,' Ed said. He dug in his pocket and pulled out his mobile. 'Oh bollocks, ten missed calls from Lydia. I've got some explaining to do.' He moved away to make the call.

'What now?' asked Emma.

'We may not have the envelope itself but I've still got my notes, so maybe we can piece some of this together.' He glanced at his watch. 'Could I tempt you to a cup of tea and some biscuits? I might be able to manage that.' He indicated the plaster on his head.

'Sounds good. Why don't you grab some clothes and stuff and then come to my place?'

'Are you sure it's OK to put us up?'

'Of course. You're both house-trained, aren't you?'

'Mostly.'

Emma laughed.

Ed returned looking pained. 'I'll be staying at Lydia's tonight apparently. I don't think she likes the idea of me staying with you.'

'OK. Dan's going to stay with me till the flat's sorted and you're at Lydia's so everyone is safe.'

'Great. Let's catch up tomorrow and decide where to go from there.'

Chapter 41

When Shepherd returned to the office, he found Burton lying back in her chair with her feet up on the desk. She'd kicked off her shoes and was waiting for him with her hands clasped across her middle.

'What have we got?' she asked.

'When you called from the hospital, I'd been going through everything I could find about David Edmonds.'

'Anything interesting?'

'He's a prominent local businessman, and as we suspected he does have his fingers in a lot of pies. He's also a wealthy man.'

'Any clues about why he would be interested in planning?'

'As far as I can see there's no specific reason. He has no businesses linked to construction or any kind of development. Yet he does seem to take a lot of interest in it.'

'What does this information tell us, do you think?' Burton leaned over precariously to hand the envelope to Shepherd. He took it and began to thumb through the contents.

'I'm no expert on planning, but whatever it is, sir, meant something to Johanna Buttle, enough to spook her and send her running straight to Sullivan.'

'Why did she do that? Why choose Sullivan?'

'Maybe she thought he would understand. Could she have known he'd been speaking to James Wilton, or that Wilton had tried to speak to him?'

'We don't even know who sent it to her but maybe she knew, and she was scared of that person?'

Shepherd looked sceptical. 'It seems a bit unlikely that she'd do anything if she was scared of the sender.'

'I was just thinking out loud.'

Shepherd frowned. 'Do you think this is what Wilton was going to tell Sullivan about?'

Burton considered for a moment. 'It's not outside the realms of possibility. She and Wilton were on the same committee so it stands to reason they must have access to similar information.'

She yawned, stretched and looked at her watch. 'Let's call it a night and start fresh in the morning.'

'Parents' evening?' Shepherd asked with a grin.

'The eldest. It's bound to be a bad report.'

'You go. I'll clear up here.'

'Are you sure?'

Shepherd's face was sad. 'It's not like I have anyone waiting for me at home.'

Burton looked uncomfortable. 'OK, well, if you're sure?'

'Of course, off you go.'

Burton looked over her shoulder as she left, watching her sergeant piling up files in the otherwise empty room.

Chapter 42

Emma's house was what an estate agent would describe as cosy. Small might have been a better word. It was a two-up two-down house that was too nice to be just a house and so was described as a cottage. The living room had very little floor space, once you took in the two small sofas set at right angles, a square coffee table in front of them and two large bookcases. A large plasma screen TV took up one corner.

'Handy for watching the football,' Dan said pointing to it.

'It was my brother's. He was always watching sport of some kind. I don't really watch much anymore, now he's not around.'

Dan was about to ask the obvious question when Emma changed the subject.

'Who do you think stands to lose the most from us knowing this?' She tapped a finger on Dan's notes, which poked out from under a takeaway pizza box on the coffee table.

'It could be anyone on the planning committee or officers in the department,' Dan said.

'Not the biggest pool of people to pick from though, is it?' Emma said.

'You think they're going to be easy to find?'

'No, not at all. So far all the loose ends have been nicely tied up and we don't know where to go next.'

'Jo Buttle gave me that envelope, and she knew that it was going to shake things up. Someone else must have known she had it and that she gave it to me.'

'They knew pretty quickly that she'd handed it over because she was killed, what, a day or two after she spoke to you?'

'Do you think she told them she'd done it?'

'Only if she thought that by handing it over she was going to save herself.' Emma paused. 'Who do you think could be involved then?'

'It could be David Edmonds,' Dan said.

'Who's that?' Emma asked.

'Another councillor. A very bad tempered one.'

'He's not involved with planning,' Emma said immediately, looking down the list of committee members names.

'He doesn't really need to be, not directly.'

'Any proof?'

'Just a feeling. I saw him with Buttle and Sanderson before the last meeting and it was weird.'

'Weird, how?'

'They seemed really jumpy and he was angry with them.'

'Why would he be angry with them?'

'Exactly.'

'Maybe Richard Drimble is looking for help with his investigation,' Emma said.

'How would he know it existed? Plus he wouldn't have killed Buttle for it.'

'He'd have just asked her to give it to him.'

'Maybe he was trying to protect the council.'

'By killing one of the councillors and attacking a local journalist?'

'Fair point. So, really, it comes down to finding out who sent it and why someone would want it back badly enough to commit murder,' Emma said.

'Maybe the person who sent it wanted it back,' Dan said. 'Maybe they regretted sending it to her. They probably didn't intend her to give it to me. She was probably supposed to give it to Richard Drimble or get the standards board involved.'

'If you're right, it begs the question of why she didn't take it to an official channel. Why bring it to the local paper? Did she say anything else to you?'

'She kept saying about wanting to tell her side of the story.'

'Right, so we need to start there. What exactly did she give you – in other words what did those papers prove – and why was her version different to someone else's?'

The next morning Emma came down the narrow-turning staircase of the cottage to find Dan sitting on the sofa, his bottom half encased in a sleeping bag, flicking through his notes.

'Did you sleep OK? Sorry I don't have a spare bed. I couldn't fit one in the other room since I'm using it as an office.'

He looked up and smiled. 'At least you have a sofa. The floor would have been much less comfortable.'

Emma yawned. 'Coffee?'

'Yes, please.'

By the time she returned from the small kitchen to the living room, Dan was fully dressed and the sleeping bag folded up in one corner.

'How long have you been up?' she asked handing him a steaming mug.

'Long enough to know that I'm still not sure what's going on.'

He noticed a vase of lilies on a side table filling the room with their perfume.

'From an admirer?' he asked with a grin.

'Yes, me. I'm a great fan of my work,' replied Emma. They laughed.

'I can see why you live on your own,' Dan said.

'Oh, yeah?'

'There isn't room to swing a cat in here, never mind a flatmate.'

'Do you frequently swing Ed?'

'You'd be surprised how often that happens.'

Emma giggled. 'So you're still none the wiser?' she said, sitting down on the sofa.

'It's like having a jigsaw with no picture on the front of the box and you know there are a couple of pieces that just don't fit. If we can find one of those pieces, I'm sure it'll all fall into place.'

'Talk me through it.Someone sent this to Jo Buttle, presumably so she'd take it to the standards board or similar,' Emma said.

'That's what I thought.'

Emma looked at him. 'You thought? As in you changed your mind?'

'She knew what the papers meant, that this showed corruption on a grand scale, so why not go to the standards committee? Why come to me?'

'Fair point.'

'And why did she keep going on about telling her side of the story and being anonymous?'

'I see. Why would she have a side unless she was involved?'

'You'd think she'd want her name all over the story about stopping corruption.' Dan puffed out his cheeks.

Emma stared down at the pages. 'How are the mighty fallen.'

'That's a bit harsh.'

'I always knew the goody two shoes behaviour was an act. Too good to be true.' She caught sight of Dan's face. 'You'd rather she wasn't involved?' she asked.

'Yes. It was nice to have a councillor who wasn't just out for what they could get. It seemed to matter to her.'

'And it doesn't help that she is distractingly gorgeous, with an immense cleavage and pointy shoes?'

'That was just a bonus,' Dan said sadly.

Emma leaned over Dan's shoulder, her hair almost brushing his face. 'So there are applications from several companies that are pretty similar. Is that not weird?'

'Not necessarily. Plans for housing estates will always have similarities. The problem is that they have all made the same mistake.'

'How do you mean?'

'Look here.' Dan held up one of the applications. 'The numbers of dwellings – they're all way too high according to building regulations on the council's website. Why would a company not check that before they submitted?'

'Why wouldn't they?'

'Because, if you look at the version that went before the committee, it's been changed to a lower number.'

'So it would get passed?'

'Yes. And then James Wilton could alter it back and they could build all those houses and make lots more money.'

Emma stayed silent for a moment. Then she asked, 'How much money?'

'God knows. I tried to calculate something in my head and gave up when I got into the hundreds of thousands.'

Emma took the planning application and looked at it. 'Always a similar number of houses and always on land that no one wanted.' She snorted. 'Until this time.'

'Exactly. This time the residents kicked up a fuss because they wanted the land as allotments.'

'But the residents almost didn't find out about the meeting.'

Dan shook his head. 'I'd love to know who tipped them off.'

'So if there have been at least seven others passed, why did this one get rejected?'

'Richard Drimble. The application that came before the committee had a higher number than in the original meeting papers. Clearly there been some sort of mix up and the original papers had been submitted instead of the new ones. He called the planning team out on it and said he had to recommend that it be rejected.'

'But he's been on the committee for nine months, why didn't he notice the problem before?'

'Unless you look at the applications all together, you don't see the pattern.'

'Now he is investigating, he should be working all this out.'

'Presumably. Maybe I should go and see him on some pretext and find out what he knows.'

'OK, well, some of us have to go to work.' Emma stood up and drained her coffee, wincing at the dregs which were cold.

'We need to speak to Paul Sanderson,' Dan said.

'Don't worry. Leave him to me.'

Dan stood awkwardly in the doorway of the mayor's office. Richard Drimble had been dodging his phone calls so Dan had just turned up at his office and charmed the secretary into letting him wait for the mayor to come back.

He needed to know what Drimble had learnt, but he didn't want to put the mayor on his guard. Suddenly Richard Drimble appeared in the open door behind him.

'What do you want?' His voice was harsh.

'Hi, I'm Dan Sullivan, I'm …'

Richard Drimble walked into the room passing close to Dan and stopped in the middle of the floor. 'I know who you are.'

Dan blinked. He hadn't expected such a frosty reception. 'I

wanted to talk to you about the planning committee.'

'I don't want the talk to you about anything.'

'The committee, you're investigating it, aren't you?'

Drimble turned towards him, the colour rising in his face. 'Who told you that?'

'Councillor Buttle, she said that—'

'Don't you think you've done enough to Councillor Buttle?'

'Me? I didn't do anything to her.'

'You're the reason she's dead.'

Dan stared at him. 'What do you mean?'

'Getting her to tell you things, to make up things, things that meant she got hurt.'

'I didn't tell her to say anything.'

'What did she give you then?'

This is what Dan had been dreading. He had to think quickly for an answer. 'The promise of an interview.'

Drimble frowned. 'She didn't give you anything else? An envelope, for instance?'

'No.' Dan tried to keep his face wide-eyed and innocent, but staring Richard Drimble straight in the eyes was hard work. When Drimble stayed silent, Dan took his chance. 'Why did you reject the Elliot's Walk application at the last planning meeting?'

Drimble frowned. 'You were there, you know why.'

'But that's not the first application to come up that was like that.'

'What you mean?'

'Elliot's Walk is the ninth application to come before the committee on your watch that breached regulations, but this was the first one that got rejected.'

Drimble took three quick steps forwards, forcing Dan back to the doorway. 'The application was rejected for the reasons given at the meeting. Any internal investigation is none of your business, and if you print one word of this, I'll sue you and your newspaper.'

He shoved Dan into the outer office and slammed the door behind him.

Chapter 43

It was by impersonating a colleague that Emma secured an interview with Paul Sanderson. He looked grey, Emma thought, as she was led through the maze of desks in the open-plan office. It was a long, wide room, lit by sharp fluorescent strip lights, and as she passed each desk the incumbent turned silently to stare and then whispering began behind her.

'They think you're the police,' explained the frumpy middle-aged woman leading the way. 'It's the suit.'

Emma smiled. Burton would have loved it if I did that, she thought. Another reason to shut me out of the case. As the woman announced her arrival, Emma took a chance to examine Sanderson. His hair seemed greyer than the pictures she'd seen of him recently, as did his skin. His eyes were dull and red rimmed as he looked up.

'What? Who?' he enquired and the woman started to explain who Emma was.

'Susan, Susan Brooker, from the *Post*?' The woman was saying. 'You agreed to see her. It's in your calendar.'

'Oh.' Sanderson looked at his computer screen. 'Oh, I haven't actually opened my calendar yet.' He was staring blankly at the screen, as if he didn't know how to open it.

'Should you be here, Paul?' the woman asked gently. 'Maybe you should have taken some time off.'

'No, no, I'm fine.' Sanderson got to his feet and offered Emma a hand.

'Sorry, do sit down, Miss ... erm ...'

'Please, call me Susan.' Emma smiled and shook the hand he held out.

He indicated for her to take the chair opposite him.

Emma took out her notebook and pen, and Sanderson looked at the woman who was hovering.

'Yes, Pauline? Anything else?'

'Would you like a tea or coffee?' she asked, clearly dying of curiosity.

Sanderson looked at Emma, who shook her head.

'Thanks, Pauline, but we're OK.'

Pauline reluctantly walked away, glancing back over her shoulder.

'So,' Sanderson clasped his hands on the desk. 'I'm sorry I've not even had time to look at the appointment so I don't know why you want to see me.' He spread his hands apologetically and then clasped them again.

'We wanted to do a feature on planning.' Emma clicked open her ballpoint pen. 'It's such an interesting process.'

Sanderson pulled a face. 'I'm not sure that's how anyone else would describe it.'

Emma smiled. 'Look at it as us trying to make it something people can get interested in.'

Sanderson tried to smile but his features were fighting a losing battle.

'Although,' Emma continued, 'with everything that's happened, some people might disagree with you.' She looked up to find Sanderson staring at her.

'What you mean?'

'There have been two deaths, both connected to the planning

committee; some might say that's exciting.'

'I wouldn't.' Sanderson's voice was harsh.

'No, I suppose not, if they're friends of yours. Were they friends of yours?'

'Colleagues.'

'I'm sorry.'

'No, it's fine, it's not your fault.'

'Thankfully, I didn't come to talk about that.' She smiled and made a note of his name and the date in her notebook.

Sanderson looked relieved. 'You must be the only person who hasn't. What did you want to know?'

'Planning is a popular committee, isn't it? Do you know why?'

'I suppose it's the place where you can make a big difference. If you're lucky, you can make or break the image of sections of the town.'

'So it's power?'

'Not quite. More the ability to make a difference.'

Emma resisted the impulse to snort derisively. She'd heard that so many times from people who didn't mean it.

'But there must be a temptation,' she said.

'A temptation to what?'

'To exploit that power?'

'How do you mean?' Sanderson looked puzzled.

'To pass something that you shouldn't?'

Sanderson froze. 'What do you mean?'

'You know, someone comes to you, who has an application in, and appeals to you to pass it, even if the rules say no.'

'I don't know what you mean.' But Sanderson's clasped hands were now shaking and his knuckles had gone white.

'That amount of power, the yes or no on some big projects – like the style of the new courthouse or building new houses, for example

– it must be tempting for people to ask you to bend the rules.'

When she looked up, Sanderson's face was also white.

Emma dropped into the chair opposite Dan across the café table. He looked up.

'I don't have long. Daisy was expecting me back ages ago.'

'Keeping you on a tight leash, is she?'

'You betcha. I've had to give up the investigation into the murders.'

'What? Why?'

'The police know that I know you, so they won't speak to me in case I share it with you. The juniors are splitting it between themselves and they're constantly overexcited. It's quite cute really.'

'Cute?'

'I remember what I was like at that age. So enthusiastic. Rushing about like a spaniel.'

Dan laughed. 'What did you get from Sanderson?'

She brought him up to speed with the conversation.

'You can tell he's up to something, you could see it in his face. He was pale, and his hands were trembling. He looks like he's not slept in weeks.'

'Did he mention if he's been interviewed by police?'

'No.' Emma smiled and accepted the coffee from the waitress. 'But I think he has; the office manager commented that the rest of the staff thought I was police.'

'Did you get anything else out of him?'

Emma shook her head and blew on her coffee. 'No, as soon as I got into the temptation of power and bending the rules, he "found out" he had an urgent meeting and so I had to leave.' She paused to sip her coffee and continued. 'But the police must suspect him. I mean, if he was having an affair with Johanna Buttle, and we're pretty sure he was, then I'd say that makes him prime suspect. Who else would be able to get her to a hotel room? Plus they're both involved with the planning applications. And another thing I've been thinking: we've got no proof that she sent you that text message. What if she was already dead when you got it?'

Dan stared. 'You think Sanderson did it?'

'He doesn't seem the type to do it in cold-blood but if he was angry enough he's got the strength. She was only little.'

'We need to have a chat with Burton, don't we? See what came out of the post-mortem. If she was already dead when I got that message, then we know someone else lured me to that hotel.'

Emma grinned. 'You think Burton is just going to tell you the results of the post-mortem?'

'She might if we can give her something in return.'

'Such as?'

'I'll think of something.'

'Let's not waste time on that. She'll go mad if she finds out you've ignored what she said about the story again. We need to think about our next move.' She looked at her watch and stood up. 'I've got to go, but keep me posted on how you're getting on. I'll see you tonight.'

Dan watched as she walked away and out of the door.

When Emma returned home that evening she was accompanied by Ed.

'Hey, mate, how's it going?' Ed asked.

'Yeah, all right. How's work?'

'Not really been in the office. Court was busy. Daisy's doing her nut trying to work out how to manage the workload, with the juniors trying to do the murder inquiry stuff between them.'

Emma snorted.

Ed laughed. 'So far none of them has thought to ask Emma for advice.'

'How was your afternoon?' Emma asked, perching on the arm of the sofa and looking at the table, which was covered in papers. She had a sudden urge to stroke the back of Dan's head, but checked herself just in time.

'Emma, you know we had that conversation about the companies and the applications being too similar to be a coincidence?'

'Yes. Do you think they are fake companies?'

'No, I don't know how they could do that without anyone noticing. Anyone could do a quick Internet search and that would be it.'

Ed flopped onto the sofa. 'So, you're stuck?'

'Not necessarily. I phoned a couple of the companies.'

'And said what? Are they bribing councillors?'

'No, don't be daft. As if that would work. I spoke to the press office and said I was a freelance journalist trying to set up an interview.'

'Clever,' said Emma. 'What did they say?'

'I got the brush off at first but then lied and said I was pitching to a national supplement and just needs a background chat.'

'And?'

'I asked if I could speak to the guy who led on the design of the Elliot's Walk development. His name was in the application papers.'

'Then what happened?' Ed asked.

'We had a general chat and I asked about the size of the developments.'

'Did he get cagey about it?' Emma asked.

'No. If there is money changing hands then he is not aware of it.'

'Or he's good actor and was lying. Or he just didn't want to tell a complete stranger,' Ed suggested.

'He did say that the council was really tough to work with, asking lots of questions and asking for changes to the plans and stuff.'

'You think this gave them more access to James Wilton?'

'Not necessarily. I think the to-ing and fro-ing was a chance to officially question and then order changes without arousing a lot of suspicion.'

'But if it's just one company then it could be that one was an honest mistake?' Emma said.

Dan shook his head. 'I called two others. On the third one, I ended up speaking to the deputy CEO and that conversation was weird.'

'How?' Ed asked.

'Obviously I was an innocent architectural journalist, but when I mentioned the size of the development and said about how difficult it is to get planning permission for large developments, he started to get annoyed.'

'And?'

'He said he didn't think a national newspaper would be interested in a story about housing estates. He said it would be better for me to leave it alone.'

'He threatened you?' Emma asked.

'Not directly, but the message was definitely that I should back off.'

'That seems to be a popular suggestion,' Ed said. 'First Burton and now this guy. But you're not going to, are you?'

'How can I?' Dan stood up and tried to pace the small living room, nearly tripping over the coffee table. 'There's something wrong at the council. It's fraud, plain and simple. Someone there must know what's going on and I need to find that out.'

Emma raised her hand, palm facing outwards like a traffic warden. 'Wait a moment; you're saying that the building companies are paying the council to pass the legal planning applications?'

'Not the council as a whole. That would be too difficult. But I think they were definitely paying James Wilton.'

'And if Jo Buttle was involved in the scam, it's likely she was being paid for her committee vote,' Emma said.

'Yes.'

'But why?'

'It's like you said before, wouldn't everyone like more money?'

Emma nodded. 'I see what you mean.'

This time it was Ed who raised his hand. 'But how would the companies know who was open to bribery? They'd only be dealing with one person, probably Wilton, but surely not Buttle.'

Dan frowned, hands on hips. 'That's true. Unless Wilton got the money and paid it on to her.'

'But how do we find out about their financial arrangements?' Ed asked.

'Do you think we could ask Burton?' Dan looked at Emma, who snorted.

'Yeah, right. You think she'll just let you look at them?'

'Fair point. And now Wilton and Buttle are both dead, I've got no source in the council.'

'How about …?' Emma spoke slowly. 'How about trying Sanderson. You said he and Buttle were close. Maybe she talked to him.'

'Good call. I need to check when the next planning meeting is and then I can tackle him.'

'He won't talk to you. He might know that you were arrested after Buttle died.'

'And he's seen you as Susan Brooker.' They both turned to look at Ed.

He groaned. 'Fine, I'll go but I think you're mad. He's never going to confess.'

'He doesn't need to. We just need to rattle his cage and give him an outlet if he wants to talk about what's happening.'

Ed sighed. 'Consider it done.'

Chapter 44

Paul Sanderson stared, horrified. 'What in God's name are you talking about?' he asked in a hoarse voice.

David Edmonds stared back at him, one hand resting on the agenda of the next day's planning committee meeting, which was lying on his desk.

'We can't carry on with the schedule. The police are all over it.' Sanderson's eyes were wide and scared.

'No, they aren't. They're busy with the murders.'

'Drimble's all over it too.'

Edmonds laughed derisively. 'He knows nothing.' He paused. 'Do it for Jo.'

'What?'

'She wouldn't want you to quit.'

'She bloody would. She wanted out herself.'

'And look what happened to her.'

Sanderson took a step back. 'Did you ...? Did you?' he stammered.

Edmonds laughed but it was without humour. 'The people we got into bed with aren't nice people,' he said. 'And clearly they don't tolerate failure.'

'But she didn't fail. She did everything they asked for.'

'You both failed. So did I. We failed to get that last application passed.'

'You're telling me that Jo died for the sake of a housing estate?'

Edmonds shrugged. 'It was more than that and you know it. It doesn't really matter now though, does it?' he asked as Sanderson collapsed into a chair.

'You're mad. How can you say it doesn't matter?' he asked, tears welling up in his eyes. 'Jo's dead.'

'Oh, pull yourself together,' Edmonds snapped.

'But it wasn't really our fault it didn't get passed; it was Drimble,' said Sanderson desperately. 'He started questioning it. There was nothing we could do.'

'And you should have voted for the application regardless of what Drimble said. If you'd both not supported him, it would have all worked out. Anyway, our job now is to protect ourselves and carry on the plans. Without Wilton we're a bit snookered but I've managed to find someone to take over from him.'

'Who?'

'Just someone who needs a bit of extra cash at the moment and is pleased to get it anyway they can.'

Sanderson stared. 'How do you find things out about people?'

Edmonds smiled. 'You don't need to know. It's probably safer that way. Just make sure the development on tomorrow's agenda gets passed.'

'Or what?'

Edmonds raised an eyebrow. 'Have you forgotten about Jo already?'

'Poor Jo,' said Sanderson, his mouth turning down at the corners as tears brimmed on his eyelashes.

'Just hold your nerve.'

'What if I decide I don't want to be a part of this anymore?'

'You don't have a choice. Jo tried to walk away and she was silenced.'

'But she's gone. You don't have anything on me.'

Edmonds laughed. 'Oh, believe me, Paul, I have enough on you to keep you in your place. What about the gambling debts you ran up before you became a councillor?'

Sanderson's face became two shades paler. 'How did you find out about that?'

'I have my sources.'

'But they're all paid off. No one will care.'

'Want to risk it? They'd never let you stay on the accounts committee.' Sanderson was silent. 'I didn't think so. Your job is to make sure the application goes through and believe me it'll be worse for you if you don't. These aren't nice people, as Jo found out.'

Sanderson sighed and rubbed his face. 'This certainly isn't what I thought it would be. An easy way to make some money, you said, not putting lives at risk. It's getting too obvious, we have to stop.'

'No one has noticed so far.'

'Except Drimble.'

'I've told you to leave him to me. Just hold your nerve and you have nothing to worry about. Screw up and I don't fancy your chances.'

As the door closed behind Sanderson, Edmonds stood silently looking out of the window. He didn't have much of a view, just the bustling High Street, where people scurried about like ants but he liked it. It made him feel superior to look down on them as they went about their boring lives. Then his mobile burst into life, making him jump. He snatched it up.

'How are things?' asked the voice.

'I think I've plugged the holes. But we may have a problem at tonight's committee.'

'Why?'

'One of our applications is up and Sanderson is getting cold feet.'

'That could be a problem.'

'Could? Of course it's a problem. He's our last line of attack and without him we've got no chance.'

There was a short silence. 'Perhaps we should warm his feet up a little bit,' said the voice quietly.

Edmonds felt his skin go cold. 'I don't think we need to go that far. I've had a word and convinced him to go ahead with the plan.'

'If anything goes wrong, I'll hold you responsible.'

Edmonds closed his eyes. 'I've done my best but he's got a mind of his own. He's still grieving about Jo Buttle.'

'If it doesn't go our way tonight there will be repercussions.' The call was disconnected, leaving Edmonds with shaking hands.

Chapter 45

'Paul Sanderson is the priority,' Dan told Ed as he stood in front of the mirror knotting his tie. 'That's the main point of going to this meeting.'

'I know. That's the only reason I'm going, remember. Why are they having another meeting so soon anyway?'

'It's an extraordinary meeting. There's another dodgy-looking housing development on the agenda and the council's website says it's an urgent application.' He held up the committee notes that he had printed out.

'Probably trying to get it past the committee before anyone looks into it too closely.' He paused as he gave his tie one last tug.

'Do we need the decision on the application as well?' he asked.

'It'd be worth staying and finding out which way it goes. See if you can grab a set of papers that are there tonight, I'd quite like to see whether they've been tampered with. But you need to get to Sanderson first, before he goes to the meeting.'

'Why before?

Dan frowned. 'I suppose it's better to get him when he's on his own. We know he might be involved in the scam and was also having an affair with Jo Buttle. Maybe she told him what was going on. She might also have told him who sent that information she gave to me.'

'I can't believe that she was involved.'

Dan shrugged. 'It's pretty out of character, but the way she was talking about it, the more I think about it, the more it looks suspicious. Why was she talking about getting her side of the story out there?'

'Reckon Sanderson will tell me anything?'

'I don't know to be honest, but if we can rattle him a bit, he might. It's more a case of gauging his reaction. If you can soften him up a little bit, we might be able to work on him a bit later.'

'I suppose it depends how you phrase the question,' Emma said.

'Your mission is to get in there and talk to him without being seen by anyone else,' Dan said.

'How important is it not to be seen?' Ed paused as he gave his tie one last tug.

'I'd just rather no one really found out that we were talking to Sanderson. They've already shown that they're not against trying to stop us.'

'What about Richard Drimble?'

'Probably best to try and avoid him too. He warned me off investigating the planning department in no uncertain terms when I last spoke to him, so I'd rather he didn't know we were sniffing around this application.'

'You think he's hiding something.' Ed wasn't asking a question as he put on his suit jacket.

'Exactly, so I think we need to play our cards close.'

Paul Sanderson froze, his hand inches from the council chamber door, as there was a cough behind him. There was another cough. He looked around and saw a sandy-haired man beckoning to him from the stairwell to the public gallery. Sanderson looked up and down the corridor and then approached cautiously. The man held the door open and then closed it behind Sanderson.

'You probably don't know me,' began the man.

'You work at the *Post*, don't you?'

'Yes.'

'I thought I'd seen you before. What's with all the cloak and dagger stuff?' Sanderson gestured back to the door.

'I didn't want anyone to see us talking,' the young man said in a low voice.

'Why not?'

'I need to ask you a question.'

'And you have to drag me into a stairwell to ask it?'

'Yes.'

Sanderson raised an eyebrow. 'What is it?'

'How well did you know Jo Buttle?'

'We were colleagues and I was sorry to hear about her death.'

The young man pulled a face. 'I'm not here for a press statement, Councillor Sanderson.'

'Oh? What are you after?'

'Information.'

'About what?'

The man paused. 'About what's happening in the planning committee.'

A muscle twitched in Sanderson's cheek. 'What is happening in the planning committee?'

'You know. You know about the planning applications. Was Councillor Buttle involved in it? Or did she find out that you were involved and try to stop you?'

Sanderson's jaw worked three times before he could speak. 'I don't know what you think is going on, but why would Councillor Buttle be interested in what I was doing? We were hardly bosom buddies.'

'That's not what I heard.' The man arched an eyebrow. 'I'd heard you were quite close. Maybe even a little too close.'

'That's idle speculation. If you print that I'll sue you for libel.'

The man held up his hands, palm outwards. 'Libel only works when it's not true.' Sanderson stared at him and the man continued. 'She found out, didn't she? She found out what was going on and threatened to blow the whistle. That's why you killed her, isn't it?'

Sanderson looked up quickly. 'What? No, I— I never laid a finger on her. I wouldn't.' The last word came out in a whisper.

'But the planning committee is corrupt, isn't it? The question is, were you or are you still involved?'

Sanderson stood up straight suddenly, making the other man step back. 'I don't know what you're talking about, and if you print that, I'll deny everything. You have no proof.'

The man smiled. 'Councillor Buttle cared about you taking bribes then?'

'Are you implying that I'd—?'

'Yes. I'm implying that you're being paid to pass planning applications. I think Buttle found out and you killed her to stop her saying anything.'

Taking a deep breath, Sanderson pulled himself up to his full height. 'I know nothing about any planning applications or money, and I certainly had nothing to do with Johanna's death.'

'Murder.'

'What?'

'She was murdered.'

Sanderson's eyes filled with tears. 'I— I've got to go.'

He walked away pushing open the door into the council chamber, wiping the back of his hand across his face. The door slammed behind him, the noise echoing down the corridor.

As he watched Sanderson go, Ed smiled grimly. Things were getting interesting.

Chapter 46

The start of the meeting was very dull.

How did Dan cope with the tedium? Ed wondered. He'd taken a seat in the public gallery, which was thankfully empty. He could see the Post reporter – one of the juniors – at the press table down below looking bored, and he sat back out of sight. The last thing he needed was the youngster telling Daisy he'd been there.

'This meeting is tinged with sadness,' Richard Drimble told the room as he opened the meeting. He glanced at the empty seat next to Paul Sanderson, usually taken by Jo Buttle. 'One of our members and an officer have been callously murdered, seemingly without reason, and I urge anyone who knows anything about the deaths of Councillor Buttle or Mr Wilton to go to the police as soon as possible. It's your duty to share any information you have.' He glanced at the reporter who was scribbling busily. He waited until the young man looked up expectantly and continued.

'Keep the police in your prayers. Hopefully they'll have a result soon.' He shuffled his papers, cleared his throat and then looked up. 'Ordinarily I would have postponed this meeting, but we have an urgent application and I think both Mr Wilton and Councillor Buttle would have liked us to get on with it.'

A ripple of agreement ran around the councillors seated in the horseshoe of wooden benches.

Sanderson was staring fixedly at the agenda, his hands clasped tightly in front of him. He wiped his eyes on the back of his hand, then shook himself and sat up straighter.

Ed kept an eye on Sanderson throughout the meeting and he wasn't the only one. David Edmonds was staring at the younger man as if he expected him to suddenly disappear, but Sanderson remained empty-eyed. He barely seemed to hear the meeting and had to be reminded several times to vote.

At last the Riverton Gardens proposal was announced. Ed noticed both Edmonds and Drimble stiffen slightly but Sanderson stayed slumped in his seat staring blankly at the agenda in front of him. Ed listened and watched as the officer read through the details. It was recommended for approval, but it had been called in by the ward councillor who gave an impassioned speech about why it should be turned down. Sanderson barely seemed to hear a word. Two committee members gave their views – enjoying the sound of their own voices, thought Ed, as neither really added to the debate – and Drimble put the recommendation to approve to the committee. Ed sat forward. Four hands were raised including Drimble's. When Drimble asked about refusal there were another four hands. The vote was tied but Paul Sanderson hadn't moved.

Drimble was staring at him, an eyebrow raised. 'Councillor Sanderson? Councillor Sanderson? Paul? Are you voting or abstaining?'

Sanderson started as if he'd been electrocuted. He stared around wildly.

Drimble tried again. 'Paul? Are you for or against?'

Sanderson muttered something. 'Sorry? What did you say?'

The councillor to Sanderson's right switched on the microphone in front of him and smiled encouragingly. Sanderson paused and took a deep breath.

'Against,' he said softly, but the microphone made his voice echo around the room, which had fallen silent. Ed looked at Edmonds, who looked frozen in his seat, and then at Drimble who was still staring at Sanderson.

'Application refused,' said the mayor slowly. Ed got quietly to his feet and scooted down the stairs. As he passed the pile of committee papers on the table outside the council chamber, he grabbed a copy. A quick glance at the papers made him raise his eyebrows. Slipping out his mobile he tapped out a text to Dan.

'It seems you were right, mate,' he said aloud as he clattered down the stairs. 'You were right.' He hurried out of the building as quickly as he could.

Paul Sanderson's stomach clenched. His eyes stared unseeing at the agenda in front of him. They knew. That reporter knew what was going on. If they knew enough to publish, then his career – possibly his life – would be over. His hands shook and he tried to wipe the sweat from them onto his trousers. He had to stay calm. But he could feel Edmonds' eyes burning into him.

But what was he supposed to do afterwards? Now Jo was dead, he had no one to turn to. His mum wasn't well and he couldn't drag her into this. He was scared, very scared. All he'd wanted to do was stop Jo from doing what she planned to do, to stop her from talking. But it had all been too late. He gave a quick glance towards the public gallery. The reporter was still there, scribbling in a notebook. No, Sanderson decided, he wouldn't do what Jo did. At least, he wouldn't do it now. He needed time to think.

The meeting passed in a blur, with his neighbour elbowing him discreetly each time he forgot to vote. Then he cast his vote against the application he was supposed to support, feeling almost as if his body were reacting without permission. He could feel the weight of

Edmonds' glare and realised he needed to get out of there.

As the meeting began to pack up he glanced at the gallery. The reporter had gone. Not caring, he pushed his way through the crowd and ran from the room. He had to get away before the story was filed. He also needed to get away before Edmonds caught up with him.

Fumbling with his car keys he bleeped the alarm and scrambled behind the wheel, locking the door behind him. The engine failed to fire on the first two attempts but on the third it leapt into life. Crunching the gears he sped from the car park, almost leaving twin tyre tracks on the tarmac.

As he passed the town hall he saw Drimble and Edmonds at the top of the steps outside, looking up and down the High Street. They saw him as he sped away but he was free. He needed to find somewhere to think.

Twelve hours later, holed up in an anonymous bed and breakfast in Tildon, Sanderson stared at his mobile phone. He had just turned it back on and it was beeping like crazy. Looking at the brightly flashing screen he realised he had fourteen missed calls and three voicemail messages. The first was from his mum.

'Paul? Paul? Where are you?' came the strident tones. 'I'm sick with worry. You were due here an hour ago to visit me and you've not shown up.' As if he didn't already know that. 'I'm very disappointed, Paul.' Again, no surprises there. 'You know I've not been well. Make sure you call me as soon as you get this message. Your brother and sister wouldn't have left me like this.' That would be the brother and sister who'd moved 300 miles to get away from her. Six of the missed calls were her number. Still, she would have to wait. He had more important things to worry about than disappointing his mother yet again.

The next message was from David Edmonds. 'Paul? Where the

hell are you? What the bloody hell were you doing in that meeting? You said you were going to do it for Jo and now you've bloody well screwed this up for all of us. Look, I need to speak to you urgently. Call me.' Hmm, thought Sanderson, another person who would have to wait for a call back. The third message surprised him.

'Paul? Paul, it's Richard Drimble. Look, I realise you're going through a tough time and I'd like to help. The police have been here looking for you. They said you'd been reported missing. We're all really worried, Paul. Call me, please, even if it's just to let me know that you're safe. Please, just let me know you're alive.' There was a beep and a woman's voice told Sanderson he had no more messages.

He saved Drimble's message and put the telephone down on the table in front of him. He stared at it, his brain racing. The plan wasn't totally formed in his head. He had to get the story out without anyone knowing it was him. Going to the police was simple enough but he would be arrested for fraud. He knew he couldn't handle prison. If he couldn't go to the police, then who could he trust?

He could tell the truth and everyone would know why he'd done it. His mother would be disappointed but then she always was. Taking a deep breath he thought back to the voicemail messages. There was only one person who he could call for help.

Chapter 47

Loitering by the back entrance of the town hall, Dan checked his watch. It had taken two days of observing to work out the security guards' patterns.

'They change over watching the front entrance and the CCTV at two forty-five every day,' Ed had said as they sat in the café. He had been hovering near the entrance and thinking up spurious reasons to go and speak to the security guards. 'There's a camera on the back entrance but for five minutes it'll be unwatched as they change over and sign paperwork. So you'll have to be fast.'

It was Emma who'd spent two days watching the back entrance of the town hall to get the access code to the door. Now it was written on a piece of paper in Dan's pocket.

'I think the estate agent in the office opposite thinks I fancy him,' she said ruefully as she joined him at the café table.

'Why?' Dan asked laughing.

'Every time he came out for a cigarette I was standing there and I didn't really have a good enough excuse for loitering around.'

Now Dan was on his own. A glance at his watch told him it was exactly two forty-five.

'Here goes nothing,' he said to himself and quietly climbed the steps. Keying in the four-digit code he was relieved when the door clicked and he was able to push it open. But he was so intent on what he was doing he didn't notice that the door hadn't quite closed behind him.

He took the stairs to the second floor as lightly as he could, his trainers squeaking slightly against the parquet floor. This floor was mostly meeting rooms but it also housed David Edmonds' office. Dan peeped round the corner at the top of the stairs. The corridor was empty and voices murmured behind closed doors. He was creeping along it when he heard footsteps.

He ducked into an alcove behind a large marble statue. The footsteps seemed to be coming from both directions. A draught down the corridor brought a familiar floral scent to his nose.

As one set of footsteps approached, Dan shot out an arm and, seizing Emma's wrist, yanked her into his hiding place, just as David Edmonds strode around the other corner.

He clapped a hand over her mouth just in time to prevent her uttering a frightened squeak.

'What are you doing?' he hissed after Edmonds had passed. Emma's brown eyes were wide and scared but her shoulders had relaxed.

Pulling his hand away she replied, 'I came to help. You nearly gave me a heart attack.'

'You being here isn't part of the plan.'

'I know, but—'

'And you almost got us caught.'

'I know, but I thought you might need some backup.' Her head jutted forward like an angry goose and her hands were planted on her hips. 'You haven't even got to the office yet.'

'Shhh, I was playing cautious.' Dan peeked out from behind the statue. 'Right, he's gone. Follow me.' They crept along the corridor to Edmonds' office. Dan turned the handle and pushed the door. Nothing happened.

'Bollocks, it's locked,' he said.

'Let me try.' Emma pushed him aside.

She turned the handle all the way to the right and then all the way to the left using both hands. There was a resounding click and the door opened.

'It's all in the wrist action,' she said, ushering Dan through the door. 'Now what?'

'Keep a lookout.' Dan was already at Edmonds' desk clicking the laptop's mouse buttons. They both winced as the computer emitted a loud beep as it whirred its way into life.

Dan stepped back. 'He's not locked it,' he said. 'Why wouldn't he lock it?'

'Maybe he's not going to be away for very long,' Emma said. 'Hurry up.'

'Right,' said Dan double-clicking on the 'My Documents' icon. 'Let's see what we have.' He paused. 'Interesting.'

'What is it?'

'There's a subfolder that's password protected. We'll have that.' Dan slipped a memory stick into the USB socket on the computer and waited for the connection to open. 'Come on,' he hissed at the computer. 'Quicker!' An icon popped up saying 'Transfer complete'.

'Right, what else do we have?'

'Check his emails.'

'Good plan.' Dan double-clicked on Outlook Express but all he found were emails relating to council business. 'Damn it, I was sure there would be some dodgy stuff on here.'

'Would he really hang onto risky stuff? Especially since anyone can get access to it? I mean, we got in very easily.'

Dan nodded and then frowned. 'This is odd,' he said.

'What?'

'This file. He's not given it a name and it's just a list of words. They're not in sentences or anything, and they don't really make sense.'

'Let me see.' Emma left her post by the door and joined him. 'Weird. You don't think it could be in code do you?'

'I don't know.'

'Copy it anyway, just in case.' She tiptoed back to the door but as she reached it she froze. 'Someone's coming.'

Dan drummed his fingers on the desk rapidly, willing the computer to work quicker. A quiet ping indicated the work was done and he snatched the memory stick out of the computer. He began shutting down the computer as Emma hissed, 'Quickly! The footsteps are definitely coming this way!'

The computer had barely stopped whirring when Dan dashed to the door. They froze and dived to the right of the door hoping to hide behind it as a hand rattled the door handle. Suddenly they heard a mobile phone burble. Dan slapped a hand to his pocket.

'It's not mine,' he breathed in Emma's ear. On the other side of the door they heard David Edmonds' voice.

'Hello? Yes, I was just about to go into my office. No, not to worry, I'll come straight away.' He sighed angrily and they heard his footsteps tap away along the corridor. Emma sagged against the wall, her hands shaking.

'I thought we were for it there,' she said. 'What on earth would we have said?'

'We could have pretended to be the cleaners,' Dan said with a grin.

'What, cleaners with no dusters or polish?' she asked raising an eyebrow.

'Fair point. I think the coast is clear.' He poked his head around the door and peered up and down the corridor. 'Let's get out of here.'

As they walked quickly away, they didn't see the mousy-haired woman coming out of a nearby committee room. She frowned for a moment and then went back into the room.

Chapter 48

Dan and Emma had not long been back at the cottage when there was a knock on the door.

Ed stood on the doorstep with his laptop tucked under his arm and grinning.

'You look smug,' Dan said as Ed sat down on the sofa.

'I have a reason to look smug.'

'Such as?'

'When you know what I know …'

'Stop being annoying. What do you know?'

'Guess.'

'Ed, I'm not bloody guessing. What do you know?'

'Someone's just emailed me.' Ed was clearly enjoying himself.

'Who?' Emma asked.

'Councillor Paul Sanderson, that's who.'

Emma sat down next to him and watched as he logged into his laptop.

'Can you not just show us on your phone?' Dan asked impatiently.

'No, it needs a bigger screen.'

'What does Sanderson want?' Emma asked.

Ed swung the computer screen to face her and opened up an email to the full-size screen. 'That.' He pointed. Emma read aloud.

'By now you'll already know what I've done. I couldn't let Riverton Gardens go through, it was a step too far. Jo gave her life trying to out these people, and I'm not going to let that be the end. Do what you like with the attached. It should give you your story, but try to keep Jo's and my affair out of this. Her husband deserves to keep his good memory of her.'

Emma paused and looked from Ed to Dan, who was sitting on the armchair opposite and leaning forward with his elbows on his knees.

'He's admitting he did it,' Dan said slowly. 'He's telling us that they were all involved. First Wilton, now Buttle and Sanderson.'

Ed was looking from one to the other. 'Want to see what else he's sent?'

'What else?' Dan got up and came to perch on the arm of the sofa, leaning over Ed's computer.

'There's some attachments. There's this spreadsheet and some emails.'

'Does it say who the emails are from?'

'No, the name's been redacted.'

'Sanderson did that?' Dan asked.

'I reckon so,' Emma said.

'Why?'

'He probably doesn't want to be responsible for giving us everything.'

'Fair point,' said Dan. 'As he said, Jo Buttle decided to blow the whistle and ended up dead. It's no surprise he's gone into hiding.'

'What happens when they find out that he's sent this to us?' Emma asked.

'Why would they find out what he's sent us?'

'When we start asking questions for the story. What happens then?'

'That's probably why he's gone to ground.'

'No, I mean what happens to us? I agree this is great stuff from our point of view, but they won't want us running around with it, will they?'

Dan frowned. 'At the moment we keep all this to ourselves. We'll only start asking questions when it's absolutely necessary.'

'OK. What's in the spreadsheet?' Emma asked.

'It's a load of numbers, with no titles on the columns, but I'm working on the assumption that these longer numbers are applications numbers.' Ed indicated the first column.

'Certainly looks like it,' Dan said. 'It's got the right sort of combination of letters and numbers.'

'And what are these?' Emma pointed to the other columns.

'I think they're sums of money.'

'Money?'

'Yes, I think this is the amount Sanderson was paid for giving the nod to each of the applications. It certainly adds up to a nice little nest egg.'

Emma and Dan stood up at the same time, making Ed roll to one side on the sofa. He steadied himself and only just managed to keep his laptop from falling on the floor.

'So, we have one officer and at least two councillors taking bribes for planning applications,' Dan said, walking to the end of the room and turning back.

'But neither Sanderson, Buttle nor Wilton was in charge,' said Ed.

'In charge? How do you mean?'

'Someone must be organising it, telling them which applications and how they should vote. They must have been managing the money too. We know it can't have been any of those three because they wouldn't have come to us with the information.'

Dan stood for a moment staring into the distance.

'What did you get from Edmonds' office?' Ed asked.

Emma pulled the memory stick from her handbag. 'Some files but they're password protected.'

'My favourite type of files,' Ed said with a grin, taking the stick from her hand. 'Let me take a look.'

David Edmonds' shoes clacked against the stone floor as he strode along the corridor muttering under his breath. He was a formidable figure and council staff scuttled out of his way. Incurring his wrath was easy enough on a daily basis but today an explosion of temper seemed even more likely.

He slammed open the double doors at the end of the corridor causing a young woman who was about to open them from the other side to shriek and drop the files she was holding.

He didn't stop to help her pick them up. In fact he barely registered her presence before striding over and banging on the door of the mayor's parlour. Without waiting to be told to come in, he barged inside.

'Drimble, I must protest at being summoned like this,' he began but stopped suddenly. Drimble, sitting calmly behind his desk, was not alone. Burton and Shepherd sat opposite him. The latter stood as Edmonds entered and indicated for him to take the spare chair. Edmonds sat reluctantly and the detective hovered behind him.

'What's going on?' he demanded.

Drimble sat forward. 'Paul Sanderson's car has been found abandoned,' he said quietly. 'The police believe there was blood on the seats.'

'What? Suicide?'

'Why would you think suicide?' Burton asked, eyebrows arching in surprise.

'Do you know something, we don't?' Shepherd asked.

'But— I— we—' Edmonds blustered. 'Why would you think I know anything?'

Drimble's face hardened.

'Apparently you were very angry with him after the last planning meeting,' said Shepherd, speaking from directly behind him. Edmonds tried to turn to see the detective but Shepherd stayed just out of sight whichever way he turned.

'Was I? I don't remember.' Edmonds tried to regain his composure.

'You chased him from the building.'

'I didn't chase him from the building. He ran off straight after the meeting and I went after him.'

'You did seem very angry with him,' Drimble put in. Edmonds glared at him.

'I was worried about him. He seemed very gloomy when I spoke to him earlier in the day.

'What did you speak to him about?' Burton asked.

'The committee meeting. We discussed the applications. Paul was talking about Jo and questioning why we were having a meeting so soon.'

'I wondered about that.' Burton was looking at Drimble. 'Could you not have postponed it?'

'We could have, but it would have thrown the schedule all off. Plus Jo would have said for the show to go on.'

Shepherd raised an eyebrow. 'Really?'

'She was very committed to planning.' Drimble sat back in his chair, hands on the armrests of his chair. 'She'd never have wanted things to slide.'

'But you said Sanderson seemed gloomy. Did you think he'd harm himself?' Burton was looking at Edmonds.

'Of course not. If I had I'd have kept a closer eye on him.' Edmonds looked from Drimble to Burton. 'Now it seems I had good reason to be worried. What happened? With his car, I mean.'

'A family out walking their dog in the woods saw the car in the car park and reported it to the police. We're still carrying out tests to see if the blood is Mr Sanderson's.'

'Why did you chase him?' Shepherd asked.

'I didn't chase him.' Edmonds' voice rose angrily. 'Like I told you, I was worried because he was behaving strangely during the meeting but he drove off before I could catch up to him.'

'What do you mean behaving strangely?'

'Paul usually loves planning but he wasn't in the room, mentally speaking. He kept missing the votes and it was like he wasn't even listening to what was happening.'

'Why were you at the meeting?' Shepherd asked. 'Was there an application you were interested in?'

Edmonds frowned. 'I often attend committees in the evening if I have nothing else in my diary.'

Shepherd raised an eyebrow as if he could imagine a thousand other things to do other than sit in a planning meeting.

'That's very dedicated. I wish I could get my officers to be so keen to volunteer for overtime,' Burton remarked.

'Why aren't you out looking for Paul?' demanded Edmonds standing up and turning towards Shepherd. 'He could be out there having hurt himself or even worse killed himself and you're just sitting here asking us questions.'

'We've got uniformed officers combing the woods, but we're more concerned that someone else might have wanted to hurt him. That's why we're asking questions.'

'We're checking out again anyone who might have had reason to hurt him,' said Shepherd, eyeing Edmonds.

'I had no reason to hurt him,' Edmonds blustered.

'You were angry with him,' said Shepherd.

'I was not!' shouted Edmonds, causing Shepherd to raise his eyebrows. 'I was not angry,' Edmonds said again, struggling to control his voice.

'Can you think of anyone who would have a reason to hurt Mr Sanderson?' asked Burton looking at Drimble.

'No, I can't,' said the mayor. 'He was very popular with the other councillors. In fact everyone liked him.'

'You said the same about James Wilton and Councillor Buttle. Now they're both dead,' said Burton bluntly. 'There have now been two – possibly three – deaths, all connected to your planning department.'

'What are you saying?' Drimble asked.

'I'd be happier if you stopped your investigation for now,' Burton said. 'We have reason to believe Wilton, Buttle and Sanderson were involved in a fraud connected to planning. It now looks like someone is tidying up loose ends.'

'But Jo and Paul would never—' began Edmonds.

'It would appear they were, both of them,' said Burton.

'What do you want me to do?' Drimble asked.

'Do nothing. Carry on with your day-to-day business and stop asking questions. We'll find out what's going on.' Burton got to her feet.

'Thank you, I—' the mayor began.

'We'd like a word with Councillor Edmonds,' she said. 'In private.'

Edmonds swallowed hard. 'You'd better come to my office.'

Shepherd held the door open for Edmonds and Burton and then nodded to Drimble as he left the office.

The mousy-haired woman looked up from her papers. There were voices in the corridor again. Even with the door closed she still recognised the stentorian tones of David Edmonds. As she peered into the corridor she saw him striding towards her, flanked by a man and a woman in suits. They all stopped outside Edmonds' office door. The woman stepped forward.

'Councillor Edmonds?'

He rounded on her as if she had jabbed him with a red-hot poker. 'Harriet, you startled me. What is it?'

'I was working in there.'

'Sorry, did we disturb you?' asked Burton.

'No, well, yes, but that's not the point. I thought you were already in your office.' She was looking at Edmonds.

'Why would you think that?'

'I saw some people leaving it about ten minutes ago.'

'People? What people?'

'A couple. A man and a woman.'

'I wasn't here and I wasn't expecting anyone either. What did they look like?'

'Both in their mid-twenties, I'd say. The girl had long red hair. The man had a white plaster on the side of his head. I didn't really get a good look at them but they looked a bit shifty.'

Burton and Shepherd exchanged a glance.

'Shifty? How?' asked Edmonds.

'They sort of peeped out of the door, well, the girl did, as if they were looking to see if there was anyone in the corridor. Then they snuck out and hurried away.'

'How long were they in there?' Shepherd asked. The woman shook her head.

'I don't know. I only saw them coming out.'

'And they were definitely coming out? They weren't just

knocking on the door?'

'No, I saw them looking out from inside.'

'We're you expecting anyone?' Shepherd asked.

'No, I was working alone. I had some paperwork to finish.'

'Do people often call unannounced?'

'They do sometimes.'

'So these people might have waited inside for a couple of minutes and then left?' Burton looked at Harriet.

'That's possible. Although I didn't hear anyone knocking on the door.'

Shepherd looked at Edmonds. 'Shall we step inside and check that everything is OK?'

Edmonds started to open the door while Burton thanked Harriet for her help.

Shepherd paused in the doorway of Edmonds' office as Harriet went back into the committee room and closed the door. His eyebrows were raised. Burton's face was an angry mask.

'I'll kill them both,' she hissed. They went into the office and found Edmonds examining some cardboard files.

'Nothing seems to be missing,' he was muttering. But when he turned back to his desk his face fell. He pointed to his laptop. 'The lid's closed,' he said. 'It was open when I left it.'

'Are you sure?' asked Shepherd, crossing to the desk.

'Yes, I was only going to be gone for a couple of minutes so I left it running.' He scowled. 'If only I hadn't answered the mayor's call I might have caught them.'

'Try not to touch it, sir,' said Shepherd holding out a hand to stop him opening the lid. 'We can test it for prints.'

'You don't think anything is missing?' asked Burton.

'I don't know but if they've been on my laptop ...' Edmonds' voice trailed away.

'Any way of checking what's been done to it?' Burton asked.

'I could get our techie guys to see if they can—' Shepherd began.

'No!' shouted Edmonds. The two detectives looked at him, surprised.

'No?' asked Shepherd. 'You don't want to know if someone has tampered with your laptop?'

'No, it'll be fine. I'll give it the once over and if there's anything wrong or missing I'll let you know.' The phone rang on his desk and he snatched up the receiver. He seemed about to cut the other person off but they said something that caught his attention. He asked the caller to hold and said to Burton and Shepherd, 'I'm sorry, this is important. Can we talk another time?' Burton looked furious, but had no option other than to leave.

Outside the office, Shepherd looked at Burton.

'We didn't get much of a look around, did we? I can't believe you let him get away with that.'

'I know. But he'll keep. Right now I want a word with our sneak thieves.'

As soon as the door closed behind the detectives, Edmonds was booting up his laptop, with the landline phone tucked between his shoulder and his chin.

'We've got a problem. Someone broke into my office and they've accessed my computer. No, I don't know.' He listened for a moment. 'Yes, I realise the significance, but at least I managed to get rid of the police. I'll keep you posted.'

Chapter 49

Emma set the cup of tea next to Ed's right hand and paused behind him. She was pleased he'd been able to stay to help. She might know how to use a computer for work, but she couldn't do anything like this. Her brow furrowed as she watched the cursor whizz around the screen.

Ed clicked open a new window and tried to open the locked file.

'Password required,' said the screen.

'How on earth do you understand all this stuff?' she asked gesturing to the computer screen.

Ed grinned. 'It's simple really.' He frowned for a moment. 'We just have to work out what his password is.'

'That's going to be a mammoth task,' she said sitting down in a spare chair next to him.

'It could be. We just need a couple of lucky guesses really.'

'But it could be anything.'

'Let's try and look positively, shall we?' Ed grinned.

'We don't know Edmonds well enough to know what random words he might choose,' Emma pointed out.

'Hmmmm.' Ed paused a moment.

'We really appreciate you doing this,' Emma said.

'Doing what?'

'Helping with the investigation. I know you're not convinced about the story.'

'I believe that Dan believes it and you'll need all the persuasive tactics we've got to stop him flying straight into the face of danger.' He stared fixedly at the screen. 'I'm surprised you got involved. You and Dan haven't always seen eye to eye.'

Emma grinned. 'I think never saw eye to eye is a better phrase.'

'I didn't think you even liked him.'

Emma took a deep breath. 'To be honest, I didn't.'

'So why help?'

'Honestly? I thought it would be a terrific story, him being involved in a murder. That was why I got involved in the first place. But I don't think I ever really believed he was capable of murder,' she said.

'I knew there had to be a real reason,' Ed said with a grin. 'Where is Dan, anyway?'

'In the kitchen. He had to take a phone call.'

''OK. Now if I could just work out this guy's password, we would be good to go.'

'What have you tried?'

'All the obvious stuff, like his own name, Allensbury, council related words, planning scam.'

'You actually tried planning scam?'

'You never know.'

'If that had been right I'd have given you fifty quid!'

Ed laughed. 'We need some more information on him to try and guess his password.'

'Like what?'

'Date of birth, family, their dates of birth, birthplace. That's what people usually use.'

Emma nodded as Ed clicked into the Internet and typed 'David

Edmonds' and 'Allensbury' into the search engine. After a couple of minutes of whirring the computer began to offer options. A quick visit to Edmonds' business website gave them the names of his wife and children but none of them opened the file.

'Good to see he's not using his kids to cover up his dodgy dealings,' Emma remarked. Ed grinned. But no matter where they searched they couldn't come up with his date of birth.

'How about this one? Says it's got all his vital statistics,' said Ed. The website opened to show a muscular twenty-something, naked to the waist, his chest slick with baby oil. 'That's definitely not our David Edmonds.'

'No, but I'd quite like to meet him,' Emma replied leaning closer to the computer for a better look at the muscled torso. 'Is he really from Allensbury?'

'Hey,' Ed pushed her gently to one side and she giggled. 'We've got work to do. Where are we going to find Edmonds' date of birth?'

Suddenly Emma slapped her hand on the table.

'Of course!'

'What?'

'Go to our website, the *Post's* website.'

'Why? How's that going to help?'

'Don't you remember? Susan did that story about his company winning an award and it was a "double celebration" –' she sketched quotation marks in the air '– because it was given on his birthday. We know how old he is so we can work out what year he was born in.'

Ed stared for a moment. 'Em, you're a genius. If it wouldn't get me into loads of trouble with Lydia I'd kiss you.'

Emma laughed. 'How is Lydia?'

'Decidedly frosty last time I spoke to her. Perhaps I'd better let Dan do the kissing instead.'

Emma laughed and blushed slightly. Ed started to search the paper's website.

'Here it is,' he said clicking on the story. A glance revealed the date on the story was July twenty-eight. 'And the story says his birthday was the day before so July twenty-seventh. The other information says he's fifty-six which makes the year 1960.'

'Quick maths. That's rare for a journalist.'

'Thanks.' Ed clicked back to the password box and inputted 270760. With shaking hands he hit the enter key.

A message popped up on the screen. 'Access denied.'

'Bollocks. I was sure that would work.'

'Try different combinations,' Emma suggested. 'Maybe you need to put a nineteen in front of the sixty?'

But six combinations later Ed was becoming frustrated.

'I give up.'

'That's not the attitude we're looking for.'

'Ha ha, very funny. What do we do now? Everything we've tried has come to nothing. It could be anything, any random bloody word.' Ed scrubbed at his eyes.

Emma sat up straight.

'That file,' she said.

'What file?'

'When Dan was copying those files, he said there was one that was just a list of words. What if one of those is his password?'

'Surely he wouldn't be stupid enough to keep his password right next to the file?'

'But who would look there? They'd do what we did and think he'd pick something related to himself. If he picked something really random that no one else would guess, he'd need a note of it so he wouldn't forget.'

'Surely not.' Ed was quickly clicking into the file and surveying the words in it. 'Here goes nothing.'

It took a further six attempts and six 'access denied' before Ed inputted the word 'pineapple' and was rewarded with a 'password accepted'.

'Yes!' He leapt to his feet, his elbow narrowly missing his cup of tea. 'Wow, I'd never have thought anyone could be this stupid.' Ed sat back down and began clicking on subfolders. 'Oh my word, it's all here.' He clicked on a file marked 'Accounts'. 'Whoa, look at this. He's made a fortune.'

'Why would you keep these kind of records?' asked Emma in a hushed tone. 'He's just incriminated himself.'

'He probably thought no one would ever find them. Plus, how would you link them to the scam unless you knew about it?' Ed opened more folders. One contained a list of names. 'Reckon that's the people involved?'

'Must be. We know just about everyone on it, James Wilton, Jo Buttle, Paul Sanderson.'

'I wonder who the question mark is.'

'Do you reckon there's someone involved that he doesn't know about?'

Ed pulled a face. 'How could it be if he's in charge of the scam?'

'Maybe it's someone they were going to bring into the scheme later. Maybe they needed another person.'

'After James Wilton was killed?'

'Possibly, although that's slightly ironic since they killed him.'

Emma took a slow, deep breath. 'If you think Edmonds is behind the scam, would he have killed James Wilton, do you think?'

'I wouldn't put it past him. He seems to have some anger management issues.'

'Who has anger management issues?' asked Dan, pushing open the door, mobile phone in his hand.

'David Edmonds.'

'How're you getting on?'

'We've got it open and there's some really interesting stuff.'

'Anything we've not already got?'

'Edmonds' accounts spreadsheet and a list of names.'

'Who was that on the phone?' Emma asked.

'Richard Drimble.'

'Drimble? I thought he hated you?'

'He's apologised and says he wants to meet me. Oh, and I think we're busted.'

'What? How?' asked Ed and Emma together.

'He happened to mention that David Edmonds' office has been rifled and his computer searched.'

'Shit,' said Emma.

'It gets worse. Burton and Shepherd were with Edmonds when he found out.'

'Double shit.'

'That's not all.'

'What else?' Ed asked.

'Someone saw us leaving the office.'

'No!'

'Yup. Drimble said the woman didn't get a very good look at the two people she saw but I reckon Burton and Shepherd will realise it was us.'

Emma sighed. 'We're in trouble, aren't we?'

'Yup.'

'But we can show them what we've found out,' Ed said. 'That must be enough to point the finger at Edmonds.'

'I don't think that'll work. Technically we stole it.' Dan sat down heavily on the sofa.

'Technically?' Emma raised an eyebrow.

'Alright, we stole it. That means they won't be happy with us and can't use it as evidence.'

'But it proves he's involved. In fact, it makes it look like he might be the ringleader.'

'Ringleader?' Dan sniggered. 'You sound like something from *The Hardy Boys*.'

Emma grinned. 'Does that make me Nancy Drew?'

Dan laughed but Ed was frowning.

'You know what I mean.'

'Maybe we could use it to convince them to seize his computer and look at it for themselves,' Emma said. 'That would give them some help at least.'

'I don't think they would see it that way,' said Dan.

'So what do we do?'

'I'll meet Richard Drimble tomorrow and see what he's found out. Then I suppose we just wait for the shit to hit the fan with Burton.'

They didn't have to wait long. Twenty minutes later, as Dan was about to leave to pick up a takeaway for dinner, Burton and Shepherd arrived on the doorstep.

The detective inspector looked like she was ready to breathe fire but Shepherd simply nodded as Emma stood back to let them in.

Dan and Ed sat side by side on one sofa but Burton and Shepherd didn't sit. Instead they loomed over them, making the room seem very small. Dan kept his eyes on the floor, not knowing what to say to appease the two detectives. In the end Shepherd spoke first.

'Nice place you've got here,' he said to Emma, who smiled. He earned a glare from Burton.

'Well?' she demanded of Dan and Ed.

'Well what?' asked Dan, playing for time.

'Don't give me well what!' Burton exploded. 'I don't seem to be able to get through to you, do I?' She paused and Dan took advantage.

'Sorry,' he began but Burton cut across him.

'Sorry? Sorry? That's not going to cut the mustard when I have to arrest you for breaking and entering!'

'We didn't really break in. The office door wasn't locked.'

'Trespassing then. How did you get into the building?' It was impossible to imagine Burton looking any angrier as she scowled at them with her hands on her hips. Dan and Ed looked at the floor.

'We watched people going in and out of the door and memorised the access code,' Dan mumbled. The expected tirade didn't start and Dan raised his eyes.

Burton's cheeks were flushed. She was desperately trying to control her temper.

Shepherd spoke instead. 'That's quite clever. Still trespassing and theft, but clever nonetheless.' He earned a second glare from his boss.

'I tell you to stay out of the way but what you actually do is trespass into the town hall, break into a councillor's office and copy files from his computer. I take it that's what you did.'

'Yeah, but it was totally worth it,' Ed broke in. A look from Burton stopped him in his tracks.

'Emma, I never thought you would be so stupid as to get involved like this.'

Emma perched on the arm of the sofa. 'Sorry, but I agree with Ed. It is totally worth it. We managed to open a password-protected file and it's got accounts showing how much money Edmonds has made from the scam.' Burton opened her mouth to respond but closed it again. 'I know that's technically hacking but if it solves the case it's worth it, isn't it?' Emma continued, turning pleading eyes on Burton.

'What does it prove?' Burton asked.

'They're being paid to pass planning applications,' Dan said. 'And Edmonds more than likely had Wilton and Buttle killed because they wanted out. He might have even killed them himself.'

Burton was thinking fast, her face creased in a frown. 'If we could find evidence that they wanted out,' she said quietly to Shepherd.

'It certainly explains where Wilton got the money to pay off those debts,' Shepherd replied in an undertone.

'Let me show you what else we've got,' Ed jumped to his feet but Burton raised a hand like a traffic warden directing traffic to stop him.

'No, don't. You came by it illegally, and if we know about it, I'll have to arrest you for trespassing and theft.' Burton paced the room, hands on hips. 'OK, for the final time, leave this alone. You've already pointed out that two people have died because of it. Leave it alone.'

Dan reluctantly agreed and Burton swept from the house followed by Shepherd.

'What a bloody mess,' Burton said, as they got back into the car.

Shepherd frowned. 'What if we came by that information legally, sir?'

'What do you mean?'

'Edmonds reacted really oddly when we offered to examine his computer before, almost as if he had something to hide.'

Burton was smiling. 'Go on.'

'Why don't we seize his computer officially? Pretend we want to check it for prints or something and search it to see if anything is missing, and just happen to come across the files? That way if we find anything it'll all be legit.'

'And we already know there's something to look for because of these guys,' said Burton slowly, jerking her thumb towards the front of Emma's house.

'Exactly.'

'Good plan.'

Chapter 50

'Why are we meeting here?' Dan asked looking around the crowded coffee shop. The tables were close together, which would make talking privately difficult. The café was also full of pre-school mothers and their screaming small children. Already Dan felt like his head was going to explode.

'Security has been tightened at the town hall,' Richard Drimble said, setting down a coffee for Dan and a camomile tea for himself. 'Since the break-in –' he looked at Dan – 'You've been in the wars,' he said, indicating the plaster on the side of Dan's head.

'It's not as bad as it looks.' Dan frowned. 'Why did you want to meet? Our last conversation wasn't very friendly.'

Drimble pulled a face. 'I wanted to apologise for the way I spoke to you. It was unprofessional.'

'You told me never to come near the town hall again.'

'I can only say how sorry I am. I was under a lot of pressure. James Wilton had just been killed and people were looking to me for answers that I just didn't have. It's no excuse but I suppose I just took it out on the first person I came across.' He smiled and blew on his cup of tea. 'I hope you'll accept my apologies.'

Dan peered into Drimble's cup as he set it down, wrinkling his nose. 'What is that?'

'Camomile tea. I've not been sleeping well so I've stopped drinking tea or coffee to see if it helps.'

'And does it?'

Drimble poked at the dark circle under his left eye. 'What do you think? I'll just be glad when all this is over.'

'So your sleeplessness isn't a guilty conscience?'

Drimble sighed. 'My only guilt is that I didn't help James Wilton. I might have been able to save him. The police are being impossible. You were right that I've been carrying out an internal investigation and they've told me to stop, but I don't know if I can. I don't know if I want to.'

Dan blew of his coffee. 'What have you found out so far?' he asked, trying to keep his voice light.

'Very little. I had my suspicions about a couple of applications but, with James gone, I lost my potential main source.' Drimble spread his hands wide. 'No one else seems to want to talk to me.'

'They've closed ranks?'

'Exactly. Now Buttle and Sanderson are gone so I can't ask for their help.' Drimble stared into his cup and then said, 'How's your investigation going?'

Dan looked at him. 'I didn't say I was investigating anything.'

'Oh, come on, you came to my office asking all kinds of questions about planning, implying that you know something. Don't tell me you just gave up.'

Dan paused, not sure what he should say.

Drimble gave a snort. 'Another person who won't talk to me. David Edmonds is the only person who will and he's driving me crazy.'

'What's he doing?'

'He keeps going on and on about his break-in, demanding increased security but then blocking the police when they try to help.'

Dan flicked at a piece of sugar wrapper on the table. 'Was anything taken?'

'Not that I know of.' Drimble raked a hand through his greying hair. 'I'm so frustrated by this wall of silence. It's like they're all afraid of something.'

'Or someone.'

Drimble looked up and met Dan's eyes steadily. 'What do you mean?'

'You might want to ask yourself who could be keeping everyone quiet.'

'You mean David?'

'That's your assumption. But you also might want to ask Councillor Sanderson for his thoughts.'

Drimble chuckled without humour. 'That would be a great idea if he hadn't gone missing.'

Dan spluttered into his coffee and slopped some onto the table. 'Missing? Who told you that?'

'The police did. I had to announce it to the staff yesterday. Everyone was very upset. He was a popular man.'

Dan looked up from where he was mopping the table with a napkin. '*Was* a popular man?'

'The police found his car in the woods with blood on the driver's seat. They didn't say how much blood but you assume the worst, don't you?'

'They don't know what happened?'

'They're searching the woods as we speak looking for clues.'

Dan sat back and stared into space.

Drimble rapped on the table to get his attention.

'What? What is it?'

Dan drained his coffee mug. 'I've got to go. All I'll say is look at the planning applications and see if you see the same pattern I did.' He got to his feet. 'That's what Burton and Shepherd are investigating.'

He picked up his bag and walked away, weaving through the tables.

Dan was pacing the floor waiting for Ed and Emma when they got home from work. His nervous energy made them both realise something was up.

'What did he tell you?' Emma asked, hanging her coat up on the peg beside the door. Dan quickly related the conversation about Sanderson.

'Oh, bollocks,' said Ed.

'You don't think he's killed himself?' Emma asked.

Ed looked horrified. 'Was it my fault? I did push him before that meeting.'

'No. I think he's gone to ground. You said he looked really scared and that Drimble and Edmonds chased him after the meeting. He's probably disappeared so everyone will leave him alone.'

'But what about the blood in the car?' Emma asked.

'That's easy to fake. We need to check the time of the email he sent to Ed.'

'Do you think Sanderson had anything to do with Wilton's death?' Ed asked.

'My gut instinct says whoever killed Wilton also killed Buttle and I can't see Sanderson doing that. I think he really did love her.'

'But what if she was going to get him done for fraud? We've seen the sums of money they were making. That's quite a reason to shut someone up,' said Emma. Dan grimaced and shook his head.

'Sorry, I still don't see Sanderson as a killer. He seems a bit too soft to kill someone, especially the woman he's having an affair with.'

Emma shrugged. 'I think he's capable of it. Men have killed their mistresses before. Anyway, did you find out anything else from Drimble?'

'Not really. He said he's getting stonewalled by everyone.' He paused and frowned.

'What?'

'I don't know. I got the impression that he was trying to get information out of me. He seems really frustrated but I'm not sure exactly about what.'

'The murders at the council would be a good starting place,' Emma said, a puzzled expression on her face. 'I thought that would be obvious.'

Dan shook his head irritably. 'I can't explain it but I didn't want to tell him anything.'

'Why?' Emma asked.

'There's was something about the timing of him asking to meet me. Last time he ordered me off council property and said not to come back. Now he's asking me for coffee and being nice.'

'Maybe he was trying to work out whether you were going to publish anything and try to stall you?' Ed suggested.

'I don't know.' Dan rubbed at his eyes with his knuckles. 'I had the impression he was perhaps pretending he didn't know anything, to try and get me to tell him.'

'You think he was just trying to find out what we know?'

'He was making a big deal about Edmonds and how he must be mixed up in this because of the prowlers in his office.'

'He didn't know it was you then?' said Ed with a laugh.

'Obviously not. He seemed to think Edmonds was creating a scene but nothing was actually missing from his office.'

'That's good. They don't know that we took stuff,' Emma said.

'Told you,' replied Ed.

'Either that or they don't want anyone to know that stuff was taken,' Emma said.

Dan explained about Drimble being forced to give up his internal investigation by Burton.

Ed puffed out his cheeks. 'Do you think that will stop him?'

'No, but I think we leave him to it. We need to try and find Sanderson,' Dan said.

'Find out if he's finished his thinking, you mean?' Ed asked.

'Exactly. We just have to hope that Drimble and Edmonds don't get to him first for their separate reasons.'

'One to look out for him, the other to potentially kill him, you mean?' Emma asked.

'Exactly. How was the office?' Dan asked.

'Daisy is still grumpy.'

'Oh, dear ... missing me, is she?' Dan pulled a face.

'She's pissed off that I can't work the crime beat because Burton won't talk to me officially, and it means she's got to keep a really close eye on the juniors to make sure they don't mess anything up.' Dan scowled. Emma laughed. 'Don't be sulky, it doesn't suit you.'

Ed laughed. 'At least the juniors can't be let loose at court, so I'm safe for now. Although that security guard who fancies you ...' Ed grinned at Dan. 'He keeps asking after you.'

'Glad I don't need to go to court any time soon.'

'He'd have loved it if you were up for murder.'

'Shut up.'

'If you're quite finished with your saucy talk.' Emma was holding out a brown A5 envelope to Dan. 'You've got mail. Daisy said it arrived yesterday but she hadn't had a chance to try and send it on to you.'

Dan looked at the front of the envelope. It had been fully addressed but not stamped.

'Is it weird that it was hand delivered?'

Ed shrugged. Dan ripped open the top of the envelope and pulled out a single sheet of A4 paper folded once in half. Dan read the typed words and handed it to Emma who read it aloud.

'Meet me in Coppin Woods at six o clock tomorrow evening. Come alone. No police. It's very important that I speak to you.' She frowned at the piece of paper and then turned it over to look at the back. 'That's it? That's all it says?'

Dan held up the empty envelope for her to look at.

'Who's it from?' Ed asked.

Emma peered at the signature. 'I think it says Sanderson,' she said, looking at Dan.

'That's what I thought too.'

Ed looked from Dan to Emma and back again. 'Why has he written to you?'

'He doesn't have my mobile number.'

'But why didn't he email me? It's me he's been in touch with,' Ed said.

'I don't know.'

'He obviously doesn't know that you're not in the office,' Emma said. 'That letter could have been there for days if Daisy hadn't seen it.'

Ed frowned. 'What are you going to do?'

Dan took back the letter and read it again, his stomach flickering. 'I'm going to meet him.'

'In the woods? Are you crazy?'

'I have to go. He says it's important. He might have more information for me.'

'Why would he want to meet in the woods? Do you think he's hiding out there?' Emma asked.

'Very possibly,' Dan said.

Ed snorted. 'Does Sanderson strike you as the roughing it type?'

'If he was hiding at home, Drimble or Edmonds would have found him by now and he wouldn't be missing, so he must be hiding somewhere else,' Dan said.

'But the police are combing the woods, so they'd have found him by now, wouldn't they?' Emma asked.

'Unless they're only searching near where his car was found,' Dan said. 'He could be hiding somewhere they're not looking at.'

'They're big woods,' Ed put in. 'Remember when we used to go in there, building dens?' he asked Dan.

'Yeah, we could have been lost for days.'

'Once we've dragged ourselves back from a trip down memory lane,' Emma said sharply. 'You can't seriously be considering going alone. Sanderson may have murdered Johanna Buttle and James Wilton. He could be dangerous.'

'Like I said, I don't think he killed anyone,' Dan said.

Emma punched him on the arm. 'No story is worth risking your personal safety,' she said loudly.

Dan smiled. 'That's why you've never made it to the nationals, Em. You're not prepared to go all out for a story.'

'I've worked at the nationals,' Emma said quietly. 'And I'm not prepared to go back to risking everything to beat someone else to an exclusive.'

'I didn't know you'd—' Dan began but Ed cut across him.

'Em's got a point. We don't know much about this guy or what he might do.'

'But when I break this story, it'll be no more fuchsia shows or who made the best jam. Daisy will have to give me better jobs and then I'll be off to the nationals.'

'She won't be able to give you better stuff if you're dead,' Emma shouted. 'Why can't you get it through your thick head that this is a huge risk?'

But Dan turned his back. 'I'm going to get changed. I've got a date at six.'

As he left the room Emma gave a frustrated squeal.

'Best leave him to himself,' Ed said, sitting down on the sofa. 'Once he's got his stubborn face on there's no talking to him.'

At five fifty-five, Dan got out of the car at Coppin Woods car park. He leaned back inside and said to Ed, who was in the driver's seat, 'I'll give you a call when I need picking up.'

'Why don't we come with you?' Emma asked from the back seat. She moved to open the door but Dan put his hand against it.

'No, he said come alone. If he sees you, he might get spooked and run.'

'We'll just wait here then.'

'No, he might see the car. Just drive away and I'll shout when I need you.'

He slammed the door and walked away. Emma watched him from the back window of the car as Ed executed a neat three-point turn.

'Why do I feel like we're making a huge mistake letting him go alone?' she asked.

Dan began to pick his way through the trees. He'd started off on the path, but after checking his watch soon realised that going through the trees would get him there quickest. Daylight was fading fast and he soon wouldn't be able to see where he was going. He tried to move quietly but a raised tree root caught his foot and he fell heavily.

'So much for a stealthy approach,' he said to himself as he got to his feet brushing leaves off his jeans. The trees were now shutting out any daylight that remained and he switched on the flashlight app on his phone to see whether any more roots were coming up. He soon switched it off as he got closer to the clearing. He didn't want to wait in the middle of the clearing so he crept around the edge to watch for Sanderson to arrive. He checked the time on his watch. Sanderson was late.

Suddenly a heavy weight hit him from behind and he went sprawling on his face. A man leapt on his back, pinning him to the ground. Dan tried to breathe but all he got was a mouthful of dirt and dust. He coughed and struggled but the man's weight was pressing down on him. His arms were spread at right angles to his body and the man's knees were digging into his shoulders.

'Don't fight or I'll dislocate both your shoulders,' a rough voice said close to his ear. Dan heard the sound of a flick knife being opened and waited for the pain of it being used.

A hellish scream ripped through the quiet evening air. There was a solid thud and the weight fell from Dan's back.

'Quick!' yelled Ed, grabbing Dan's arm and trying to haul him to his feet. 'He's only stunned.' A heavy log lay on the ground near to where the man was struggling to his knees, shaking his head to clear it. Dan staggered to his feet.

'Where did you come from?'

'You didn't think we'd let you come on your own, did you?' Ed grinned.

The man was reaching into his jacket. They saw a flash of metal and a gun appeared in his hand. He pointed it at them, but Emma charged over from his left hand side and kicked him hard in the arm. The gun flew into the undergrowth. The man gave a yell and dived after it.

'Run!' yelled Ed. He grabbed Dan's arm, dragging him along behind him. All three sprinted into the trees as best they could. Crashing sounds behind them told them the man was in pursuit, with or without the gun.

'Shit, where's Em?' Dan yelled, glancing over his shoulder.

'Get back to the car. I'll go and find her.' Ed darted away through the trees. There was a whistling noise and bark exploded from a tree close to Dan's head.

He zigzagged away trying not to lose his bearings and miss the car park altogether.

He heard two more shots, a woman scream and a heavy thud. He skidded to a halt at the edge of the car park, peering back to see where the others were.

Suddenly Ed exploded from the trees to his right, running and carrying Emma over his shoulder.

'Shit!'

'Get the bloody car started!'

Ed threw the keys at Dan, who raced to the driver's door and leapt in. His hands were shaking so badly he didn't think he'd be able to start the engine.

'Is she … is she hit?' he asked as Ed wrenched open the back door and bundled Emma inside.

'I don't know. Just drive!'

Dan's three-point turn was a haze of dust and squealing tyres and he roared onto the main road.

Chapter 51

Councillor David Edmonds' phone gave a sharp staccato ring, making him jump. He snatched up the receiver.

'Hello, sir, it's the front desk. The police are here for you.'

Edmonds froze. 'What?' he whispered. He'd thought he was safe. His heart thumped. 'What do they want?'

'They say they'd like a quick word.'

Edmonds paused. He had no choice. 'OK, send them up.' He placed the phone back in its cradle and stared at it for a moment.

What on earth could the police want now? That bloody fool must have messed up the job. What if he'd been caught? What if he'd talked? But just as Edmonds got to his feet, a loud knock echoed around the room.

'Hello, Councillor Edmonds,' said Burton stepping inside the room. Shepherd appeared behind her like a bulky shadow.

'What do you want?' Edmonds asked, sinking back into his chair trying to cover up his shaking knees.

'There's more to all this than meets the eye, isn't there?'

'More to what?'

'This latest incident.'

'I don't know anything about anyone being attacked.'

Burton's eyebrows shot up and she looked at Shepherd. 'Who's been attacked?' she asked.

Edmonds stared. 'I … I don't know,' he blustered. 'I just assume when you come striding in here that something like that has happened.'

The detectives looked at each other and Edmonds took a deep breath.

'What is this about?' he asked.

'Your break-in,' said Shepherd. 'We've been told there have been a number of similar incidents where nothing appeared to have been taken but computers were targeted.'

'So?' Edmonds asked.

'We'd like to take your computer for analysis,' Shepherd explained.

Edmonds' fingers beat a rapid tattoo on the table. 'You want my computer? Why?'

'We're investigating two murders,' Burton said. 'James Wilton's computer was wiped when he was killed and we don't know whether the killer took the files away or just deleted them. It could have been the same person who went through your computer.'

'You mean he might not have found what he was looking for from Wilton?' Edmonds asked. 'Why would you think that I would have the information? I have nothing to do with the planning department.'

'We're just considering all our options,' Burton said.

'Can we take your computer?' Shepherd asked.

Edmonds was silent for a moment. 'Do I have a choice?'

'You can say no but we'll just get a warrant and come back.'

The councillor frowned. 'What am I supposed to do without a computer?'

'I'm sure you'll manage,' said Shepherd approaching the desk and closing the laptop's lid with a click.

When Burton and Shepherd came back to the office from their lunch break, clutching takeaway coffees, the computer technician was slumped in a chair at one of the empty desks, tapping a pen against his chin and staring at the wall.

'Steve?' said Burton as she and Shepherd entered the office. The man started and jumped to his feet.

'Oh, you're back already. They said to wait here for you but that you might be a while.'

'Good of you to wait. I hope this means you have something for us.'

'Yes and no.'

Shepherd frowned. 'What do you mean?' he asked sitting in a swivel chair, which creaked ominously under his weight.

'I checked out that computer you gave me. They found several sets of fingerprints on it by the way. The information is in here.' He handed over an A4 envelope. Burton dragged out two sheets of paper stapled together.

'Hmmm, Edmonds' prints,' she muttered and then sighed. 'And Mr Sullivan's.' She passed the paper to Shepherd with a snort of irritation.

'Not smart enough to wear gloves,' remarked Shepherd.

'But, the computer,' Burton said, turning to the technician.

'Well, sir –' the man looked uncomfortable '– I don't think you're going to like this.'

'Why not?' Burton's eyes narrowed.

'Those files you said would be on it, they're not there.'

'What?'

'They're not on it. There was a lot of stuff to go through but those ones weren't there.'

Shepherd frowned. 'So where did Sullivan get that information from?' he asked, looking at Burton.

'Oh, he would have got it from the laptop,' the tech interrupted. 'It was there before but it's not there now.'

Burton and Shepherd stared. 'What?' Burton asked.

'They've been deleted but not very thoroughly.' The tech allowed himself a slight smile. 'They thought they'd cleaned it out properly but it didn't take long to find evidence of the files.'

'Where are they?'

'They've been deleted so that you can't actually see them but you can see where they were. Someone knew you were coming.'

'But how?' Burton turned to Shepherd. 'How did he know we were coming?'

'Maybe he deleted them to be on the safe side,' Shepherd said. 'If he knew someone had read the files and possibly made a copy of them, he thought he should get rid of it, just in case.'

'Can you tell if the files have been copied?' Burton asked.

'Sure, the computer's history will tell you that. It'll even tell you where it was copied to.'

Burton looked at Shepherd. 'So even if Edmonds doesn't know who's taken it, he knows someone has seen it.' She turned to the tech. 'Is there any chance you can recover the files?'

The man frowned. 'I can certainly try.'

'Brilliant, Steve. Let us know how you get on.'

As the door closed behind Steve, Shepherd got to his feet.

'Edmonds has some files on his computer which basically explain he was involved in the scam,' he said. 'Someone – and only we know who – broke into his office and copied the files onto a remote device.'

'We assume that he knows they've been copied but not by whom,' Burton said, watching Shepherd pace the floor.

'He knew we were interested in the files, so he deleted them to make sure no one sees them on his laptop. But he must have copies somewhere else, where no one can find them, for safe keeping.'

Burton grimaced. 'Let's just hope he doesn't work out who took them,' she said. Just then her mobile phone rang. She answered, spoke for a few moments and then hung up. 'Oh, for God's sake.'

'What's up?'

'You're not going to believe this.'

Chapter 52

'You just can't keep away, can you?' Dr Christine French's smile wasn't an entirely cheerful one. 'Not back in the wars again, are we?' she asked, raising an eyebrow.

'No, it's Emma this time,' Dan said. 'We think she's sprained her ankle.'

'And how did she do that?' asked the doctor, smiling at Emma. 'I need to take off your shoe.' Emma paled as the doctor moved her foot. 'Sorry,' said the doctor seeing her wince. 'How did it happen?' she asked.

'Well ...' Ed began but Dan cut across him.

'We went for a walk in the woods and she tripped.'

The doctor raised an eyebrow. 'Walking in the woods? In the dark?'

'We were out walking and didn't realise how quickly it was going to get dark,' Dan said glancing at Ed.

'We needed fresh air,' Emma interrupted. 'Long day at the office. I wasn't looking where I was going and I fell.'

The doctor didn't look convinced. 'I don't think it's broken,' she said examining Emma's ankle. 'But I'd like to get it X-rayed to be sure. It may take a while, but it's best to be on the safe side.' She left closing the curtain.

'Why didn't you tell her the truth?' Ed hissed.

'Do you want to explain to her that Emma got hurt when we were chased through the woods by a man with a gun?'

'Who the hell was he?' Emma asked.

'I didn't see his face,' Ed said. 'I was too busy running away.'

'Where did he come from?' Dan asked.

'He just appeared out of the trees. He was on top of you before I realised what was happening,' said Ed. 'I couldn't see what he was doing to you but I just grabbed that log and hit him with it. He saw me coming and he ducked so I didn't get him properly.'

'He definitely wasn't Paul Sanderson,' Emma added.

'Where did you guys come from? I thought you'd driven away.'

'We doubled back and parked in the same place. You didn't think we'd actually let you go to that meeting alone, did you?'

'Well, I thought that—'

'You could handle it and keep the story for yourself?' Emma's tone was sharp. 'I told you not to go alone and now I've been proved right.'

'We went through all this in the car. I admitted you were right.'

'OK, enough of this. Did he say anything?' Ed asked.

'Nothing, just threatened to dislocate my shoulders.' Dan rubbed his left shoulder and wincing. 'It's quite painful actually. I hadn't noticed until now. He had a knife too, I think.'

'It could have been much worse than some nice bruises in the morning,' Emma said with a shudder but Ed cut across her.

'It would appear that Sanderson lured you to the woods and then sent someone to kill you,' he said.

Dan looked at him. 'It appears?'

'We don't know for certain that letter did come from Sanderson. It was typed so there's no way of checking handwriting. Plus it was me who spoke to him at the planning meeting, so why didn't that letter come to me?'

'That's a good point,' Emma said.

'You think it might be someone else who did it?' Dan asked.

'That guy was pretty keen to kill all three of us,' Ed said. 'That makes me think we must have been looking in the right place and we must be getting close to the truth because someone doesn't want us investigating anymore.'

'Two more steps and the sofa is right behind you,' Dan said as he helped Emma to hop to the sofa.

'I can't believe we were at the hospital for so long,' Ed said, yawning.

'So much for NHS waiting targets,' Emma said with a laugh.

'I'll put the kettle on.' Ed headed into the kitchen.

'Are you really OK?' Dan asked, putting a cushion under Emma's ankle and propping it on the coffee table. She winced but smiled.

'I could get used to all this personal service. It's only a sprain.'

'I thought he'd shot you.' Dan sat down on the table facing her.

'So did I for a moment.' She almost laughed. 'I heard the crack and then I fell. Then my shoulder felt really hot, but it's just a bruise, look.' She slid her cardigan off her shoulder. Just below her right collarbone was a large purple bruise. 'I think I landed on a tree root,' she said grinning. 'Being shot would have been a bit more dramatic.'

'And potentially fatal,' Dan said quietly.

Emma was silent for a moment.

'I'm really sorry,' Dan rushed on. 'I should never have gone there. I risked all our lives and for what? We didn't find anything out.'

'What were you expecting to find out?'

'Sanderson might have been able to give us something new but it wasn't even him.'

'I thought it was him at first,' Emma said. 'But that bloke was too tall and slim to be him. It isn't your fault.' She reached out towards him but Dan got up and began to pace the room.

'Of course it's my fault. I got careless. I thought it was Sanderson, I didn't think he would send someone to try and kill me.'

Ed returned at that moment with three cups of tea and a packet of Penguin biscuits clamped in his mouth.

'Mate, you couldn't have known that it wasn't Sanderson. We all thought it was. But next time you get invited to a meeting in the woods at night, just say no.'

'I got cocky and I nearly got us all killed.'

'It wasn't cocky,' Emma said and then paused. 'Well, maybe a bit cocky, but maybe we should be focusing on what we do next.'

'It doesn't make sense,' said Emma. 'Why would Sanderson send Ed that email, giving us the ammunition to blow the scam wide open, and then send someone to kill us? He just wouldn't do that. What would be the point?'

'Maybe he regretted telling us,' said Ed. 'He might have changed his mind about making the story public.'

'But he didn't need to have us killed to do that,' Emma said. 'He could have just contacted you and asked you to hold off on the story.'

Ed snorted. 'Come on, Em, you're a journalist. Would you sit on something like this?'

'You have a point. No, I wouldn't. But he must know that we don't have enough or we'd have published by now.' She paused and Dan stood up.

'All I wanted was a big story to get my teeth into,' he said, walking to the end of the room. 'I never wanted us to get shot at, pushed down stairs or run over.'

'Ever heard the phrase "be careful what you wish for"?' Emma grinned.

'Let's think this through logically. Who would want to stop you from finding out more for the story?' Ed asked.

'Any number of people in this case.' Dan sighed.

'Fair point. We've established that Sanderson has probably told us everything from his side, so it has to be Edmonds,' Emma said.

'It could be the question mark on Edmonds' list,' Ed added.

'You think there's another person involved?'

'I suppose we have to assume that there is,' Dan said.

'But if Edmonds is running the scam, then there may not be anyone else.'

'Burton isn't going to like this,' Emma said.

'I don't care, we have to tell her,' Dan said. 'That guy nearly killed you.

'I say we turn over the note and leave it all up to them,' Dan said.

'What? No story?' asked Ed.

'We can't give up now!' Emma sat forward.

'Em, you nearly got shot! A maniac with a gun chased us through the woods. I think we have to play it safe now.'

'But what about the story?' Emma said. 'We don't have enough to run it. We need more.'

Dan stared at her. 'I dunno, Em, the more I think about it, the more I wonder if it's worth it.'

'Come on, it's your big story. You can't quit now. We need to find out who the mystery person is. I hate leaving loose ends.'

Dan smiled grimly. 'Unfortunately I think the person who runs this scam is thinking exactly the same thing. But in their case, we're the loose ends and I don't want to get tied up any time soon.'

A couple of hours later a knock at the door roused Dan from where he'd fallen asleep on the sofa.

Burton and Shepherd stood on the doorstep taking in Dan's rumpled hair and extremely creased T-shirt.

'You didn't need to dress up for us,' Burton said, raising an eyebrow as Dan showed them through into the living room.

'Sorry, you just woke me up.'

Burton looked down onto one of Emma's sofas where Ed's fair head stuck out of a sleeping bag. He hadn't moved.

'Sleeping like a baby,' said Shepherd with a grin.

'A bomb could go off next to his head and he wouldn't hear it,' Dan said. The third prod of Shepherd's meaty fingers woke Ed, who jumped about a foot when he saw the detective standing over him.

'Blimey, where did you two spring from?' he demanded, pulling his sleeping bag up primly over his T-shirted chest.

'We got your message,' Burton nodded at Dan. 'I'd have preferred you to come to the station but we were passing.' She perched on the other sofa and Dan hovered in front of the TV. 'Well? We're waiting.'

Dan told the detectives about the letter and the meeting in the woods. Both sat in silence until he'd finished, although Burton made an angry sound in her throat when he mentioned being shot at. When Dan had finished, there was a silence. It was Shepherd who broke it.

'You're telling me that you went to a meeting in the woods at night? What kind of stupid idea is that?'

'We ... I thought it was Sanderson. He's usually pretty friendly, he'd already shared some stuff with us and I thought he wanted to talk about it.'

'But you weren't sure it was him?'

'I was as sure as I could have been.'

'Do you still have the note?' Burton asked.

Dan pulled it from his bag. 'It seemed like a good idea at the time,' he said quietly.

'But it wasn't Sanderson?' Burton passed the note to Shepherd.

'No, it definitely wasn't.'

'Did you get a look at him?'

'He jumped me from behind so I was face down. Once I was up I didn't hang around long enough to really look at him.' He looked at Ed who looked back at him with a shake of the head.

'He was tall, well, about two inches taller than Dan.' Emma's voice from the stairs made them all jump. She was delicately hopping down the stairs.

Shepherd crossed the room, seized her under the armpits and carried her across to the sofa, seating her next to Ed.

'Oooh!' Emma cried, looking flustered.

Shepherd grinned and took up a standing position at the bottom of the stairs with notebook in hand.

'You saw him?' Burton asked.

'Yeah, when he dived on Dan. He was quite thin but wiry, strong enough to knock Dan down easily.' She thought for a moment. 'He was mostly bald with a few strands of hair on top and he had a thin face.'

'What was he wearing?' Burton asked.

Emma frowned. 'It was very dark and he had dark clothes on. That's why we didn't see him until the last minute. There was only moonlight in that clearing.'

'Good job we had that,' Ed agreed.

'I think he had a black cloth coat on,' Emma said. 'It didn't make any noise like a leather coat would have done.'

'Anything else?' asked Shepherd.

'Yeah, he smelt funny.'

'Smelt funny?'

'Kind of a damp smell, like his coat had been wet and hadn't dried properly.'

'He smelt damp?' Dan asked. 'I didn't notice anything like that.'

'I noticed when I kicked the gun out of his hand. I was quite close to him.'

'I hit him with a tree branch to get him off Dan,' Ed put in. 'And when we ran away he started shooting at us.'

All three journalists looked quietly at the floor.

'You realise how lucky you were,' Burton said. All three nodded. 'OK, this is how it's going to be. You're all going to stay here—'

'What about work?' Ed protested.

'You'll just have to miss work. I need you to stay away from this.'

'Do you have any suspects?' Emma asked, as Burton got to her feet, smoothing her suit jacket.

'Several, and at least one has just leapt to mind,' Burton replied.

Chapter 53

David Edmonds' hands shook. 'What do you mean he got away?'

The man looked up at him. A chunk of blood stained cotton wool was clamped to the back of his head.

'He got away. You said he'd be alone.'

'He was supposed to be.'

'Well, he wasn't. I had Sullivan on the ground, right where I wanted him, when one of his mates popped up and clobbered me over the head with a chunk of tree branch.'

'Why didn't you chase them?'

'I did. Have you ever tried to chase three people through the woods in the dark? I thought I'd got one, the girl, but it was too dark to get a clear shot at her.' The man paused and peered at the cotton wool, prodding at the wound with a dirty finger, testing to see if it had stopped bleeding.

Edmonds wrinkled his nose in disgust.

'So what's next?' the man asked.

The councillor paced the office, trying to think fast. What was he going to do? He had failed to get rid of Sullivan again. The news would not be well received.

'Have you had your head checked?' he asked, trying to buy some time.

'Nah, I don't want no one asking questions. Besides, it's not that bad.' He paused. 'What do we do next?' he asked again.

'I don't know,' Edmonds admitted. 'Look, you get home and rest. I need to think. I'll be in touch if I need you again.'

The man got up and moved towards the door. Then he turned back and cleared his throat. Edmonds looked up. The man raised his eyebrows.

'Oh, yes.' Edmonds picked up a bulky envelope from the desk and threw it to the man. 'It's all there.'

'Cheers, guv.' The man glanced back as he went out of the door. Edmonds had slumped into his chair, staring dejectedly at the desk.

The door clicked shut and Edmonds sighed into the silence of his office.

It had all seemed so simple and it was all working out right until that one bloody application. Then that reporter started to stick his nose in, asking questions and, worse still, he seemed to have nine lives. Now he was going to have to admit he had failed again. He wasn't looking forward to this conversation but it was best to get it over and done with. He seized his mobile phone and began to look up the familiar number.

Burton rapped on the thick oak office door.

'We seem to be spending a lot of time at the town hall, sir,' Shepherd remarked.

'You tempted to become a councillor?' Burton replied.

'Nah, I could never get used to the politics.'

Burton laughed and rapped smartly on the door a second time.

'Come in,' said a distracted voice. As they opened the door David Edmonds was throwing a lump of cotton wool into the bin. Parts of it were stained red. Shepherd looked at Burton.

'Hurt yourself, Councillor Edmonds?' he asked, pointing to the bin.

'Bit of a nose bleed,' said Edmonds sniffing. 'Nothing serious.' He turned towards his desk and knocked over a coffee mug. Liquid spilt across the surface. 'Oh, shit!' he yelled, grabbing some tissues from a box and trying to stem the flow. Shepherd glanced at Burton again.

'We're sorry to bother you,' Burton began, making no effort to help Edmonds who was desperately shifting papers and mopping at the coffee spillage. Her tone was that of someone about to announce bad news. 'But we've made some progress with the case.' She settled herself in a chair and smiled.

Edmonds' head snapped up to look at her.

'Oh?'

'Yes, we think some files were stolen from your computer.'

'Files were stolen? How do you know that?' Edmonds threw the handful of soggy tissue into the bin and sat down, his eyes never leaving Burton.

'Our tech guys found some deleted files.'

'What? How?'

'Our guys are experts in that kind of thing,' Shepherd put in. 'Apparently the computer keeps a record of the files in its memory even after they've been deleted. I think that's clever because it means you can never really lose anything.' He looked from Edmonds to Burton and back again. His tone seemed to be making Edmonds very nervous.

'Didn't you notice they were gone?' Burton asked.

'No. Well ... I ... no, I didn't.' But Edmonds couldn't quite meet the detective inspector's eye.

'The funny thing is, sir, that these same files were copied to a remote device at the time of your break-in.'

'They copied the files and then deleted them?' Edmonds asked.

'Interestingly no,' put in Shepherd. 'They weren't deleted until the day we asked to see your computer.'

'That's odd,' said Edmonds.

'I agree,' replied Shepherd. 'Where did the files go, Councillor?'

Edmonds' mouth opened and closed a few times like a startled fish.

'I have no idea.'

'You expect us to believe that some files vanished from your computer and you didn't notice?' Burton paused, but Edmonds said nothing. 'Who else has access to your computer?'

'I don't always lock my office door unless it's overnight so I suppose someone could have sneaked in. Do you know what was in the files?' Edmonds' eyes narrowed.

'At the moment, no. Any chance you could help us with that?'

'It can't have been anything important if I didn't notice it was gone,' said Edmonds. 'You said you'd made progress on the case. You know who actually broke in here?'

'Not yet,' said Burton. 'There were other fingerprints on it but we've not found a match yet.'

'Those files must have been important if someone sneaked in here to copy them, and then came back to delete them,' Shepherd said. 'Are you sure you don't know who it was?'

'Correct me if I'm wrong, but this is a crime and I'm the victim,' Edmonds said. 'Isn't it your job to solve it rather than just asking me?'

Shepherd's face darkened at the other man's tone. 'Yes, sir, it is and we will solve it, but if you're honest with us the culprits will be caught a lot quicker.'

'At present the murder cases are our top priority, which I'm sure you can appreciate,' said Burton, with a warning look at Shepherd.

'Yes, yes of course.' Edmonds looked awkward for a moment. 'Are you any closer to solving either of those?'

The detectives looked at each other. 'We're following a number of leads,' said Burton.

Edmonds snorted. 'Not doing very well at all, are you?' he said.

Shepherd took a quick step forward but Burton stood up and stopped him. When Shepherd backed off, she sat back down.

'We think they might have been killed because of their association to the planning department, so we're looking into that,' Burton said.

'And we're looking into everyone else connected with that department,' said Shepherd, his dislike of Edmonds clearly showing in his face.

'You see, we've heard allegations that both Buttle and Wilton were involved in some kind of cash-for-applications fraud and the more we find out, the more elaborate it seems,' Burton continued.

Edmonds stared at her in silence.

'We don't think they were acting alone and we're going to be questioning everyone connected to planning.'

'I've never been on the planning committee,' Edmonds said quickly.

'And yet you attend almost every meeting,' Shepherd remarked.

Edmonds' cheeks flushed.

Burton got to her feet. 'We've still got a lot of work to do, but we'll be in touch soon, I've no doubt,' she said.

'In touch with me? Why?' Edmonds blustered.

'Like I said, we're speaking to everyone involved with planning and I have the feeling we're close to a solution.'

'It's weird how she gets those feelings.' Shepherd held Edmonds' gaze. 'And she's nearly always right.'

The detectives both moved towards the door. 'I'm sure you're a busy man,' said Burton. 'We'll let you get on.' She ushered Shepherd to the door but then turned back. 'Oh, one more thing ...'

'Yes?'

'Don't leave town, will you?'

She closed the door with a click that echoed around the silent room, leaving Edmonds staring after them.

'Don't leave town?' Shepherd asked outside the door. 'You've been watching too much American crime drama, sir.'

Burton laughed. 'I've always wanted to say that,' she said. Her mobile phone suddenly burbled in her pocket as they walked down the corridor.

'Yes, Steve?' he said. The tech on the other end of the phone spoke for a couple of minutes. 'Damn it!' Burton swore under her breath. 'No, no, Steve, it's not your fault. Is there anything else you can do? Well, let me know if you do.' She slammed the phone's leather cover shut.

'What's up, sir?'

'They found those deleted files and opened them but the bloody things were empty.'

'Empty? How?'

'Someone deleted the contents before deleting the actual file. Clearly they're cleverer than we thought.'

Chapter 54

Pamela Sanderson was startled by the ringing telephone. No one usually rang at this time of the morning. It was almost ten o clock. Perhaps it was Paul, but she wasn't hopeful. He'd left her to fend entirely for herself. The voice on the other end wasn't one she recognised.

'Hello, can I speak to Paul Sanderson?'

'No, he doesn't live here.'

'Oh.' The voice sounded disappointed. 'Sorry to have bothered you.'

'I'm his mother, can I help?'

'You might be able to,' said the voice. 'My name is Ed Walker, from the *Allensbury Post*. I had an appointment with him today to do an interview for a story but he didn't turn up and I can't get hold of him on his mobile. I've been trying to find his home number.'

'You won't find him in the phone book, he's ex-directory. What is the story about?'

'Oh, it was just something about the planning committee,' said Ed. 'Do you know where he is?'

'Unfortunately no, I've not seen him for a couple of days, since the last planning committee meeting oddly enough.'

'Did he usually come and visit you a lot?'

'Yes, he was very good at keeping me company. I have heard from him though.'

'You have?' Ed's voice was excited.

'Yes, he called me to say he was all right. He said whatever I heard, whatever anyone told me, that he was all right. It was a bit of an odd thing for him to say actually.'

'Did he say where he was?'

'No, he said he had to go away for a few days on business but he would be back soon. I told the police the same thing when they asked.'

'Oh, brilliant, could I leave a message for him then?'

'Yes, I've got paper and a pen.'

'Just tell him Ed Walker needs to speak to him urgently, he'll know what it's about.' Ed reeled off his mobile number.

'OK, I'll pass that on when I see him.'

'Thanks.' Ed hung up. He looked at Dan and Emma.

'What did she say?' asked Dan.

'He called her a couple of days ago.'

'So he's definitely not dead?' said Emma.

'He wasn't a couple of days ago and he called her after the police found his car.'

'I knew they were barking up the wrong tree,' Dan said.

'But why would he disappear?' Emma asked.

Dan frowned for a moment. 'Could he be behind the whole planning scam?' he asked.

'I thought you thought it was David Edmonds,' Ed said.

'But I keep coming back to the fact that he's not on the planning committee. If it is Sanderson then it fits together more logically. Ed freaked him out when he spoke to him at the meeting because Sanderson didn't realise how much we knew. He "disappears" once he knows we're looking into it, lures us to the woods and has someone try and kill us.'

'You're forgetting that he sent me that email after the planning meeting so he must have wanted us to have those papers,' Ed said.

'He usually seems so mild mannered,' Emma said. 'I thought we'd decided that he wasn't capable of murder.'

'Just because he didn't do it himself doesn't mean he didn't arrange it,' Ed remarked.

'I agree with Em,' Dan said. 'He doesn't seem the type, but maybe that's how he's getting away with it. You said he was pretty stressed at the planning committee and he would be if he was watching his scam fall apart in front of his eyes. The more I think about it the more I reckon he'd attack if he thought someone was trying to break up such a carefully covered up plan.'

'Do you think he killed James Wilton as well as Jo Buttle?' Emma asked.

Dan nodded. 'Buttle, yes, I think he did. She was about to reveal the whole scam to me, whether she was involved or not, and that would have been an end to the gravy train.'

'But they were having an affair, surely that would stop him from killing her?'

'Not necessarily. Maybe he wanted out and she wouldn't let go.'

'Or she wanted out and he wouldn't let go,' said Ed. 'Maybe her murder had nothing to do with planning?'

'That would be one hell of a coincidence, wouldn't it? Wilton is murdered for fraud and then Buttle, who's connected to Wilton, gets randomly killed by her lover who's also connected to planning? Their deaths are linked. They have to be.'

'Maybe he just couldn't take any more stress?' Ed suggested.

'But she had more to lose from the affair being found out,' Emma put in.

Dan ran his hands through his hair. 'We're not getting anywhere,' he said. 'I say we focus on finding Sanderson or at least finding out why he attacked us. That'll answer a lot of questions.'

Chapter 55

Burton pushed open the office door. It collided with Shepherd's meaty elbow and knocked a stack of papers from his hands.

'Bugger it,' said Shepherd, trying to catch the cascading papers.

'Sorry. What's that?'

'David Edmonds' bank records.'

'Anything interesting?'

Shepherd scooped up the papers and dumped them on the desk next to his which had some clear surface. 'Yup. You were right.'

'About what?'

'He has a lot of income. His business is doing very well, but there are some odd payments.' He started to sort through the papers and handed one sheet to Burton.

'Odd?'

'Yeah, there's some large sums being paid into his personal accounts here and there. Always roughly twenty thousand. Then he transfers it in pieces and I can't tell where it goes.'

Burton gave a low whistle.

'Offshore bank account, do you think?'

'I don't know. Maybe he's trying to avoid tax. Maybe he's hiding it from his wife.'

'He must have a fair amount stashed away. The payments are

regular, each month always around the same date. There's about eight or nine of them going back over the last year. There'd probably be more if we looked further back.'

'Any pattern to the payment dates?'

Shepherd smiled. 'It's usually just after planning meetings according to this calendar.' Burton smiled too.

'That would tie in with Sullivan's planning applications theory, wouldn't it?'

Shepherd nodded. 'Certainly suggests that Edmonds is involved in that, whatever he might have told us.'

Burton frowned. 'Involved in, or in charge of.'

Shepherd raised his eyebrows. 'In charge of? You think he's the brains of the outfit?'

'You said that the money gets transferred onwards from him in pieces? What if he's paying the other people involved?'

'You think he keeps a portion of it, but has to pay the others as well? That would certainly make sense.'

'He's powerful within the council, but how did he get two councillors – Sanderson and Buttle – who are straight arrows by all accounts, to join in something like this?'

'He knew about their affair. He told us that. Jo Buttle wouldn't have wanted that to come out because of her husband.'

'Good point. He must have had something on Wilton too.'

Shepherd nodded in agreement. 'But it seems risky to leave a paper trail like this. Why not pay the others in cash?'

'You wouldn't be able to take that much cash out of any bank, especially on a regular basis.'

'So the murders are definitely tied up with the planning scam.'

'Yes, I think Sanderson's disappearance is a bit too convenient.'

'Making a run for it before he's next?'

'Or to avoid being arrested for fraud and murder,' Burton said.

'What did you get from the mother?'

'She seemed more worried that he'd left her on her own than that he was being treated as missing. But then she told us she's heard from him and he said he was fine. Wouldn't tell her where he was but presumably he knew she would tell anyone who asked.'

Burton pondered for a moment. 'Was there anything that linked Wilton, Buttle and Sanderson, apart from the planning committee?'

'Buttle and Sanderson were having an affair, but Wilton kept himself to himself and they don't seem to have ever crossed paths outside work.'

'The only common denominator as I see it is David Edmonds. He must have known something about them all and used it to get them to commit fraud.'

'In other words, he uses blackmail to get them involved in passing the applications and then pays them to do it?'

'I agree that it's a bit weird. Clearly the vote is secured by blackmail but then they're rewarded financially.'

'But what does he get by bribing them, apart from a vote? Why would he need that?'

'Maybe he's paid by the housing construction companies if he can get the applications passed. He gets paid per application that gets passed.'

'And then he pays the others,' Shepherd said.

Burton nodded. 'We know Buttle wanted to get out by telling someone about the scam because she went to Sullivan. Whoever knew she was going to do that, obviously thinks that she told him everything because they killed her and started going after Sullivan.'

'They went after Sullivan before she told him anything.'

Burton stared out of the window for a moment. Then she stiffened. 'Sullivan had an email from Wilton, didn't he?'

'Yes.'

'And it contains planning application numbers?'

Shepherd nodded, smiling. 'Yes, so the person behind it suspects that Sullivan knows which applications have been involved, but presumably the list included applications that are coming up soon. He could report it to the standards board, or something like that.'

'He could just report it in the *Post*.'

'I don't think he could report on the scam unless he had proof of it, but they must think he knows enough to put the pieces together. They start trying to silence him,' Shepherd said.

'The attempts to stop him have got more and more desperate so it makes me think either he must be getting closer to the truth or someone thinks he's closer than he is.'

'Sullivan clearly thinks Paul Sanderson has something to do with it.'

'I know but I think he's barking up the wrong tree. It was too clumsy for that note to have actually come from Sanderson.'

'You mean the rest of it has been too slick so far?'

'Exactly. There wasn't a lot of forensic evidence at either killing, and we've never found the murder weapon that stabbed Wilton.'

'He might blame Sullivan for Buttle's death.'

'If he killed her himself?' Burton pulled a face. 'That doesn't quite stack up.'

Shepherd shrugged. 'I'm running out of theories.'

'We suspect that Buttle was involved in the fraud, but let's get hold of her financial records and see how involved she was.'

Peter Buttle looked a bit sheepish when he opened the door to Burton and Shepherd.

'Sorry I shouted at you last time.'

Shepherd smiled. 'Not to worry. We've had much worse.'

Buttle led the way into the kitchen where the table was covered in paperwork.

'I looked these out after you called,' he said. 'Help yourselves. Either of you want a cup of tea?' The detectives shook their heads. 'I seem to be existing on tea at the moment,' he said flicking the switch on the kettle.

Shepherd gave a slight smile. 'I know how you feel,' he said. 'I lost my wife too.'

'Murdered?'

'A hit-and-run.'

Buttle winced. 'Tell me, does it ever stop hurting?'

'Not really, but as time goes on you find that you can cope better with the pain.'

There was a slightly awkward silence and then Burton cleared her throat.

'Did you have joint accounts?' she asked pointing to the paperwork. Shepherd turned back to the pages on the kitchen table, looking uncomfortable.

'Yes. Everything we had we shared.' He paused. 'Well, I thought we shared everything.'

'Did your wife have any accounts in her own name?'

'Not that I knew of.'

'Knew? Past tense?'

'Yes. I found this while I was looking out all the paperwork. Most of it was together where I was expecting it to be, but I found this in another drawer.' He handed Shepherd a thick white A4 envelope, which showed their address through a cellophane window. Shepherd took it and pulled out the sheets. He whistled. 'No need to even go looking for the payments,' said Buttle sourly.

Shepherd held out the top piece of paper to Burton who peered at it. Her eyes widened.

'Mr Buttle, there's seventy-five thousand pounds in this account. How could you not have known?'

'I've never seen that paperwork before in my life.'

'The payments weren't being put through your joint account?'

'Certainly not that amount of money. Although Jo dealt with our personal accounts. I did the business accounts.'

Shepherd, who had picked up the previous month's current account statement, gave a quiet cough. 'Mr Buttle, have you seen this payment before?' He pointed to a credit of five thousand pounds.

'No, I … she never said anything about it. Where did it come from?'

'It doesn't say. It's just a number, not a name,' Shepherd said.

'Are there any more?' Burton asked.

'Same amount, same pattern. Transferred out straight away too. Look at the date,' said Shepherd under his breath to Burton. 'It was two days after the withdrawal from Edmonds' account.'

'What is going on?' asked Peter Buttle peering over Shepherd's shoulder in disbelief.

Burton took a deep breath.

'I'm sorry to have to tell you, Mr Buttle, but we think your wife was involved in a planning scam.'

'What? No, she wouldn't, she couldn't!'

'We think she and some of the other councillors were accepting bribes to pass certain planning applications that shouldn't have been passed.'

Buttle was staring with his mouth open. 'No, not Jo, surely. She wouldn't do something like that. I would have known. We shared everything.'

Burton and Shepherd exchanged a look. 'Not everything it would seem,' Shepherd said quietly. 'Can we take copies of these?'

'Yes, of course, there's a photocopier on the printer in the study.' He started towards a door leading off the kitchen.

'That's OK, I can manage,' Shepherd said, disappearing through the door.

'What happens now?' Peter Buttle asked Burton.

'We're still carrying out investigations.'

'I just don't understand why she did it. It wasn't like we were short of money,' said Buttle with a sour grin.

'We think someone may have forced her into it.'

Peter Buttle frowned. 'Who would do that? Why would they do that? Why would Jo let them do that?'

'We believe there were a number of councillors involved and that someone was using personal secrets to get them to participate.'

Buttle frowned. 'But what could they have on Jo? She had no secrets.'

'We're still looking into that,' Burton lied.

'She was so idealistic about trying to make a difference. Changing the council from the inside, that's what she always used to say. Making people trust councillors again.' Buttle forced an ironic laugh. 'She never gave a hint of being involved in corruption.' He spoke the word with disgust.

'Did she have anything happening in her personal life which could have been used to make her take part in this?'

'No, like I said we had no secrets.' Peter Buttle gave a short humourless laugh. 'Or at least I thought we didn't, but what would I know?'

Burton didn't know how to answer him. Both looked round as Shepherd stepped back into the room.

'The money will be seized as proceeds of crime but we'll be in touch about that in due course,' Burton said.

They left Buttle sitting there with his head in his hands.

'Did you tell him about Paul Sanderson?' Shepherd asked when they got outside.

'I didn't have the heart to do it,' Burton admitted. 'It'll come out in time.'

Shepherd nodded. 'And here's another thing.'

'What?' Burton asked as they climbed into the car.

'There's a lot more involved than nine applications. She had at least one other account with seventy-five grand in it and I suspect, if we dig, we'll find more.'

'Let's get digging,' Burton said grimly.

Chapter 56

'I can't believe Dan volunteered to do the shopping and cook dinner,' said Emma, flopping onto the sofa.

'I think it was an excuse to get out of the house. He feels like he's been cooped up for weeks,' Ed replied.

'It's only been a couple of days,' Emma laughed. 'He likes being active, doesn't he?'

'I wouldn't get too excited about dinner though. His speciality is beans on toast with cheese, and he usually burns that.'

Emma laughed. 'I miss working,' she said looking around the living room. 'The day feels wrong without it, and this place has never been so tidy.' She got to her feet and slowly limped to the bookcase. She began pulling out the books and putting them in alphabetical order.

'That's very obsessive compulsive,' Ed remarked with a grin looking up from the laptop screen. 'They look better in size order anyway.'

Emma laughed. 'I've got to have something to do,' she said. 'I'll go mad otherwise. What are you doing?'

Ed frowned. 'I'm trying to find some evidence that Paul Sanderson is behind this, something conclusive.'

'What if there isn't anything?'

'How do you mean?'

'What if Dan's right and Sanderson didn't do it?'

'He's flip-flopping around. I don't think he wants to believe Sanderson could have been behind it.'

Emma sighed. 'I suppose I'm just trying to play devil's advocate and say what if there isn't anything to prove conclusively it was Sanderson?' When Ed said nothing, she continued 'Think about how you'd sell it to Daisy as the story. How would you convince her of your argument?'

'I'd start by saying that we know Sanderson is on the planning committee.'

'That's pretty obvious.' Emma spoke with Daisy's slightly pompous 'Tell me the story' voice.

'I've started from the basics. From the details of certain planning applications, we believe a number have been passed fraudulently.'

'How many?'

'Eight or nine that we know of for certain, possibly more. James Wilton's email to Dan suggests he knew what was going on and he was changing the applications so that he could rubber-stamp them and they wouldn't have to come before the committee.'

'Where does Sanderson fit in?'

'Dan overheard a conversation between Buttle and Sanderson after the Elliot's Walk decision, saying their consciences were clear. Then they ran away from David Edmonds.'

'Does this really implicate Sanderson though?'

'James Wilton is murdered and Johanna Buttle gives Dan some information that proves Sanderson was part of the planning scam.'

'Part of the scam doesn't prove he's leading the scam though, does it?'

'OK, it suggests that he was involved and also that Jo Buttle was as well. Then she gets murdered.'

'OK, he is starting to look a bit suspicious.'

'I tackle him about it at a planning meeting, he freaks out and disappears. He then emails me with information that backs up our theory that he was involved in the scam.'

'While he's missing and presumed dead?'

'Yes, which proves he's not dead. He then pops up again to lure us to the woods for meeting and has someone try to kill us.'

'That's where your theory fails. Why would Sanderson give us information that proves there's a scam if he's part of it?'

'He tried to kill us. Or Dan at least, because he didn't know we would be there. He might have regretted giving us information that implicated him.'

'I still don't buy that he'd have tried to kill Dan more than once and then just give him the information that blows the scam open if he's spent so much time on it. It just doesn't fit. Plus he'd been working entirely with you and emailed the information to you. Why would he then write to Dan and ask him to go to the woods, without mentioning you at all?'

Ed frowned.

'She's got you there.' The door opened and Dan entered, hands full of shopping bags.

Ed tried to stand up to help him but he was waved away.

They heard him dump the bags with a thump onto the kitchen counter and then he returned to the sitting room, pulling off his jacket.

Ed slumped back into his chair, pulled up against table in the corner of the room.

'Do you have a better idea?' he asked.

Dan paused. 'I think it's David Edmonds.'

Emma stared at him. 'But he's not on the planning committee,' she said, frowning.

'He isn't, but he seems to have been at every meeting in the last year, even when it's not related to his ward. No one goes to planning unless they have to. Why has he been so interested?'

'Is it unusual for councillors to go to meetings where they aren't on the committee?'

Dan grinned. 'There speaks a woman who's never had to sit through a council meeting. They're usually so dull that even the councillors avoid them, unless they have to go because it affects their ward or their party or to boost their own meeting attendance figures.'

Emma considered for a moment. 'So you're saying there isn't really a reason for Edmonds to be there?'

'Unless he's in charge of the scam and was making sure everyone voted the way they'd been told to,' Dan said. 'In fact, judging from Buttle and Sanderson's reaction to that meeting where Elliot's Walk was passed, he's got to be in charge of the scam. They practically ran away from him as soon as the meeting was over and he seemed keen to get to them.'

Emma nodded. 'How do we prove it's him?'

'That's just the problem,' Dan said. 'I've got no idea.'

The desk sergeant looked up. The man in front of him was dishevelled and wild-eyed.

'I need to speak to DI Burton,' he said. 'I want to confess to a murder.'

Chapter 57

Burton looked at the man across the table. His chest heaved as he tried to draw breath.

The door opened and Shepherd entered with a cup of tea. He put it down in front of the man and deposited three sugars and a plastic stirrer beside it.

'Good for shock,' he said, sitting down. But the man shook his head. He stirred the tea twice but didn't take a sip. He continued to gasp for breath. 'Maybe I should have brought a paper bag as well,' said Shepherd, raising an eyebrow. Burton glared at him.

'So, Councillor Sanderson,' said Burton. 'You want to confess to a murder?' She leaned across the table. 'The question is, which one?'

Sanderson's head snapped up. 'What do you mean, which one? Jo's, of course.' His eyes filled with tears.

'You killed Councillor Buttle?' Burton glanced at Shepherd who raised an eyebrow.

'What I mean is that she's dead because of me.' Sanderson's voice tailed off into a sob.

Burton tried not to sigh audibly. 'Why don't you start from the beginning?'

'I liked Jo as soon as I met her.' Sanderson took a deep breath to steady himself. 'She was so pretty, but without really knowing it, y'know. She had such beautiful eyes and a warm smile.' He paused and stared off into the distance for a moment. 'She was such a good person too. I was getting pretty disillusioned with all the councillors who are only in it for themselves and their stupid party politics. Jo was different. She really cared about the people who voted for her.'

'When did your affair start?' Shepherd asked.

Sanderson looked startled for a moment. 'You know about that?'

'It seems to be common knowledge,' Shepherd replied.

'It was probably about six months after we met. I'd always liked her but I'd met her husband too and he's a great bloke. I didn't want to hurt anyone.'

'What changed?'

'It was one night after a late meeting. A group of us went to the pub for a quick drink and Jo and I got talking. People gradually drifted away and before we knew it we were on our own. We hadn't even noticed people leaving. We had quite a lot in common, mostly the way we wanted to use our positions as councillors.'

Burton raised an eyebrow.

'Use them to help people, I mean,' Sanderson added. He sighed. 'Nothing actually happened that night but we both knew it could. Then a couple of days later, it did.'

'What happened?' Burton asked.

'She kissed me and I didn't stop her. Well, you wouldn't, would you?' He looked at the detectives, appealing for their support. 'We didn't mean it to happen but then we couldn't stop.'

'That's what they all say,' Burton said, glancing at Shepherd. The detective sergeant's jaw had tightened.

'I don't think Peter found out and I don't think she would have left him.'

'You never asked her to?'

'It was discussed, but to be honest we were both happy with the current situation. I saw no reason to change it.'

'So you just carried on risking hurting her husband,' Shepherd said sharply. Burton ignored him.

'You're not married?' she asked Sanderson.

'No, I never met anyone I wanted to marry. I've never really been a fan of the whole institution, to be frank. But if I had got married, I'd have wanted it to be someone like Jo.' He sighed and fell silent. Shepherd's lip was curled in disdain.

'How did you come to murder her? Did you lure her to the hotel?' Shepherd asked.

'I didn't actually kill her …'

Burton got to her feet. 'Mr Sanderson, there's something called wasting police time.'

'What I mean is I might as well have done.'

'How do you mean?'

'Jo came to me in a blind panic. Someone had sent her an envelope with documents showing what was going on. They were threatening to release the information publicly if she didn't do something about it.'

'What did you do?'

'She wanted to put an end to the whole thing, to blow the whistle, but I tried to persuade her out of it.'

'Why?'

'It was mainly selfish. I wanted time to get my affairs in order in case it all did come out. I told her to wait a while and that we would talk it over.' He paused. 'I think I was going to try and persuade her to run away with me, somewhere safe, but before I had a chance to speak to her again she'd spoken to that reporter and handed all the information over to him.' He stopped and took a sip of his tea grimacing. 'Can't bear lukewarm tea.'

'What did you do when she told you she'd passed on the information?' Burton asked.

'I tried to persuade her to get it back, to tell the journalist that she'd changed her mind.'

'But she wouldn't?'

'No, she kept saying it was all for the best, that it would put an end to it.'

'You didn't agree?'

'This isn't something you walk away from. We'd made too much money from it, been involved for too long, for anyone to believe we'd been coerced. There was too much evidence.'

Burton leaned forward, resting her elbows on the table. 'What did you do?'

'Something I'll regret for the rest of my life.'

Up in the CID office, Burton was staring fixedly at the wall. Shepherd sipped his coffee and waited. When the governor was thinking, it was best to leave her to it.

'If it's not Sanderson, that puts David Edmonds in the frame, doesn't it?' Burton said. 'We know from Sanderson that Edmonds knew about the affair, and that he was using it as a way to control them and keep them involved.'

'Do you think that was the only reason they were staying? I'm sure the money was a nice little sweetener,' Shepherd said.

'You think they were just staying for the money?'

'I think Buttle had a lot to lose in hurting her husband, but that wouldn't have been half as damaging as the fraud. If they were such straight arrows, as we've been told, they'd never have got involved.'

Burton frowned. 'We need to find out more about where Councillor Edmonds was when the murders took place.'

'He seems to have alibis.'

'Let's see how watertight they are.' Shepherd waited silently. Burton drained her plastic cup of vending machine coffee, grimaced at the sharp taste of the contents and threw it towards the bin. It fell smoothly inside and she grinned. 'Right, let's go and have a word with Sanderson about the attack on Sullivan.'

They pushed open the door to the interview room. Paul Sanderson looked up.

'OK,' said Burton sitting down heavily. 'Just a few more questions. How well do you know Daniel Sullivan?'

Sanderson looked surprised. 'He's one of the *Post* reporters, isn't he? I've been interviewed by him a couple of times but I wouldn't say I knew him.'

'Why did you order someone to try and kill him?'

Sanderson's mouth fell open. 'Kill him? Me?' he stuttered. 'I didn't. Why would I?'

'You knew that he had all the information about the scam. Councillor Buttle made sure of that. You'd be in big trouble if he printed a story.'

Sanderson stared. 'But I wanted him to print it, once I was ready.'

'And if he'd decided to print it sooner than you wanted?'

Sanderson looked down at his hands clasped on the table.

Shepherd put a plastic bag on the table. It contained the note inviting Dan to the meeting in the woods. Sanderson peered at it and then looked at them.

'I didn't write that,' he said.

'It's signed by you.'

'That's not my signature,' Sanderson said peering at it. 'Not even close. Plus I would have handwritten the note, not typed it.'

'The personal touch?' asked Shepherd.

'You could say that.' Sanderson paused. 'This letter was sent to that reporter, was it?'

'Yes, and when he went to this meeting he was attacked and shot at. One of his friends was hurt.'

Sanderson sat up straight. 'Shot at? Why would you think that was me?'

Shepherd tapped the note.

'I don't even know anyone with a gun.' Sanderson looked desperately from one detective to the other.

Burton and Shepherd looked at each other and said nothing.

'Why would I want to kill a reporter?' Sanderson continued.

'If you thought the scam, and your part in it, was going to be exposed? We're talking about quite a serious fraud charge. How would you cope in prison?' Burton held eye contact until Sanderson looked away.

He frowned. 'I know how serious the charge is,' he snapped. 'I'd not spoken to Sullivan. I'd been dealing with one of his colleagues, Ed Walker, but to be honest I was trying to avoid them.'

'Why were they after you?'

'Not after me, as such, just wanting information. I didn't want to give it to them.'

'So you abandoned your car?'

Sanderson allowed himself a smile. 'The blood on the seats was inspired, wasn't it?'

'Yes, until our forensics lot got their hands on it.'

'You drive a black Audi, don't you?' said Shepherd.

'You know I do if your people have been all over it. Why?'

'A black Audi tried to run-down Mr Sullivan a couple of days after James Wilton died. You wouldn't know anything about that, would you?'

Sanderson stared. 'No, I wouldn't. Why would you think that?'

'The trip to the woods was the third time an attempt on his life was made that could be traced back to you.'

'It wasn't me.'

'A lot of people think you're dead,' Shepherd remarked.

'That was the plan. If they thought I was already dead, then they wouldn't try and find me.' He looked from one detective to the other. 'What happens now? You do believe me, don't you?'

Burton and Shepherd exchanged a look.

'I haven't made my mind up about the attacks on Mr Sullivan, but I'm arresting you for fraud. You'll be held in the cells for further questioning,' she said, getting to her feet. Shepherd followed her to the door. Looking back, Burton added, 'I'd get yourself a good solicitor. You're going to need one.'

Chapter 58

'Wow, your culinary skills are much better than Ed had me believe,' Emma said, as they tucked into chicken and red pepper risotto. 'This must have taken ages. It's lovely.'

Dan grinned. 'Oh yeah, ages,' he said, forking up a bit of rice.

'Mmmm, getting it out of the box can be really tricky,' Ed commented, nodding towards the 'ready to eat' packaging poking out of the kitchen bin.

'Oh.' Emma frowned. 'I thought you said you were making dinner.'

'This is about as close as I get.' Dan laughed, spearing a piece of chicken and pointing it at her. 'Otherwise there's too much of a risk of people getting food poisoning.'

Emma laughed. 'It's very well reheated,' she said, grinning.

'Thank you.'

Ed began poking at his rice, chasing a piece of chicken around the plate with his fork.

'Is it fighting back?' Dan asked, looking at him.

'Just a bit.' Ed finally stabbed the chicken rather hard and his fork squeaked on the plate. Both Dan and Emma winced. 'Sorry,' he said.

'What's the chicken ever done to you?' Emma asked.

'I was just thinking …'

'Poor innocent chicken,' Emma said.

Ed frowned at her. 'I was just thinking ...' he repeated. 'If Edmonds is behind this—'

'Hurrah, you're on board,' said Dan, through a mouthful of rice.

'Not quite. Why is Sanderson acting so weird, disappearing and then having us attacked in the woods?'

'The note was obviously fake and it was meant to look like Sanderson sent it,' Emma said.

'I still can't believe I fell for that,' Dan said, looking at Emma.

She smiled. 'No harm done.'

'So what's your theory?' asked Ed. 'How do we prove it was Edmonds?'

'Sanderson has disappeared because David Edmonds is after him,' Dan continued. 'Well, you would, wouldn't you?'

'Maybe he's acting strangely because his girlfriend has just been murdered,' Emma suggested. 'He can't grieve properly because they are only supposed to be colleagues.'

Ed continued to frown. At last he raised his hands in surrender.

'Well, I still don't like it, but I have to admit we're running out of other options. There's no one else left.'

'He must have used the affair as a way to get them involved,' said Emma. 'There's no other way he would have talked them into it.'

'He's not on planning though,' Ed said.

'Yeah, but we've seen how many times he attends the meetings, more than anyone would want to go to a planning committee. There's got to be a reason,' Dan said.

'He was keeping an eye on them,' Emma said. 'That's why Buttle and Sanderson ran away from him after the Elliot's Walk application got turned down. They knew they'd gone against him and he'd be furious.'

'It's ironic he picked the two most idealistic people to get involved in corruption,' said Dan.

But Emma was frowning. 'Hang on, the numbers don't add up,' she said.

'We're journalists,' Dan replied. 'We don't do maths.'

She laughed. 'No, the planning committee. There's eight members plus the chairman, and he has the casting vote in the event of a tie. If Edmonds was on planning they would be able to push through any decision, but there must be another person involved to give them a majority.'

'What are you saying?' Ed asked.

'We need to find that extra person,' said Emma. 'They're another loose end that would need tying up but if we get to them first we might get some answers.'

When Emma came into the living room, she found Ed sitting on the floor surrounded by sheets of A4 paper.

'What are you doing?' she asked.

Ed gestured around. 'I'm reviewing everything we know so far and something doesn't feel right.'

'Are you supposed to be a mind map?' Emma asked.

'Ha ha, very funny. But I think I found something.'

Emma sat down on the sofa looking over his shoulder and took the sheet of paper he held out to her. She skimmed through it and then looked back at him.

'What is this?'

'I'm glad you said that. I've not seen it before.'

'It's an email. Where did it come from?'

'I'm not certain but I think it came from the information that Johanna Buttle gave to Dan.'

Emma looked back at the page. 'Look at the name here,' she said, pointing. 'Bilton Lancaster? What sort of name is that?'

'It's certainly not one I've ever heard locally before and I've

324

worked for the *Post* for five years.'

'You can't be expected to know everyone, especially if he or she has never been to court.'

'I know, but I read the paper and I'm sure I'd remember a name like that. Now if you read the email, it's related to the planning applications. He's emailing Wilton asking about an application that his company has put in. He is asking what Wilton is going to do about it.'

Emma frowned. 'What does that mean?'

'It's obvious. Bilton Lancaster must work for one of the building companies. He must've been liaising with Wilton to make sure that their application got passed.'

'Which company is he from?'

'His email doesn't say where he's from, but with a name like that he'd probably be quite easy to find.'

'This is really useful. This is the first bit of evidence we found that shows someone outside the council knew what was happening. Other than this all we've got is information showing who is involved inside the council.' Emma's eyes were shining.

'Now we just need to work out which company this Bilton Lancaster works for and we can track him down,' Ed said.

'What's going on?' Dan stepped into the room, his hair wet from the shower, staring at the piles of papers on the floor.

'Ed's had a breakthrough,' Emma said, struggling to feet. As she wobbled Dan grabbed her arm and steadied her.

'Better a breakthrough than a breakdown,' he said.

'Oh, shut up,' said Ed with a smile.

'Look at this.' Emma was waving a piece of paper in Dan's face. He took it from her and she watched as his eyes scanned down the page. A frown creased his face. He looked from her to Ed and back again.

'Where did you get this?' he asked.

'It was in with some papers,' Ed said. 'I think it came from that bundle that Johanna Buttle gave you.'

'I thought we gave all that to Burton and Shepherd?'

'So did I. I was looking through these planning applications and it was there.'

'Bilton Lancaster?' Dan asked.

'Have you heard that name anywhere before,' Emma said.

Dan shook his head. 'No, and you'd remember a name like that, wouldn't you?' He frowned as he read the email a second time.

'What do you think?' Ed asked.

'I can't believe this has been sitting under our noses all this time.'

'What do you mean?'

'This opens up a new avenue of investigation, doesn't it? James Wilton is dead, Buttle is dead and Sanderson is missing. Now we've got a new lead.'

'You're thinking the same as us, we need to track down Lancaster?' Emma asked.

'Yup.' Dan pulled out his phone.

'What are you doing?' Emma asked.

'Googling him. Quickest way to get an idea.' He stared at the screen and frowned. 'Hmmm, it comes back with a prep school, a tourist guide for a town in Lancaster and a monastic site, whatever that is, called Bilton Grange.'

'So he doesn't exist,' Ed said.

'He doesn't exist on Google,' Dan replied.

'Meaning you think he exists somewhere else?'

'Exactly. We know he's got something to do with housing contractors, maybe he works for one. Let's invent a story and try to get a comment from him for that. That way we can sound out as to what his connection was to James Wilton.'

'But we know his connection with Wilton, they were working on a planning application together.'

'But we don't know how well they knew each other or whether they were involved in other applications.'

'They can't have been very good friends,' Emma said.

'What do you mean?' Dan asked.

'That last line of the email, that's pretty heavy stuff. "Do the job, or we'll make sure your reputation is destroyed. You'll never work again."'

Dan read the email again. 'I take your point. He's threatening Wilton, isn't he?'

'Yes, and look at the date.'

Ed was now on his feet too and reading over Dan's shoulder.

Dan's fingers tightened on the piece of paper. 'That's two days before Wilton died,' he said.

'And the same amount of time before the Elliot's Walk planning application got turned down,' Emma said.

Dan turned to her, the sheet of paper crumpling as his fingers gripped it. 'You think Bilton Lancaster works for the Elliot's Walk construction company?'

'They are the ones who lost the most by the application being turned down, aren't they?' Emma asked. Dan nodded. 'Maybe they got rid of Wilton to make sure that the mistake wouldn't happen again, to make sure that next time their application was passed.'

'And no one at the council did anything to stop them?' Ed asked.

'People at the council already knew what was happening,' Emma said. 'They knew about the planning applications, they knew about the bribes, and they did nothing about those.'

'James Wilton signed his own death warrant then?' Ed asked.

'As soon as he decided to put the wrong numbers on that last application,' Dan said. 'He must've thought that he could stop the scam and I doubt he thought they'd kill him because of it.'

'What do we do now?' Emma asked.

Dan glanced at his watch. 'It's too late to start ringing the building companies now. They'll all have closed for the day. First thing tomorrow we need to get on the phone and track down Bilton Lancaster. We need to find out what he knows. I get the feeling this might be the lead we've been looking for.'

The voice emanating from Dan's speakerphone had a tinny sound.

'I'm sorry, we don't have anyone called Bilton Lancaster working here.'

'Are you sure?'

'I think I would know.' The woman sounded annoyed.

'OK. Thanks very much for your help.' Dan hung up the phone and rubbed his eyes.

He heard a key in the door and Ed and Emma entered carrying a tray of takeaway coffees. When she saw Dan's face, Emma frowned.

'Oh dear, is it going that well?'

'I phoned six of the companies and none of them have Bilton Lancaster working there.'

'And you tried FGB Contracting?'

'They were my first call, but they've never heard of him.'

Emma headed towards the kitchen with her shopping bags, passing Ed in the doorway.

'It was always a bit of a long shot, mate,' he said. 'There was nothing in that email to say that Lancaster worked for one of the construction companies.'

'Who else could he be?' Dan asked. 'Who else would be interested in a planning application?'

Ed frowned. 'I don't know. I agree that it's weird he was emailing Wilton about an application, and specifically about one of the dodgy applications.'

'It couldn't be someone who had found out what Wilton was doing and was trying to blackmail him?' Dan asked.

'Who would bother to do that?' Emma said, returning from the kitchen.

'Good point. I'm clutching at straws, really, aren't I?' Dan said.

'I don't blame you. We've come this far and now you've hit a dead end. It's frustrating.' She came into the room and sat on the sofa. 'If it isn't this Bilton Lancaster, then who is it?'

'That's just it, the only person we've got left is David Edmonds,' Dan said.

'Then it must be him,' Emma said.

Chapter 59

'I'm telling you, the police know something.' David Edmonds' hands were shaking. 'They keep coming back to me.'

'Keep calm, David,' said the voice on the other end of the phone. 'They don't know anything. They're fishing and if you start acting like you've got something to hide, they'll come after you. We're nearly there, just hold your nerve.'

'What you mean we're nearly there?'

'One more application and we can wind this up.'

'What the hell are you talking about? The police are all over this.'

'We made promises, David. We have to honour them.'

'It's too much of a risk. The committee is already under scrutiny; damn it, the whole department is under scrutiny. We'll never get away with it.'

'No one will notice.'

'You're crazy.'

'No I am not. If we stop now, we will lose out.'

'So I have to put up and shut up?'

'That's right. Remember I hold all the cards, David. If you don't keep up your end of the bargain, I'll destroy you, your business, your family.'

'You wouldn't do that.'

'Wouldn't I?' A silence hung in the air. When the voice spoke again, it was very calm. 'We carry on as normal. There's one application left and then we can shut up shop. You're OK with that.' It was a statement rather than a question and Edmonds knew better than to argue.

'Fine. One more application.' He found himself listening to the dialling tone and he put the phone down on his desk. All he had to do was keep his nerve and keep away from the police.

A loud knock at the door made him jump.

'Councillor Edmonds?' Shit, it was the police. He recognised the detective inspector's voice.

He cleared his throat twice and sat in the chair behind his big mahogany desk, running his hands through his hair.

'Come in,' he called, his voice shaking slightly.

Burton appeared, followed by Shepherd. Edmonds tried to look like the unscheduled visit was messing up a busy day.

'What can I do for you?' he asked, checking his watch. 'I have a very busy morning.'

The detectives sat in chairs opposite his desk and Shepherd looked at Burton, waiting for her to begin.

She took a deep breath.

'We've been doing some more digging,' Burton said.

'Into the murders?' asked Edmonds.

'Partly, but also partly into what's been happening in the planning committee.'

Edmonds raised his eyebrows. 'And what's been happening in the planning committee?' he asked.

'You mean you don't know?' Shepherd asked, looking surprised.

'Don't know what?'

'Come on, Councillor. You know perfectly well what we're talking about,' Burton was getting irritated. 'The planning applications.'

'Oh that.'

'Yes, that. I'm sure Councillor Drimble has discussed it with you.'

'No. Why would he?'

'He is investigating, or rather he was investigating. He said he was speaking to everybody connected with the planning committee.'

'Then why would he talk to me? I'm not connected to the planning committee. We've already established that.'

'Your interest in planning has always looked a bit unhealthy, hasn't it?' Shepherd asked.

'What you mean by unhealthy?'

'You seem very interested in the committee, and in its decisions, but you claim to have no connection to it.'

Edmonds shrugged. 'I can attend any council meeting I want to, so what if I choose to attend planning?'

'Did you know about the false applications before Councillor Drimble revealed what happened?' Burton asked.

Edmonds looked surprised. 'Why would I?'

'By all accounts you were quite close to Councillor Sanderson and Councillor Buttle. Did they mention anything to you?'

'I didn't know them that well.'

'That's surprising.'

'Why?'

Burton smiled. 'We've heard from several people that you were regularly seen together. Whispering in corners was how it was described. What was that about?'

'That's none of your business.'

Burton leaned forward. 'This is a murder inquiry. Everything is my business.'

'If you must know, it was about their affair.'

'You discussed their affair regularly?'

'No, of course not. I simply made them aware that I knew about it, and so did others.'

'But we were told that you been seen together repeatedly. I'll ask you again, what was that about?'

Edmonds said nothing, but stared at the detectives.

'You can play it that way, Councillor Edmonds, but we will find out. Even if we have to do it without your help.'

Edmonds held her stony gaze without speaking.

Shepherd spoke next. 'Did you know that James Wilton and Councillor Buttle were receiving money for passing those applications?'

'No I didn't.'

'That wasn't what you were discussing in corners?'

'No. I've just told you I know nothing about it.'

'The odd thing is we've seen their financial records and there's a pattern to the payments that were being made to them.' Edmond's face remained impassive. 'The payments were always made straight after a committee meeting where one of the housing applications had been passed.'

'Really?'

'Yes. There are significant amounts of money, which Councillor Buttle hid from her husband.'

'I don't see what that's got to do with me.'

Shepherd took a plastic evidence bag containing some sheets of paper from his inside jacket pocket. He handed them across the desk to Edmonds; he glanced down at them. His face reddened.

'This is my bank statement. How the hell did you get that?'

'By first getting this.' This time Burton handed him a piece of paper. 'We weren't sure that you would give permission immediately, so we got a warrant.'

'Your bank statement's very interesting,' Shepherd said. He leaned forward and indicated a payment with a stubby forefinger. 'Do you recognise this payment?' Edmonds pursed his lips and said nothing. 'That's five thousand pounds. Did you not notice it going from your account?'

'I transfer money quite frequently. Between my business account and my personal accounts.'

'But five thousand pounds? There are two payments going out of your personal account, but the account number isn't your business account.'

'I really don't see why this is any of your business.'

'You see, according to James Wilton's and Councillor Buttle's bank accounts, they both received payments of five thousand pounds and, do you know what, that was a day or two after that money went out of your account.' Shepherd sat back and stared at Edmonds. 'Do you have an explanation for that?' Edmonds said nothing, but stared down at the bank statement rather than meeting Shepherd's gaze. There was a long silence before Burton spoke.

'We believe that someone killed James Wilton and Councillor Buttle because they wanted out. They couldn't take the weight of being involved in fraud and decided to blow the whistle.' She waited for Edmonds to speak but he said nothing. 'Remind me, where were you on the night James Wilton was killed?'

Edmonds stared. 'You surely don't think that—'

'Just answer the question.'

'I was at home with my wife. We had some friends over for dinner.'

'And you were there the whole night?'

'Yes.' Edmonds looked uncomfortable.

'We can check,' Shepherd reminded him.

'I stepped out at about nine o'clock for some more wine.'

'How long were you gone?'

'I went to the local off-licence so I was only gone about twenty minutes. It wasn't long enough to get to the town hall and back,' Edmonds said quickly.

Burton raised an eyebrow. 'And when Johanna Buttle was killed?'

'I was at an awards dinner, but I'm not sure of the time. I'd need to check in my diary.'

Burton frowned and stared pointedly at the desk diary in front of Edmonds. 'Go ahead,' she said.

'This is my council diary. The dinner will be my business diary. I don't have it with me.' Again Edmonds struggled to make eye contact but he saw the look passed between Burton and Shepherd.

'I don't know why you're asking me these questions.'

'We're investigating two murders, Councillor Edmonds. Two people are dead and another is missing and they were all involved in fraud. They didn't die of their own accord; they were silenced because they broke ranks.'

'And you think that was me?' Edmonds asked.

'If I could prove that, you'd already be in the cells.' Burton's eyebrows were drawn into an angry line.

'So, you have nothing on me.'

'Oh, I wouldn't say that,' Burton said. 'If I can prove that you weren't where you said you were when either of the murders were committed, we'll be discussing this at the police station.' She got to her feet. 'We'll be speaking to you soon.' She left the room followed by Shepherd who closed the door sharply behind him.

Edmonds took a deep breath and looked down at his trembling hands. It was time to look after his own interests. There was no such thing as the common good any more.

'Do you really think he killed them, sir?' asked Shepherd as they drove back to the police station.

Burton nodded. 'The money transfers are too much of a coincidence. He claims he knew nothing about the money and applications before the murders, but I just don't buy it.'

'The whispering in corners?'

'We're being asked to believe too much. Why would he be talking to Buttle and Sanderson if not for that reason? Sullivan told us that they ran away from him after the planning meeting that started all this, why would they do that without good reason?'

'But he seems to have alibis for both.'

Burton frowned. 'His alibi for Wilton's murder is his wife and some friends. They might not be wholly honest if they want to protect him. Plus he was very quick to point out that it wasn't enough time for him to have got to the town hall and back.' She paused. 'The alibi for when Buttle died is hazy given that he can't recall what time he left the awards dinner. He could easily have met up with her somewhere.' She was silent for a moment. 'I don't like it when someone who seems as guilty as sin has a watertight alibi.'

'Too convenient, you mean?'

'Exactly. We need to check out those alibis.'

'Do you really think a respected local businessman would kill people?' Shepherd asked.

'Maybe not by his own hand, but he's got too much to lose to let them ruin his reputation. People have been killed for less than that.'

Maureen Edmonds took a step back from the front door, a hand clasping the front of her cardigan together. On the doorstep stood a burly man holding out a police warrant card.

'Mrs Maureen Edmonds?'

'Yes?'

'I'm Detective Sergeant Mark Shepherd from Allensbury CID. May I come in, please?'

Maureen Edmonds stepped back and held open the door. 'Has something happened? Is it my husband?'

'Not at all. I just need to ask you some questions.'

'Oh, why do you need to speak to me?' She waved the detective into the hallway and led the way into a chintzy-patterned living room. It felt very crowded, with sofas and little tables in all directions. Every surface seemed to be covered with miniature cottages, making Shepherd feel as if he'd wandered into Lilliput. Maureen Edmonds indicated the sofa, seating herself in an armchair opposite and patting her grey curls before pushing the steel rimmed glasses up her nose. As Shepherd turned to sit down he knocked over a small, empty china vase.

'Sorry,' he said, managing to catch it and put it back on the table. Mrs Edmonds laughed and waved it away.

'David always does exactly the same thing,' she said. Shepherd sat down opposite her, noticing that she sat with her back straight and her legs crossed at the ankle. 'What is this about?' she asked.

'You know about the two murders that have happened at the council?'

'Oh yes, David told me all about those. Why do you want to know?'

'We're just fact checking about all the people who knew James Wilton and Johanna Buttle. I understand your husband knew them both well?'

'I'd never heard him mention James Wilton, but I know he's worked with Johanna Buttle for a while. Such a lovely woman.'

'In what capacity did he work with Councillor Buttle?'

'Well, at the council.'

'Were they on the same committees?'

'I don't believe they were, but David said she had a lot of potential in local politics. I'm sorry I don't know much more. I've never been particularly interested in council business.'

'But you are a councillor's wife?'

'I don't really understand all that kind of thing. I leave that to

David.' Her glasses had slid slightly down her nose and she pushed them back again, eyeing Shepherd almost suspiciously. 'But you didn't want to talk about local politics, did you?'

'No, I need to ask you some questions about your husband.'

'He is OK, isn't he?'

'He's fine. I saw him about an hour ago.'

'If you've seen him this morning, I don't understand how else I can help you.'

'Do you remember where you were on Tuesday twenty-sixth of September?'

Maureen Edmonds looked puzzled for a moment. 'I don't know, probably at the charity shop. I do a few shifts there in the week. It's good to do your bit, isn't it?'

'It certainly is. What about in the evening?'

'Let me see, oh yes. That was the night we had Gordon and Andrea for dinner. I remember now because David was late home from work and he'd forgotten to pick up the wine I had asked him to get.' Shepherd scribbled some notes and she continued. 'Yes, I said we'd try to get by with the wine we already had but Gordon does like a drink. It's a bit of a sore point with Andrea, but you can't say no to a guest, can you?'

Shepherd nodded sympathetically. 'What did you do?'

'By the middle of the evening we were running out, so David said he'd pop into the village to get some. I tried to stop him but he insisted. Gordon is a good friend of his, you see. He didn't drive,' she said, seeing Shepherd look up. 'He took a taxi to the local off-licence.'

'What time was that?'

'Probably around nine o'clock. Although he took a bit longer than I expected.'

'How do you mean?'

'The shop is only about ten minutes along the road, but he was gone about thirty-five minutes.'

'Did he say why?'

'He said there was a big queue.'

'And did he have the wine when he came back?'

'Yes. Well, that was why he'd gone.' Maureen was eyeing Shepherd suspiciously. 'He bought two bottles of a very nice red wine, which Gordon almost finished off himself. I don't know how Andrea copes with him.' She pursed her lips. 'David isn't like that,' she added smugly.

'How did Councillor Edmonds seem when he came home?'

'What you mean?'

'What sort of mood was he in?'

'He was annoyed that he'd had to go out and that there'd been a queue in the shop.'

'Did you notice anything else?'

She frowned. 'Well, now you mention it, I did. He seemed a bit unsettled and kept looking at his mobile.'

'Is that unusual?'

'He does tend to keep the phone on in case people want to get hold of him. He is a very important man, you know.' Shepherd nodded and she went on. 'But he doesn't usually watch it. It was as if he was waiting for a call, but he said he wasn't. Then of course we heard about that poor man a couple of days later.'

'James Wilton?'

'Yes. So sad, him with a wife and a little girl as well. David was very upset about it, although as I said I'd not heard him mention Mr Wilton before.'

'What about Johanna Buttle?'

'That was such a terrible shock. Such a lovely woman. But I don't think politics is the right place for a woman.' She pursed her lips again and shook her head.

'And how did Councillor Edmonds seem after he found out she was dead?'

'He was very upset, obviously. He kept saying "I only saw her today". But I suppose what was more of a shock was the fact that he'd only been at the Turpin Hotel a few hours earlier for the Allensbury Business Awards.'

Chapter 60

Half an hour later Burton and Shepherd were struggling to get information out of the Turpin Hotel's duty manager. The man was short and greasy-looking and had a nervous habit of rubbing his hands together as if they needed cleaning.

'Tell us about the Allensbury Business Awards,' Burton said. 'They were the same night the Councillor Johanna Buttle died, weren't they?'

'Yes, they were. We were very busy that night.'

'You didn't mention that before.'

'To be honest, I was more worried about someone dying in my hotel. I didn't think it was relevant.'

'Everything is relevant in a murder inquiry. What time did the awards party wrap up?'

'About half-past midnight. Most people had left by one o clock in the morning. We needed a lot of taxis that night; the champagne had been flowing.'

'The bar and function room area would have been very busy then?' Shepherd asked.

'Yes, at one point I thought I'd have to call in more staff. The restaurant got very busy as well.'

'You didn't see Councillor Johanna Buttle?' Burton asked.

'No, I didn't. I know her by sight, but I didn't see her that evening. She certainly wasn't booked into the restaurant.'

'How did she end up in one of the rooms upstairs?'

'How would I know that?'

'She hadn't booked a room?'

'I don't think so. I haven't seen any documentation for that.'

'Did you know all of the people attending the awards?' Burton asked.

'There were a few familiar faces, but I won't pretend to recognise everyone. There are a lot of business people in this town. They've probably all been here at one time or another, but I only really recognise the regulars.' He paused from moment. 'I'm sure the business awards organisers could give you a list of everyone that was here.'

'We've already got that, thank you. You didn't see anyone who looked like they didn't fit in?'

'It was all dinner jackets and ball gowns at the awards dinner, but we also had people less smartly dressed in the bar and the restaurant. With so many people milling around I wouldn't have noticed, even if the person looked out of place.'

Shepherd held up the photograph. 'Do you recognise this man?'

The manager looked at it and smiled. 'Yes, that's Councillor Edmonds. I know him very well; he's often in here. Lovely man.'

'He was here the night of the business awards?'

'Yes, I even complimented him on his dinner suit.'

'How did he seem?'

'He seemed to be having a good evening. The champagne was flowing and every time I saw him he was talking to someone.' He smiled. 'He wasn't in such a good mood later in the evening though.'

Burton and Shepherd looked at each other.

'Why was that?' Burton asked.

'Because he didn't win an award. I think he was expecting something, but it didn't go his way.'

'What time did he leave?'

The man frowned for a moment. 'I don't know. I saw him in the reception area shortly after one o clock and he asked me to call a taxi. The receptionist was doing that duty so I asked her to ensure that he got one.'

'Did you actually see him leave?' Shepherd asked.

The man frowned. 'Now that you mention it, I didn't. I went to attend to an issue in the bar, and when I came back he was gone. I assumed he got in a taxi.'

Burton smiled. 'Thank you. You've been very helpful.'

From where she sat in her office, Burton could hear laughter. It was a male voice and a female. As she looked up, Shepherd walked to his desk followed by a pretty brunette in a checked shirt and black trousers. The woman gestured as she told a story and Shepherd laughed even more. Then the woman looked at her watch, made a final joke and patted Shepherd on the arm. She turned to go and Shepherd's eyes followed her all the way to the door. Burton got to her feet and walked round her desk to the office door.

She cleared her throat, making Shepherd jump. 'A friend of yours?' she said, jerking her head towards the door where the brunette had left.

Shepherd blushed. 'No, she's one of the new techs. She brought us this.' He held up a brown cardboard folder.

Burton moved forward to take the folder from him. 'What is it?'

'Something they got from David Edmonds' laptop. They found something new when they were going through his emails.'

Burton's eyes were scanning down the sheet of paper. 'And this email was just sitting there on the laptop? How had they not already found it?'

'We told them that the priority was to find the missing files. They've been shorthanded and they've only just got round to his emails.'

'Bilton Lancaster? Who is Bilton Lancaster? I've never heard that name before.'

'Me neither. He certainly never came up in this investigation. A name like that, you'd remember it.'

'This email is very interesting. Edmonds is telling him which applications they're working on. Why would this Bilton Lancaster want to know that?'

'The only reason I can think of is that he works for one of the developers. It would be useful for them to know what the committee was working on.'

'Whoever he is, Edmonds is offering to "fix it" for him.'

'Look at the date.'

Shepherd looked at where Burton's finger was pointing. He raised his eyebrows. 'Two days before the planning committee meeting,' he said.

'And about one day before James Wilton was killed,' Burton added.

'So we've got David Edmonds agreeing to get the application that Bilton Lancaster is interested in passed, even though it's fraudulent.'

'Presumably he still thought that James Wilton was on their side.'

'What if he didn't?'

Burton looked at Shepherd. 'What you mean?'

'What if Edmonds already knew that James Wilton was jumping ship? That would have a serious impact on their ability to get the application passed. With only two votes sewn up on the committee they could have run into trouble.'

'And they did, because James Wilton had changed the numbers.'

'But Edmonds didn't know that, did he? We know he was

threatening Buttle and Sanderson to vote the way they were supposed to; Sullivan practically overheard that. Maybe he killed James Wilton without knowing that Wilton had already changed that application?'

Burton rocked back on her heels. 'You think that James Wilton told Edmonds that he wanted out, but Edmonds wouldn't let him. So Wilton changed the numbers to make sure that it all came out in public and Edmonds killed him after the changes had been made.'

'That's what I'm thinking. In the email he tells Bilton Lancaster that he'll fix it. What if the fix wasn't the application, it was James Wilton.'

Burton held her breath for a moment and then puffed out her cheeks. 'The one problem is at the moment we don't have any physical evidence to tie Edmonds to the crime scene.'

'Maybe not,' Shepherd said. 'There's no reason why he would have done it himself. We know he wasn't away from home long enough to kill James Wilton, take the car into the woods and dump it before getting back home with two bottles of wine. His wife said he seemed irritated. I can't imagine he'd have been so calm if he'd just killed somebody. But that's not to say that he didn't get someone else to do it for him.'

'It gives us a very good reason to pick him up and interview him,' said Burton. 'Let's go.'

Richard Drimble stared as Burton and Shepherd strode up the town hall steps towards him.

'Good morning, Mr Mayor,' Shepherd said with a nod.

Drimble put out a hand to stop them as they drew level with him. 'Morning. What can I do for you?'

'It's not you we're after, sir,' said Burton.

'Oh? Who are you "after"?'

'We're actually looking for Councillor Edmonds. Is he here today?'

Drimble frowned. 'I don't know. I haven't seen him.'

'OK, we'll look elsewhere.' As Burton and Shepherd turned to leave, Drimble held out a hand.

'Why are you looking for David?'

'It's part of an investigation,' Burton said. 'We are hoping he can answer some questions for us.'

'What sort of questions?'

'That's for Councillor Edmonds to answer.'

Drimble frowned. 'I'm the mayor, the leader at this council, and I'd like to know why you're harassing one of our councillors.'

'It's hardly harassment, we just want to speak to him,' Shepherd said.

'You might be a leader at the council, but I'm leading this investigation,' Burton said coldly. 'I'll decide who needs to know what and when.'

Drimble looked angry, but didn't say anything.

'If you'll excuse us, we need to go and look for Councillor Edmonds,' Burton said. This time she turned her back and clicked away down the stairs. Shepherd turned as well but Drimble's voice stopped him.

'Shall I tell David you're looking for him?'

'Best not,' Shepherd said. 'We'll find him.'

Chapter 61

When Emma heard the front door slam, she walked downstairs. 'Who was that?' she asked Dan as she entered the living room.

'It was only Ed.'

Emma glanced at her watch. 'What was he doing here at this time of day? Why was he not at court?'

'He'd spilled something on his tie and he came back to get a clean one.'

'Typical Ed.'

'Exactly.' She walked round the sofa and sat on the armchair looking at Dan. 'What?' he asked.

'What do we do now?'

'Well, I still think this Bilton Lancaster is involved.'

Emma's eyes widened. 'I thought you decided it was Councillor Edmonds?'

Dan scratched his head. 'Maybe they are in it together.'

'But we don't know who Bilton Lancaster is.'

'If we don't know who he is, how do we know he's not involved?'

'Slightly warped logic, but I see where you're coming from.'

'I just wish there was somewhere finding out who he is. Ringing all those companies was a waste of time.'

'But it had to be done.'

'If he doesn't work for a developer, then who could he be? Why would anybody else be interested in a housing planning application?'

Emma frowned. 'I'm running out of ideas,' she said.

Dan leaned forward and rested his elbows on his knees, rubbing his face with both hands. Then he sat back and looked at Emma.

'There is someone, someone else who would be interested in a planning application.'

She frowned. 'You were so convinced earlier that David Edmonds was involved,' Emma said. 'Why has that changed?'

'I'm not saying that I don't think it was him. But I think we just have to bite the bullet and go and have a word with him.'

Emma stared at him. 'You want to talk to Councillor Edmonds? Why?'

'I've just realised, he's the only one who we haven't spoken to properly. We've chased everyone else, even ...' He stopped, silent for a moment, then exhaled heavily and slapped a hand to his forehead.

'What?'

'I can't believe I've been so stupid. Of course it's him.'

'Who him?'

But Dan wasn't listening. 'I'm going to tell him that I know exactly who Bilton Lancaster is.' He was on his feet, shoving his wallet, phone and keys into his pockets.

'What are you talking about?'

'You heard me.'

'You know who Bilton Lancaster is?'

'Yes. And you'll never believe me when I tell you.'

Emma grabbed her handbag and followed Dan out to the car, pausing to lock the front door carefully and rattle it four times. Dan had already unlocked the car door and was climbing inside.

'Come on! We don't have time for that.'

Emma climbed into the passenger seat, only just managing to shut the door before Dan slammed the car into reverse and backed out of the parking space.

'Where are we going?'

'The town hall.'

'How do you know he'll be there?'

'He'll be there. They'll both be there.'

Chapter 62

David Edmonds' phone was playing the *Jaws* theme again. Sitting in the office of his business premises on Allensbury industrial estate, he had thought he was safe from interruptions. For a moment he considered ignoring the call, but he knew it wasn't worth the hassle.

'What is it now?' he asked.

'David, we have problem.' The voice was cold.

'This whole scheme has been a problem from beginning to end.'

'You're blaming me for that? You chose the people; you swore you had them under control. If anyone is to blame, it's you.'

'It was your idea. I told you it wouldn't work.'

'There was nothing wrong with the plan. The problem has been in the execution.'

'You've been as involved in that as I have.'

'I know. I've had to be more involved than I should have been.'

'What's wrong now?'

'We need to wrap this up.'

Edmonds frowned. 'What? When I suggested that earlier you said no.'

'Things are changed since then. We need to prepare ourselves and get rid of any evidence. We need to meet.'

Edmonds glanced at his watch. 'I can be free in an hour.'

'No, that's not enough time. Meet me at your office in the town hall tonight. We can destroy everything together.'

'And then what?'

'That's up to you, whether you choose to stick around or leave.'

'You know I can't just leave. I have too many roots here.'

'That's your problem. Just make sure you're in your office later today and that you've got all the evidence.' There was a moment of silence. 'Have you spoken to the police today?'

'No, I haven't. Why?'

'I would make yourself scarce for the day. Make sure they can't find you.' The phone line went dead.

Edmonds dropped the phone onto the desk and reached into his top drawer for a USB stick. He inserted it into the socket on his computer and began to copy files onto it. He heard the phone in reception ring, and Mandy very competently answering. Then the phone on his desk buzzed.

'Yes?'

'There's a call for you,' Mandy said. 'It is Detective Inspector Jude Burton. She says it important.'

Edmonds rubbed his nose. 'Please can you tell her I'm out of the office and you don't know how to contact me?'

If Mandy was surprised by his request, she didn't show it.

While the files were copying, he went to the filing cabinet in the corner, opening it with a key. Pulling out the top drawer he rifled through the contents until he found the files he was looking for hidden at the back. He extracted them quickly and bundled them and his laptop into his briefcase. He stood there with the USB stick in his hand. He had a bad feeling about tonight, the feeling that it wouldn't be entirely simple. But there was no one he could trust. He dropped the USB stick into an envelope addressed to himself. Then he left the room crossing the hall to Mandy's desk. 'I'm going out now. Please could you post this?' He handed her the envelope and although Mandy's eyebrows rose when she saw the address, she didn't ask any questions.

'You're still uncontactable?'

'Yes, for the rest of the day.'

'Is that for everyone?' Mandy knew the rules.

'Yes. I don't want to speak to anyone today.'

'OK.'

Edmonds smiled at her. She was incredibly competent. 'Thanks, Mandy.'

'See you tomorrow.'

Edmonds wasn't sure whether that was a question or a statement but he nodded and said, 'Yes, see you tomorrow.' Then he turned and left the building.

It was barely half an hour later that the door opened and Mandy looked up to see a man and a woman approaching the front desk. She smiled at them.

'Can I help you?'

She wasn't entirely shocked when they both showed warrant cards.

'I'm Detective Inspector Burton and this is Detective Sergeant Shepherd. We'd like to speak to Mr Edmonds, please.'

'I'm sorry he's not here. He's at a meeting and he is not contactable.'

Burton remained stony faced. 'I can't believe that in this day and age anyone is not contactable. Where is his office?' But Shepherd had already spotted the right door and was heading towards it.

'Sorry, you can't go in there.' Mandy was on her feet and following him, trying to reach the door before he did. He gently imposed his body between her and the door without touching her.

'That's fine, I can manage,' he said. He knocked gently and then pushed door open. He walked into the room and looked around then came back out the office. 'He's not here.'

'That's what I just told you,' Mandy said.

'Was he when we called earlier?' Burton asked.

Mandy blushed. 'I ... I don't know.'

Burton frowned. 'Have you heard of perverting the course of justice?'

Mandy met her eyes but said nothing.

'If I find out that you are hiding information from us, and a murderer goes free, you will be prosecuted.'

Shepherd offered Mandy a business card and she took it mechanically. 'If you see him, or you think of anything you'd like to share with us, just give me a call.' Clutching a business card, Mandy watched them leave the building and climb into the car. She walked back to her desk and sat down. She took a deep breath and reached for the phone. But then she stopped. This was his problem, not hers. She'd best stay out of it. She dropped Shepherd's business card into her desk drawer and pushed it closed.

Burton was scowling as the detectives climbed into their car.

'He's not at the town hall and he's not here. Where next?'

'I think we should go and have a word with his missus again,' said Shepherd. 'Maybe she'll know where he is.'

But Maureen Edmonds was as much at a loss as they were.

'He said he was going to the office this morning, but he didn't say exactly what was in his diary,' she said as they sat in the crowded front room.

'He didn't mention going out to any meetings?' Burton asked.

'No, but then he doesn't usually tell me about the business. I don't really understand it all, you see.' She gave a little laugh. 'It annoys him when I don't know what he's talking about.'

'It's very important that we speak to him, so if you hear from him during the day, can you please ask him to call me?' Burton handed her a business card.

'Yes, of course. He's not in any trouble, is he?'

'No.' Shepherd smiled. 'We just need his help with something.'

They said their goodbyes to her.

Burton looked at Shepherd over the roof of the car.

'Councillor Edmonds has done a very good job of hiding from us.'

'Where next?' Shepherd asked.

'Back to the station. We can have a think when we get there.'

Chapter 63

Dan and Emma climbed the steps to the town hall, trying to cross the reception area quickly without drawing attention to themselves. Committee meetings were held in public, meaning anyone could attend, but it might have looked suspicious to be seen attending the Innovation Panel, where nothing was ever decided, innovative or not.

As they reached the foot of the stairs, they overheard the security guards talking.

'Right, there's just the one meeting taking place tonight. It should be a quiet one for you. All the rooms that should be locked are locked.'

'Thanks, mate. You get home to your wife. How's the kiddy?'

'Much better, thanks. Her temperature's come down so hopefully she'll actually sleep tonight.' The guard rolled his eyes as he pulled on a jacket. 'See you in the morning,' he called, slamming the door behind him. The security guard on duty paid no attention to Dan and Emma, clearly considering them to be no threat.

Dan began to take the stairs two at a time, Emma limping and trying to keep up. He strode along the corridor, muttering, 'I can't believe I was so stupid.'

'Wait for me. It's not stupid, it fooled everyone.'

'Come on, let's get to Edmonds' office.'

'Do you think he'll be there already?' Emma asked as she scurried after Dan as fast as her ankle would let her.

Just as she spoke, a shot rang out.

Chapter 64

Burton was queuing in the canteen for a coffee when Shepherd barrelled through the double doors.

'Sir, you've got to see this.' He held out a sheet of paper.

'What is it?'

'Remember that email, from Bilton Lancaster?'

Burton's eyes were scanning down the sheet of paper. 'What about it?'

'I ran his name through the database and this is what came out.' He tapped a finger at the sheet of paper. Burton was scanning through the tightly clustered printed words. Suddenly she went very still. She looked up at Shepherd, lips parted in surprise.

'Are you kidding me?'

Shepherd shook his head. 'Nope. I even called the team that dealt with it and checked. It's definitely him.'

Burton moved out of the queue and began to hustle Shepherd towards the canteen door. 'We've got to warn Sullivan.' She was already reaching into her handbag for her mobile phone.

Ed rubbed his eyes hard with his knuckles. He peered at the computer screen blinking furiously. The lights at one end of the room had been turned off and the fluorescent bulbs above his head seemed incredibly bright. He wasn't used to being the last one in the office, but thanks to an over-running court case, it was gone six o clock and he was still filing copy. The phone on his desk started to ring. He groaned. It was never a good idea to answer the office phone at this time of night. There was usually a crazy person on the other end of it.

'Hello, newsroom.'

'Can I speak to Emma Fletcher, please?'

'Sorry, she's left for the day. Can I help or take a message?'

'It is Detective Inspector Burton here. It's urgent. I need to contact Emma immediately.'

Ed was surprised. 'Why? What's going on?'

'Sorry, we don't have time to do this.'

'I can try calling her now on a mobile.' As he spoke Ed was tapping the screen of his phone until he reached Emma's number. He dialled but the phone just rang. 'That's odd, it's just going to voicemail.' He scrolled through the screen and selected Dan's number. 'Oh, that's odd. Dan's mobile is going to voicemail too. I thought they would be finished by now.'

There was a pause on the other end. 'Finished what?' Burton asked.

'They were going to talk to Councillor Edmonds. Dan thought he might know who Bilton Lancaster is.'

'How do you know about Bilton Lancaster?'

'We found an email—'

Burton cut across him. 'They were going to the town hall?'

'Yes but—'

'Right, we're on our way.' The line went dead as Burton slammed down the phone.

Leaving his computer logged on, Ed grabbed his keys and ran out of the room, down the stairs and into the street. His heart pounded as he ran up the hill towards town hall.

Chapter 65

'Was that gunshot?' Emma hissed as they stood frozen in the corridor.

Dan nodded. 'I think it came from Edmonds' office.' He walked up to the door, and then gently pushed it open.

David Edmonds lay back in his chair, his eyes wide and staring. There was a red hole in the left side of his head and blood was dripping into a pool on the floor. Emma gasped and clapped a hand to her mouth. All Dan could do was stare in horror.

Standing over Edmonds, clutching a small pistol, was Richard Drimble.

He swung around when they entered, a fearful look coming into his eyes.

'Thank God you're here. He tried to kill me. We were struggling and the gun just went off. I tried to …'

'Save it, Mr Mayor, we know it was you. Or should that be Mr Lancaster?'

'I don't know what you mean. What was me?'

'You've been behind this all the time, the planning scam, everything.'

'What scam? I don't understand.'

'Cut the crap. I thought you were better than that, better than hiding behind excuses.'

Drimble's face hardened.

'Yes, everyone has such expectations of me. As the mayor, I'm expected to suffer fools gladly.'

'Why compete to become mayor then?' asked Emma.

'For the power,' Drimble said. 'You'd be amazed what you can get by holding a position like this.'

'Like control of the planning committee, you mean?' Dan asked.

'Yes. It's surprising what you can do in planning. It seems like such a dull committee that no one ever watches it.'

'And you managed to get yourself elected onto it?'

'I was asked to by my party after Alan Horgan's heart attack.' Drimble allowed himself a smug smile.

Emma frowned. 'That was a bit convenient, him having a heart attack just when you needed him to.'

Drimble's face contorted. 'Stupid girl! Do you really think that was natural causes? I engineered that! He was a fool, but he was starting to notice the plans that Wilton was slipping through. He began asking questions and we couldn't have that. So I saw to it that he had to step down and then selflessly agreed to take his place, after the right amount of persuasion to make it look legitimate. That way no one was looking into the committee and we could carry on as before.'

'And once you were on the planning committee you could keep a closer eye on it?' Dan asked.

'Yes. Buttle and Sanderson were shaken by Alan Horgan being taken ill so conveniently just when he seemed about to expose what we were doing. Of course, they didn't know about my involvement in the scam.'

Dan stared. 'They didn't know?'

'No one did, except David.' Drimble nudged Edmonds' chair so it swung back and forth, his arms dangling limply over the arms. He smiled. 'Such a shame David couldn't hold his nerve. The police were preparing to arrest him, so poor David came here and killed himself.' He shook his head in mock sorrow.

'They'll never believe that,' said Dan. 'Not if you shot him from over there.'

'Ah, but I didn't. I've done this thing properly, the way I do everything. David will be found dead with the gun in his hand and only his fingerprints on it. Or at least he would have done until you two turned up. Now there's going to have to be a little change of plan.'

'Such as?' Dan nudged Emma to move behind him towards the door. They had been inching closer to it as Drimble talked.

'I think the police might find that David killed you two after finding you ransacking his office.' Drimble paused and swept a couple of files off the shelf onto the floor and overturned the desk tidy, spilling pens, paper clips and drawing pins onto the desk. 'Then, consumed with guilt, he shot himself.'

'There's just one problem with that,' said Dan, his back pressed against the bookcase next to the door.

'What's that?'

'You'll have to catch us first!' With one movement Dan grabbed a heavy book from one of the shelves and hurled it at Drimble, pushing Emma out of the door. A shot exploded into the ceiling, showering the room with plaster. Dan slammed the door.

'Go!' he said, grabbing Emma's hand and dragging her along the corridor. She hobbled along, whimpering as she tried to keep up. But when they reached the end, instead of the staircase, they found themselves with only a fire escape ahead.

'Oh balls, we've taken a wrong turning,' Dan moaned. They could hear running footsteps behind them and Dan pushed open the door. Greeting them was a set of stairs that only led to the roof.

'We'll get trapped up there,' Emma said as Dan began to push her up.

'We've got no choice. Hopefully the security guard will have heard the shots and called the police.'

The door onto the roof seemed to be locked but Dan threw his body weight against it and it burst open, banging against the wall.

Out on the roof, it was raining heavily and they were soon soaked through.

'Quick, I need to—'

But before Dan could do anything but tap in the emergency number on his phone, the door behind them exploded open and Drimble stood there, gun pointing at them.

'Well, that wasn't very clever,' he said.

'The guard will have heard the shots. The police will be on their way.'

But Drimble shook his head. 'No, they won't. I told him all he heard were doors slamming and he believed me.'

Dan could feel Emma shaking next to him. He just needed to keep Drimble talking, just for long enough.

'If you were in on the scam, why did you turn down the Elliot's Walk application?' Emma asked, her teeth chattering.

'I can tell you that,' Dan said. 'James Wilton fooled you, didn't he? He wanted out so he deliberately put higher numbers into the plans than were in the briefing you'd given Anderson for the meeting. He knew that when it came up at committee it would become obvious what was going on.' Drimble made a growling noise in his throat. 'You knew he wanted out but you just thought he was going to tell someone about it. He called you and told you that.'

'No, he called David. David panicked and called me. "He's going to blow everything",' Drimble spoke in a whiney voice. '"What are we going to do?" Well, I fixed that the way I fixed it every bloody time something went wrong.' He gestured towards them, pointing the gun as he emphasised his point. 'Of course, I had someone else dispose of the body. The mayor couldn't be seen to get his hands dirty.' He spoke in a mock-pompous voice. 'But I know enough people who can help with things like that.'

'Wilton tipped off the residents too, didn't he? He put the note through Kevin Turtle's door telling him that the plans had come round again knowing full well that the residents would come to the meeting and kick up a fuss. You didn't know about that either, did you? That's why you looked so shocked at the meeting when there were so many of them.'

'He'd lost his bottle,' Drimble spat. 'He'd paid off his debts and thought he could just walk away like that.' He snapped his fingers. 'I wasn't finished!' He shouted the last word. 'It's different now, all the loose ends are tied up, and I can move on.'

'Don't you think they'll come looking for you?'

'They won't know where to start.'

While Drimble was talking, Dan and Emma had been gradually backing away from him around the base of the clock tower, but now they were pressed against the corner of the parapet. As Drimble raised the gun, Dan's mobile began to ring in his pocket.

'Get rid of that,' said Drimble.

'Here, take it.' Dan hurled the phone towards Drimble, making the man duck, and then ran at him, shoving him against the wall as hard as he could. Drimble gave a grunt as all the air was forced from his lungs and the gun flew away, clattering against the wall.

With a roar, he dived at Dan, grabbing him by the lapels. He shoved Dan back against the side of the parapet that ran around the edge of the roof. Dan's hands scrabbled against the wall trying to get enough of a handhold to push back at Drimble, but the other man was bigger and stronger. Dan was gradually being lifted up and would soon be over the wall.

Emma dashed forward and began to punch Drimble's back. He

turned to shove her away and she fell heavily to the ground.

Drimble threw his weight towards Dan again, but in the split-second Drimble had been distracted, Dan had wriggled to one side.

Drimble's momentum carried him forward; he slipped and disappeared over the wall. He grabbed Dan's jacket as he slid over the parapet and was left dangling by one hand.

Dan tried to brace himself against the wall to prevent being pulled over, but his trainers weren't giving him any grip against the wet roof surface.

Emma screamed and flung herself at Dan, grabbing the waistband of his trousers to prevent him being pulled over the wall.

'Just don't let go!' Dan yelled.

'If I'm going, I'm taking you with me!' Drimble roared.

'No!'

The shout came from behind them and the roof was suddenly filled with policemen.

Burton dashed over and grabbed Dan and Emma. Shepherd reached over the wall and, with the help of two uniformed officers who were of a similar size to him, seized Drimble's jacket and hauled the mayor back over onto the roof.

'You cut it a bit fine,' Dan gasped, clutching at Burton's coat. The strength went from Emma's legs and she sank onto the ground, shaking. Dan flopped down beside her and put an arm around her shoulders.

'You OK?' he asked. She nodded silently.

'Dan!' Ed cried dashing over to them. 'Emma! Are you OK?'

'It was him,' said Dan pointing at Drimble. 'He was behind the scam. He's Bilton Lancaster.'

'We were right about Bilton Lancaster being involved,' Ed said.

They were sitting in the lobby of the town hall, sipping mugs of tea rustled up by the security guard. Emma and Dan were wrapped in blankets and Emma's teeth had almost stopped chattering. They'd been examined by paramedics at the scene and given a clean bill of health.

'It was a pretty good plan pretending to investigate his own scam,' said Dan.

'But you said you had a feeling something wasn't right, didn't you? When he invited you for coffee,' said Emma.

'True.'

'He's not been in town very long. How did he know so much about the people on the planning committee?'

'I can answer that one. David Edmonds,' said Shepherd, 'he knew the people. It seems like he had dirt on everyone. We found deleted files on his computer of emails going back two or three years that had evidence he could use against people. Drimble thought they'd bend to Edmonds' will easier than his. He was right too. All he had to do was make sure he kept Edmonds in line. It was working too, until Wilton got cold feet and decided he wanted out.'

'Has Drimble – sorry – Bilton Lancaster, admitted what he's done?' Emma asked.

'Not yet, we've still got a lot of work to do to crack him but at least we've got evidence already,' said Burton.

'What I don't understand,' said Ed, 'is why he chose Allensbury? Did he have family here or something?'

'We haven't got to the bottom of it yet. We've heard from Hampshire police and it seems they've been looking for Bilton Lancaster for some time in connection with fraud.'

'Let me guess, planning applications?' Dan asked.

Burton smiled. 'Got it in one.'

'And no one else knew that Drimble was involved in the scam?' Ed asked.

'Paul Sanderson has coughed to his part but the only person he'd spoken to about it was Edmonds,' said Shepherd. 'That's why we were sure he was in charge.'

'But there was someone else pulling his strings,' Dan said.

'Exactly.'

'The irony is we found another set of prints on the envelope that was sent to Jo Buttle,' said Burton.

'Really? Whose were they?' asked Dan.

'James Wilton's. He must have sent it to her, thinking that she would help expose the scam, but it got delayed in the internal mail.'

'Did he know she was involved in the scam too?'

'We're not sure yet. Hopefully there'll be something in the paperwork that'll tell us that.'

'So she needn't have done anything,' Dan said. 'The person who was threatening her was already dead.'

'Another of life's little ironies,' said Burton, tugging at the ends of her hair.

'I still can't believe it's all over and we can go back to work,' Dan said.

'I never thought I'd hear you sound so pleased about that,' said Ed.

'It'll be nice to get back to normality,' said Dan. 'Anything for a quiet life.'

Emma stared at him. 'Hang on a minute, don't you have a story to write? I thought that's why we risked our lives? For your story?'

'I'm exhausted. I don't know if my heart's still in it,' Dan admitted.

'So why did you do all this, if not for the story?' asked Burton, sweeping her hand around the town hall lobby.

'Isn't this supposed to be your big break?' asked Ed.

'I don't think I'm ready for all that just yet.'

'You may never get another chance like this,' Ed pointed out. 'And how many reporters can say they've been in the middle of the story?'

'You can't back out now,' Emma said angrily. 'I almost got shot for you! Twice!'

Dan grinned and took her hand. 'How about a joint by-line?'

She grinned. 'Sounds ideal. Come on, let's go home and get writing.'

He smiled at her. 'Is there pizza and beer?'

She laughed. 'I'm sure that can be arranged.'

Chapter 66

MAYOR JAILED FOR MURDER
By Ed Walker

Allensbury Mayor Councillor Richard Drimble was today jailed for a minimum twenty years for murdering three people as part of a planning scam.

Drimble, tried under his real name Bilton Lancaster, was convicted of the murders of Planning Officer James Wilton, Councillor David Edmonds and Councillor Johanna Buttle, who were implicated in the scam, which netted each participant more than seventy-five thousand pounds in bribes from building companies over the course of the last eighteen months.

He was also convicted of a further thirty counts of fraud.

The four, along with Councillor Paul Sanderson, were taking bribes from building companies to pass planning applications for housing on valuable sites. The councillors also profited when fake companies, set up by Drimble, sold on the land with planning permission already granted to developers.

Sentencing him, the judge told Lancaster: 'You demonstrated a callous lack of empathy for the people you forced into taking part in this fraud. They were no less complicit in the execution of the scam but you abused your position, using information they did not want to be made public to force them into it. Some may say it was a fraud without victims as money was not taken from individuals, but the families of the three murdered people would say otherwise.'

He described Lancaster as a very dangerous man who 'became wilder and more violent as the net closed on him'.

Councillor Paul Sanderson admitted four counts of fraud at an earlier hearing and was sentenced to fifteen months for each offence to run concurrently.

For further story see pages four and five.

COUNCIL ROCKED BY MAJOR FRAUD INVESTIGATION
By Daniel Sullivan and Emma Fletcher

It was an investigation by the Allensbury Post which saw murderous Mayor Richard Drimble, also known as Bilton Lancaster, brought to justice.

James Wilton contacted the newspaper while trying to extricate himself from the scam. Tildon Crown Court heard how Lancaster had been able to draw Wilton into the scam after discovering he had financial problems. He had also used information gathered by Councillor David Edmonds about Councillors Buttle and Sanderson to blackmail them into taking part.

It was Wilton's conscience which led to the unravelling of the scam. He not only contacted the Post, but also sent a package of information to Councillor Buttle who unbeknown to him was also involved.

Charles Fordham, prosecuting, told the court: 'We believe Mr Wilton chose to inform Councillor Buttle by whatever means he could, as he believed she would be the most likely to act and prevent the scam from continuing. Sadly he did not know that she was part of the scam and that his information was wasted.'

However, Councillor Buttle, who was also looking for a way out of the scam, chose to share the information with the Post, asking that her name be kept out of the story. It was not until later that the Post learned of her involvement in the scam.

The court heard how Councillor Buttle was killed after she threatened to go public about the fraud.

Mr Fordham said: 'We believe Lancaster initially planned to simply take the information from Mrs Buttle, but on learning she had already passed it on to a reporter he killed her and moved on to trying to recover the information from the reporter before he was able to use it.

'We understand that Councillor David Edmonds was deputised by Lancaster almost as an enforcer, carrying out the majority of the dirty work through some low connections he had formed earlier in his business life. Lancaster only took things upon himself where there was a personal score to settle.'

Lancaster even admitted poisoning former planning committee chairman, Mayor Alan Horgan, causing him to have a heart attack to take over the running of the committee.

Mr Horgan said: 'I was shocked when I heard what he had done. It beggars belief that someone would sink so low just for a position on a committee. I suspected something was going on in the committee when I examined some of the papers before committee meetings but before I could start to investigate I fell ill. Of course I now realise why he went to such extremes but it sickens me to think I could have died because of his greed.'

Lancaster even pretended to launch his own investigation into the planning committee to allow him to question everyone, maintaining his control of them through fear, and also to try to keep tabs on the police investigation.

Detective Inspector Jude Burton said: 'Bilton Lancaster managed to cover his tracks very well, pretending he was as keen as we were to solve the murders and uncover the fraud. We are grateful to Councillor Sanderson for turning over information to us which enabled us to bring this case to a conclusion.

'Lancaster told us that once the net began to close, Councillor Edmonds began to panic and that he killed himself, but we are confident that he was another of Lancaster's victims.

'We are working with police in Portsmouth where we understand Lancaster was involved in a similar incident and we hope to be able to bring charges in that case as well.'

The fraud has fundamentally damaged Allensbury Borough Council's reputation and a full-scale internal investigation has begun.

Matthew Pitchford, the council's chief executive, said: 'We are all very shocked about what has happened in this council. Our thoughts and prayers are once more with the innocent families of the three victims. We are confident that no one else at the council was aware of what was happening apart from those involved in the fraud but an investigation has been launched. It would be inappropriate for me to comment any further.'

Councillor Buttle's husband Peter said: 'I had no idea what she was up to and it breaks my heart that her principles couldn't keep her on the straight and narrow. She hadn't even spent any of the money and this has now been seized by the police. I don't want it; I don't want any of it. I hope they give it to charity where it can be used to do some good.'

The family of Councillor Edmonds asked to be left to mourn their loss in private.

Councillor Sanderson's family declined to comment on his involvement.

Thank you so much for reading *A Deadly Rejection*.

If you enjoyed it, please tell your friends, or leave a review on your chosen platform or Goodreads.

You can follow me on Twitter @lmmilford or keep up-to-date with what's next by following my blog www.lmmilford.com or signing up for my newsletter.

Printed in Great Britain
by Amazon

18641921R00222